East End Honour

By Kim Hunter

East End Honour
Copyright © Kim Hunter 2010

The right of Kim Hunter to be identified as author of this work has been asserted in accordance with sections 77 and 78 of the Copyright, Designs and Patents Act 1988.

All rights Reserved

A CIP catalogue record for this title is Available from the British Library.

This is a work of fiction.
Names, characters, places and incidents originate from the writers imagination.
Any resemblance to actual persons, living or dead is purely coincidental.

Table of contents

OTHER WORKS

WHATEVER IT TAKES
TRAFFICKED
BELL LANE LONDON E1
EAST END LEGACY
EAST END A FAMILY OF STEEL
PHILLIMORE PLACE LONDON
EAST END LOTTERY

Web site   www.kimhunterauthor.com

Preface

One day I'll fly away.
With my wings spread wide I will soar through
the sky.
With the sun on my back and the wind in my
face,
I will glide through the air with speed and grace.
Freedom is yours I will hear the wind cry.
Make the most of your time for we all must die.
Not me I shout back, I've waited too long,
For this moment of splendour,
Now hush or be gone.

Lisa Frasier (nee Murphy)

Prologue
Summer   1960
Bethnal Green, London

It was a hot and humid September day when Vera Frasier found out she was pregnant. Temper wise she was a volatile woman at the best of times but the baby news, coupled with the stickiness of the day made for not a very nice person. Even though she was approaching her twenty fourth year, she still lived at home with her mother and that fact alone made matters all the worse. Beatty Frasier was old school and an unmarried pregnant daughter was going to bring shame on her. It didn't matter that things were changing fast and it was now a time for free love, to Beatty it was all absolutely disgusting. Vera knew that the moment she broke the news she would have to leave the family home. With no money of her own, and the father unknown, the situation was becoming more difficult by the day. Deciding that she had at least three months grace before she had to tell her mother, she went down to Roman road market and purchased three smock dresses. Luckily for her they were the height of fashion, so for the time being at least her mother wouldn't make any comments regarding her changing shape. On her way home Vera decided to stop off at the local council offices and inquire what she had to do to get a flat. In 1960, corporation properties were in abundance, with hundreds more being built every year. The kindly looking man behind the counter guessed at her predicament. In the last couple of years it was something Arthur Meadows had begun to see on a regular basis, though only heaven knew why these girls kept allowing it to happen. Since the introduction of the birth pill there just wasn't any sense or reason to it but as angry as he got, he couldn't help but pity the poor things. After all the young may have felt liberated but their parents were still from a generation that had been raised as straight laced as the Victorians.

"Well let's have a look shall we?"

Vera was grateful that at least someone was helping although she still felt her blood begin to boil at the questions he started to ask.

"Do you know who the father is?"

"I beg your pardon?"

"How many times did you have sex and do you like multiple partners?"

Suddenly Vera could see that this perverted little man was nothing more than a voyeur and if given half the chance would have jumped at any invitation to watch her.

"Does it turn you on asking about my sex life?"

"My dear girl how dare you even ask such a......"

Vera slammed her hand down onto the counter top and instantly stopped the man from speaking.

"Now you listen here you fucking perv! Find me a flat or I'm going to start shouting at the top of me bleeding voice that you was trying to interfere with me."

Arthur Meadows began to sweat profusely and his hands shook as he shuffled the papers in front of him.

"My dear girl I was doing nothing of the sort and besides no one would believe you. Now if you don't mind I have a lot of work to do."

As Arthur stuttered and stumbled over his words Vera couldn't help notice that the sweat he was producing was making his national health glasses slip down his nose. Every time they almost reached the tip, his hand would fly up and push them back into place. The sight was so comical and she knew that the more she stared at him the more he perspired and the more he perspired the more his glasses would slip. Seeing the state he had got himself into only confirmed to Vera that she had him right in the palm of her hand.

"Bleeding work! You dirty old tosser. I want to see your manager and I mean like right now!"

Once again the sweating and glasses fiasco began again and Vera couldn't hold her laughter inside.

"Well if you think this is all a joke young lady then you can think again."

Vera slammed her hand down onto the counter top again. "A fucking joke! I want to make a complaint and I want to do it now, do you hear me or are you bleeding deaf?"

Arthur Meadows was only a couple of years away from retirement and couldn't afford any scandal. Rather than risk his pension he removed some details from his meticulous filing cabinet and thrust them at Vera.

"Now get out of here you conniving little bitch and don't let me see you in here again. Your sort, have a way of degrading this place and it makes me want to vomit."

Vera snatched the details from his hand and as she turned to leave, smirked and winked at the bespectacled little man. Outside she glanced at the papers and realised she knew exactly where the property was. The man at the council hadn't studied Vera's details very well or he would have seen that it wasn't far from where she lived now. If he had of noticed he would probably have sent her to an area far away from all that was familiar to her. The brand new development on Rickman Street was better than she could have imagined and Vera had moved in within a couple of days. Apart from the basics of a bed, chair and cooker, her flat was sparse but to Vera that meant nothing. At least she had somewhere to call her own and from now on whatever happened in her life was solely down to her. On one particular visit her mother at last commented on Vera's size. The bulge had seemed to appear almost overnight and it was a bulge that Vera swore was getting bigger by the hour.

"So you're up the duff then?"

Vera had been making tea and luckily had her back to Beatty. She stopped momentarily while she thought of the right answer to give.

"Look mum it's not as bad as you think. I have this place and I'm working a couple of evening shifts down the Marsden so we'll get by."

"Get by! Whose going to look after the poor little bastard while you're pulling pints? 'Cause you don't want to think you can come fucking running to me for a babysitter. I've had four kids and you're the first to bring trouble to me door. If you can't stop yourself from opening your legs to all and sundry, don't expect me to be around wiping 'shitty arses and snotty noses just to help you out."

With that Beatty Frasier stood up and left the flat. The question of who the father was never got asked and as far as Vera was concerned it was a blessing. More than partial to the odd gin or two she wouldn't have been able to name the culprit even if she'd wanted to. Her mother's reaction was little more than Vera had expected but what she hadn't reckoned on was Beatty never setting foot over the Rickman street threshold again.

Jason Frasier came into the world on a warm night in April of the following year. Vera had been alone as she was most days and delivered her baby unaided. Luckily for her the birth was easy and after cutting the cord, she laid Jason on her naked breast and felt nothing but pure love.

"It's just me and you now son and I ain't ever going to let anyone hurt you."

Times were hard but somehow Vera Frasier managed without any help from her mother. She continued to work at the Marsden and the landlord was happy for her to leave the baby in the back room. Jason was a good kid and caused his mother little grief. Always happy to see a smiling face, he wore a permanent grin and was loved by everyone who came into contact with him. When Jason was eighteen months old Vera started to see one of the regulars on an add hock basis. She knew that Denny Raven was married and she had even accepted that there was no future with him but something stopped her from ending the relationship. Vera craved love and if that love came from a man who would never leave his wife, then that would have to do. Denny was always kind to Vera and treated her with respect, the type of respect that she hadn't experienced before. Coupled with the fact that he slipped her a few quid here and there seemed to make the relationship work but that was all about to change. The romance came to an abrupt halt the evening she told him she was pregnant. A nice meal at the steak house had been followed by a stroll in the park. When they took a seat on one of the benches and Denny placed an arm lovingly around her, Vera mistakenly thought the time was right. Suddenly Denny pushed her away and he glared at her with nothing but contempt.

"Fucking pregnant! You leery cow. I'll tell you this for nothing Vera; you can get down those bloody back streets to one of the old girls 'cause you ain't saddling me with another fucking brat."

Vera couldn't believe what she was hearing. Her kind and caring Denny had instantly disappeared and been replaced with a monster. His words had cut her to the quick but it didn't take more than a few seconds for her fiery temper to erupt.

"I'll tell you what Denny Raven, you can just fuck off right now and leave me be."

"What so you can come crawling to me for money and bring aggro to me door?"

Not wanting him to see her hurt Vera laughed out loud. "Come running to you? I wouldn't piss on you if you were on fire. No, I'll bring this baby up and I'll provide for it without any help from you or anyone else." Without a seconds hesitation Vera Frasier stood up, smoothed down her dress and headed off in the direction of Rickman Street. Denny Raven didn't see her tears and didn't want to. He didn't chase after her; in fact Vera had very little contact with him in the ensuing years. The former friendship became so strained that if she even saw him on the street she would cross over to the other side. Just after Jason's second birthday his brother Vincent came kicking and screaming into the world. As with her eldest Vera delivered the child alone but whereas Jason had been an easy birth Vincent was the exact opposite. Vera's labour went on for hours and all the time she had to care for Jason as well. When she finally couldn't hold back any longer, she gently put Jason into his play pen. He stared in amazement as his mother got down on all fours and began to grunt and groan. Jason thought that she was playing horsey and started to cry when she wouldn't lift him out.

"I know sweetheart but it won't be long then mummy will play with you. Be a good boy for me please!" When Vincent at last emerged onto the floor his brother stared in wide eyed amazement. If Vera had thought she felt love when Jason was born it was nothing compared to what she was feeling now. After doing all the necessary things which Vera was now a dab hand at, she lifted up her baby to show him to his brother.

"Look Jay this is Vinny. He fought so hard and so long to come into this world and now we have to take special care of him. Say hello."

Jason could just about manage to say the word 'ello but it was enough for his mother and she smiled down at both her sons. 'We'll manage' was what Vera Frasier had told her mother and Denny Raven and manage she did. For the next forty years there would be no more men on the scene. No family came to her aid when she needed them and no words of comfort were offered. The struggle only made her stronger and the realisation that the only people she needed in the whole world were her boys, hardened Vera Frasier to any outsiders. Some thought her bond with the boys was unnatural but to Vera they were her life. She tried not to show any favouritism but sometimes she couldn't help it. Jason was a good boy through and through but there was something about her Vinny, something different and to Vera in a way very special.

CHAPTER ONE
2005

The small council flat on Rickman Street felt oppressive. The East End, in particular Bethnal Green, had been Jason's Frasier's home for more years than he cared to remember but today it seemed cold and alien. Today he would rather be anywhere else on earth than here. Jason or Jay as he was known to everyone lit up his umpteenth cigarette of the day and placed the kettle back on the hob for the third time. It was only eight thirty but he'd been awake since the early hours. In the past sleep had never been a problem to him; in fact his mother had often remarked that her eldest could sleep on a linen line but that had all changed recently. Even in his early forties and with his jet black hair beginning to take on the early signs of grey at the sides he was still good looking. Tall and with a strong physic Jason was the epitome of most women's dreams but the lack of sleep was beginning to take its toll on Jason's normally handsome face. Opening the cupboard he removed two more mugs and placed them onto a tray. Looking round he smiled at the pristine kitchen his mother prided herself on. Vera Frasier loved her family to the point of obsession and at times Jason felt suffocated. He knew that with Vinny now gone things would only intensify and it was something he neither wanted nor could handle at the moment. He had already decided that once today was over they would head back to the Camel. It would break his mother's heart but if he stayed here it would destroy him. Staring into space, guilt began to slowly invade his thoughts but he was saved when the door opened and a plump gray haired woman entered the room.

"Morning son, sleep well?"

"So so mum. Tea?"

"Umm lovely. Is that lazy bitch out of her pit yet?"

For such a gentle looking woman Vera Frasier had a tongue as sharp as a knife. It had rarely been used on her boys but as far as friends and neighbours were concerned, they came up against it daily.

"For fucks sake mum, leave it out. Lisa's been through the wringer these last few months; cut her a bit of slack will you?"

"And what about me! Ain't I been through it as well? Of course I fucking have but you don't find me huddled up with the covers over my head ignoring the world and his wife."

Keeping the truth from her had been hard but he knew that if she was aware of everything it would finish her, so Jason didn't argue. It would be a futile exercise as far as his mother was concerned and today of all days was going to be hard enough, without her not speaking to him. Picking up the two mugs of tea, he placed one on the table in front of his now tearful mother and walked into the hallway with the other. Tapping gently on the bedroom door Jason waited for a reply. When none was forthcoming he turned the handle and entered the dark room. Instantly her perfume filled his nostrils and he took a second just to smell the scent of the woman he loved.

"Here you are Lisa a nice cup of rosie."

Jason solemnly shook his head at the lack of a reaction and walking over to the window he drew back the curtains. Light flooded into the small space and he glanced around at what used to be his and his brothers room. The bed was a dishevelled mess and he could just make out his wife's body which was curled up into a tight

2

foetal position. She looked so frail and tiny and Jason just wanted to take her in his arms and tell her everything would be alright. That wouldn't happen as he couldn't tell her everything would be alright, things would never be alright again and backing off he placed the mug on the bedside cabinet.

"You'd better start getting ready soon love, the hearse will be here in a couple of hours."

There was still no response but he knew today of all days she wouldn't let him down. By ten that morning Vera and Jason Frasier were suited and booted and ready for the day ahead. Lisa had managed to force herself into the new black dress Jason had bought but her tear stained face did nothing to enhance the outfit. Vera Frasier sat tight lipped. She hadn't uttered a single word to her daughter-in-law in the past week and she didn't intend to start now. For the sake of appearances she would hold her tongue until it was all over but once they were back home in the flat all hell was going to break loose. From now on everyone was going to follow her rules and with that thought just the smallest hint of a smile crept across Vera's face. Perhaps today wasn't going to be so bad after all.

The three figures looked a solemn sight as the funeral limousine drove through the streets. Jason stared ahead at the hearse but no thoughts of love were forthcoming. The Crematorium in Plaistow was a bleak sad place and as the car pulled up Jason could see that there were no other mourners. It had always been difficult for his brother to make friends and the few that he had acquired, or at least that's how Vinny saw them, were in reality only civil to him out of respect for Jason. Vincent Frasier had been a cold and nasty man. A man who cared only for himself and to hell with everyone else. There were

3

only two people who had ever bothered if he lived or died and one of them was now glad that he had gone. Vera was the only one who still loved her son; she saw him as some kind of saint and couldn't understand why there weren't any people here waiting to see him off on his final journey. In true motherly style she suspected that it was all Lisa's fault. She was convinced that no one liked the girl and what Jason had ever seen in her only god knew. At the same time she was also convinced that her daughter-in-law, somewhere along the line must have had a hand in what had happened to her boy, she was sure of it. Jason stood by the door as his brother's coffin was taken inside. Out of respect for his mother he would stand and greet anyone who showed up but in reality all he really wanted was to be as far away from here as possible. Minutes before the service was about to begin, two cars drew up and Jason was surprised when three men got out of each. Pauly South, Mango Smith and Terry Tyler were the first to appear and the sight of them brought a smile to Jason's face. He had seen Mango on and off but as for the other two, it had been years. Mango held out his hand and Jason grasped it firmly. The years had been kind to Mango Smith and his afro Caribbean skin was as smooth as a baby's backside. Unlike Jason, Mangos jet black dreadlocks were still as dark as ever and it only enhanced the man's appearance. "Thanks for coming lads, me old mum will be made up. Nothing worse than an empty crem!"
Terry stepped forward and Jason had a premonition of what he was about to say.
"Save it Tel! He was a cunt and he got what he deserved. Pity it wasn't years ago, it would have saved a lot of heartache all round."
The men were stunned at their friend's words. True none

of them had ever liked Vinny but today of all days these were harsh words they were hearing. Not knowing how to follow on from what had just been said, they bowed their heads and went inside. The occupants of the second car had held back. They had seen the conversation taking place but had not been able to hear what had been said. Fred Blatch, Stevie Day and Tony Tibbs had worked with the brothers at the Kings factory over on Hackney way and were all of the same opinions regarding Vinnie. Jason on the other hand was a different kettle of fish altogether. He was a diamond, a mukka, a pal that you could turn to in times of trouble. He had always seemed to draw the short straw where anything to do with his brother was concerned but Jason was the type that never seemed to mind. To him family had been everything, at least up until a few months ago. Tony was the first to speak, as was the norm he always spoke for the trio. It had been the same right through school and then on into the work place.

"Everything alright Jay?"

"Yeah fine Tone, just some old mates from way back."

"Cool, for a minute I thought you was having some aggro."

"Nah just said a few things that needed to be said. Tone I'm only here for me mum and if it was down to me I'd have left the fucker on top and let him rot like he deserves. Anyway boys how's things at the factory?"

Unusually it was Fred who spoke.

"Not the same since you left and after the takeover, well to be honest its shit with a capital S. Mind you the blokes still can't get their heads round what you did."

Tony and Stevie gave their friend a black look as much as to say 'Why did you bring that up?' Seeing this Fred realised he'd dropped a clanger and tried to back pedal as

5

fast as he could.

"Sorry Jay, no offence mate."

"None taken Fred."

"But fuck me mate you did pull a blinder. I think you and Vinny's little escapade will go down in local fucking history."

Tony and Stevie rolled their eyes upwards. Fred was supposed to stop talking, not go on again just because Jason hadn't taken umbrage. Jason Frasier grinned. He wasn't proud of what had happened but all the same it was good to see that it had brought a smile to people's faces. It was now a standing joke but at the time it had been a nightmare. Once again it had all been down to Vinny but as usual Jason had been left to take the flack. This thought alone brought back the sombre reason why they were all here today and no other words were spoken as the four entered the tiny chapel. Seeing the men walk inside made Vera smile with pride. At least her boy wasn't going without a proper send off. It was good to see people loved him, a fact she'd doubted for a long time but had never had the heart to voice. Now at least the wake could go ahead and without embarrassment. Being so close to the flat, The Camel Public House had been the ideal venue for Vinny's send off. Over the years it had become Vera's regular and if no one had shown up today she would never have been able to live it down. With these lads and thanks to the few regulars who were never out of the place, it should be a good turnout. Maude Shelton had run The Camel on Globe Road for over forty years. She had watched Jason and Vincent turn from boys into men and she'd also seen their characters emerge over the years and they were as different as chalk and cheese. A stranger would never have been able to guess that they were brothers, possibly through their

6

lack of physical resemblance but mostly down to how they lived life with such totally different views. Jason was good looking, kind and friendly. The kind of man any mother would be proud of and any future mother-in-law even prouder. Vincent on the other hand had always had a chip on his shoulder, had always envied his brother and wanted whatever he had. Not prepared to work for anything he thought the world owed him a living and if things didn't materialise, well Vinny was happy to just take what he wanted. To Maude he had never seemed quite the ticket but it was no secret that out of the two he was the apple of his mother's eye.

Years back when Jason reached fifteen, Maude Shelton had given him a part time job. It wasn't much, just a few hours each day after school. It was only restocking and cleaning up but she soon noticed that the boy loved every minute of it. Everything went well for a few weeks until Vinny started to turn up with his brother and then things changed almost overnight. Stock began to go missing but Maude was unable to prove anything. It wasn't just the odd soft drink and a few packets of crisps; that she would have turned a blind eye to. No this was bottles of whisky and cigarettes on a regular basis. Confronting the boys had been a waste of time even though she had known that Vinny was behind it all. Maude knew she had no alternative but to let her young helper go. Jason just bowed his head in a knowing way when she informed him his services were no longer required. It was as if he was used to taking the blame and collecting his coat and bag he had left without another word. Now almost thirty years later and she was holding a wake for the little bugger who had stole from her all that while ago. Well at least this time someone would be paying for the drinks he'd taken, she would see to that personally even if it was

7

a little late in coming.

The main doors opened at twelve on the dot and Vera Frasier was the first to enter. Nodding to Maude in a not so friendly manner, she proceeded to take a seat in one of the wrap around booths. As much as the landlady disliked Vinny, she hated Vera even more. The woman was a witch as far as she was concerned with never a good word to say about anyone. Knowing that today would be no exception she didn't want her pub slagged off for its hospitality and food. The spread had taken her all morning to prepare and even if she did say so herself, it was a real feast.

"Everything go off alright Vera?"

"Yeah thanks. Loads at the Crem but then I never thought it would be any different. Everybody loved my boy, you know that."

Maude smiled gently and nodded. Today wasn't the time to tell home truths, today was for a grieving mother to see her youngest son off. Even if that son was a complete shit, Maude knew she had to show compassion. As Mango and the few other mourners entered the Camel, Jason was taking Lisa back to the flat. Every single second of the day had been torture for her and Jay knew that to return to the pub and listen to his mothers ravings would just about tip his wife over the edge.

After placing the kettle on to boil Jason made a hot drink and all the while his wife just stood in the kitchen staring into space.

"Why don't you go and have a lay down sweetheart? You must be knackered."

Lisa Frasier didn't reply but her husband saw the tears begin to well in her eyes. Leading her by the hand they both entered the bedroom and he turned down the top sheet. God! every second of this was tearing him apart, every time he looked at his beautiful Lisa he couldn't believe what had happened to her. Jason knew that she just wanted to curl up and shut the world out and that was exactly what he would help her do. Slowly he undressed her and she offered no resistance. It was as if Lisa was drugged into almost a stupor and he didn't know how to make things better, couldn't make things better. It was a death sentence and no one could do anything about it. After making sure she was tucked up and warm enough, he quietly closed the door and went back into the kitchen. Jason intended to return to the wake but as he lit another cigarette his mind began to wander. Sitting at the table he tried to shake the images from his mind. He didn't want to regress but as hard as he tried it wouldn't stop. Maybe it was something he needed to do; maybe it was the only thing that would enable him to make sense of this whole sorry situation. Before he realised it Jason was back in nineteen eighty two and it was the night of his twenty first birthday.

CHAPTER TWO
1982

The night was warm and balmy. The kind of evening all
youngsters want if they're on a night out and April the
twenty fourth was no exception. Jason's pace was so
quick that he almost ran along the pavement in
anticipation at where they were going. Mango, Pauly and
Terry where finding it difficult to keep up and constantly
moaned for their friend to slow down. As always Vinny
hung back from the rest. For once Jason hadn't wanted
him there but as normal Vera had put her parts on and
Jason had given in. It wasn't that he didn't love his
brother because he did but whenever Vinny was invited
along, for some reason things always seemed to turn sour.
Tonight was Jason's and he didn't want anyone or
anything to spoil it. You were only twenty-one once and
he had been looking forward to this outing for months.
Camden Palace situated on Camden Road was the place
to be seen, or so the boys had heard. It was expensive
and not somewhere they had been before and tonight they
were buzzing.

"Slow down Jay, this ain't a fucking route march."
Jason began to laugh but soon stopped when the Palace
came into site. Its large white structure topped with a
green deco dome appeared to take over the skyline and
Jason felt a shiver run down his spine.

"I tell you something boys; from now on this is going to
be my regular Saturday night venue."
Mango laughed.

"Listen to Lord fucking Rothschild here! Just how you
going to pay for a place like this every weekend? You
can't even afford a pint at the Camel let alone a night

club. It's ok for a birthday treat, but it's out of our league mate, at least on a regular basis."

For the first time that night Vinny now stood level with the others. The anger on his face was evident and Jason whispered under his breath 'here we go again'. Vincent Frasier was only two years younger than his brother but it sometimes felt to Jason as if he was looking after a baby.

"Who are you fucking talking to you black bastard. If my brother says he's coming here then he will."

The racial words brought more tension between the lads than ever before. Suddenly Mango made a dive for Vinny but as usual Vinny stepped behind Jason. This was the norm, Vinny shouting his mouth off and Jason having to deal with the fall out. The older brother put out both arms as he tried to placate Mango and defuse the situation.

"Take no notice mate you know what a gob shite he is. He's so fucking thick that he don't even understand half of what he says."

With that remark, Vincent dug his fingers into his brother's ribs. Jason ignored the pain and continued talking. He wanted peace again, at least until they were inside. If the bouncers saw there was trouble, their feet wouldn't touch the pavement let alone the wooden dance floor. Mango Smith understood what his friend was trying to do and decided to let the remark go, at least for the time being. To ignore it went against the grain in the most painful way but he thought the world of Jason and his friend's birthday was more important. Mango raised his palms in a gesture of acceptance and the men continued to walk. This time instead of Vinny lagging behind he stood close to his brother's side. He knew that he'd overstepped the mark and for safety's sake he would stick like glue to his personal minder. The queue was

11

already starting to lengthen but the boys didn't mind.
Joining on at the back they couldn't wait to get inside.
The dull drone of the music could be heard outside and
Jason, high on life, began to sing out to ABC's Poison
Arrow. Terry Tyler grabbed his friends shoulder.
"Shut the fuck up Jay. If they think you're pissed they
won't let us in."
Vinny was again about to open his mouth but one look
from his brother told him to do otherwise. Finally they
made it inside and the place was packed to the rafters
with bodies gyrating to the beat. Girls dressed up to the
nines in the latest fashion of footless tights and overlong
shirts, eyed the boys up as they entered. Typically they
ignored the women and showed no interest, even if they
would all be desperate for a quick fumble by the end of
the night. Pauly and Jason went to the bar for drinks
leaving Vinny alone with Mango and Terry. You could
cut the atmosphere with a knife, Mango was still seething
over Vinny's remark earlier and Terry wasn't really in
the mood for conversation with either of them. Suddenly
Mango began to laugh and Vinny and Terry followed his
eyes to see what was so funny. In the middle of the
dance floor stood a man of at least sixty but trying
desperately to fit in with the younger crowd. His tight
polyester trousers hugged every part of his lower body in
a way that he thought sexy but in reality showed off
every lump and bump of his portly frame. A crimson
shirt open necked to the waist, was topped off by the
obligatory gold medallion. The man threw his arms into
the air as he danced and the girls surrounding him were
laughing hysterically at his antics. Taking the mockery
as interest, he intensified his moves in a desperate attempt
to resemble his hero John Travolta.
"Fucking hell Tel, if he carries on like that I'm going to
12

split me sides. I hope I don't act like such a twat when I get to his age."

"No need to worry Mango you already act like a twat."

"Well thanks a bunch mate."

Like a vulture Vinny scanned the dance floor and spying a dowdy looking girl decided to go in for the kill. She wasn't attractive and he didn't fancy her but he was interested in a quick shag. Susie Morgan glanced in his direction and Vinny smiled at her. Susie didn't need any more encouragement and was standing in front of the boys in seconds. It was weeks since anyone had shown an interest in her and she wasn't about to let this opportunity pass. In the light of the bar area her acne was now more visible and Vinny had to fight to keep his disgust inside. He looked in every direction other than hers as he spoke.

"Do you come here often?"

Mango burst out laughing and Vinny shot him a look of anger. The tension was explosive and Terry Tyler could see that it was about to kick off. Getting in between the two he whispered in Vinny's ear.

"Look mate not tonight alright. We're here for Jay and if you get us all fucking kicked out the night will be a wash out. Now none of us want that and I'm sure Jay would never forgive you, so why don't you take the bride of Godzilla here outside and give her a good seeing to. Maybe that will calm you down and we can all get back to enjoying ourselves."

Reluctantly Vinny agreed and grabbing Susie by the arm led her towards the exit. She didn't object, quite the opposite in fact and if he hadn't of taken the lead then she most certainly would have. Susie Morgan was desperate, desperate to be wanted by a man. She didn't care who it was, as long as someone was interested and she could let her friends see that she had pulled. As they passed the doorman at the main entrance Vinny noticed that they were grinning but he decided to ignore it. About to walk out of the door, he stopped when he realised that he may have to stand in the queue again. Shag or no shag he wasn't prepared to do that and Jed the head bouncer saw there was a problem.

"Everything alright guv'nor?"

Vinny turned so that Susie couldn't hear what was being said.

"Look mate I'm just off outside for a quick screw but I don't want to have to stand in line again to get back in. It's me brothers birthday and I need to be with him besides which she ain't worth queuing over."

Jed playfully punched Vinny on the shoulder.

"No problem pal, just come straight up to the front."

As Vinny led his conquest outside the four doormen burst out laughing. They had all been witness to this seedy scenario regularly and Susie Morgan was as dirty as they came. Jed hoped the young lad had a Johnny or it would be a visit to the clap clinic in the next few days. Outside Suzie led him to a quiet corner under the fire escape. It was an area she had used many times and they would be sheltered if it started to rain. There was no getting to know each other and neither of them bothered with any conversation. Hungrily Susie pulled at his belt and zipper and didn't relent until she found what she was looking for. Vinny wanted to be aroused but no matter how hard he tried nothing would stand to attention. He told himself that it was her fault. That her ugly boat race full of yellow spots was putting him off but in reality he knew differently. Recently this was happening more and more. There was a time, when a glimpse of a fanny in one of Jason's Fiesta magazines would make him as hard as

14

rock in seconds but now, nothing. The curious thing was
his old boy would stand to attention whenever he was
reading his weightlifting magazines. The sight of well
oiled muscular men had started urges inside him that he
didn't like. At almost nineteen he couldn't see why this
was happening; for god's sake it wasn't as if he was a
faggot or anything. The idea sickened him and he
roughly pushed Susie to one side. This hadn't happened
to her before and she didn't like it. True some of the
men she had been with in the past would have frightened
a blind woman but no one had ever pushed her aside, at
least not until they'd had what they wanted.
"What's wrong with you? Some kind of poofter are
you?"
Her insult was like a red rag to a bull and before she
knew what was happening he'd slammed his fist into her
face. Susie Morgan groaned out in pain but her cries only
fuelled Vinny's fire, he liked to hurt people, especially
those who couldn't retaliate. Back handing her across the
face forced Susie to the ground and Vinny proceeded to
ferociously kick her over and over again. When he
finally felt that a just punishment had been administered
he rearranged his clothing. Looking down on the now
bleeding excuse for a woman, Vincent Frasier sneered as
he hawked as much phlegm into his throat as he could
muster. Spitting directly into Susie Morgan's face, he
gave her one final kick for good measure before heading
back inside. Her whimpers were muffled and no one
heard her cries due to the fact that the people outside the
club were so noisy. Jed was a little surprised to see the
man back so soon and wondered where dirty Susie was.
It was only a passing concern as the place was too busy
tonight to worry about anything but your job.
"Fuck me pal that was quick!"

15

Vinny only sneered as he walked past. The air seemed to thump with the heavy sound of music and coupled with him receiving some much needed relief by way of hurting Susie, he was now up for a good night. Jason had scored them all an E each and as the effects took hold Vinny began to dance. The sound and colours of the room were so much more intense and it would be a further three hours before his high started to subside. When the boys finally left Camden Palace, Mango was the first to notice the paramedics pushing the stretcher into the ambulance. As human nature dictates, they all had a quick glance but it was Mango who recognised the patient.

"Hey Vinny, ain't that the girl you was with earlier?" Vinny shrugged his shoulders indifferently but as he continued to walk his pace quickened. Mango noticed this and he ran to catch Vinny up.

"That was her Vinny I remember."

"So fucking what! She was a scrubber anyway. Probably got what she deserved, teach her to keep her spotty trap shut in future."

Mango couldn't believe what he had just heard and dropped back a place to rejoin Jason.

"Did you catch that Jay? I think Vinny did for that poor girl."

Jason Frasier smiled and gently shook his head.

"Don't be a twat, of course he didn't. I know my brother can be a right wanker sometimes but hit a woman? Never!"

"Well if you're so fucking sure birthday boy let's go ask him."

Jason couldn't understand what all the fuss was about. Admittedly he hadn't managed to score any pussy but all the same he'd had a really good night and now it was all about to kick off again between his brother and Mango.

16

"Look! If I ask him will you let it drop? I've just about had a gut full of you two tonight. All I wanted was a good time but you've both done nothing but bitch at each other like a couple of queens."

Mango didn't like what was being said and wished Jason would wise up to his brother once and for all.

"Ok but I tell you Jay it was him."

Jason called after his brother and Vinny slowed down until all five of them walked along together.

"Vin this tosser has the weird fucking idea that it was you who did that girl. Tell him it weren't so we can all get home in peace will you."

Now completely down from the E, Vinny was feeling really tired and he was pissed off at having to defend himself. He didn't answer his brother's question and stopping dead in his tracks Jason grabbed Vinny by the arm and swung his brother round to face him.

"Tell me you didn't!"

Vinny stayed silent.

"You stupid fucking idiot! Did anyone see you?"

Vinny shook his head.

"Are you sure Vin?"

Vinny nodded. The question his friend asked rocked Mango Smith to the core. Where was the anger and sadness at what had happened to the girl? It seemed to Mango that Jason's only interest was in making sure that his brother was safe and there was no chance of him getting his collar felt by the Old Bill. There was no concern for the girl or the fact that Vinny had left her hours ago and she could have been dead for all they knew. Mango, Pauly and Terry Tyler were all disgusted at what they'd just heard and after letting the brothers know their feelings in no uncertain terms, crossed over to the other side of the road and walked home without them.

17

It wasn't until Jason was home and in his own bed that thoughts of the girl entered his head and for that alone he was overcome with guilt. The poor cow didn't deserve what she'd got and Jason couldn't for the life of him think what had possessed Vinny to do such a thing. Still for the moment they were safe and he prayed that his brother hadn't given out his name to anyone.

It would be a couple of weeks before the five friends met up again but the upset was soon forgotten about and everything was back to normal. Over the years it became common practice for Vinny to get into scrapes and it was always Jason who came to the rescue. Mango Smith soon gave up trying to warn his friend, he'd realised early on that anything he said would fall on deaf ears. Mango just hoped that one day Vinny wouldn't be his brother's downfall.

CHAPTER THREE

Through the eighties and into the late nineties the brothers drifted from one shady job to another. Things never amounted to anything and although Vinny was always full of bright ideas, most were doomed to fail before they had even got off the ground. Vera Frasier never seemed to mind, as long as the rent was paid and there was food on the table then for Vera, everything was fine with the world. It was a family ritual that on Saturday nights the boys would take their mother down to the Camel for a few drinks but to anyone who took the bother to notice they were a sad looking trio. Maude Shelton felt it was a crying shame that someone as handsome as Jason was wasting his life. A life that she would have given her back teeth to live again. The one and only time she had ever broached the subject with the boy's mother had ended with such a barrage of abuse that she hadn't bothered again.

"My boys are happy as they are. We don't want any slappers coming in and spoiling our family thank you very much. In future Maude Shelton I'd ask you to keep your fucking big nose out of my business. You might rule the fucking roost in here but not where mine are concerned. If you ever fucking mention it to me again I'll knock seven bells of shit out of you. Understood?" Maude didn't take kindly to threats and she was no coward by anyone's standards but she was also an astute business woman. Maude was wise enough to realise that if she got into an argument the outcome would be the Frasier family getting barred and that would make no sense at all. Silence was the best policy as far as she was concerned, silence and the hidden smugness that said

19

'Slag me off all you want Vera Frasier and I'll just keep on taking your money'.

Over the years gossip had been rife about the Frasier family. The brothers were always up to something dodgy and it was common knowledge that for a short while when the boys were younger Vera had been on the game. She had never married and both her boys had different fathers so it was assumed that they were probably the result of some punter or another. To Maude it had answered the question as to why Jason and Vinny were so different even though they were not in reality the children of curb crawlers.

These days Jason didn't see that much of Mango Smith and nothing at all of the other men. Pauly South worked away in Scotland for most of the year and Terry was going serious with a girl called Mandy Conner. Back in school Mandy had gained the reputation of being a slapper but as the years passed that reputation had faded. It certainly had as far as Terry was concerned; he was well and truly loved up. As for Mango, well nothing much ever changed with his circumstances, except the fact that his ability to tolerate Vinny had reduced to such a level that he couldn't even bear to be in the same room as the man. The two brothers came as a package so it stood to reason that he couldn't see that much of his old friend. The turning point in Jason's life came in the form of a wedding invitation, a small white card that brought everything to a head. It was nothing fancy, in fact Terry and Mandy were on such a miniscule budget that their wedding feast would have to be held at the Camel, it was the fact that people's lives were moving forward and his seemed to be stagnant with no hope of change. Jason scanned the card once more and there and then he made a decision. When Vinny came home Jason called his brother into the kitchen and got them both a drink. Handing his brother a can of Fosters his face wore a serious expression.

"Lighten up Jay you look like the worlds about to cave in on you."

"Not far wrong there bro."

Vinny removed the ring pull from his can and after taking a large gulp, proceeded to burp out loud.

"What the fuck are you talking about?"

"Vin, just look at us! Look at where we've ended up."

Vinny Frasier laughed at his brother's turn of phrase.

"Well Jay I've got to admit I was at the front of the queue when the looks were being dished out but you ain't that bad mate."

"Stop fucking about I'm trying to be serious here. I got this today it's an invite to Terry's wedding."

Jason handed his brother the card but after just a glance he placed it on the table. Vincent Frasier couldn't even be bothered to read it. His name hadn't been included so as far as he was concerned it wasn't worth looking at.

"You mean you want to get married?"

"Don't be a tit Vin of course I don't. It's just that our friends are out there doing something with their lives and look at us. No Jobs or none that you care to speak off and still shacked up with our old mum. Is it going to be like this when we're fifty?"

"Fucked if I know, ain't that bothered to tell the truth. Now are you coming down the Camel for a quick pint?"

Jason groaned out loudly.

"You haven't heard a fucking word I've said have you? Well I'm telling you this Vin, things have to change. Tomorrow I'm going to get a proper job, a job that brings a decent wage home and something I can be proud of. I'm sick to death of ducking and diving."

Smoothing down his hair in the small kitchen mirror, Vinny shrugged his shoulders.

"Please yourself mate, now are we going for that pint or what?"

As it happened going to the Camel with Vinny had paid off and Maude was sympathetic when Jason had started to tell her how he was feeling. Vinny couldn't be bothered to listen to anymore of his brothers garbage so had begun a game of pool in the other bar. Luckily for Jason Maude was far more understanding than his brother.

"Jay I've thought for years that you was wasted. I even tried to bring the subject up with your mum once but I don't need to tell you where that got me. So what's brought about this change of heart?"

'I don't know really Maude. I suppose finding out that Terry was getting hitched made me feel as if I was missing out on something. Do you know I'll be thirty six this year and I've never even had a proper girlfriend?"

The landlady looked surprised at this and it didn't go unnoticed by Jason.

"No not like that Maude! I've had plenty of one night stands and fumbles round the back of this place but nothing that lasted past a week."

"And why do you think that is? Could it have anything to do with that little shit in the next room I wonder?"

Jason didn't like what he was hearing but he guessed it was true all the same. Well for once in his life Vinny would have to stand on his own two feet. For once Jason Frasier was going to put himself first and do what he wanted.

"I suppose it would be easy for me to blame someone else Maude but the fact of the matter is I'm the only one who can do anything to change it. Nobody really forced me to keep bailing Vin out and no one forced me to be Jack the lad instead of living a decent life like everyone else."

That last sentence confirmed all that Maude Shelton had believed for years. That Jason Frasier deserved much more than this life was giving him.

"I don't know if it's any help love but a regular of mine was saying yesterday that Kings are hiring over in Hackney. It's not rocket science but its honest work and the pays good. Well I've never heard any complaints and some of the workers drink in here regular on a Friday afternoon."

"Thanks Maude, maybe I'll give it a try."

The following morning Jason was true to his word. Up before anyone else in the flat, he made his way over to Hackney. As he walked along the air was crisp and dry and with the sun shining on his face it felt good to be alive. Kings packaging, a large tin roofed building surrounded by a high fence, was situated on Cassland Road. After ringing the bell, Jason had to wait several minutes before anyone answered. Finally the large steel gate was slid open just enough to reveal a pair of dark brown eyes almost hidden under a flat cap. The wearer sported a roll up in his mouth, was unshaven and didn't appear to be the friendliest of people.

"Yeah?"

"Sorry to bother you mate; only I was wondering if there were any jobs going?"

"Wait here."

The gate slid shut and Jason could hear the man walk away. It was a good ten minutes before any signs of life from the building were shown again. Leaning against the fence Jason had begun to wonder if this had all been a waste of time when suddenly the gate reopened.

23

"Guv'nor will see you now. Go in that building marked office, down the corridor to the white door that says Roly Peterson. Knock but don't go in until he calls you."

"Thanks mate, err what's your name?"

The man in the flat cap totally ignored the question and after closing the gate behind Jason, disappeared down a narrow walk way. Doing as he had been instructed Jason Frasier stood outside the door and waited. This was getting weirder and weirder by the minute. Finally he heard the words 'enter' bellow out from behind the white door. The office was small and sparsely decorated. The smell of strong cigars filled the air and Jason wrinkled his nose at the offensive aroma.

"I hear you're looking for work?"

"That's right Mr?"

The man didn't offer his name.

"We run a tight ship here. It's just repackaging of household goods such as irons and knives etc. Now I don't have any packing vacancies but I am looking for a couple of janitors to keep the place clean and let the Lorries in and out, that sort of thing. You interested?"

It wasn't the sort of work Jason had been hoping for but then again it was a start and he knew he had to prove himself. Remembering that the man in front of him had said a couple, he immediately thought of Vinny. Maybe if his brother was doing regular work as well, things might change.

"You bet I am. In fact my brothers looking for a job as well so maybe you could kill two birds with one stone so to speak!"

Roly Peterson was a big man but not in height. What he lacked vertically he more than made up for in girth. Weighing in at twenty stone the man struggled with his every move. Jason could see the large circles of sweat under each arm and thought that by the end of the day his new boss must smell more than a little ripe. Roly ran his hand over his rapidly receding hairline.

"Fair enough I'll give you both a go. Happy Bottle will show you round and you can start tomorrow."

"Thanks and me names Jason, Jason Frasier if you was wondering?"

Roly didn't reply and looking down at the papers on his desk, dismissed Jason without another word being spoken. Outside in the yard Jason looked round for anyone that might resemble Happy Bottle, whoever that was. The only person in sight was the miserable little sod that had let him through the gate. Well it was worth a try, so Jason made his way over.

"Is your name Happy?"

The man eyed Jason up and down and his expression said in no uncertain terms that he was suspicious to say the least.

"That's me, who wants to know?"

"Roly's just taken me on as a janitor and he said you'd show me around."

"Follow me and its Mr Peterson to you. No one but the big bosses call him Roly, got that?"

Jason didn't argue. What had started off as a good morning was fast turning out to be a washout. He didn't know how long he would be able to stick this place but if it was just until he got a few quid in his pocket and found another job, then it would at least be something. Getting Vinny on board wasn't as easy as Jason had imagined it would be. When he returned to the flat his brother was still asleep and didn't rise until after eleven. Jason sat in the small kitchen with Vera and waited until finally the door opened and a bleary eyed Vincent Frasier entered. Both had solemn faces, Jason's due to anger at his

brother laziness and Vera's because she knew that her
boys could soon be having a row.

"What are you two doing? You both look as if you're
waiting for a jury to return and how come you're dressed
and ready to go out Jay?"

"I'm dressed because I've already been out. In fact little
brother I've gone and got us both a job."

"Yeah right!"

"I'm serious Vin. We start at Kings tomorrow morning
at eight sharp."

Vinny walked over to the cupboard and began to tip
cereal out into a bowl. He didn't speak straight away as
he was trying to take in what his brother had just said.
Suddenly he burst out laughing.

"You're having a fucking laugh if you think I'm going to
work in some sweat shop for a couple of hundred a week.
No fucking chance mate!"

Suddenly Vera joined in the conversation and it didn't
please her eldest son one bit.

"Well I don't see why you both have to get a job. Ain't
we managing good as we are?"

"Mum I don't want to just fucking manage and will you
butt out, this is between me and Vin."

"Well there's no need to speak to me like that I was only
trying to help."

Jason Frasier stood up and bending over the woman,
planted a kiss on the top of her head.

"I know you was mum but just for once stay out of things
Ok?"

Jason stared directly at his brother as he began to pull on
his jacket that had hung on the back of the kitchen chair.

"It's your call Vin. If you want to sit and rot in this flat
all day, well that's up to you. Me? I want a bit of
decency for once. It's down to you Vin but I'll be setting

the alarm for seven in the morning. If you join me good, if not then you can just fucking get on with it."

With that Jason Frasier walked out of the kitchen and out of the flat. Still in shock at being spoken to like that from her eldest son Vera remained silent.

"Well ain't you got anything more to add mother? You're not normally fucking stuck for words."

"Nothing to say son. It ain't my decision but I will say one thing."

"Thought you might, here we fucking go!"

"Do you know something Vincent? Sometimes you can be a nasty little shit. Well I hope your brother goes to that job, I hope he likes it and gets on well. Then it'll be you left out in the cold for a change 'cause you won't have anyone to wipe your snotty little nose for you."

Vera was the second to leave the kitchen and as she walked out Vincent just shrugged his shoulders in an indifferent manner. Outwardly it appeared to be two fingers up to his family but inside he was worried. Without Jason he was nothing and no one on the street would take him seriously on his own. Oh he could look after himself but that wasn't the problem, without Jay by his side people always crossed the road rather than have to make conversation. Vinny decided that today would be spent in thought. Today he would mull over and digest the situation, telling himself that once he had got his mind straight then he would make a decision. Vinny couldn't even admit to himself that he would always be in his brother's shadow and wherever Jason went then Vinny would follow. Even with his show of bravado, he already knew what he would do, tomorrow he would be up at seven; tomorrow he would start a poxy job and all because he was nothing without Jason.

27

CHAPTER FOUR

The start to their first morning had been a disaster. Vinny wouldn't get up and it was seven forty five before they even left the flat. It was cold and raining and no matter how hard Jason tried he couldn't get his brother to hurry up. When they finally arrived at Kings fifteen minutes late, Happy Bottle wouldn't let Vinny in. Jason was allowed entry but until Happy had clearance Vinny had to wait outside the gate. It took ten minutes to sort the confusion out and when Vincent Frasier was finally let in he was less than pleased. Jason could see by the look on his face that he was ready to explode; he just hoped Vinny could hold it inside. For once his brother kept his calm and when Happy showed them to a small room that was to be theirs, Vinny's mood quickly lightened. To have somewhere to sneak off to and be able to put his feet up made the job seem not as bad as he'd first thought. The boys were given overalls and basic cleaning tools. It would be their duty to keep the factory floor and outside areas clean and tidy. When Vinny saw the buckets and brooms he couldn't believe that he had been coerced into this and he shook his head and sighed. Uncharacteristically, for once he didn't utter a word which his brother was grateful for. The rest of their first day passed uneventfully as did the next three months. Gradually Vinny started to act like he didn't mind the job and it was something that pleased his brother. Jason on the other hand found the work mind numbing. The majority of the workforce consisted of foreigners who made the conversation difficult but a handful of locals did work at Kings and after a week Jason had eagerly sought them out. He wasn't one to talk that much but after eight hours of listening to only Polish or Lithuanian, it made for a very long day. Fred Blatch and Stevie Day both worked on the end of line six and as this was an area that Jason had to clean, the men quickly became friends. Tony Tibbs was a foreman of sorts, though never insisted on anything being carried out. The three were childhood friends and because of this Fred and Stevie took little notice of him. Tony was always being called into Roly's office and hauled over the coals because things weren't going quickly enough but Roly Peterson would have done just as well to save his breath. Jason found the whole situation hilarious and referred to the lads as the three musketeers. Vinny didn't bother with the men and when his brother tried to include him in things he would just give a look of contempt and walk off in another direction. Fred Blatch had been at Kings the longest, though they had all joined in the same year and he liked to keep an eye on the foreigners and help them out whenever help was needed. His friends couldn't understand his concern and only saw the migrants as intruders to their country. They knew that Fred was second-generation Ukrainian but didn't see why that should influence him either way. Fred on the other hand, saw a different side to these people. He saw the homesickness, the hard work and the difficulties that they faced every single day just trying to be accepted but his friends looked on him as an old woman and would ridicule him at every opportunity. When things were quiet and the three had time for a chat Fred would always start to talk about the foreigners and say that there was something not quite right with the setup at Kings. Since Roly Peterson had sold out and was now only the manager things were different and Fred was sure something dodgy was going on. Whenever this topic arose it was an opening for Stevie to wind his mate up

29

and start talking to Tony about Enoch Powell's river of blood speech and how all the foreigners should be deported back to where they came from. Fred would never rise to the bait but it didn't stop Stevie trying whenever he got the chance. Jason joined in with the banter but soon got bored with the same old thing. To Jay it was as if the men had become institutionalised and he was weary of it happening to him. Still time did fly by and before they knew it the brothers had been working at the factory for five years. Recently Jason had started to become more and more disillusioned and wondered if hard work was really worth the effort after all. In all honesty, the only thing that kept him at Kings was the thought of seeing the little blonde girl who had recently started work on the packing line. Lisa Murphy had made an impact on Jason within her first few days but he was yet to speak to her. He had noticed that she was overly quiet and only spoke if spoken to. Lisa sat outside alone on her breaks and Jason could tell by her eyes that she was filled with sadness. His mother had always told him that the eyes were the windows to the soul and Lisa's eyes were the most heartbreaking he had ever seen. Jason decided to begin his courtship slowly. He would just say good morning when he saw her and a week or so later began to take his breaks outside too. After several days of silence he plucked up the courage to ask her what her name was even though it was something he'd already found out. Timidly she told him it was Lisa and he offered her his name without being asked. Their friendship blossomed and Jason found himself buying her little presents. Nothing much, just the odd bar of chocolate or packet of sweets but he could see that it meant the world to her. He couldn't work out what it was with this girl, there was no doubting that she was pretty

30

but that wasn't it. For as long as he'd taken an interest in the opposite sex there had never been a short supply of women as far as Jason Frasier was concerned and it was something he'd always prided himself on. With Lisa Murphy it was different. Jason was the one doing all the chasing and no matter how hard he tried, nothing seemed to be working. He'd brought her gifts, paid her compliments for which he could see that she was grateful but there was always something missing. He couldn't put his finger on it and that alone intrigued him even more. Vinny was no help in the matter and when Jason tried to talk to him his only advice had been 'For fucks sake Jay, shag her and move on. What is she for Christ sakes, some kind of super model?' That was just the point, Lisa Murphy was nothing of the kind. Unlike the usual airheads that he went for, this girl seemed to have a special quality, a quality that he'd never come across before but it was something he liked. The more she resisted his advances, the harder he tried. Finally when he had run out of ideas and had asked her out for the umpteenth time she surprised him in her reply.

"It's not that I don't like you Jason and in different circumstances I would love to go out with you but it's my family."

"What do you mean?"

Lisa didn't answer and he didn't push things, at least she was now entering into conversation with him and he wouldn't jeopardise that for anything. Over the next few weeks she began to open up to him more and more and when Jason again asked her out on a date she quietly told him that her father would never allow it. True, Jason Frasier was at least fifteen years older than her but that didn't seem to be the problem. Lisa explained that her father was a staunch catholic and would never allow her to date anyone. Jason knew that he would never give up, couldn't in fact. No one had ever made him feel like this little timid princess did. Lisa was tiny and slim and standing only five feet tall Jason towered over her. He loved every single thing about her and just wanted to sweep her up into his arms and take care of her. Vinny didn't bother where his brother spent his break time; he was too wrapped up in his own little world. Everyone except Jason had noticed how he had befriended one of the other workers and for want of a better word, had formed a special closeness. Stephan was Lithuanian and as camp as they came. Morning breaks and lunchtimes the two would spend holed up in what Vinny liked to call his office. The door was firmly locked and other visitors were discouraged. Fred Blatch who had taken a fatherly interest in Stephan became increasingly worried about the two men's behaviour but didn't know how to intervene or warn Stephan off. Fred didn't really know Vincent Frasier that well but he was a good judge of character and was sure this one was rotten to the core.

On one of his Saturday lunchtime visits to the Camel Jason happened to mention Lisa to Maude. More than a little interested Maude asked question after question until she suddenly went quiet.

"What's up Maude?"

"Look Jay it's not for me to interfere but I know the family you're talking about and a bigger bunch of low life's you ain't ever met."

Jason didn't say anything but he had an idea he wasn't going to like what was coming next.

"If it's the same family I'm thinking about, they live over Hackney way on Morpeth Road."

"That's them. Lisa said where she lived and...."

Before he could continue Maude swiftly cut him off.

"Jason you really don't want to get mixed up with the likes of them. Eamon Murphy, that's the father, well he's a real nasty bastard. Mind you the two brothers ain't much better, treat that little girl like a dog, or so I've heard."

"Why do you say don't get involved, they can't be that bad can they Maude?"

"You don't know the Murphy's like I do Jay. They started to drink in here for a while, mind you that was going back a few years now. Eamon's Irish and old school, nice as pie to begin with but once he's got a few scotches in him he changes. He's a real bleeding Jekyll and Hyde that one. The last time the three of them were in here a fight broke out. There was an argument between the old man and another of me regulars called Percy. I wouldn't even say it had time to get overheated. I mean a few choice words were exchanged but that was about it and then before I knew it they were on top of poor old Percy like a pack of wild animals. It was nothing short of a blood bath in here. No one could stop them, they just kicked the shit out of him. Finally when it was over I told them that if they ever came back again I'd phone the Old Bill. Of course that never would have happened, even poor old Percy didn't report it when he finally came round. Do you know Jay he was in a comma for a month and to this day he's never really gotten over it. Doesn't even come in here now but then who can blame him, they blinded him in one eye, the bastards!"

Jason exhaled deeply. He hadn't been expecting this but then again he couldn't let a thing like someone's reputation put him off, not without at least meeting them first. Before he left the premises Jason purchased a bottle of the Camels finest malt whisky. Maude realised what he was going to do but didn't attempt to talk him out of it, she could see by the look in his eye that there was little point in trying.

Walking slowly over to Hackney he mulled over all that he had heard and tried to work out the best way to handle the situation. By the time he turned into Morpeth Road he was no nearer to a plan. The street was run down and the row of Victorian terraces looked in need of some serious renovation. Number six was the worst with peeling paint and permanently closed curtains that hadn't had a wash in years. Hesitantly Jason knocked on the door. Minutes later he could hear someone walking down the hall towards him and hoped it was Lisa. Unfortunately that wasn't to be and a large man with thinning ginger hair appeared. He was dressed in only a vest and trousers which were held up by braces and a large worn leather belt. A shadow of dark stubble on his face told Jason that the man didn't bother much with personal hygiene. Jason held the bottle behind his back and put on the friendliest smile he could muster.

"Yeah?"

"You must be Mr Murphy; Lisa's told me so much about you."

"Who the feck are you?"

Eamon Murphy's accent was strong and Jason had to listen hard to understand what the man was saying.

"I'm Jason Frasier and I work with your daughter. We've recently become friends and I wanted to ask your permission to take her out on a date. My intentions are strictly honourable and I think Lisa is a smashing girl Mr Murphy."

As his last word was spoken Jason brought the bottle of whisky to the front. Eamon Murphy's face lit up and straight away his attitude changed.

"Come inside lad and we can have a chat. Lisa's not here now but then I don't suppose she needs ta be."

Over the next few minutes the two men discussed pleasantries but all the time Eamon's eyes never left the bottle. Jason could see that they weren't really getting anywhere but he did get the impression that he would now be able to see Lisa outside of work. After shaking her father's hand Jason left the house and began the walk back to Rickman Street with a happy heart. It felt as if a weight had been lifted and he couldn't wait to see her on Monday morning. Coming from the opposite direction Lisa arrived home shortly after Jason had left. Placing the heavy shopping bags on the front step she struggled to find her keys. Seconds later the front door flew open and before she knew what was happening Lisa was being dragged inside. The bags of groceries fell over and vegetables rolled into the gutter but Eamon Murphy wasn't the least bit bothered about the food. He'd already downed a good amount of the whisky and now he was about to teach his whore of a daughter a lesson she wouldn't forget in a hurry. His grip on the collar of her coat never loosened as he frog marched her along the hall. Reaching the sitting room he threw his daughter to the ground and began to kick her.

"Please Da Da what have I done?"

"What have ya been up to ya feckin' whore. Ya brought shame to me family that's what ya done. Strange men comin' round to me feckin' home and askin' if they can take ya out. Want to get their feckin' hands down ya drawers, if they ain't already."

"No Da it ain't like that honest! If you mean Jason? We're just friends."

"Just friends! I'll give ya feckin' friends."

Knowing better than to try and fight back, Lisa clasped

35

her head as she received blow after blow. Take the
punishment without a fuss and it would be over all the
quicker. It was a painful lesson she had quickly learned
as a child and a lesson that had been repeated many times
over the years. As her father continued to thrash her, the
door opened and Sean Murphy walked in. He was the
oldest child and favourite of his father. He didn't bat an
eye lid at what was going on and his only comment was
to remark about the spilt food outside in the street.
"I know son and when I've finished with this little mare
she can go and collect it."
"Well don't take too long Da I'm feckin' starving!"
With that both men began to laugh and Eamon's temper
at last started to subside.
"Now get up off the floor ya lazy little cunt and make ya
brother here some dinner."
Lisa obeyed her father's orders; she didn't dare do any
other and with shoulders slumped over went outside to
retrieve the shopping.
Later in the tiny back kitchen as she peeled the potatoes
she wondered what had brought all this about and what
on earth had possessed Jason to call round. Lisa couldn't
be angry with him though, he didn't know how she lived
and she hadn't offered the information. She knew this
wasn't how families were supposed to be but she was too
ashamed to confide in anyone, least of all Jason Frasier.

Monday morning came and went as did Tuesday and
Wednesday. With no sign of Lisa, Jason was becoming
more and more concerned. He decided that if she didn't
show tomorrow then he would call round on his way
home from work. It didn't turn out to be necessary but
after his initial happiness at seeing her, Jason couldn't
believe the state she was in. Lisa's beautiful face was a

yellowish purple. One eye was so badly swollen that it was almost closed and if it hadn't of been for the fact that Eamon Murphy wanted her pay packet at the end of the week, then she still wouldn't of been allowed out of the house. It was lunch time before Jason got to talk to her but as he went to take her in his arms Lisa pulled away.

"For fucks sake girl what happened?"

Her eyes filled with tears and Jason could feel his own heart begin to break.

"You shouldn't have come round Jay; you don't know what they're like. If my father sees you anywhere near me again he'll kill me."

Jason moved a step closer.

"Kill you! Lisa what on earth are you talking about? Don't tell me your own dad did that to you?"

When she didn't answer he knew he'd hit the nail on the head.

"Right give me till the end of the day to come up with an idea."

"Jason you haven't got too."

"Lisa let's not even go there alright? You're my girl and I'm going to put a stop to this, I just need to think about things for a while that's all. Meet me outside the gate after work."

Lisa began to cry and Jason grabbed both of her arms. She winced in pain and he felt sick at what he could only imagine she had been through.

"Promise you'll be there?"

Nodding slowly she quietly whispered 'I promise'. Vinny as usual had been using the store room as his own personal office but Jason had become so obsessed with Lisa that he didn't take any notice of the magazines that were lying on the shelf. The boys had been getting on well with each other lately so Jason had no reason to question what his brother was up to. Locking the door, Jason spent the whole afternoon in the room deep in thought and by the time it came to knock off for the day he had hatched a plan. As promised Lisa was waiting for him and he told her that they would talk as they walked so that she wouldn't be late home. Instead of turning off into Terrace Road they travelled in the opposite direction and going the Meynell Road way would add fifteen minutes to their journey if they didn't walk quickly. Jason reasoned it was a calculated risk worth taking, at least this way they had less chance of being seen.

"Lisa I want you to listen to me carefully and apart from this one question I'm going to ask you, I don't want you to comment until I've finished. OK?"

"OK"

"Right here goes. Do you have any real feelings towards me?"

"Feelings? Of course I do Jason; I'd even go as far as saying you're my knight in shining armour."

"Good that's all I needed to hear. Now then this is what I want you to do. Every day over the next week I want you to smuggle a few of your things out of the house. By Friday you should have as much as you're going to need then you never have to go back to those bastards again."

Lisa stopped dead in her tracks and turning to face him she started to cry again.

"They will hunt me down and drag me back home Jay, it doesn't matter where I go they will find me."

"Maybe they'll try babe but if you're my wife there ain't much they can fucking do about it now is there?. I'm going to take a couple of hours off work tomorrow and go and get us a special licence. That's only if you want to of course?"

Lisa didn't answer, instead she threw her arms around

38

Jason's neck and hugged him for dear life. The next few days were scary but exciting and by Friday everything was in place.

CHAPTER FIVE

On Saturday morning Lisa set of as usual to do the weekly shop. Under her old coat she wore a beautiful cream dress that Jason had given her the day before and for the first time in her life Lisa Murphy felt like a million dollars. The bus drive over to Whitechapel was nerve racking. As it passed by the top end of Roman Road Lisa ducked down in case anyone saw her who might know the rest of the Murphy clan, anyone who could alert her father to the fact that his daughter was acting strangely. There were too many nosey people in these parts and many so scared of Eamon Murphy that they would do anything to get into his good books. It took a while for her to realise that to everyone else she was just the Murphy girl doing her weekly chores but still Lisa had never felt so relieved when her stop finally came into sight. The register office was situated on Stepney Way and there was a public toilet a couple of doors down. Ducking inside Lisa applied some light makeup and studied her face in the mirror. Her father had never allowed her to own makeup let alone wear it but recently she had begun to buy the odd item and hide it in her room. Never daring to apply it she would look at the pretty colours of the eye shadows each night before she went to sleep. Finally she walked up the steps to the registry office and when Jason saw her he couldn't believe his eyes. He had always known that Lisa Murphy was pretty but today she was stunning and today she would make him the happiest man in the world. Twenty minutes later and the couple emerged from the building as Mr and Mrs Jason Frasier. Staring deep into each other's eyes, they both knew that from now on no one could stand in their way but then again they hadn't banked on the reception they were to get from Vera just a short while later. After going for a meal and spending a few precious hours together, it was late afternoon by the time the newlyweds returned to the flat on Rickman Street. Placing his key in the lock Jason swept Lisa up into his arms to carry her over the threshold.

"I know this isn't our home but it will do for a couple of nights just until I get something else sorted out."

"I'd live in a shed Jay as long as it's with you."

Placing a kiss tenderly on her lips, the moment was soon interrupted by the sound of Vera Frasier's shrill voice echoing down the hall.

"Is that you Jay? And about fucking time I've had your tea ready for over half an hour."

Lisa giggled at the woman's words, totally unaware of the battleaxe she was about to encounter. Sheepishly Jason poked his head around the kitchen door. Vinny and Vera were seated at the table and about to tuck into a meal of steak chips and peas. Still full up from earlier he didn't want to disappoint his mother; if she was anything at all she was a good cook but the thought of eating again so soon made him feel sick.

"Come on in son and tuck in before its stone cold."

"Sorry mum but I've already eaten and I've got someone with me I want you both to meet."

"Now Jay you know I don't like strangers round here at meal times, whoever they are they'll just have to come back later."

"That's going to be a bit difficult mum as she's going to be sleeping here."

"What!"

Before Vera could continue Jason held up his hand.

"Mum, Vin, I want you both to meet my wife."

41

Momentarily Vinny choked on the small piece of steak he had managed to put into his mouth before his brothers startling revelation and before all hell was about to break loose. Vera dropped her knife and fork and just stared open mouthed.

"Come on in Lisa and meet your new family. Mum, Vinny this is Lisa."

Vera forced her plate across the table with such force that the contents spilled over and onto the floor.

"Are you fucking winding me up son, because I ain't in the fucking mood?"

"Look mum, I know it's a bit of a shock but it's what we want and we're really happy ok?"

"What you fucking want! What about me? I ain't having some little slapper coming into my house and laying down the law. I ain't having it Jason do you hear?"

Vera knew exactly how to push her son's buttons and this time they were well and truly stuck down.

"Now you listen here and listen good Mum. Lisa ain't a slapper and she ain't laying down the law as you put it. We only need to stay for tonight after that we'll be out of here."

Jason grabbed Lisa's hand and led her from the flat. He was so angry that he couldn't speak. Expecting a little trouble from his mother had been one thing but this time she really had overstepped the mark.

"Come on babe we'll go for a few drinks and come back when the old bats had a chance to calm down."

Lisa didn't reply. It wasn't that she expected anything different, because in her world the confrontations were far worse. It was more that today had been like a fairy tale and like all brides she had wanted the fairytale ending and not to be slagged off by her husband's mother. As usual the Camel was busy but Maude still had time for the couple and when she heard they had tied the knot it was drinks all round. Jason told her what had occurred back at the flat but she wasn't surprised at the reception they had received from Vera.

"Are you sure you know what you're doing Jason. I mean the Murphy's are hard bastards and I'd be surprised if Eamon took this lying down."

"I'm sure and anyway what can he do? We're married now and as far as the law is concerned he has no claim on her."

Maude Shelton was still concerned but the couple looked so in love that she couldn't do anything but join in with their happiness.

"Look Jay I don't know if it will be of any use to the pair of you and it wants a good clean but there's a room at the back of the pub you can have for as long as you like."

Jason's face beamed with happiness as Maude led them through the rear corridor to have a look. The room was a good size with a small kitchenette at one end. A toilet was situated next door and Maude said she was happy for them to use her bathroom in the flat above for washing. Lisa couldn't stop grinning; her own little place at last and she could decorate it just how she wanted. Suddenly she began to cry and Jason wrapped his arms around her. Maude Shelton knew some of what the girl had been through and gently closing the door made herself scarce.

"Come on now babe, whatever's the matter?"

"Nothing Jason I'm just so happy. I've never felt so good or so loved in all my life."

"You soppy cow, whatever are you like. Come on we best go back and see mum and Vinny, it's going to be a busy day tomorrow."

With a final thank you to the landlady, Jason and Lisa headed back to the Rickman Street flat and another onslaught of abuse that only ended when Vera Frasier went to bed. As they lay curled up on the living room floor they both felt invincible. Vera's ranting had been totally ignored and Jason had managed to hold his tongue, for tonight at least. Vinny had been silent but then again that was nothing unusual of late. Jason held onto his bride for dear life. He didn't try to take things further as it didn't feel right, not here in his mother's home. Tomorrow would be a different matter, tomorrow when they were in their own place he would make love to his wife all night long.

Up with the larks the newlyweds made their way to Roman Road market where a handful of shops opened on a Sunday. With nothing but excitement they purchased as much second hand furniture as they could afford. A double bed was first on Jason's list followed by a small sofa and at Lisa's insistence a coffee table and vase. The shop owner took pity on them and offered to deliver it all for a fiver. By nightfall they had cleaned the place from top to bottom and the furniture had been installed. Along with the curtains and bits and pieces that Maude had given them the room now had a warm glow. Jason led Lisa into the bar for a celebration drink and to sort out the rent with Maude. His landlady was having none of it and after a friendly argument it was decided that he would do a couple of evening shifts in the pub as payment. Jason couldn't keep his eyes off Lisa and an hour later he began to yawn making Maude laugh to herself. The lad was so obvious it was comical but then she had been exactly the same when she and her Geoff had first wed, god rest his soul. Admittedly Jason was a lot older than most first time husbands but his excitement at what was to come was no less than a younger mans.

Jason Frasier was undressed and in bed within seconds

but when Lisa hadn't returned from the toilet twenty minutes later, he became concerned. Wrapping the duvet around his naked body he walked into the hall and tapped gently on the door.

"Lisa darling, are you alright?"

"Yeah I'm fine I just need a few minutes that's all."

Jason went back to the still warm bed and after another ten minute wait, began to drift off to sleep. He was woken by his wife getting in beside him but when he reached out to touch her he could feel that she was still fully clothed. As his hand brushed over her covered breast Lisa recoiled in horror. Jason moved closer and he could feel her whole body tense up.

"Whatever's the matter babe?"

"I don't want you to touch me. All I want is to go to sleep."

Jason couldn't understand. This was supposed to be one of the best nights of their lives and his wife of just over twenty four hours had gone stone cold on him. Again he tried to touch her putting her fear down to first night nerves but stopped when Lisa began to sob uncontrollably.

"Baby I only want to love you like a husband should." Slowly he began to move on top of her but she didn't respond, her whole body was ridged.

"I should have told you before we got married." Wearily Jason moved back onto his side of the bed.

"Told me what? Come on now Lisa you're starting to scare me."

Lisa Frasier took in a big lungful of air and straight away her story began to unfold.

"My dad and brothers have raped me almost daily since I was twelve years old. They have even done it all together in the same room. I have been forced to perform terrible

45

acts Jason, terrible terrible things that you couldn't imagine would even go on in a family."

Her words disgusted Jason to the core but he knew that to show Lisa how he felt would only cause her more pain and that was something he would rather die than do. Not knowing how to continue he slightly stuttered with his next sentence.

"I'm ok with this babe really, if you want to tell me that is?"

"I don't know if I can Jay but I suppose I at least owe you an explanation."

"You owe me nothing darling, all I want to do is help you."

They were now both sitting up and gently he placed an arm around her shoulder and spoke in almost a whisper.

"Take your time love.'

Lisa wiped her eyes but her bottom lip still quivered as she spoke.

"It all started when my mother passed away. I was only nine and I suppose deep down for some ridiculous reason my father blamed me."

"Don't make excuses Lisa."

"I'm not but you have to understand what it was like Jay."

"I don't know if I can."

"You have to if not I might as well kill myself here and now."

"Lisa don't ever say that please! It's just that I can't bear to hear that people hurt you so bad and you've kept it all bottled up for so long."

"But I need to tell you now!"

"Ok I'm sorry, take your time."

"I was desperate for love Jason, so desperate that when they began to cuddle me it was all I craved. To begin

46

with that was all it was and even though my dad drank heavily he was never cruel to me but over the next three years things started to slowly change. I suppose you could say that they began to groom me. It was just touching my leg to begin with then one night just before my twelfth birthday I was sitting alone on the couch when my dad came in drunk. He sat beside me reeking of whisky and the look he had in his eyes scared me. I tried to move away but he was on me in a second and before I could scream he had forced his hand between my legs. I've never felt pain like it; well not until they raped me anyway."

The way her revelations came out so matter of fact bothered Jason as much as what she was telling him. Oh he was outraged at what they had done to her but how it was being portrayed, seemed that to Lisa it was almost normal but then maybe it was. Pulling away from her Jason placed his head in his hands.

"This is so wrong Lisa, so very wrong."

"I know it is but please Jay don't hate me. I tried to hide from them, I tried everything I could think of but even when I began my periods they wouldn't stop they were at me all the time like animals."

"Baby I could never hate you but stop now you've told me enough."

"Enough! You can't begin to imagine what I went through. Don't tell me you've heard enough when I've lived a nightmare for the last fourteen years."

"I didn't mean to I...."

"No you didn't mean anything but I suppose you're just the same as them aren't you? You just want to get your end away, that's all it means to you don't it?"

Her words were like a knife in his heart and he instantly became angry. Jason grabbed her by the shoulders and

47

roughly shook her.

"No it doesn't Lisa and I thought you knew me better than that. I love you and I only asked you to stop because I thought it was pushing you too far."

"Pushing me too far! Have you heard a word I've said? I've been to hell and back Jason. No one, no matter who they were could push me any further than I've already been."

"Ok! I'm sorry. If you want to talk then talk, it doesn't matter if it takes all night. Come to that Lisa if it takes a lifetime then I will still be here listening, at least for as long as you need me?"

Slowly she started her story again but this time she stared deep into his eyes searching for any sign of the disgust that she was sure he must be feeling.

"My mother had died of a broken heart or so my father said but in reality I think she had just had enough. My elder sister died in tragic circumstances when I was five and from then on my mum just gave up. My dad had always treated her like dirt and I suppose without our Mary she didn't want to go on anymore."

Jason Frasier's young wife suddenly went silent as her thoughts drifted back through the years. He didn't want to make the situation any worse so decided to stay quiet until she was ready to continue. As Lisa recalled the last fourteen years she thought of her first time on the streets. Eamon had taken her by bus to Kings cross and told her he'd wait in the Grange café across the road. He warned her not to get into any cars and to keep to the side streets of the station. Lisa was petrified and felt as though she stood out like a sore thumb. Up until that night her abuse had only been carried out at home by her family. Now her father was widening the market and wanted her to sell herself to anyone willing to pay. Lisa's first customer couldn't have been any worse. Raymond Tibbs was a regular with the other girls and every single one of them hated him with a vengeance. His shortness in stature was more than made up for in his extrovert manner. Raymond or stinky Ray as the girls called him hardly ever washed and his ejaculation time was legendary. To earn a quick twenty wouldn't have been too bad but Raymond Tibbs always lasted a good half hour. When business was slow the girls had little choice but to entertain him, that or get a beating from their pimps. Luckily the night was young and punters were plentiful. Recognising that Lisa was a first timer made the regular girls take pity on her but pity in the working game only went so far and when Raymond Tibbs appeared most of the girls scattered. Shirley Thomas an aging pro who had worked the Cross for years steered him in Lisa's direction.

When stinky Ray set eyes on the new blood he almost fainted with excitement and if it had of happened it would have been a lucky escape for Lisa. Sadly that wasn't the case and as he led her down the side of the Cross she began to tremble. Ray's firm grip on her elbow enabled him to feel this and her fear excited him even more. To have fresh meat was Raymond Tibbs's dream and tonight he had well and truly come up trumps. When they reached one of the archways and Ray was confident that they wouldn't be disturbed he moved in closer and smiled in a leering way. In the dim light Lisa could see his yellow teeth and his breath smelled rancid. She turned away but that didn't deter Ray. His hand moved swiftly up her skirt and when he discovered she wore no knickers he let out a sigh of appreciation. The no underwear idea had been Eamon's as he thought it would make business faster, how wrong he was. Lisa was so naive that she

49

didn't know it was the law of the streets to get your money up front. When she had endured a good thirty minutes of his rough mauling and when she thought he had at last come she asked for her money. Raymond Tibbs did up his trousers and laughed at her words. "Girlie you have a lot to learn. You're so fucking green that it should be you paying me. Now I ain't one to renege on a deal but twenty's far too much."

He forced a tenner into her hand and walked off as Lisa stood there with tears streaming down her face. She couldn't stomach the idea of seeing her father but knew she was in for a beating if she didn't. Slowly she made her way to the café and sat down beside her dad.

"Well? Hand it over then."

Lisa pulled the crumpled brown note from her pocket and passed it across the table. All the time she stared down at her shaking knees, never once daring to look her father in the eye.

"You're having a feckin' laugh ain't you! Come on empty your feckin' pockets, if you think ya can have one over on your old Da you can feckin' think again."

"Please Da that's all there is. I told the man it was twenty but afterwards he wouldn't give it to me."

"Jesus girl have I not taught ya anytin? You always get the feckin' reddies up front. Well you'll just have to work twice as hard, now get your bony feckin' arse back out there and don't come back until ya have at least a ton in ya grimy little hands."

Lisa didn't argue and with bended head went back out to join the other girls. It took hours for her to earn what she had been told to and by the time she returned to the café it was past midnight. The premises were now shut and Eamon leant against the windowsill. His face was like thunder and she knew that she had taken far too long.

50

Handing over her earnings she stared at the ground and waited for the onslaught to begin. It never came; instead her father grabbed her arm and led her home. The next two weeks followed much the same pattern but Lisa was a quick learner and her earnings soon increased to a level that Eamon was happy with. Her youth made her the preferred choice for many and Lisa was soon bringing in a hundred and still getting back to Morpeth Road by ten. This pleased her father as it left enough time to make last orders in the pub after taking her home. On the first night she had thought that her father would make her find her own way and many a night he had wanted to but then he couldn't risk her getting mugged or attacked. This little golden goose was far too precious to risk that happening. One morning not long after Lisa had been on the game, she woke with a thick green discharge that had penetrated her nightdress and gone onto the sheets. Knowing that something was wrong she took the soiled garment downstairs and showed it to her father. Instead of sympathy she felt the full force of his slap as it made contact with her cheek.

"You dirty little bitch, now you've feckin' ruined everytin'. Put your feckin' coat on and get down the quacks."

Lisa didn't argue she just did as she was told and made her way to the surgery. Dr Myers had treated the family since before Lisa was born. Aware what was going on in the Murphy household, he had more sense than to cross Eamon. He sympathised with the girl but so much of this type of thing went on that he reasoned to interfere wouldn't change anything. After examining Lisa, Doctor Myers informed her that she had Gonorrhoea. It meant nothing to the young girl so he went into graphic detail of how she had contracted it. Her treatment was a month's

51

course of antibiotics. No one else was informed and no help was offered. Finally when Lisa had finished recounting all the gory details to her husband she looked for a reaction but none came. A few minutes later and after swallowing hard he knew he had to speak.

"So you became their victim?"

"Yeah I suppose so. Anyway by the time I was fifteen things had really gotten out of hand. I wasn't sent out onto the streets anymore but my dad would bring back blokes after closing at the pub. He didn't know them and was only interested in the score a time he got for selling me."

"What!"

"Yeah I know it doesn't sound so good does it? but then again the truth rarely does."

"You mean he continued to sell his own daughter for sex, after everything you'd been through?"

"Don't seem so shocked Jay; it happens a lot more than you think. Anyway their little game plan didn't last long. Not after the pregnancy scare, no after that it was restricted to the family only and they always took precautions. What a hypocrite my dad was. He's supposed to be a staunch catholic but he isn't against contraception at least not when it comes down to shagging his own daughter that is."

Jason couldn't begin to imagine how they were ever going to overcome this. Their first night of wedded bliss in their own little home and his wife was revealing to him all about the sexual abuse she had suffered.

"So what do you want to do?"

"Do? What can I do?"

"Well you can go to the Old Bill for a start. Tell them what you've just told me and at least your dad and brothers will get what they deserve."

52

"I couldn't do that Jay, no way could I."

"Why on earth not?"

Lisa thought for a moment before she answered.

"I suppose because of my mother's memory, that and the shame I would feel at knowing everyone was aware of what they had done to me. No Jay I just want it left alone then maybe slowly it will all just go away."

"My darling I doubt that very much but if it's what you really want then its fine by me. Would you like me to sleep on the sofa?"

Lisa Frasier turned to face her husband.

"Jay I just want you to hold me and make me feel safe. I don't know how this will all turn out and I don't know if I will ever be able to have sex with you, so if you want to leave I'll understand."

"Babe I could never leave you and I'm sure we can work through all of this. It may take some time but I know we can do it."

Jason didn't give up and every few weeks the couple would try again but no matter how much they both wanted it; the outcome would always be the same. He had been so wrong in his assumption that he could make things better and over the years they continued attempting to consummate their marriage but it never came to anything. Lisa would either go as ridged as a board or start to sob uncontrollably.

CHAPTER SIX

The couple celebrated New Years Eve two thousand and one at the Camel along with Maude and a few of the regulars. Jason was now full time at the pub and had given up working at Kings. It was an idea that had come into Maude's mind a few months earlier and it had suited all concerned. Now here they stood united and waiting for the toll of big Ben to signal a happy future for them all. Maude leaned over and quietly spoke to Jason but it was still within Lisa's earshot.

"Jay I'm not getting any younger and I could do with a holiday. I want you to take control for a couple of weeks."

"Are you sure?"

"Of course I am and anyway Jay when I retire I want the two of you to have the pub."

"Don't be daft Maude, you can't do that!"

"Why can't I?"

"'Because it's worth a bloody fortune, that's why."

"Listen! I have no kids and you two have been like family to me. What else can I do with it, pour pints in a bleeding shroud?"

Maude Shelton placed an arm around each of their shoulders and pulled Lisa and Jason close to her.

"I love you both so much and you've made my life a lot happier since you came here, there's no way I could ever risk losing that."

Lisa's grin spread wide across her face. She loved living at the Camel but it had always worried her that one day they would have to move out. Now that everything was secure, it was going to be a great new year. From day one Maude had taken to the young girl. Over the past three years she had seen Lisa change from a timid little girl who was scared of her own shadow into a beautiful young woman who idolised her husband. Lisa reminded her of what it was like to be a newlywed although she understood that the girl's troubles ran a lot deeper than she let on. Still Jay took good care of her and it was plain for anyone to see that he totally doted on his wife. Mr and Mrs Jason Frasier had never managed to consummate their marriage but it was something no one was aware of but them. The situation had caused problems over the years but it had also brought the two closer together. Lisa knew of her husband's small infidelities but that's all they were, small indiscretions that she was content enough to overlook. Jason didn't cheat on a regular basis and it never meant anything to him when he did but after all he was only human and sometimes he needed relief. It was a man thing and as hard as he tried he couldn't help it. Guessing that his wife was aware of what was going on, he was always very careful not to bring any hurt to her door.

Lisa remained working at Kings Factory and even though Jason had been against it in the beginning he had finally agreed with his wife after a few lengthy arguments. Each day she would walk to work but always took the long route round. Over the years she had only bumped into her father once and that was on a Saturday down Roman Road market. As he approached Lisa could feel all the old terror begin to build up in the pit of her stomach but she needn't have worried, he walked straight past her as though she didn't exist. Standing still she had waited for the hurt to begin but it didn't. When anger hadn't shown its face she smiled deeply, at last she was free. Vinny and his mother still drank in the pub at weekends but

55

relations were strained. Vera never spoke to her daughter in law and only to her son when it was to order a drink. Jason and his brother were still friendly but nothing like it had been in the past. Soon after he started full time at the pub Jason had thought Vinny would leave Kings but to his amazement his brother was still there. Without prior knowledge, no one at the factory would ever have known that Lisa and Vinny were related. The two didn't speak although Lisa was aware of her brother in laws life style. It wasn't something she had discussed with Jason, she didn't even know if he knew but she could imagine the hurt it would cause if it ever came out into the open. Vera was another matter altogether. She would never of believed it and Lisa would have been the biggest low life under the sun for saying such a thing about her precious boy. Vincent Frasier had banked on his sister in law keeping her mouth shut and it had paid off. Jason would never have let things lie if he had known the truth, so when no outbursts occurred Vinny was happy with how things were going. His special friend Stephan whom he had met soon after joining Kings had suddenly left. Fred Blatch tried to get to the bottom of the man's disappearance but had drawn a blank at every corner. He knew deep down that it was something to do with Vinny but couldn't prove anything. Everyone assumed the missing man had returned to Lithuania but nothing was further from the truth. Stephan Karspowsky resided at the Mildmay Mission Hospital in Shoreditch. It was a hospital come hospice and dedicated itself to the transition from hospital to community living. In Stephan's case that wouldn't happen and he would be a resident of the hospice until he died of a viral disease that had slowly stripped him of everything. Vincent Frasier had promised to visit but as was the norm when there was nothing in it for him, Vinny didn't want to know.

The social scene that Vinny so desperately craved hadn't reciprocated his wanting. Most people in the gay community shunned his advances but it didn't stop him spending ever Friday night trawling gay pubs looking for that brief encounter that he so yearned for. To begin with it was time mostly spent at Compton's of Soho. On his first night out he had found the atmosphere electrifying and no matter how hard he tried he hadn't been able to stop staring at the men. To him they were all gods, every single rippling muscle but it didn't take long for Vinny to realise that he didn't fit in with the traditional gay scene. Men would take one look at him and then back off as fast as they could, even the ones who were married with families and only out for fast seedy sex. It was something that they could see within, a cruel nasty streak that he didn't do a very good job of hiding. Where most were out for fun and the possibility of a relationship, Vinny just wanted hardcore and it was enough to frighten off most decent gay men. Realising that he had no chance of pulling, Vinny soon saw the place as too tame and not really for him so he moved onto the club scene. Starting at Heaven in the West End, he soon realised that this wasn't for him either. Everywhere he looked the men seemed to be in couples and that was something he was definitely not interested in. Vinny felt disgust with himself but at the same time he couldn't control his urge, like a drug addict he was forced to seek out the one thing that repulsed him. From his first act with Stephan he had never received only given and in Vinny's mind this didn't make him queer. Maybe he was just promiscuous and one day he would settle down like his brother but somehow he couldn't see that happening. Women did nothing for him; in fact he would go as far as to say they

57

repulsed him. His next attempt was at G-A-Y on the Charing Cross Road. Immediately Vinny liked the feel of this place. It was sweaty and sexy, the kind of atmosphere he had been looking for and best of all catered to a large selection of the European community. Since Stephan's untimely demise and his first initiation at Compton's it hadn't taken him long to realise that men from Eastern Europe was his preferred taste. He found black people attractive but he didn't want to have sex with them, he was definitely only interested in white skin. Vincent Frasier would frequent G-A-Y as often as he could and it got to the point where even Vera began to question him.

"Vincent where do you keep going to? You ain't got some fucking trollop on the go like your brother have you?"

Vinny touched the side of his mothers face.

"Never my queen. There's only one woman in the world for me and she's standing not a million miles from here." Vera glowed with pride, at least one of her boys still cared about her.

"You're a smooth talking bastard just like your old man was. Now are you going to take your old mum out for a drink?"

"I can't mum I've got to go see someone."

Vera's mouth turned downwards as she tried to use the show of disappointment to make her son feel guilty. It didn't work.

"Now don't start, this is all I fucking need! If I get back in time we'll go out if not it will have to wait until the weekend alright?"

Vinny didn't wait for her to reply and was out of the flat as fast as his legs would carry him. Although the lure of G-A-Y was strong he was eager to experience something

58

new. An acquaintance he'd met at the club had told Vinny about the bathhouses. Up until now it was something he'd heard of but never dared to try but as he was now becoming more and more experienced on the scene and as his confidence grew, Vinny decided to give it a go. Chariots Sauna was situated on Cowcross Street in Farringdon so it wasn't far to walk. From outside it resembled an office building and what went on inside was very well hidden. Although nervous he could feel the excitement beginning to build as he entered through the highly polished glass doors. Vinny was greeted at the reception by Oliver Elliott a large muscle-bound man in a tight fitting black vest. Inquiring about membership he was told that the sauna was open to all and was well known for its discretion by not asking people any personal details. This was sounding better by the second and after Oliver had given Vinny the guided tour he was left to his own devises in the changing room. The place was very quiet and apart from a couple making out in the sauna there was no one else about. Vinny had a quick swim in the small pool then headed for one of the relaxation cabins complete with glory holes. Peering at the three fist sized holes in the wall Vinny was intrigued and bending down was about to peer through when a large penis emerged. Disgusted he stood up and nearly fell over the central wooden bench in his haste. Mutual masturbation and oral sex definitely wasn't for him. He was interested in nothing more than someone's arse and to even contemplate oral sex made his stomach turn. He muttered under his breath though not loud enough to be heard 'Dirty bastard!' The door to the room opened and a large bald headed man entered. He resembled a marine and when he spoke in a Russian accent Vincent Frasier thought all his Christmases had come at once. The man let his towel drop to the floor, revealing a massive penis and suddenly Vinny became scared. Nodding to the naked man he walked towards the door but a strong arm gripped him by the shoulder. The Russian pushed his victim over the wooden bench and with one huge muscular arm held him there by pressing down on the back of his neck. Vinny's arms flailed about wildly over the edge of the bench but he wasn't able to lift them as the Russian held him down with such force. The towel was snatched up from the floor and before Vinny knew what was happening it had been forced across his mouth and was being held tightly at the back of his neck almost like a garrotte. Sweat ran down his forehead as he realised what was about to happen. Vinny screamed and tried with all his might to spit the towel out but it was useless. No one came to his rescue as his abuser roughly entered him from behind. Tears streamed down Vincent Frasier's face as he felt pain seer through his body. He'd heard of male rape but it had never occurred to him that one day he would experience it. Vinny knew that his skin was slowly tearing with every thrust that the Russian inflicted. When the rapist at last finished he calmly stood up and releasing the towel from Vinny's mouth, wrapped it around his waist and arrogantly walked from the room. Droplets of blood slowly made their way down Vinny's legs and it took all of his strength just to stand up. Dressing as quickly as he could he gasped at the pain that shot through his body with every movement. Ten minutes later and he at last made it to the reception and asked Oliver to call him a cab. By the look on Vinny's ashen face the receptionist guessed what had occurred but still he asked no questions. Sometimes this sort of thing went with the territory if you were stupid enough to get yourself into a vulnerable situation. Oliver knew that

60

today this man had learned a valuable lesson, one that he himself had gone through several years earlier. Vinny felt every hump and bump of the journey home and when the cab at last pulled up in Rickman Street he almost fell out of the door. Staggering up the cold concrete stairwell he breathed a sigh of relief when he finally closed the front door of the flat behind him. Sobbing out loud and at the same time desperately trying to silence the noise Vinny had to force his fist into his mouth. The last thing he wanted was for Vera to see the state he was in and start the Spanish Inquisition. The television blared out from the living room as he quietly made his way to his room without being seen or heard. The experience had filled Vinny with rage, the kind of rage that even he had never felt before. Now it was him against the world and he was going to take whatever he wanted. Laying in the darkness, his body engulfed with a burning pain, he silently made a promise to himself. No one, no matter who they were, would ever do anything like that to him again. No one would ever force him into a corner, not without paying a heavy price. Where it had once been the Frasier brothers against the world, Vinny now realised that he was on his own. In the solitude of his room Vincent Frasier swore vengeance on the entire human race.

CHAPTER SEVEN

In his own lifetime, Freddie Gant would become a legend
to some and a nightmare to others. Born in the summer
of nineteen fifty-two, his mother Pearl couldn't wait to
have him expelled from her body. She saw him as
nothing more than an inconvenience and the sooner she
was able to earn again the better. Pearl Gant was an
unusual breed of Tom, she was only in it for the money
but at the same time she also enjoyed her work. On
occasion, if a punter didn't have enough reddies then she
would allow tick, something unheard of to the rest of the
working girls. Most in the trade knew that a pro could
earn in a day what it took a shop girl to earn in a week
but unfortunately that wasn't the case with Pearl Gant.
Having not been blessed with good looks, she made her
money wherever she could and that would sometimes
come in the guise of things more sinister. Lesbian acts
and threesomes were tame in comparison to what Pearl
would offer. It was common knowledge that she had
even performed acts of bestiality, in fact whatever the
customer wanted she would provide without question.
Freddie grew up being cared for by any brass that was on
hand and not working at the time. His mother always
found a knack of seeking out the girls that were on their
monthly's and couldn't tout for business. At other times
when there wasn't anyone to mind him he would be told
to sit quietly in the corner while she plied her trade. One
of his earliest memories was of watching an overweight
Greek bloke go down on his mother. Over the years
Freddie learnt every con trick in the book and not only
did he know how to hide from the rent man but any
disgruntled customers who had the nerve to return for

their wallets that had been swiftly lifted by Pearl and there were many. Pearl Gant showed her son no love but she did teach him how to survive and it was a lesson that would stand him in good stead in his adult years. Only once in his life, did he ever ask his mother the question of why she didn't love him. It had happened late one Saturday night. Pearl had just seen off her last punter of the day and had poured a large glass of gin. As usual Freddie was sitting quietly in the corner. His mother was in a foul mood and as she passed him she lashed out for no reason. The side of Freddie's face stung where his mother had slapped him and he couldn't hold back the tears any longer.

"Why was I born, why did you have me?"

Lighting a cigarette, Pearl Gant curled her lip back into a snarl.

"I was unlucky alright! You just happened, just fucking happened that's it. Now shut the fuck up and get to bed before I do you some real damage."

He never questioned or wanted love from his mother again, in fact after that night he quickly came to hate the very sight of her and any other woman who sold their body for cash. School was a hit and miss affair but Freddie learned enough to cover the value of money. Reading and writing wasn't his forte but no one could fiddle him out of a penny.

His early teens were spent ducking and diving and pick pocketing was a lucrative business in the swinging sixties. As soon as he could walk Pearl had taught him how to dip and as yet he hadn't been caught. The tourist trade was rich pickings in Soho and a young Freddie quickly learned the easiest way to mug off anyone who didn't have the nous to know any different. As soon as he was old enough he left Pearls flat on Old Compton

Street and moved into a rented room just off Greek Street. To most it would have been seen as swapping one slum for another but to Freddie it was a palace. Myrtle Greggs ran a tidy ship and as long as her guests paid the rent on time, then she didn't bother what they did for a living. A full English breakfast was always on the table in the mornings and a hot meal ready at night for whenever they returned from what they'd been doing. Freddie had never known such luxury and soon began to look upon Myrtle as a kind of second mum, the kind of woman his mother should have been. Eventually most of Myrtle's paying guests moved on, all except Freddie. He was happy with how things were and managed to squirrel away a few pounds every week for his nest egg. Things took a sudden upward turn when Myrtle died after a short illness and left the boarding house to her only remaining guest. It had come as a shock to Freddie and to say he missed the old girl was an understatement but he also saw it as an omen for his future. Deciding it was now time to move up a notch Freddie sold up quickly and purchased his first shop on Jermyn Street. In the ensuing years Freddie Gant would trade in many things, all of which were illegal but the one he gained the most pleasure from was the sex trade. Maybe it was a deep seated hatred of his mother but Freddie just loved to take cash from the Toms. Pornography was on the increase and Freddie Gant sought out the best suppliers he could find. It was hypocritical to say the least but in Freddie's eyes porn was totally different to prostitution and he had even been heard to say that he admired the women. Before long he had a massive turnover and a reputation for the hardest core in the smoke. In a very short space of time he had opened two more shops and secured the office on Bridle Lane. This above all his other properties was Freddie's pride and joy; after all it was now his home.

Wally Evans had been on nodding terms with Freddie for several years but it wasn't until Wally fell on hard times that the two men's friendship developed. Known locally as a fixer, he could make anything happen or disappear and that included people. When his wife passed away suddenly it had just about finished Wally. Rene had been the love of his life and had never questioned his line of work. As hard as he was and no one ever dared dispute that fact, with Rene he was as gentle as a lamb. Without her he didn't see any reason to carry on and the bottle beckoned to him daily. It takes a long time to build a reputation in London but a short while to lose it and it didn't take Wally Evans more than a few weeks to lose his. Soon no one showed him the respect he had previously commanded through fear, but being drunk most of the time, he wasn't able to change their minds. He spent day upon day walking the streets of Soho drinking from a bottle until he could no longer stand. A sad looking figure, he would then fall asleep wherever his body fell.

Not long after Freddie purchased his office and home, he had been in the middle of putting a blind up at the front window when he spotted Wally swaying from side to side. Beckoning him over, Freddie opened the door and invited Wally in. Several strong coffees later and after Freddie had offered the man a shower, the two began to talk. It had been years since anyone had really shown an interest in him and to Wally this act of kindness instantly formed a bond between the two men. When Wally Evans recounted the loss of Rene, Freddie showed a sympathetic side that over the next few years would rapidly disappear. He gave Wally a stern talking to and told him he would be dead himself if he carried on the

65

way he was.

"Look mate as hard as it is to fucking hear, nothing's going to bring her back. Now you can carry on as you are and join her pretty quick or you can sort yourself out and make a new life."

Wally didn't know if it was because someone was showing him concern or just the fact that he'd had enough of living like this but either way he wanted to live. Freddie hadn't said anything he didn't already know but hearing it from a stranger gave Wally the push that he needed. Employing him on the spot had made Freddie Gant a God in Wally's eyes and there wasn't anything he wouldn't do for his new boss.

As history dictates when things are going good something bad always happens and that bad thing turned up in the guise of Pearl Gant. In a small place like Soho it had been a miracle that mother and son hadn't regularly bumped into each other. Freddie saw it as a blessing that he hadn't been constantly forced into seeing his mothers face or watch her ply her trade. Recently hearing that her only son was doing well had prompted Pearl to seek him out and see if there was any spare cash to be had. Wally was about to open up the office for the morning and was waiting for his boss to appear when the front door suddenly burst open. A woman of maturing years and wearing thick pan stick makeup walked in. Wally was stunned for a minute and considered at great length what his boss would say. The woman shocked him further when she asked for Freddie by name.

"Sorry love but the Boss ain't up yet and there's no way I'm going to be the one to disturb him. Now if you want to leave your name or call back later I......"

"Fucking call back later? You cheeky cunt!"

Wally grabbed her by the arm, fully intending to forcibly

throw her from the building.

"Listen whore! Don't fucking come in here shouting the odds or you'll soon see a side to me you won't fucking like. Now out of here before you really start to piss me off big time."

"Look you nonce! I'm his fucking mother, so get your hands off me and get him down here now!"

Wally didn't know what to say and doing as he was told made his way up to the flat. Tentatively he knocked on the door and was about to walk back down again when a bleary eyed Freddie answered.

"What the fuck Wally! This had better be good."

"Sorry Boss and I wouldn't have disturbed you but there's some dizzy old bat downstairs says she's your mum?"

Wally Evans could see the colour visibly drain from his Boss's face, which caused the great lump of a man to stand there not knowing what else to say. The thought that he had just called the woman an old bat, not to mention laying his hands on her was something he was starting to regret. If it turned out that she was Freddie's old mum, then he had stirred up a shit load of trouble for himself.

"Ok Wall, give us a minute and I'll be down."

Not needing to be told twice Wally descended the stairs as quickly as possible. When Freddie Gant finally appeared he was washed, clean shaven and sporting the latest in designer gear. Always one to be dressed smartly, he had made an extra effort today as he wanted to show Pearl just how far he had come. She stood looking out of the window as he walked down the stairs and just the sight of her made the hairs on the back of his neck stand to attention.

"Hello there Pearl, how are you keeping?"

Pearl Gant turned with such speed that Wally Evans instantly bowed his head down towards the counter. Low on intelligence but a hard man through and through, even he realised when to keep quiet and now was definitely one of those times.

"How am I fucking keeping? You cheeky little bastard! I've been flogging my fucking arse off, that's how I've been. All them fucking years I fed and clothed you and you don't even tell me when you're having good times. I ask you, what sort of fucking son behaves like that?"

Her question was aimed in the direction of Wally but he knew better than to reply, instead he continued to concentrate on some non-existent paper lying on the counter before him. Freddie hadn't envisaged his mother turning up and now that she had he was becoming more agitated by the second. Grabbing Pearl by the elbow he swiftly opened the door and shoved her outside.

"You were never a mother to me and you ain't now, so fuck off out of it! If you ever darken this fucking doorstep again I'll do for you, do you hear?"

Pearl Gant didn't bother to answer. It had been worth a punt and nothing ventured nothing gained was all she told herself. Freddie watched her totter along the street in her trademark stiletto heels and her legs were so bandy, that he laughed to himself as the image of her trying to stop a pig in an alley entered his mind. Back inside Wally now looked up at his boss but wasn't ready for the onslaught that was about to come.

"What the fuck do I pay you for?"

About to answer Wally didn't get a chance to defend himself.

"Wal, if you ever put me in that fucking situation again, you can find yourself another job. From now on, if anyone comes in here no matter who the fuck they are without an appointment, then tell them to sling their hook. I don't care if it's the fucking Queen herself. Understood?"

Wally only nodded but the point had been made and that was all that mattered. He had let Freddie Gant well and truly down by letting Pearl into the office and he would make sure that it wouldn't be repeated. The subject of Freddie's parentage was never raised again and looking at the woman Wally could see why. He felt sadness for his friend and just the glimmer of understanding as to why the man was like he was. Even though there wasn't a huge difference in age, Wally Evans always looked on his boss in a fatherly way and for some reason he wanted to protect the man beyond what he was paid to do. As the years passed he became obsessed with Freddie and it was known by all, that he'd made it his job to defend his boss to the death, if that's what it took.

CHAPTER EIGHT

Freddie Gant ruled his empire out of the office on Bridle
Lane. Running vertical to Brewer Street it was deep
within the heart of Soho and near enough to all his
businesses for him to keep his finger on the pulse and be
immediately aware of anything that was happening.
Having grown up in the area and being the only child of a
brass Freddie knew every scam there was. Slowly over
the years he had expanded his empire of sex shops and
even purchased a couple of small clubs. Not the kind of
places that many decent people would frequent, though
many tourists found themselves lured into the seedy dens.
An exorbitant entrance fee would be charged and it was
compulsory to purchase champagne for the girl that was
seated with them. Many found out the hard way, that it
was easier to pay the sky high price for a bottle of
champagne than to argue. To dispute the fee would end
up with the person being physically thrown from the club,
minus a few front teeth and not before their wallet had
been emptied of its contents. 'Fanny's Place' was the
second club purchased and where Freddie Gant and
Lance Bowers would first be introduced. Lance had
recently moved to the capital after graduating from police
training school. He had excelled in every task and exam
he'd taken and was now being fast tracked within the
Metropolitan force. His naivety of city living had
somehow seen him end up at the club on a rare night
when Freddie and Wally were paying a visit. The young
policeman had wandered in off the street and after sitting
with one of the girls named Sandra for over a half an
hour, now refused to pay for the drink she had consumed.
As Freddie walked past on his way to the manager's

office he heard one of his bouncers arguing loudly with the young man.

"Look here you little tosser! She had the drink and you've had the pleasure of the lady's company, now cough up or I'll call the Old Bill"

"You can try your bully boy tactics on me all you like and as for calling the police then go ahead. I'm sure they will take a dim view of someone trying to extort money from one of their own."

On hearing this Freddie's ears pricked up like radar. Stopping dead in his tracks he beckoned Sandra over. "Look I don't want any fucking trouble in here tonight, take him out the back and give him a blowjob to calm him down. The last thing I need is to have the Old Bill crawling all over the club."

Sandra Graham obligingly did as she was told and after whispering into the ear of her guest, he willingly followed her outside to the back of the club.

"Wally? Got your camera on you?"

"Sure have Boss."

"Then go and take a few snaps. I think they just might come in handy in the future."

Doing as he was told Wally quietly walked out of the rear fire escape and after positioning himself by one of the large waste bins, happily snapped away. The couple, who were by now so engrossed in what they were doing, didn't see or hear the constant click of the Kodak.

Freddie Gant wasn't the hard but fair kind of gangster that's often portrayed on film. He was a cruel and selfish villain whose only interest was how many reddies could be earned no matter what the cost or who got hurt.

For years now Wally Evans had been Freddie's right hand man and the only other person he trusted in the world. Wally was a thug, a body to be called on when punishment needed dishing out and anyone who tried to have a go at Freddie Gant and there had been many over the years, had to go through Wally first. Standing over six feet tall and weighing in at twenty two stone the man instilled fear just by looking at you. Wally truly was a force to be reckoned with and his face was hardened with a gnarled look about it and smiling was something he rarely did in public. The sex industry that the two men traded in was a lucrative business but you had to keep permanently on your toes. There was always someone trying to muscle in and take a piece of your action. Most of the trouble came from local young upstarts who had no backing. They fancied their chances and over the years Freddie had found out that these could be every bit as dangerous as another firm trying to muscle in. The blacks were the worst with over seventy percent of shootings being carried out by gang members. Freddie hated them with a vengeance and wished he could send them all to kingdom come, let alone back to their home land. Soho was on a different level in comparison to anywhere else in the country. The majority of youngsters carried guns, had real front and seemed to have no concept or fear. Lately Freddie had realised that he needed to up the ante as far as his businesses were concerned and he was going to have to rule with more violence than ever before. Choosing to live above the office had not been out of necessity but a personal choice. It was dangerous to be seen too often coming and going on a regular basis from one place but to him living and working in the same building was an added bonus. His office was plain, no luxuries whatsoever but that wasn't the case when it came to his home. Freddie's flat was the latest in designer chic and had every mod con imaginable. No one, except Wally, was ever invited into his inner sanctum and that was just how he wanted it. The front door was three inch steel plate and every window was blacked out. When Freddie Gant was in residence it was as if the rest of the world didn't exist. Lately profits had increased three fold due to his involvement with the Russians. Hesitant when first approached, Freddie had soon seen how much money could be earned from laundering. His ownership of a factory over in Hackney had proved a perfect front and now he was truly in love with the queen's head. Kings was a dismal grey building that didn't stand out aesthetically. Unless you needed to go there you would pass by without a second glance and that was exactly how Freddie liked it. At first it had been his own personal greed to accumulate as much cash as possible, now the mighty pound had turned into his mistress and she ruled with an iron rod. Even Wally had noticed of late how consumed his boss had become with all the money that was rolling in but he was shrewd enough not to mention it. Freddie Gant had an account with Newham's and the bank address was Nauru in the pacific. The island had such stringent privacy laws that it stopped not only foreign investigators but even local ones from knowing who really controlled a company. The set up was brilliant and allowed Freddie to hide vast amounts of illegal income without any questions being asked. When Roly Peterson began to run up a tab at one of his clubs Freddie had just let it ride. Roly had a liking for brasses and Freddie had given the word that he could have whoever he liked whenever he liked. When the bill had run into a few grand Freddie Gant sent Wally to collect. Knowing that the fat old perv wouldn't be able to pay, Wally was told to make the man an offer he couldn't refuse, his life or his factory. Reluctantly, just as Freddie had imagined, Roly gave in and Kings passed over in ownership to Freddie. Not wanting to seem a complete bastard Freddie kept Roly on as manager and knew that the man would run things as if his life depended on it. It also meant that he could distance himself from the place and if things ever went tits up then he would be able to deny all knowledge of what had gone on. The company's finances were run through the Nauru bank and as far as anyone was concerned everything was legal and above board. On the day that Boris Worzinze from one the Russian firms approached Freddie asking for him to launder their money, he knew he had hit the jackpot. The Russians wanted to bring cash into the country but weren't able to show that it was legitimate. Together the two men came up with a plan. Russian money would be paid into Freddie's Nauru bank and then Boris would open up an employment agency in London. The Russians would provide an immigrant workforce, who would then be sent on to Kings via Boris's agency. The unprecedented level of eastern European's coming into the country everyday was nothing short of brilliant for them. Labour fees would be paid from Freddie's Nauru bank account and hey presto the Russians money was now clean. Freddie Gant took a twenty five percent fee and everyone was happy all round. Occasionally Boris would require a payment to be made in cash. The money was transferred on a regular basis so that there was never any delay when it was requested. Once collected it would be stashed at Kings until Boris was ready to make a visit. This hadn't happened for several months but the money had still been regularly coming in and was beginning to mount up. When these special transactions took place it always made Wally Evans feel uneasy. Wally knew only too well that if his boss ever crossed theses people, then he would be looking for new employment and Freddie would be looking for a cemetery plot. Even Freddie was wise enough to realise that he was no match for the Russians and at times this thought played heavily on his mind.

Vincent Frasier made his way to work and as usual he was late. Since Jason had left the factory, the Russians had been trying to clean more and more money but it was getting increasingly difficult to find the amount of workers needed. Luckily for him and due to the manpower shortage, Vinny's lateness went unchallenged. Happy Bottle let the man in through the gate but his unfriendliness didn't go unnoticed. Like most, Happy after a time had taken to Jason but it was a different matter when it came to his brother.

"The guv'nor needs you to work late today, we've got a big order on and the top brass are coming. Make sure that the corridor to Mr Peterson's office is kept clean and tidy."

Vinny Frasier saluted behind the man's back but said nothing. Since his encounter at Chariots, he was just biding his time waiting for a golden opportunity to strike. Unbeknown to him that opportunity would present itself within the next few hours. By six that day the majority of the workforce had left for home and Vincent Frasier was doing his final inspection of the office building before clocking off. The door to Roly Petersons office was firmly shut but Vinny noticed the door to the stationary cupboard at the end of the hallway was ajar. In all his time at the factory he had never seen it open and not one to miss an opportunity, he slipped inside in the hope that there would be something worth nicking. After snooping around for a few seconds he was about to leave disappointed when a tall thin cupboard situated to the left caught his eye. Not immediately visible it had been

75

draped with an old sheet to appear inconspicuous. Drawing the sheet back Vinny cagily opened one of the doors and couldn't believe his eyes at what he saw. The whole unit was stacked from top to bottom with twenty and fifty pound notes. Vinny quickly shut the door and replaced the sheet. This needed to be thought about in great detail and by the looks of the dust on the sheet the cash had been there for some time. He quietly closed the stationary cupboard door and was about to continue sweeping when he saw Happy standing at the bottom of the hall watching him.

"What are you doing Frasier?"

"Only what you told me to do, keep this area clean you said."

"So what the fuck were you doing in that room then?" Vinny glanced behind him at the now closed cupboard door.

"Nothing! It was open that's all and I just shut it. Fuck me what's with all the third degree?"

Happy motioned with his arm for Vinny to leave and scared that he'd been caught out Vinny did as he was asked. He knew that this was what he'd been waiting for and guessed that there was something illegal going on. As the two men walked across the concrete that stretched out in front of the building, Vinny tried to make conversation in the hope that what Happy had thought he'd seen would soon be forgotten.

"So then mate after all this time are you going to let me in on the secret?"

"What secret?"

"Why they call you that?"

"Call me what?"

"Happy Bottle."

"Because I'm a miserable cunt and only smile when I've

76

had a drink, though what the fuck it's got to do with you I don't know."

Vinny could see that he was fighting a losing battle, however nice he tried to be the man was having none of it.

"No need to be like that mate, I was only trying to make a bit of conversation."

"Well if I was you I wouldn't fucking bother! Now are you going to fuck off home so I can lock these gates or what?"

Vinny didn't answer instead he just walked out in silence. His mind was now too busy thinking about all that cash to worry about trying to get on the good side of this miserable little sod. Walking home he couldn't stop mentally picturing what he had seen and imagining what it would be like to have that amount of money, there must have been at least a half a million. He realised that if he robbed the place then he would probably have to leave the area but then that didn't really bother him. The idea of spending the rest of his life coped up in that poxy flat with Vera was enough to spur him on. Not wanting to act rash, he decided to monitor the situation over the next couple of weeks. He mentally weighed up what the consequences could be of waiting and accepted that he could lose out big-time if this was a one off but somehow he didn't think it was. To let things be for a while would be best, and then at least he wouldn't immediately draw suspicion to himself. Happy would eventually forget about what he had seen and if Vinny brought Jason on board it should be a piece of cake. Apart from the large front gates there was no real security at the place; maybe it was a lesson that the fat bastard Roly Peterson needed to learn and Vinny hoped it would be quite soon.

The following few days seemed to drag but Vinny still

did exactly as he had planned. Whenever an opportunity arose for him to be in the office building he would jump at the chance and each time he tried the stationary door it was firmly locked. This didn't deter him, in fact he rationalised that it must be locked due to the cash inside. Keeping well out of Happy's way had been easy and when he wasn't scouting the building he was tucked up in his own little office making plans. The approaching weekend was a bank holiday and Vinny knew this would be the perfect opportunity. Tonight he would call on Jason to see if he was in or out of the deal, either way in the next week Vincent Frasier was going to be richer than he had ever dreamed of.

The Camel was quiet for a Tuesday night. The usual pool team were on an away match and a lot of the regulars had gone on a day trip to Clacton that Maude had arranged. Jason stood at the bar reading the Evening Standard and Lisa was in the back washing up after their meal. Not hearing the side door open, Lisa froze with fear when she finally turned round and saw her brother in law standing in the doorway. She didn't know why but he always gave her the creeps and after what she'd been through, that was really saying something.

"God Vinny you scared me, how did you get in here?"

Vinny ignored her question.

"Where's Jay?"

Drying her hands on the tea towel that until a second ago she had been gripping in fear, Lisa tried to speak without sounding scared.

"He's in the bar but you didn't answer me Vinny, how did you get in?"

Totally blanking her, Vinny made his way along the hall and into the bar area. Jason looked up and couldn't help but smile when he saw his brother. They hadn't been so

78

close in recent years but he still loved Vinny like a brother should.

"Hello mate, what brings you over here?"

"Alright Jay! Just thought I'd pop in and see how me big bruvver was doing."

Jason laughed.

"Since when have you ever just popped in? Come on mate what's on your mind?"

"Well to tell the truth I've got a bit of a proposition."

Jason decided not to comment until he'd heard Vinny out but if this proposition was anything like the normal hair brained ideas his brother usually came up with then he could forget about it. Pouring them both a pint of larger he motioned for his brother to join him at one of the tables. Jason knew Lisa wouldn't disturb them as she couldn't stand Vinny. Ever the diplomat, she had never mentioned the fact but the look in her eyes said it all every time Vincent Frasier was within a hundred feet of her. Her body language was normally tense but went to almost rigid whenever Vinny was around and it spoke volumes to her husband. After taking a mouthful of beer Vinny proceeded to tell Jason about all that he had seen.

"So what do you think?"

Jason puffed his cheeks out and thought for a moment.

"I'm not sure Vin, I mean I have a good set up here. If we get caught then I can kiss goodbye to all of this."

"All of this! Fuck me bro do you want to be a pot man all your life?"

"I ain't no pot man and Maude's giving us this place soon."

"Yeah and I'm going to be the next president of America."

"No straight up Vin, the Duchess told me and Lisa this place will be ours."

His brother's words stunned Vinny. He had always thought Jason got everything given to him on a plate and now he was even more determined than ever to rob Kings.

"Look if you don't help me then I can't do it. Please Jay just this once fucking help me out."

"Just this once! Fuck you make me laugh Vinny you really do."

Jason Frasier could see the pleading in his brother's eyes but at the same time he thought of Lisa and all that they had. If he ended up getting his collar felt, then what would she do? Then again he had never been able to deny Vinny anything.

"Let me hear what you've got planned, then I'll make me mind up."

Vinny smiled to himself, he knew that he had his brother on board.

"Well I want to do it Saturday night. I can do everything from inside but I need you to hire a car and bring a large holdall and I mean large! If you can remember, there's a wooden gate down the side of the fence and the stupid fucks only pull a bolt across it at night. I'm going to hide inside the storeroom on Friday night and when everyone's gone I'll unlock the gate from the inside. All you have to do is be waiting in the car when I come out."

"And it's as easy as that!"

"Don't be fucking sarky Jay! You know as well as I do that they're a bunch of fucking muppet's at that place. I suppose they don't think anyone will ever rob them and I reckon they don't think anyone knows about the cash either."

"Have you thought for a minute what they're doing with that much money on the premises? I mean we need to know what were dealing with here Vin. We don't want to end up in the Thames because we've pissed off some face or another."

Vincent Frasier had already thought about everything his brother was saying but he didn't care. After all he would be out of the Smoke almost immediately and as for Jason, well for once he would have to follow Vinny, that or suffer the consequences.

"Fuck me Jay you sound as if you're shitting yourself. I've already done a bit of investigating and its nothing more than a tax scam. The only one whose going to feel the pinch is that fat bastard Peterson."

Jason was still unsure but his brother's complete look of honesty finally swayed him.

"OK do what you have to but not a word to Lisa or mum all right?"

"For fucks sake Jay, give me a bit of credit will you." Getting up from the table Vinny didn't say goodbye, he just walked straight out. Jason was well aware that he would be hearing from Vinny in the not too distant future and was already starting to have a niggling doubt about agreeing to any of his brother's plan.

CHAPTER NINE

Over the next two days Vinny kept his head down but closely observed anything that was happening at Kings. A few strangers were noted coming and going but apart from that it was business as usual and nothing out of the ordinary. Happy was his normal miserable self and the work force had no more exceptional orders. Vinny was concerned that he had missed his window of opportunity but he wouldn't know for sure until Saturday, the suspense and excitement was killing him. Friday morning at six thirty am Vincent Frasier's alarm burst into life and he was instantly up and out of bed. Vera had cooked him eggs and bacon every morning for as long as she could remember but today he had no appetite.

"What the fucks wrong with you? That little lot didn't grow on trees you know."

"Give it a rest Mum for god's sake."

"Don't you take that fucking tone with me or you'll be cooking your own fucking grub in future."

"Sorry but I just ain't hungry."

Despite her harsh words Vera Frasier was the ever doting mother and walking over to her son placed the palm of her hand on his forehead.

"Well you ain't got a temperature boy but maybe you're coming down with something. Why don't you take the day off?"

Vinny almost jumped down her throat with his reply.

"Day off? No way!"

"Alright boy calm down, a bit bleeding touchy this morning aint you. What's up?"

There was no reply and picking up her mug of tea Vera rolled her eyes upwards.

Vinny continued to stay silent and grabbing his jacket from the back of the chair, he stormed out of the flat. Vera glanced at the clock, it was only just seven and her sons shift didn't start until eight. Whatever was riling him she hoped would be sorted by the time he came home. He could be a right miserable little bastard if he had a mind to be and just lately that was happening more and more often. At first she had put it down to Jason leaving and her youngest missing his brother but as time passed and things didn't improve she realised it had to be something else. Well as far as she was concerned he could just piss off out of it, she wasn't in the mood for any of his tantrums today. Vinny walked slowly to the factory and trying to kill time, stopped to buy a newspaper on the way. Nerves were starting to get the better of him and he knew that once tomorrow night came there would be no going back.

As usual everyone at Kings was in a good mood. The Lithuanians were rabbiting on ten to the dozen and like every other day he couldn't understand a word they were saying. It was always the same on pay day and Vinny couldn't wait for it to be over. By five that evening all but a skeleton crew had clocked off for the long weekend. Quietly Vinny made his way to the rear of the factory. An old fire exit, that hadn't been used for years and was partially covered by empty cardboard cartons, would be perfect for getting back inside later. Moving the boxes he pushed down on the release bar and was relieved when the door opened freely without making a noise. Pulling it almost shut again he breathed a sigh of relief as he slid the cartons across the floor. They easily covered the now open gap and he was content that to any unsuspecting person everything looked normal, Vincent Frasier made his way back and entered the canteen. Popping his head around the tearoom door where Happy Bottle sat deep in thought, he spoke in an overly loud voice, though it was something he'd never done before.

"I'm off now mate see you Tuesday."

Happy didn't reply but it made no difference to Vinny, he only cared that someone knew he had left the premises. Sneakily he crept into his private office come storeroom and locked the door from inside. There was a small hole in the frame that let a beam of light into the room and it would enable him to peer through and see when Happy closed up for the weekend. This turned out to be longer than he had expected. At six Roly Peterson had driven out of the gates but there was still no sign of Happy. Another hour passed and Vinny was just about ready to give up when the man came into sight. Vincent Frasier had to stifle a laugh that was desperate to escape. No wonder the creepy little sod was late going home. Struggling to get to his old Lada with a large box, Vinny could see that it contained toilet rolls, reams of paper and a large canister of instant coffee.

"You crafty, robbing little cunt!"

Vinny's words were only a whisper but at the same time Happy turned round and glanced back at the building. Vinny ducked sideways and then reprimanded himself for being so stupid. Happy hadn't heard anything and he certainly couldn't see Vinny but it was probably his own fear at being caught that had made him do a double check. At last the man drove out of the yard and when he jumped out of the car to close and lock the gate, Vinny once more sighed with relief. Not wanting to tempt fate he waited until he heard the Lada drive away. Slipping out of the store room it was now becoming overcast but the thought of getting soaked didn't worry Vinny. He was coiled as tight as a spring and getting wet was the

84

least of his worries. Making his way over to the old wooden side gate, he had a moment of panic when to begin with the bolt wouldn't budge. A few seconds spent wiggling and cursing and the metal at last moved. Now on the outside, Vincent Frasier closed the gate and removing a small piece of wire from his overalls, proceeded to secure the bolt to the iron fence. Satisfied the job was neat enough and that a passerby wouldn't see anything had been tampered with, he made his way home in anticipation at what tomorrow would bring.

The following morning Vinny got up at the usual time. Vera had again cooked a full breakfast and this time he forced it down. His mother could be nosy at the best of times and if he didn't eat again today she would start with her Miss Marple routine.

"That's what I like to see, a good fucking appetite. Feeling better today are we?"

Vinny just nodded.

"I thought we could go down Roman Road and do a weekly shop. I need veg and meat and it's a struggle trying to carry it on my own. What do you say?"

"Well I've got a bit on today myself mum and...."

Deciding that she wasn't about to put up with any of his nonsense, she instantly cut him off. Vera needed help and he was bloody well going to give it to her. If she'd learnt only one thing in life, it was that she knew both of her boys like the back of her hand. She had a knack of knowing how to wind them up and also of how to get her own way. Jason was putty in her hands most of the time; well he was until he'd gotten in with that little trollop. Now Vinny was different altogether and could be a bit more difficult, she had to be careful when she worked on him. Holding her back Vera winced in pain and knew that her son would immediately feel guilty.

85

"All right! all right! Enough of the fucking drama queen routine, I'll come with you."

"Good lad. How about if your old mum treats you to a pint at the Camel afterwards?"

This was perfect as Vinny needed to check on the details with Jason in readiness for tonight.

"You've talked me into it. Mother you know the way to a man's heart and no mistake."

Vera grinned to herself as she took the two large shopping bags from the kitchen drawer. Three hours later and with the weekly shop at last done, Vinny was about to drop. His mother had a knack of bumping into everyone she knew and the idle gossip drove him up the wall. For some reason old people talked about nothing but illness and death and Vera was no different. By the time they reached the Camel he was almost ready to burst. Struggling in with the bags he rolled his eyes in Jason's direction and the brothers both silently laughed but well out of their mother's eye line. Lisa was behind the bar with her husband as Maude had gone for a lay down and the sight riled Vinny as it was now going to be difficult to talk to his brother. Jason on the other hand was only too aware what today was and deep down he was glad that his wife was within ear shot. He knew that Vinny would never talk about his plan in front of her and Jason had his fingers crossed that it would force things to fall through. That wasn't to be and just before leaving Vinny sidelined his brother and told him what time to be at the factory.

"Now don't let me down Jay!"

Jason only nodded but his body language didn't go unnoticed by Lisa. She could see that her husband was unhappy about something but decided not to push him. By now Lisa knew her husband well and whatever it was,

Jason would confide in her when he was good and ready and not before.

Later that evening Jason waited by the side gate of Kings but he hadn't hired a car as Vinny had asked. Reluctant to give his personal details or show his driving licence, Jason had instead borrowed Mango Smiths clapped out mini. After a small amount of arguing Vinny had reluctantly given in and agreed it was a better option. He had purchased a cheap set of licence plates so that the car would be difficult to trace if anyone ever reported seeing it. Jason still wasn't feeling any better about the job, in all honesty the last few days had given him time to worry even more about everything he was risking. Once again it was what his brother wanted and what Vinny wanted he always, one way or another, seemed to get. Vinny walked to the factory and was already inside when his brother pulled up. Switching off the headlights Jason could feel himself shaking. Being a jack the lad and doing the odd dodgy deal was miles apart from this. He didn't know why he'd allowed Vinny to talk him into such a stupid thing but now he was here, he had no alternative but to see it through. Ten minutes later and after staring at his watch for what seemed like forever, he saw that it was seven forty and Vinny should have been out by now. If his brother was in trouble how would he know? Should he go and look or just wait it out, sometimes he really could throttle Vinny. When his watch read seven forty five, he was about to start up the engine having decided that this just wasn't worth the aggro and Vin would have to take care of himself, when the gate at last flew open. Vincent Frasier struggled through the opening with the large box and the weight made him lean over as he walked. Jason didn't know how much was inside but guessed it had to be a fare amount. Getting out of the mini he made his way to the rear of the car. Mangos vehicle was small to say the least and after the brothers had transferred the money into a holdall, they attempted to place it in the boot. Jason hadn't bother to check and as he lifted the tailgate was faced with a mound of Mango's old junk.

"What the fuck!"

"Alright Vin there's no need to get stroppy. I should have looked before but I didn't, I'll just have to throw it all on the back seat."

A few minutes later and the space was now clear. Fortunately for them the bag just squeezed in but it was a tight fit and it took a few seconds of pushing and shoving before they were able to close the boot.

"There I fucking told you to hire a van, you twat!"

"Oh don't start Vin; it's gone in ain't it?"

"More by fucking luck than judgement."

Vinny kicked out at the car in pure frustration before returning to secure the gate. Getting into the passenger's side he wasn't in a talkative mood but it didn't matter as Jason was too on edge to notice.

"Right I'll take you back to the Camel then I need to get this heap of shit back to Mango. Stash the bag in the outside coalhouse, I've put a new padlock on the door and left the key in it. When you've done that go and see Lisa and for fucks sake don't go upsetting her."

"Would I?"

Jason didn't reply and the brothers set off in silence. Turning onto Terrace Road they hadn't got more than a couple of hundred yards when disaster struck. From out of nowhere an elderly woman stepped off the curb and straight into the path of Mango's old car. The impact was loud and threw Vinny and Jason forward in their seats. Dazed but unhurt Vinny fumbled for the handle and after getting out walked round to the driver's side and opened the door. Not seeing or hearing anything from his brother, for a few seconds Vinny could only stare open mouthed.

"Jay! Jay! Speak to me mate."

Jason had hit his head on the steering wheel and was now unconscious. As blood began to run down the side of his face his brother became hysterical and started to panic. Pulling Jason from the car, Vinny knelt on the cold wet tarmac and cradled Jason's head in his lap. Vincent shook Jason over and over again but there was no response.

"Jay! Jay! Oh god no, please say something Jay." Staring down into Jason's motionless face he instinctively decided that his brother was dead. Glancing both ways down the street he didn't know what to do and hated the idea of having to leave Jason here alone but he quickly realised that he had to look out for himself now. Standing up and without any thought for the other victim, he stepped over her broken body and tugged open the cars boot. Shock was beginning to set in and he had to concentrate hard to muster enough strength to remove the holdall and place it over his shoulder. Glancing down he noticed the fake number plate that Jason has seen fit to put on. Leaning down he yanked it off and walking to the front of the car did the same before pushing both plates into the holdall. His weakness was making things difficult but he was determined not to get his collar felt for this and with great difficulty he moved away from the scene as quickly as his legs would carry him. Two streets later and Vincent Frasier was done in. He realised there was no way he was ever going to get back under his own steam, so he stopped a passing mini cab and asked the driver to take him to the Camel. The driver was foreign and luckily for Vinny he had no idea what was in the bag or Vincent Frasier would never have arrived at his destination. Needing time to get his head in gear about what to do next, Vinny put the money in the coalhouse as he'd been told. Remembering his brother's words he decided against entering the Camel. He didn't want to be in the same pub as his sister in law let along make pleasant conversation; instead he sat on the wall outside trying to decide what to do.

Back at the crash Jason was starting to come round and his groans were heard by a man out walking his dog. Soon the whole street was overrun with police cars and two ambulances. First to be treated was the woman but the paramedics soon realised that she was beyond help and pronounced her dead at the scene. Luckily it was a different story for Jason and after a spinal board was put in place, he was whisked off to the nearest hospital escorted by an over enthusiastic patrol car. Three hours later following an x-ray and after his facial wounds had been tended to, Jason Frasier against the doctors wishes, discharged himself. As he walked out of the emergency room he was immediately arrested.

"Jason Frasier I am arresting you in connection with causing death by reckless driving. Anything you say will be taken down and...."

"Fucking arrested! You are having a laugh aint you? I ain't got the foggiest what you're on about."

All memories of the crash had disappeared, though he did remember why he was in the car in the first place. He was desperate to ask about Vinny but thought better of it. If Vin had managed to get away then good luck to him, there was no point in dragging him into all of this. The only thing Jason couldn't work out was why no mention had been made of the cars cargo and why he'd been travelling with such a large amount of cash. If Vinny had managed to have the money away then all the better but then again if it was a tax fiddle as his brother had said the money wouldn't be traceable anyway. No, Jason decided there and then to just sit tight and see what happened. After being taken to the local police station he was placed in a cell for the remainder of the night but not before he was given his obligatory phone call. Anxiously waiting for a reply, he was more than a little relieved when it was Maude who answered.

"Listen Maude I have to keep this short but I've been arrested. There's nothing you can do until the morning but I just wanted Lisa to know I was alright."

"Arrested! Oh Jason whatever for?"

"I can't explain now and in any case it's better that you don't know. Make some sort of excuse to Lisa and I'll phone you again as soon as I can."

"But Jason....."

"Maude I have to go, just please tell Lisa not to worry."

With that the line went dead and Maude Shelton was left staring into the receiver. Replacing the handset she turned to face the bar and could see that luckily Lisa hadn't heard the conversation. The regulars were having a singsong and to say they were loud was an understatement. All the golden oldies had resurfaced and at the moment Arthur Yallop was doing his own unique rendition of 'Underneath the Arches'. Lisa had begun to get anxious about Jason's whereabouts but when she looked in Maude's direction the older woman just smiled and she relaxed. He'd be home soon and in the meantime she was actually starting to enjoy herself. Maude decided to delay being the bearer of bad news until after closing. With only her and Lisa on duty it would have been a nightmare trying to console the girl and serve pints at the same time. When the front doors were at last locked, Maude led Lisa out into the yard for a breath of fresh air and after deciding that honesty was the best policy, broke the news to her.

"Arrested! But why?"

"My darling you now know as much as I do. He didn't go into any details so I suppose we'll find out more in the morning. For now I suggest we both need to try and get some sleep."

"I just need a few minutes on my own Maude and then I'll be in. You go up; I'll make sure every where's locked and secure before I turn in."

"You're a good girl Lisa; try not to worry too much."

"I'll try but it ain't going to be easy."

"I know sweetheart, night night."

"Night Maude."

Standing in the back yard with tears streaming down her face Lisa Frasier silently stared up at the sky and wondered where her life was going. Slowly as she turned and walked back into the pub she shuddered. A feeling of foreboding seemed to engulf her and she silently prayed that it didn't mean she would never see her husband again. Wearily she climbed fully clothed into bed. The tears came thick and fast but finally she drifted off into a fitful sleep.

CHAPTER TEN

Vincent Frasier ran home and quickly packed a bag without his mother even knowing he'd returned. Phoning a mini cab he asked to be taken to the station but wanted to stop off at the Camel first. Quietly letting himself into the rear yard, Vincent removed the holdall from the coal house and after throwing it on the back seat of the cab, told the driver to put his foot down. The next train out of Kings Cross, which just happened to be going to Cambridge, was the one that Vincent chose to board. He had never been to that particular City before but at the moment just getting out of London was the most important thing. Checking into a hotel the man hardly acknowledged anyone; all that he could think about was Jason as his feelings went on an emotional rollercoaster. One minute his heart was breaking at his loss and the next he was in his elements. He had more money than he had ever known and to top it all off he never had to see that bitch Lisa's face again. Not a second thought was given to Vera and to tell the truth Vinny couldn't care less about his mother. He never had, the only person in his life who had mattered to him was his brother and now that he was gone, well Vinny just had to get on with things. Life was going to be difficult and lonely from now on but somehow all this money would ease Vinny's pain or so he tried to convince himself.

The Cumberland Hotel was mid range and Vinny had only chosen it because it was the first one he came to after leaving Cambridge station. Calling it a hotel was a bit of an overstatement as it was only marginally better than a bed and breakfast. The rooms were not fancy but they were spotlessly clean and although there were no luxury facilities, the hosts more than made up for this with their warm welcome. Trevor Hayes and his partner Melvyn had run the place for the past five years and it was their pride and joy. A civil ceremony earlier in the year had cemented their future and the men were blissfully happy. Blissfully happy except for one bone of contention, Trevor still had a roving eye and it was the only thing to cause trouble between the pair. When Vinny had signed the register Trevor hadn't been able to keeps his eyes off the new guest and Melvyn had dug his husband sharply in the ribs. Vinny at last felt safe and smiling to himself at his good fortune was oblivious to what was going on in front of him. After showing their most recent guest to his room, Trevor and Melvyn left him to settle in. After quickly looking around Vinny placed his bags on the floor and then fell onto the bed. Suddenly he broke down and cried like a baby at the thought of never seeing his brother again. Two hours later and after a long hot shower, Vinny at last made his way downstairs to the restaurant. He was now feeling flash and wanted something special, something that would tell any other diner that he was a man of means. Starting to splash the cash around he asked for the most expensive thing on the menu as well as a bottle of champagne. To Vinny's hosts, this injection of money was a much needed boast for the hotel. Most guests ordered the meal of the day but when Vinny's choice came through to the kitchen, Melvyn was forced to dig deep in the bottom of the freezer and retrieve the last lobster left over from his own wedding banquet. Melvyn Hayes had taken on the female role of the partnership and as such was overly inquisitive. He hoped that their new guest was gay as it would make a nice change to have some of their own people staying for a change. Vinny

94

gave no hint of his sexuality and ignored any of Melvyn's innuendos. Melvyn was desperately disappointed when he realised that their new guest probably didn't bat for his side. That said, it didn't stop him from asking one question after another. Over dinner Melvyn's questions became so intense that Vinny started to worry. When asked what he was doing in Cambridge, he had a knee jerk reaction and said he was a construction worker. Finally when he hadn't really got anywhere with his prying Melvyn became bored with the conversation and minced off in the direction of the kitchen. Vinny began to have a silent conversation within his own head and everything he said was challenged by his alter ego.

"What the fuck did you say that for?"

"Listen I didn't have much choice. The nosey cunt would have kept on otherwise."

"So now what?"

"Now I get a job, at least until I know the coast is clear." Vinny slammed down his knife and fork and the whole room went quiet.

"Get a fucking job! You're having a laugh ain't you. I didn't just rob half a million quid to turn round and go back to work."

"Well mate I don't think you've much choice in the matter. Now I suggest we get an early night, because tomorrow we start looking for some fucking work!"

Vincent Frasier realised that people were staring at him and hoped that he hadn't spoken out loud. With his head bowed low he made his way upstairs and went to bed. The next day passed relatively smoothly and Vinny was able to secure some site work at one of the local universities. It would be enough to keep the nosey Melvyn Hayes at bay and stop the man asking so many questions. Even though Cambridge was so close to

London, Vinny still looked upon everyone as carrot crunchers. Reading in the local paper, that 'The Junction club' held a gay night once a month cheered Vinny up. Dressed to the nines he made his way to the place that for one night only was called 'The Dot Cotton Club'. The music was loud and pumping and just as Vinny thought that maybe Cambridge wasn't too bad a place after all, he spied Trevor and Melvyn Hayes arriving. Creeping along in the shadows that fell onto the outer walls Vinny made a hasty retreat but unbeknown to him he'd been spotted.

"Melvyn I think I just saw our new guest over there."

"Where?"

"There beside the bar."

"Well he isn't there now, you must have been mistaken."

"I could have sworn it was him."

"For goodness sake Trevor will you stop thinking about other men just for one second?"

Once outside, Vinny took in a deep lungful of air in relief that he hadn't been spotted, or so he thought. The last thing he needed was to be accosted by those two faggots. Walking along he was at a loss as to where to spend the rest of the evening when he came across the Kite Club. Only just visible at the top of a small alleyway, he knew instantly that this was more to his liking. Two men were propped up against the wall kissing passionately and this sight alone had Vinny chomping at the bit to get inside. Back in London, Lisa woke with a blinding headache and made her way upstairs to Maude's kitchen. About to swallow two aspirin, she nearly jumped out of her skin when she noticed her landlady huddled on the floor in the corner.

"Whatever are you doing down there Maude?"

"Just thinking. Sometimes when I'm feeling bothered I like to get in the corner and I'm able to sort out in me head any troubles I might be having. I know it must look stupid but it seems to do the trick, well mostly anyway."

"And has it worked today?"

"Not quite but I'm working on it. Now first thing we need to do is get down the nick and find out what the hell is going on. We should get dressed!"

In a second Maude was on her feet and making her way to the bedroom. Lisa just stared at the older woman, sometimes this place was nothing short of an asylum.

"Come on girl chop chop. We're not going to get that man of yours home while we stand around chewing the fat, now are we?"

It was a rhetorical question and Lisa was bright enough not to answer. Instead she did as she was told and the two women were dressed and heading out of the door within fifteen minutes. At the Police station Maude immediately realised that whatever was going on was serious. They were treated with courtesy but informed they didn't have a chance of seeing Jason until after he had been interviewed. The desk sergeant told them that as the duty solicitor hadn't deemed to show his face, it could be hours yet but they were welcome to take a seat if they wanted to wait. Maude and Lisa both took up the offer and even though she knew it would do no good, Maude continued to question the policeman.

"Surely the least you can do is tell us what the charge is."

Sighing deeply the desk sergeant was about to reply but was instantly distracted by the commotion happening behind Maude's back. Suddenly the doors swung open and a scruffy looking man carrying a worn out briefcase under his arm almost fell inside the building. After taking a second to catch his breath and compose himself the best he could, Clive Heath finally walked over to the counter.

97

"Ah Mr Heath! How nice of you to finally grant us your presence."

"Sergeant!"

Instantly Maude Shelton was on her feet. Guessing that this was the man who was holding everything up, she marched over to the counter and now stood directly in front of Clive Heath.

"You don't know me but I'm a good friend of the man I think you are about to see and this is his wife."

Clive Heath nodded in Lisa's direction and then turned back to Maude.

"Charmed I'm sure."

"Enough of the smarm, what the hell is going on here?"

"Madam I don't know if you are aware of the situation but an elderly lady was knocked down and killed. Now I am unable to give you any further information as I haven't even seen my client yet. Until I have taken instruction I...."

Maude didn't like his tone and she didn't like the way he obviously looked down on her.

"Listen to me Mr! Don't presume to know what I'm thinking or about to say, as you ain't got the foggiest idea."

Thrusting a card that held the Camel's details into his hand, she walked towards the exit. Lisa silently got up and followed, leaving the solicitor staring open mouthed and the desk sergeant grinning from ear to ear. Outside Lisa turned to face Maude.

"Did that man say a woman had died?"

"Now don't go getting carried away darling, at least not until we know all the facts. When that leery sod in their calls me later we'll find out what's what but for now all we can do is go home and wait."

Jason's interview took place shortly after and when

everything was in place and the solicitor had left he was shown back to his cell by a custody sergeant who was known as Banny. Jason Frasier didn't recognise the man but just as the cell door was about to close the Sergeant spoke.

"You don't remember me do you?"

Jason just stared blankly.

"No I didn't think you did, well let me enlighten you. I was a beat plod when you and your little brother ran riot around Bethnal Green. My son Ronnie even went to the same school as you."

"Well thanks for the history lesson Sarg but I can't see what any of this has...."

"Shut the fuck up and listen! For the sheer fucking hell of it you decided one day to beat my boy to a pulp. He walks with a permanent limp now and you bastards never paid the price. Well I'll tell you something for nothing, you fucking will now. You're in my territory and I'm going to do my best to make sure that your stay is as uncomfortable as possible. Sleep tight!"

With that the cell door slammed shut and Jason flopped down onto the concrete plinth that was to be his bed for the second night in a row. Racking his brains it all suddenly came flooding back to him. The man called Banny was sergeant Banister and father of Ronald Banister. Once again it was something that Jason had taken the blame for and he could remember it all so clearly now. It had been a cold winter's day just a few weeks before he left school. Late home from a detention, he had come across the boy lying in the street. Vinny was standing over him with a piece of two by two wood hanging loosely from his hands. Ronnie Bannister was a nobody; a quiet lad who never said boo to a goose but for some reason Vinny had taken a dislike to him. As usual

99

it had been down to Jason to clear up his brother's mess and luckily on this occasion they were never brought to justice. Either from not wanting to be labelled a grass or purely out of fear, Ronnie Bannister had kept his mouth shut, for a number of years at least. Jason sat with his head in his hands and wondered if he would ever stop taking the blame and receiving the punishment for something Vincent had done.

Maude knew that once Jason had been interviewed he would instruct his brief to get in touch with her and until that time came they would just have to sit back and wait. Just as she had predicted the call came at five thirty that afternoon. Clive Heath informed her that the charges were manslaughter by gross negligence and due to the fact that as it was a Sunday, his client wouldn't be up before the magistrate until the following day. The seriousness of the offence meant a special hearing was being held on a Bank holiday but it was just a formality as bail was going to be opposed. In all likelihood Jason would be placed on remand in Belmarsh prison.

"Why would bail be opposed? Surely they don't think that Jay is a threat to anyone!"

"It's not a case of that Mrs. Shelton. When Mr Frasier was arrested he became abusive and the officers took exception to his behaviour. The custody Sergeant is being overzealous in saying that he feels Mr Frasier may abscond if set free."

"Jason would never do a runner!"

"That may be so Mrs Shelton but as we both know and especially in the smoke, the last thing you need to be doing is upsetting the police. Now I can make arrangements for you and Mrs Frasier to see him in a couple of day's time. Once the hearings over and they've got him settled somewhere he can receive visitors."

Clive Heath could hear her sighing on the other end of the phone.

"So Mr Heath what are we looking at here?"

"Well it's down to the prosecution to prove gross negligence and that's not an easy feat by any means. Thankfully their most difficult task will be in trying to define the degree of negligence and after speaking to Jason I don't think that's going to happen. That said I'm not a gambling man so I wouldn't be able to tell you either way. All I can say is that the best case scenario would be for him to walk out of court a free man."

"And the worst?"

"I think we can safely say six months."

"Six months! Bleeding hell."

"Mrs Shelton it's not as bad as it sounds. With good behaviour he could be home in three and then there's the time he would have spent on remand to be taken off."

"Not as bad as it seems! You try telling that to his young wife because I don't think she will see it that way. Let me know when there's anymore news can you?"

With that Maude hung up and made her way into the bar to tell Lisa. The Camel had only been open for half an hour but already there were at least ten of the regulars standing at the bar.

"Lads I need to have a little talk with Lisa, so if any of you want a pint you'll just have to pull it yourselves."

The men had been frequenting the place long enough for Maude to know that she could trust them and in any case they were all too scared of the landlady's sharp tongue to try and pull a fast one.

"Lisa lets go up to the flat and have a chat."

Lisa Frasier didn't question Maude and meekly followed behind her. Once seated in the kitchen Maude Shelton relayed all that the solicitor had told her. As expected

101

Lisa broke down and Maude didn't say anything else until the crying had subsided. After the girl had dried her eyes and noisily blew her nose, she was able to muster a smile when told about the impending visit.

"Lisa we haven't heard anything from Vinny. Now is there anything you haven't told me?"

Lisa shook her head but Maude could feel that there was something going on that just wasn't right.

"Are you sure? Just think for a minute."

Again Lisa Frasier shook her head.

"Look darling I ain't a fool. I know something's going on with Jason and that brother of his and with Vinny keeping a low profile, well there could be a shit load of trouble coming our way."

Lisa began to cry all over again and Maude's heart instantly went out to her.

"Honest Maude I don't know what's going on. Last night they didn't tell me anything, they just went."

"Ok darling we'll leave it there for now. Take the night off and have a rest, we've got a busy couple of days ahead of us."

"If it's all the same to you Maude I'd like to carry on as normal. The last thing I need is to be shut away in that room on me own."

"Darling I think you're right. It's the last thing that either of us need. Now shall we go and see if that group of piss heads have drunk the place dry?"

Lisa giggled and after kissing Maude tenderly on the cheek, the two women made their way back into the bar.

CHAPTER ELEVEN

The day after the robbery and still unaware of any problems, Freddie Gant phoned Roly Peterson at home. A small child answered the telephone which was a pet hate of Freddie's at the best of times but this child's manners were appalling.

"Yeah, who is it?"

"Could I speak to Mr Peterson Please?"

"Who are you, what do you want?"

"I'm Mr Gant, now go and fetch your father sonny."

Without taking the receiver away from his mouth the boy shouted loudly, deafening Freddie in the process.

"Dad! Dad! Some geezers on the phone for you."

Roly could be heard puffing and panting as he made his way across the tiled hallway.

"Who is it son?"

"Gant someone or other, Oh I don't know. Anyway, if you weren't so fat you could have answered it yourself."

Roly didn't reprimand the boy.

"Ok thank you Tyron, now go back and join our guests."

Roly swallowed hard as he took hold of the receiver. It was unusual to say the least being called on a Sunday but then in all honesty since Roly had been shafted out of his business nothing came as a surprise to him anymore.

"Hello?"

"Polite little fucker you've got there Roly."

Roly Peterson didn't try to defend his son's manner and instead carried on as if the remark hadn't been made.

"Mr Gant and what can I do for you on this fine Sunday afternoon?"

His sarcasm at being called at home didn't go unnoticed by Freddie but just this once he decided to let it go.

103

"Roly I have a collection tomorrow and I need you to be at the factory."

"But Mr Gant it's a bank holiday and I have my family....."

"I don't give a flying fuck if you've got the Queen herself as a house guest. I need a collection and you had better be there. Midday sharp and don't let me down, do I make myself fucking understood?"

"Loud and clear Mr Gant loud and clear."

With that Freddie hung up and Roly Peterson was left with a dead handset glued to his ear. Wally Evans as usual stood at his boss's side. He had heard the conversation or at least one side of it and was waiting to receive his orders. Wally had never taken to Roly Peterson and he was itching for his boss to give him the word. If given half the chance he would have gone in all guns blazing and annihilated the fat waster without a second thought. Freddie on the other hand was calm and composed. For the time being he needed Roly Peterson as a front if nothing else.

"Get over to Kings tomorrow lunchtime and collect five hundred grand. Boris will be here just after two o'clock so make sure you're back on time."

"Sure thing Boss. Is everything ok?"

"Nothing I can't handle, just that fat cunt Peterson being sarky. I feel a little lesson in manners will soon be in order to remind him just who's in charge. Let's get this delivery over with and then we'll have another look at the situation."

Wally smiled to himself, this had been a long time coming and it was a job he was relishing.

"Nice one Boss, I've waited ages to get me hands on that one."

"Wally you never cease to amaze me. I really don't

104

know anyone who's as sick as you. It goes without saying that in our game violence is part of the territory but for fuck's sake, what pleasure do you get out of pulverising someone?"

Wally wore a puzzled expression as he thought about what Freddie had just said.

"Don't know really. I've always enjoyed the sight of blood and when it's someone who's hurt one of mine then all the better. Do you know that in all the years me and Rene were married we never had a cross word."

"Yeah! Right."

"No straight up Boss. If she ever pissed me off I didn't say a word and just took my frustration out on me next bit of business. Kept me calm and off home I'd go to the little woman, maybe that's how I got a liking for it."

No other words were spoken but in a strange way Freddie understood what his friend was saying. He studied the man for a few seconds without speaking. Sometimes it bothered him just how close Wally wanted to be but then again he reasoned he would never get anyone else so loyal.

"I'm going up to the flat now so get yourself off home and don't forget, be at Kings by noon tomorrow."

Freddie didn't wait for a response and immediately walked up the stairs. He was well aware that Wally Evans would lock up and make sure that everywhere was secure before he left. On Bank holiday Monday Roly Peterson had risen early. As brave as he'd been on the telephone yesterday, he wasn't stupid and knew that to keep his boss waiting was a definite no no. It had played on his mind all of the previous afternoon that maybe he'd overstepped the mark but then he hoped that Freddie Gant had calmed down over night and forgot about the conversation. Deep down he knew that he was kidding

105

himself, people like Gant never forgot anything. After being forcibly evicted from Kings, Roly had just about managed to hold onto his Mock Tudor mansion in Basildon. He had begun to use the drive into work every day for reflection and had found that lately he was thinking more and more of ways to get his company back. The only trouble being that with a bodyguard like Wally Evans it would be more than a little difficult to get rid of someone like Freddie Gant. Roly's wife was a want want sort of woman and keeping up with all the monthly repayments was becoming a task in itself. In the beginning he loved nothing better than to give her everything her heart desired but when he started being taken for a mug his attitude changed. Any fool, married to a woman like Sheila Peterson would soon tell you that it took its toll in more ways than one. No one could deny that she was beautiful and his buddies at the golf course had commented on several occasions that she could have been a model. That said Sheila Peterson was a bitch through and through. True she'd given him a son but she had also quickly realised that Tyron was her trump card and the reason why her husband would never divorce her. If Sheila was anything she was clever and Roly had to concede that she had well and truly duped him. There was a twenty-year age gap between them and he had left his wife of thirty years to be with Sheila. Mavis Peterson had always doted on her husband and was heartbroken when Roly informed her one Sunday over lunch that he was leaving. Mavis had never asked for much and she'd been a good wife but even her pleading and begging couldn't make a difference. Thinking that the grass would be greener with a new younger wife, he had eagerly packed his bags but it hadn't turned out that way for Roly Petersons. Now he was saddled with a leech for a wife and a seven year old brat for a son who was definitely going to take after his mother. When the initial throws of lust began to wane Sheila had been quick to move into the spare room and now kept the door securely locked. Her lack of providing his marital rights had been the main instigator for him seeking out the warmth of brasses in the first place. Roly reasoned that had this scenario never of risen, then he wouldn't have gotten into debt with Freddie Gant. When it came down to the cold hard facts, Roly Peterson couldn't and wouldn't except any blame himself. No it was all Sheila's fault and if he didn't get the factory back then she would have to pay. He hadn't worked out how but just the thought of her having to go without was enough to keep him going. As it was a bank holiday and the traffic was unusually light, Roly who had allowed plenty of time, arrived at Kings roughly fifteen minutes early. The factory was deathly quiet and without Happy Bottle on duty he had to open the gates himself. Even if he didn't own the place anymore he still liked to Lord it above all his employees and opening the gates was beneath him, even if there was no one there to see him do it. For some reason walking into the office building unnerved him today and after sitting at his desk for a few minutes he decided to check the precious cargo he'd been ordered to hand over. Opening the store cupboard door, the sight of the empty shelves where once a ton of money had sat didn't register immediately and it took a few seconds for the penny to drop. When Roly finally noticed that the proverbial cupboard was bare and that all the cash had gone, he clutched at his chest as his angina instantly kicked in. Placing a chubby hand on to the wall to steady himself, Roly inhaled slowly in a desperate attempt to bring his heart rate down and get things under control. A few

107

minutes later he at last felt well enough to carry on and although now starting to sweat profusely, stepped back out into the hallway. Entering the main factory area he feared that the robbers might still be on the premises and had to force himself to look around and see where the building had been broken into. When no forced entry was apparent he immediately phoned Happy and he could clearly see his hand shake as he dialled. After what seemed like an age and the thought that Happy wasn't home had terrified him, the receiver was at last picked up.

"Yeah?"

"Happy it's me. I'm at the factory and the cash has gone."

"What?"

"You fucking heard me now get your scrawny arse over here now."

"But it's a bank holiday Mr Peterson."

"Well if you don't get over here now you'll be on a permanent fucking bank holiday. Got it?"

With that Roly hung up, slumped back in his chair and began to sweat again. Ten minutes later Happy's footsteps could be heard running along the corridor in the direction of the office. The door burst open and the little man almost fell inside. Happy's flat cap had comically slipped sideways and as he doubled over, held up his hand asking for a minute to get his breath. If the situation hadn't been of such a serious nature, then Roly would have found the sight hilarious. Happy Bottle was puffing and gasping for air as he spoke.

"How?"

"How? You moron! How the fuck should I know but I'll tell you this for nothing, when Freddie Gant finds out it will be both our heads on the block."

Happy immediately stood up straight and his face

108

suddenly wore a deep frown of confusion.

"But Mr Peterson it ain't nothing to do with me! I only work here!"

Roly shook his head from side to side and wore a smirk that riled even Happy.

"Maybe so but I doubt whether he will see it like that. Now is there anything you can tell me before I make the call?"

Happy took a moment and racked his brains. He couldn't recall seeing anything or anyone out of the ordinary, except.

"Fucking hell it's that cunt Frasier, I'd bet my life on it Boss."

"Frasier? Frasier who?"

"No Vinny Frasier. You know one of them two brothers that you hired. He's a nasty piece of work and no mistake. I fucking caught him a couple of weeks ago."

"Caught him doing what?"

"Well nothing really but I came in and he was in the stationary cupboard. Well not in it exactly but I saw him close the door. Anyway when I confronted him he said that the door was open and he was just closing it."

"So? Why do you think he wasn't doing just that?"

"Because I never leave the fucking door unlocked that's why!"

"Well someone did and watch your mouth Happy, I'm still your boss and you'd do well to fucking remember that. Now how come you're so sure he's involved?"

"I don't know Mr Peterson there's just something about him. He's weird and I wouldn't trust him as far as I could throw him."

"That ain't good enough Happy. If you tell Gant about this, the bloke will be dead in a second. Fuck me man if you're going to throw someone to the lions make sure

109

they're guilty first. I think we should hold onto this information for a while longer. At least until we've exhausted every other possibility."

"Where did they get in Boss?"

"That's just it, there's no signs anywhere and I know Gant will suspect us because of that fact."

"Well if that don't prove it's an inside job I don't know what does. Do you really think we'll get the blame?"

"I can't see how Freddie Gant will see it any other way do you? Besides men like him have to be seen to make someone pay."

"Oh fuck! Oh sweet Jesus what are we going to do?"

"Just wait a minute and let me think will you!"

"Wait?"

"It's the only thing we can do, that and pray. If the gods are looking down on us then we might just scrap out of this mess, if not; well if anyone can sort this out its Freddie. I just hope me and you ain't part of the sorting out."

Finally after a few minutes and when all avenues had been exhausted, Roly at last made the call he'd been dreading. He and Happy had searched every inch of the building but both realised early on that it was a futile exercise. Still they had tried, if only to desperately delay the telephone call that they both knew Roly had to make. The phone only rang twice before it was snatched up and the person on the other end sounded far from happy.

"Yeah?"

"Oh hello Mr Gant its Roly Peterson. I'm afraid there's a bit of a problem here at the factory."

"How so?"

"Well the money seems to have disappeared."

Freddie Gant, who had been sitting behind his bespoke desk suddenly stood up and began pacing the floor.

"Fucking disappeared are you having a laugh or what?"
"No straight up Mr Gant. I got here by twelve just as you said, in fact I was ten minutes early but I don't suppose that would have....."
"For fucks sake man, just get on with it."
"Well the long and the short of it is we've been cleaned out."
"Roly Roly Roly when are you going to fucking learn. It's you not us that's been cleaned out it's you and I along with the fucking Russians want the money back. Come one o'clock today me and Wally will be paying you a visit and you'd better fucking have what I want."
With that Freddie slammed the phone down.
"What did he say Mr Peterson, what did he say?"
"You don't want to know Happy; believe me you really don't want to know."
Freddie called Wally on his mobile and told him to come to the office before going to the factory. The last minute change of plan put the big man in a bad mood to begin with. Having only been a hundred yards from Kings, he now had to drive all the way over to Soho and he wasn't happy. When Wally arrived he could tell straight away that his boss was also angry about something.
"Change of plans Gov?"
"Fucking change of plans is an understatement. That cunt Peterson has only gone and got done over. The fucking cash has gone and Boris is going to have our arses for this. I tell you something for nothing Wal, if this goes tits up and costs me then I won't be the only one who pays."
Dialling Boris's number Freddie Gants face was red with rage.
"Boris we've got a bit of a problem at this end and it's going to take a few hours to sort out. Yes I know we said

111

two but I really need to sort this now, can I give you a call later? Great thanks for that mate."

Freddie replaced the receiver then punched his fist hard onto the desk.

"Get me to Kings as quick as you can."

Wally Evans knew there was trouble brewing with a capital T and the conversation was non-existent on the journey over to the factory. The main gate was already open and Roly and Happy Bottle were standing on the office step as the car pulled up. Walking straight into the building, Freddie Gant closely followed by Wally, didn't say a word to the men. Like lambs to the slaughter, Roly Peterson and Happy Bottle meekly stepped inside. Freddie took up residence in Roly's leather chair and both men stood in front of the desk like school boys caught smoking behind the bike shed. Wally flanked his boss's right hand side and was ready to get stuck in as soon as he was given the word.

"Well well well Roly what a fucking mess you've created here, don't you agree Wal?"

Wally stared straight at the men and slowly nodded. His eyes were hard and slightly closed, making him the epitome of fear. It was a scenario that both men had adopted over the years and it usually worked well. Mostly by the time they had finished talking, their victim would be so scared that they would willingly give up any information. On the seldom occasions that this little role play hadn't worked, Wally Evans was always ready to step in and carry out his work and it was a job he took exceptional pride in.

CHAPTER TWELVE

Vera woke at seven thirty on Sunday morning. Normally she would have been up over an hour ago but as it was a bank holiday she thought she deserved a lie in. Checking the fridge, Vera was happy to see that everything was in place for a slap up breakfast. Cooking for Vincent was nothing unusual, she had always liked to see her boys off with a full stomach but this was holiday time and just like at Christmas, Vera liked to spoil them. Every day since Jason had left had been torture and she couldn't get used to cooking for only two. Vinny was of course her favourite but her family wasn't complete without her eldest sitting at the table. That said she wasn't so desperate to have him back that she could accept the little bitch he had married. At eight o'clock Vera placed the frying pan onto the stove. When the sausages and bacon were cooked and warming in the oven she went through to the hall to call Vinny. He was always slow at waking and she didn't want the eggs to spoil. Five minutes later and after she still hadn't heard any movement, Vera once again made her way along the hall only this time she stood directly outside his room. Coughing loudly she called out his name.

"Vincent! Can you please drag your sorry fucking arse out of that stinking pit and get to the table."

For months now Vinny had seemed lonely and it had long been a hope of hers that he would bring someone home, maybe today was that day. Vera accepted that all men had to have someone but deep down she didn't really want another intruder, at least not one like that whore Lisa. Vinny was a strange lad and deep in the back of her mind it bothered Vera. Maybe that was the real reason why she was even entertaining the idea of him bringing someone new into the house. When the food began to dry up she started to lose her patience and poking her head out of the kitchen door, screamed in the high pitched voice that she had used on her son's for the whole of their lives whenever she was angry with them. "Vinceeeeent!"

Still no reply and now more than a little irate, she marched straight into his room, guest or no guest he was going to get a mouthful. The bed hadn't been slept in and the sheets were still as neat and crisp as when she had made them a day earlier. Sitting on the bed her appetite instantly disappeared. It was the first time her son had stayed out all night and the realisation that he wasn't home didn't sit well with Vera Frasier. It would have been a different story if Jason still lived with them. Her two boys had been inseparable and she would have been reassured that wherever they were, they would be together. Vinny was a special boy, his mother had known that from the minute she'd given birth to him. When it came to Jason he was a different kettle of fish altogether, always sure of himself and wise to boot. The fact that her sons were so very different made her over the years, become overly protective of her youngest. Now sitting alone in his room she glanced round at all the bits and pieces he'd started to collect. Nude statues of men filled every shelf and the bedside table overflowed with bodybuilding magazines and videos. Even when the proof was staring her in the face Vera refused to accept what her youngest son was. Walking back into the kitchen she removed all the cooked food from the oven and tipped it into the bin. When Vincent deemed to show his sorry face she was going to give him the mother of all ear bashings. The morning and afternoon passed slowly and when it reached seven o'clock Vera Frasier was little short of hysterical. She didn't have the foggiest idea where to look for her boy and the thought of having to go cap in hand to the Camel appalled her. No, Vera reasoned that she would wait at least another day before she took things any further. Knowing Vinny he was probably shacked up with a little scrubber somewhere and didn't give a toss that his dear old mum was out of her mind with worry. He had always been selfish but just this once if that was the case then it was something she wouldn't have minded.

On Monday Maude Shelton was up and about with the larks. It had been a night of terrible sleep and she was now glad that at last the morning was here. Every second of the previous eight hours had been horrendous with visions of her beloved Jason lying in a filthy prison cell. Not once had she given Vinny a thought as deep down she knew that all this aggravation was somehow connected to him. Having made herself a pot of tea she now sat at her small kitchen table and glanced at the clock. It was just after nine and she didn't know whether to wake Lisa or wait awhile. Fortunately the decision was taken out of her hands when she heard a terrible banging on the pubs back door.

"Fucking open up you whore! I want to talk to my boys, do you hear?"

There was no mistaking that voice and Maude quickly put on her dressing gown and headed downstairs. She found Lisa sitting hunched on the hallway floor behind the back door.

"Oh darling whatever's the matter?"

Lisa looked up startled and Maude knew that whatever was going on couldn't continue.

"I don't know, I swear I don't. She just turned up out of

115

the blue and the mood she's in, well I didn't dare open up. Maude why does she hate me so? She don't even really know me!"

"Darling I wouldn't take it personal, Vera Frasier hates everyone. Now come on let's get you up off that cold old floor."

Maude Shelton gently got hold of Lisa's arm and standing her up, pointed her in the direction of her room. All the while the banging on the door loudly continued. "You wait in there love, I'll deal with this. It's been years coming and I think now is about the right time to give Vera Frasier a few home truths."

The young girl didn't argue, she was just so grateful that she had someone looking out for her. When Lisa was safely tucked away next-door Maude at last opened up. Vera immediately barged in but that was nothing unexpected.

"Well?"

"Well what?"

"Where the fuck are my kids?"

"Listen to you, kids indeed! They're both grown men Vera ain't it about time you let them act like it? And besides I ain't got the foggiest where they are."

"Don't fucking lie to me because I can see straight through you Maude Shelton."

Maude still held the door open and she had no intention of closing it. She wanted this horrible woman out of her pub and as quickly as possible.

"No one's lying to you but if you stopped and drew a bleeding breath then maybe we could find out what you're on about."

"My boy ain't been home and I'm worried sick. Now I know I ain't got any hold over Jay, he made his bed a long time ago but my baby is a different matter."

116

Maude was quickly becoming fed up with the woman standing in front of her.

"For god's sake Vera I wish you'd just stop for a minute and listen to yourself. My baby! The boy must be forty if he's a day. Go home Vera and for once in your miserable life let them be the men that they've become and not the two little boys you won't allow to grow up!"

Vera Frasier lunged forward and grabbed a handful of the landlady's hair.

"I told you once before not to interfere with my family but I guess you didn't take any fucking notice, well you will this time."

Before Vera had a chance to carry on with her onslaught of words, Maude had quickly spun round and snatching the woman's wrist pulled her arm up high behind her back. Vera Frasier screamed out in pain and instantly let go of Maude's hair. Pushing her towards the open doorway, Maude gave a final shove that saw Vera fall flat on her face in the back yard.

"Now go home you old cow and don't cause anymore fucking trouble. I swear if you darken my doorstep again I'll fucking do for you."

With that Maude slammed the door shut and turned to see a grinning Lisa standing in the hall.

"Oh Maude, that was brilliant. I've never seen anyone stand up to that old bitch like you just did. I wish Jay could have been here to see it."

With one hand Maude patted the girl gently on the shoulder and with the other rubbed at her sore head.

"I'll tell you one thing, the old girls still got plenty of fight left in her."

"She ain't nothing when it comes to you Duchess."

The word 'Duchess' brought a lump to Maude's throat. It had long been a favourite name of Jason's but this was

117

the first time that his wife had referred to Maude in that way.

"It's over now love and I'm going to get back to me breakfast, I suggest you do the same."

Back inside her flat Maude began to think and with all that had gone on in the last few days her imagination went into overdrive. Jason's arrest she could handle but with Vinny involved somewhere along the line and now Vera turning up, things were starting to get a little crazy. Finally she came to a decision and after a five minute search through her address book and with shaking hands to boot, Maude dialled Vinny's mobile. She really didn't have a clue what she would say or where the conversation would lead but still she hoped with all hope that he would answer. It rang several times and she was scared it was about to go to a recorded message but at last someone replied.

"Yeah?"

"Vinny is that you?"

"Who's asking?"

"It's Maude, Maude Shelton from the Camel. I'm trying to get hold of Vincent Frasier is this the right number?"

It was several seconds before there was another sound but finally Vincent spoke.

"Yeah Maude, it's the right number and this is Vinny but why are you ringing me?"

"Your mums on the warpath and I don't think it's going to be long before Lisa snaps. I've got no idea what's gone on Vinny but if you could just come back and explain things then I think Lisa would at least be able to handle it."

"Leave it with me Maude I'll make sure she gets the full story. Have they got any details about the funeral yet?"

"Funeral? What funeral? Whatever are you talking

118

about Vinny?"

Vinny didn't reply and instantly hung up leaving Maude with the receiver still pressed to her ear. His last sentence cemented her belief that things were far from right but she also accepted that she had little choice but to trust him. All the same his mention of a funeral really bothered her and for the life of her she couldn't work out what he was on about. Feeling just a little relieved that she had at least made contact, Maude went down stairs to see if Lisa was all right. The girl had experienced a hard couple of days and Maude hoped that she would be able to handle the visit later that afternoon. Not waiting for an invitation Maude knocked at the same time as she entered the room. Lisa was propped up in bed flicking through a magazine. Her eyes were dark through lack of sleep and Maude Shelton was well aware that to mention the conversation with Vinny might just tip her over the edge. Taking a seat on the side of the bed, Maude put on her best smile.

"Hi sweetheart, excited about the visit?"

"Scared more like."

"Scared? Whatever have you got to be scared about?"

"Seeing Jay in that horrible place for one thing. The idea that I may have to leave here frightens me and I really wouldn't want to live anywhere else."

"Well let's hope things don't come to that."

"What do you mean?"

"Oh nothing darling I'm not thinking straight. You have a home here for as long as you need or want one with or without Jason."

Lisa flung her arms around the woman and held on tight. The unexpected show of emotion took Maude by surprise and for a second she didn't know how to handle it. Awkwardly she patted the girl on the back.

119

"Come on now it's time you were getting dressed. You want to look your best for that husband of yours don't you?"

Lisa nodded and was instantly out of the bed. In an almost childlike way she began to rifle through her wardrobe and the pitiful sight again brought a lump to Maude Shelton's throat. Her sudden onset of emotion was halted by someone once more banging on the back door. Standing up, Maude went to answer and hoped that it wasn't Vera Frasier again as she really wasn't in the mood for world war three. Slowly opening the door she could see that it wasn't Vera but Joey West her part-time pot man.

"Hello mate what's up?"

"Nothing Maudie, just thought I'd let you know that Kings got done over this weekend and Freddie Gant is doing his nut."

"Freddie Gant! What's he got to do with Kings?"

"He's the real owner Maudie,, didn't you know that?"

Maude Shelton shook her head.

"First I've heard of it but when it comes down to that nasty piece of work nothing would surprise me."

"Well that's all the info I have at the minute but as soon as I know more I'll let you in on it."

It was common practice in the east end to make the local publican aware of any trouble in the area and sometimes they even knew the details before the Old Bill.

"Thanks for telling me Joey and don't be late this afternoon will you?"

"You can rely on me sweetheart, you know you can."

After Maude Shelton closed the door she came over faint and leant against the inner wall to steady herself. Suddenly what Joey had just told her registered and putting two and two together she had hit the nail on the head. Desperate to find out more, she hoped with all her heart that Lisa had remembered something that would be of use. Walking into the room she sat back down on the girl's bed.

"You know when I asked you if you could remember anything about what the boys had got up to."

"Yeah."

"Well have you?"

"No not really. Well apart from I heard Jay on the phone to Mango the other day. He was asking if he could borrow the car though what he needed it for god above only knows. If he hadn't have borrowed it then there wouldn't have been an accident and we wouldn't be in this mess. Plus I bet Mango will be round here in the next few days wanting compensation but I suppose you can't blame him , it's just I ain't got no spare cash at the minute."

"Don't worry about that my love. If Mango Smith comes round here I'll sort him out. Now finish getting ready the taxi will be here in half an hour."

Maude wearily made her way back up to the flat and sat down at the table. She could feel the tension starting to set in and rubbed at the back of her neck. If she'd only had suspicions before that the boys had been doing something dodgy, now she was sure that they were the ones who'd carried out the robbery. Her time at the prison today was going to be about so much more than just paying Jason a social visit. Maude was sure in her heart that he couldn't have known Freddie Gant owned the factory and now with all the accident worry she was about to burden him even further. The trouble was, Maude knew that this latest snippet of information could turn out to be a hundred times worse than any prison sentence he may receive.

121

CHAPTER THIRTEEN

The cab driver eyed the two women suspiciously when they asked to be taken to Belmarsh. At least once a week he took someone on the monotonous drive over to the prison. They were bread and butter fares and he'd been doing it for more years than he cared to remember but this time it was different. These two didn't look like your average wife and mother and it intrigued him as to why they were visiting Belmarsh in the first place. Maurice Stokes had been a London cabbie since his early twenties and it was a job he loved. The people you met could sometimes turn out to be very interesting and if you were really lucky could even be famous. A favourite pass time of his was eyeing up his fares in the rear view mirror and trying to work out their life story. Maurice decided to strike up a conversation and see if either of the women were willing to shed a little light on their trip.

"So! Have you two been up here before?"

There was no answer from the back seat, which instantly created an atmosphere but not enough for the cabbie to stop with his questions.

"I do this trip regular and the stories I hear would make your hair curl I can tell you. So who are you visiting today if you don't mind me asking?"

Suddenly Maude shot forward in her seat and pressed her face close to the small gap in the sliding glass window.

"I do bloody mind you asking you nosy little sod. Get off on other peoples misfortune do you? Now just do what you're being paid for and drive will you."

The colour of Maurice Stokes cheeks instantly turned crimson and if his plump little body could have disappeared down the foot well, then it would have.

He didn't dare apologise and instead stared directly ahead for the next fifteen minutes. In all the years he'd been driving he'd never come up against a person like Maude Shelton and even though it was long overdue, Maurice Stokes had finally been put in his place. The lack of conversation didn't do anything for Lisa's nerves and as the large building that was Belmarsh prison, loomed in the distance Maude could see Lisa visibly begin to shake. "Pull yourself together love; if Jay sees you in a state it will only upset him. Let's keep the emotions for when we come out shall we? As far as our boy is concerned we're both coping well. Ok?"

"Ok I'll try but I can't promise anything."

It wasn't the reply she wanted to hear and Maude sharply turned on Lisa.

"Don't be so damned negative all the time. It's Jay you have to think about now and not yourself. At the end of the day you'll be walking back out, he won't."

Lisa was shocked at the words but she didn't want an argument, at least not today. Getting out of the black hackney, Maude waited to be told how much the fare was. As Maurice Stokes informed her that it would be a score he didn't once have the nerve to look her in the eyes. Handing over a crisp twenty pound note she sarcastically told him to 'keep the change' and the taxi sharply pulled away without a goodbye. It didn't rile Maurice that there wasn't a tip, in all honesty he was just pleased to be away from the woman.

"What a Wanker!"

"Sorry Maude what did you say?"

"Oh nothing love, come on let's get this over with shall we?"

Although Belmarsh was a category A prison housing murderers, terrorists and child molesters, it still had a small remand wing. The main building was impressive and having only been built in the nineties, incorporated state of the art security installations. It may have been modern compared to the likes of Pentonville and Wormwood Scrubs but it was no more inviting and the smell of institution hung heavily in the air. Lisa clung tightly to Maude's arm as they were ushered through one automatic gate after another. Prison guards seemed to be everywhere and although not rude in anyway, their manner gave not an ounce of friendliness or compassion. To Maude it was as if they looked upon every person who walked through the gates, other than the staff, as criminals. Maude Shelton had weighed up the situation within a few minutes of arriving and she didn't like the conclusion she had come to. Treat someone like a dog and sooner or later they would start to bite. No wonder the country was in the state it was if this was how the screws looked upon the population and if things didn't change, then god help them in twenty years time was all that Maude could think. Finally they reached the visiting room and were directed to a vacant table. Lisa glanced around her at all the other visitors and wondered if this was to become a regular part of her life. If it was, then she didn't think she would be able to cope. Maude watched the girl and instantly knew what she was thinking.

"Now you can get that idea out of your head once and for all young lady!"

"What idea?"

"Lisa I ain't stupid. I saw the look on your face when that woman and her kids came in. You thought that could be me pretty soon didn't you?"

"Well it could be couldn't it? Could be me every other week for the next god knows how long."

"I'll tell you why it won't, because Jason wouldn't let it happen that's why."

Lisa lifted her palms upwards as if to say 'where here now ain't we'.

"Ok point taken but I know that boy as if he were me own and something's not right with all of this. That's why I'd like a few minutes alone with him, not straight away but after a little while. You could suggest going to get us all a nice cuppa and give me time to say my piece."

Lisa nodded and seconds later a heavy metal door at the end of the room opened. Men of all shapes, sizes, colour and creeds began to emerge and Lisa couldn't help but strain her neck as high as she could in the hope of catching an early glimpse of her husband. When Jason Frasier finally walked over to the table and took a seat he could see the look of horror in both of the women's eyes. His face was still swollen from the accident and he knew he must have appeared a right mess.

"Come on you two it's not as bad as all that, it looks far worse than it is."

"Well I wouldn't want to be the other fella!"

Jason giggled at Maude's joke but his wife couldn't see the funny side. Lisa didn't speak but as she gripped his hand as tightly as she could muster uncontrollable tears began to roll down her cheeks.

"Babe please don't cry. I can't stand it when you're upset."

"Oh Jay, when are you coming home?"

"Lisa I wish I knew but it ain't going to be for some time yet."

"Why?"

"Darling you wouldn't understand but no one wants us to be together more than me."

"Then just tell them that you didn't do it Jay."

125

"If only it was that simple babe but at the minute that's just not possible."

Maude couldn't believe what she was hearing and started to think that Lisa might be having a breakdown. The girl wasn't stupid, she knew where they were and yet she was talking to her husband as if he could just get up and walk right out if he really wanted to. Maude coughed loudly and Lisa realised this was her cue to disappear for a few minutes. Wiping her eyes with a fresh tissue she smiled widely in her husband's direction.

"Who's for a nice cup of rosie then?"

"Thanks babe that would be great."

"Do you need a hand Lisa?"

"No no I can manage Maude; you stay here and have a chat with Jay."

When she at last walked away from the table Maude Shelton breathed a sigh of relief.

"So how's she really coping then?"

"She's fine Jay but that should be the last thing on your bleeding mind at the moment."

"Look I know it seems bad but the woman stepped out of nowhere and my brief said that come hell or high water he's going to do his best to prove that and...."

Maude Shelton cut Jason off mid flow.

"I ain't talking about the accident dozy bollocks! I'm talking about Kings."

Jason bit his lip and Maude sensed that he was racking his brains trying to come up with some lame excuse.

"Don't try and pull the wool over me eyes Jay, I'm far too long in the tooth for that."

"Ok I'm sorry, does Lisa know about it?"

"No but I don't know how much longer I can keep it from her. As soon as Freddie Gant finds out who's at the bottom of all of this, then you and Vinny's life won't be worth diddly squat. As for your wife, I'll do my best but I don't know if I can protect her Jason. Honestly I'm at my wits end son, what a mess and no mistake."

"Wo wo! Back track there a second Duchess. What's Freddie Gant got to do with any of this?"

Maude smiled but it wasn't a humorous smile.

"I didn't think you knew he was behind Kings, oh Jay whatever are we going to do? Faces like Gant don't let things go and he will hunt you both down to get that cash back."

"Listen Maude, I want you to take Lisa home and watch over her the best you can. As soon as I get back to the wing I'll make a few phone calls."

Maude rubbed her brow with the tips of her fingers as she spoke.

"Well if its Vinny you want to speak to, I wouldn't bother as I've already spoken to him."

"No no it's not Vin but anyway what did he say?"

"As usual not a lot. He said he'd come back and speak to Lisa to explain but as yet he ain't appeared. Then again I don't really expect anything else when it comes down to that brother of yours. He did say one strange thing though, something about a funeral. What on earth he was on about I don't know."

Jason knew exactly what his brother meant but he decided to keep quiet about the matter, this was between him and Vinny and no one else.

"Duchess Can you send me a few quid in?"

"Of course I can darling as soon as I get back. Is there anything else you need?"

The conversation came to an abrupt halt when Lisa returned to the table. Maude was dreading having to make small talk for the rest of the visit but as luck would have it that wouldn't happen. Just as Lisa had taken her

127

seat the alarms went off and the whole room was sent out. One of the other prisoners had decided to assault his wife and for today at least visiting time was over. The poor cow had travelled all the way from Swansea and her husband had taken offence at what she'd decided to wear, such was prison life!

Back on the wing it took Jason two days to secure the use of a phone card from big Larry Pond. Larry ruled the wing with an iron rod but for some reason had taken a liking to Jason. That said, when the promised cash came through from Maude Jay would of course have to pay it back and at an extortionate rate of interest. Lying back on his bunk Jason had decided to wait until late afternoon to make the calls. Most people would be out at work and he didn't want to waste his valuable credit. The hours dragged by and when five o'clock at last came and with more than a little trepidation, he dialled the first number.

"Hello! Battersea dogs home Rex speaking."

"Hi mate its Jason, how you doing?"

For a second there was silence and Jason suddenly regretted making the call.

"I'm fine mate but you were the last person I expected to hear from."

"Why?"

"Why? Fuck me mate there's murders going on here. Kings got robbed and they've been interviewing us all day."

"What's that got to do with me Fred?"

"Listen pal I don't want to be involved in any of this but I will tell you one thing for nothing, after they spoke to that miserable old bastard Happy Bottle two days after the bank holiday, all interest moved over to your brother. Who I might add ain't been around for several days."

"But I still don't see what any of that's got to do with

128

me?"

"Listen Jay, I really like you as a mate so don't take me for a mug. Now I don't need any aggro so I'd appreciate it if you didn't call again. The last thing I need is Freddie Gant on my case especially since Roly went walk about."

"Yeah I heard Gant was involved behind the scenes."

"Don't tell me you didn't know he was the owner of Kings. Fuck me Jason, you have to sort this mess out. He's one face you don't want to wind up. The Freddie Gants of this world are naughty boys and I mean real naughty boys."

"What do you mean about Roly?"

"Happy reckons no one knows where he is, which really ain't like him. Make of that what you will."

"You don't think he's......"

"Jay, Freddie Gant is a right nasty bastard and he has a lot of other nasty bastard's doing his dirty work. For fucks sake Jay he's the boss of a powerful firm and I wouldn't put anything past him."

Jason Frasier thanked his friend for the information and hung up. Walking back to his cell he was lost as to what to do next. Finally he decided that he would call Vinny. His brother had been the one to get them into this mess and now he would have to get them out of it. The phone card still had plenty of credit but dialling Vinny's mobile, Jason wondered if it would be enough or whether it would be used up with just his ranting. The number was withheld but Vincent Frasier answered all the same.

"Vin?"

"Fuck me bro it's good to hear your voice, I thought you was a goner."

"Of course you did and you didn't bother hanging around to find out did you? Anyway that s not why I'm on the blower, it's something far more important than your loyalty to me."

"Don't be like that Jay, how was I supposed to know. Where are you anyway? I've had that daft old cow Maude on the phone giving me fucking earache and I tell you, I can do without her ranting on at me."

"You're a cunt Vin! You've only gone and shafted Freddie Gant."

"Freddie Gant! What the fuck are you on about?"

"Freddie Gant my tosser of a brother, only fucking happens to own Kings. You've really stitched us up big time Vin."

Not visible to Jason, Vinny as usual shrugged his shoulders.

"So! We just don't go back, end of story."

"End of fucking story! Vinny, faces like Gant don't let things go. He'll be like a dog with a fucking bone to get that cash back and there ain't really anyplace I can hide now is there?"

"Why?"

"Why? You twat, because I'm fucking banged up that's why and if Gant wants me then he ain't going to have a hard time tracking me down now is he?"

"I'm sorry mate, really sorry but what do you expect me to do?"

"Come back and hold your scrawny little hands up that's what. Give the money back and hope that he don't fucking pulverise us that's what!"

Even with miles between them Jason could hear his brother gulp on the other end.

"That's a tall order Jay. I mean you're kind of protected but who's going to look out for me. I've heard some nasty fucking tales about that bastard and his henchman Wally Evans."

Jason Frasier couldn't believe what he was hearing.

After all the years he'd looked out for Vinny and taken the blame most of the time, this insult to the word brother was once again covering his own back.

"Look Vinny I don't give a toss whose looking out for you. All I need to know is that Lisa and Maude are safe. Me and you will have to take our chances. Will you do that for me Vinny? Vinny? Vinny are you still there?" Jason should have known that he was wasting precious card time. His brother had hung up and was now pacing the floor in turmoil over what to do. He didn't care about the women. As far as he was concerned, if Freddie Gant wanted someone to pay then it might as well be those two. No, Vinny wasn't about to lose any sleep over his sister in law but he did care about his brother. There began a battle of wills inside his own head. Finding out that his brother was alive was brilliant news but having to take the rap for robbery was asking a bit much as far as he was concerned. Whichever way he looked at it Jason was as much to blame so why should he be the one to suffer. The conclusion as usual came out in favour of saving his own skin. Maybe he would pay a visit to the Smoke after all but it wouldn't be to see Freddie Gant. Walking over to the tiny fridge that was the hotels mini bar, he pulled out a scotch and downed the miniature bottle in one.

CHAPTER FOURTEEN

Just as Fred Blatch said, the interviews had begun in
earnest only in reality they had started two days earlier
and had been nothing like what he and his colleagues
would experience. These were interrogations, the kind
that would have been happily adopted by the Gestapo.
Happy Bottle was told to get off of the premises but to be
back sharpish first thing in the morning and the screams
had started before Happy even had chance to unlock his
car door. They were bloodcurdling and caused him to
shake uncontrollably as he fumbled to get his key in the
lock. He knew that he had little choice but to return the
following day, that or they would come looking for him.
Happy consoled himself with the fact that if he was to be
punished they would have done it there and then. No, he
would come back as told and fall over himself to
accommodate Freddie Gant in any way that he could.
Roly Peterson freely urinated the second Wally took a
step towards him and that in itself angered the big man
even more. Pushing Roly down onto the chair, Wally
leered down menacingly as he wound the duct tape
around his captive's arms and secured it to the wooden
rests. Wally carefully unfolded a polythene sheet and
laid it down on the floor. Next and with as much effort as
he could manage due to Roly's size, Wally dragged the
chair until it was dead in the centre of the plastic.
Freddie Gant sat relaxingly back in his seat and waited
for the fun to begin. It wouldn't last long and he
reasoned there was no need for a gag as apart from
Happy, there wasn't anyone else around to hear the
screams. In the unlikely event that there was, it would be
a warning to them and anyone they told about it. Onto

the desk Wally placed a green metal box containing various small tools. He'd had them specially made many years earlier and they were something he was extremely proud of. His old mum had always told him that to be a good workman you needed good tools. Removing a pair of razor sharp pliers, Wally Evans began his torture by snipping off one of Roly's little fingers.

"I can't tell you anything. I don't know arghhhhhhhh."
The pain was excruciating and Roly's eyes bulged as Wally cut off the other finger.

"Arghhhhhhhhhhh! Arghhhhhhhh!"
When no information was forthcoming he moved onto the thumbs. Ten minutes later and when water had been thrown over Roly to bring him round, he looked down at his hands to see only stumps. Roly Peterson knew there was no way he was getting out of this alive and silently prayed to God for it to be over quickly. Wally was enjoying himself far more than he'd done in a long time, even though both he and Freddie knew that there would be no new information. Roly had been ready to spill his guts the moment they walked in. No this little exercise was being carried out for two reason and two reasons only. The first being that Freddie Gant couldn't be seen to lose face and not to punish Roly would have resulted in exactly that. The second was that from time to time Freddie liked to allow Wally to flex his muscles. The last thing he needed in this game was for his right hand man to go soft.

"Wal I think I've about done here, that fat cunt ain't going to tell us anything new. I'll wait in the car while you finish him off. Get rid of his fat carcass in the pit round the back. The acid will dispose of him, though God only knows how long it will take. Roly you really should have gone on a diet it would have saved us all a

133

lot of fucking time and trouble."

Wally grinned at his boss's words. As Freddie left the room he was laughing to himself and Roly knew that his time on this planet was fast running out. Wally Evans took a moment to work out how he would finish his victim off. Whenever possible he liked to try out something new and keeping your finger on the pulse was a must nowadays. Instantly an idea sprang to mind and he smiled to himself. He decided that he wouldn't finish this poor excuse for a man off after all; no he was going to put him in the pit alive. The thought excited him and he swiftly wrapped the chair and Roly's entire body except for the head in cling film. Wally tipped the chair backwards allowing Roly's body to be supported wholly by the chairs back legs. Hoping that it wouldn't snap under the man's weight, Wally proceeded to drag the chair to the rear of the factory. For a split-second Roly Peterson thought that maybe his life was going to be spared after all but as they rounded the corner and the large inspection pit came into sight, he knew that wouldn't be the case. Trying to drag his feet was futile; he was feeling so faint that he had little control over his body. As Wally hauled the chair to the steel safety covering that would soon become his coffin lid, Roly felt his bowels relax and the remains of last night's dinner released itself. Wally Evans removed the heavy metal plates and manoeuvred the chair containing his victim onto the edge of the tank. Wally stepped back, as the sheer size of the man would create a large splash and getting acid on him no matter how little was the last thing he wanted. As the chair bobbed up and down Roly desperately struggled for breath. If the screams from the office were bad, nothing could compare to the ones being emitted now. For only a second or two Roly Peterson

134

struggled with every ounce of strength he could muster but as the liquid burnt and dissolved his skin, it was over in a matter of minutes. Wally could see that he would have no more problems and slammed the lid shut on the rapidly disintegrating corpse. Twenty minutes later and all signs of trouble in the office had been cleaned away. The invention of cling film had been a blessing to people in Wally Evans's line of work. It stemmed the flow of blood and usually made the job of cleaning up a lot faster. Wally closed and locked the door to the building before joining his boss in the car.

"Fuck me Wal you took your time, everything Ok?"

"Yeah sure, sorry about the wait Freddie but the cling film split a bit and that fat bastard bled like a stuck pig. It took a little more clearing up than usual that's all. Just as I tipped him in the pot he started jabbering on about someone called Frasier but it was too late to get anything else out of him."

"Fucking hell Wal! He may have been trying to tell us what we need to know."

"I realise that Boss but what could I do? He was a nano second away from hitting the fluid. There's no way I was getting any fucking closer to that hydrochloric acid than I had to. Anyway where to now?"

Freddie Gant shook his head in exasperation.

"You never cease to fucking amaze me Wal. Well I suppose we'd better go back to the office and plan our next move. I'm not fucking looking forward to phoning Boris but because of that fat twat and now you, I ain't got much fucking choice in the matter. I think I can wangle us a bit of time but the Russian won't wait long. I've dreaded getting into bother with them for a while now; god only fucking knows where this is all going to end!"

Due to the weekend's trouble, a sign had been posted on

135

the main entrance into Kings. The place would be closed until further notice day but all workers should still report in for a meeting on Tuesday. With no signs of life at the factory Happy let himself inside the building but the quietness of the place only heightened his fear. When he noticed that Wally Evans now sat in his old boss's chair and Freddie Gant was nowhere to be seen he realised that maybe he'd made a mistake regarding his future. Maybe they were going to top him as well. There was no evidence that Roly was dead but Happy Bottle knew the score, knew how these types of people operated and if he had been a betting man would have had a large wedge on not seeing Roly Peterson alive again. Wally beckoned for the man to come inside and was about to speak when the telephone rang. He looked at Happy as if to ask 'who's that?' but Happy just shrugged his shoulders. Deciding to answer just in case it was his boss, Wally picked up the receiver and a barrage of abuse bellowed into his ear. Sheila Peterson had been sure that her husband would answer and when she heard a voice telling her to 'Fuck off! she slammed the phone down. Roly had never stayed out all night before not even when he visited his whores in Soho and she was really starting to get concerned. Sheila Peterson was well aware of her husband's indiscretions, in fact she welcomed them but Roly always returned home no matter what the hour. With friends arriving shortly she could do very little but if he didn't come home today, then first thing in the morning when the factory was busy and Roly was at his most vulnerable she would make a visit. Tyron's school fees still hadn't been paid and if her scumbag husband thought he could shirk his responsibilities he had another think coming. Happy Bottle guessed who the caller was and inwardly smirked to himself. Wally couldn't possibly have seen any response but he was sharp enough to know how people's minds worked and turning towards Happy curled his lips back as he spoke.

"Are you taking the fucking piss?"

Happy realised that the man's attention was now well and truly focused on him and he could feel his legs begin the shake.

"No! no way Mr Evans, I wouldn't do that. I've come to help Mr Gant out in any way I can."

"Well Mr Gant wants every single member of the workforce brought in here throughout the next couple of days. It'll be one at a time so make sure there's someone in the place who speaks their fucking lingo. You'll have to tell them that we've been robbed but don't go into any detail, Mr Gant likes his private business to stay just that, Private!"

"Yes Mr Evans, sure Mr Evans is there anything else Mr Evans?"

"Just fuck off out of my sight you creepy little cunt and you'd just better pray that no one incriminates you, because if they do then fuck am I going to enjoy making you suffer."

Happy almost ran from the room and once outside inhaled the fresh air as quickly as he could. Instantly the contents of his breakfast appeared on the concrete but he was at least grateful that his terror had erupted from the top end rather than the bottom. Dabbing at his mouth with an old grey handkerchief, Happy knew that he had to play things carefully and do anything that was asked of him to have any hope of survival.

By 9.30 that morning he had everyone seated in the canteen and had begun to try and explain the weekend's events. The English workers looked shocked but as far as the Eastern Europeans were concerned, their faces wore a

137

blank expression. Happy knew that they probably didn't have the first idea of what he was talking about but he carried on all the same. At the end of his informative statement he called Fred Blatch over.

"Fred I need you to help me out here mate and if you value your own skin you won't fucking argue. Freddie Gants going to be here soon and none of these twats have got a fucking clue what I'm on about."

Fred lifted his palms upwards as if to ask 'So what's all this got to do with me'.

"You speak their fucking lingo don't you?"

Fred Blatch blew out his cheeks.

"I wouldn't go as far as to say speak. I can make them understand a bit but not much. If you're planning on me saving your fucking bacon then you can think again."

"I ain't planning anything Fred but you're the best we've got and we need to show willing. Now will you give it a go or not?"

Fred nodded but as he walked away he shook his head in resentment at having been asked in the first place. By the time Freddie Gant arrived the first interviewee was sitting waiting in the office. Fred Blatch began to speak and even though Wally glared at him for even daring to open his mouth he continued.

"Mr Gant I'm going to do my best to help you out but my language skills are very limited. If you could keep the questions to a minimum, then maybe I just might be able to pull it off."

Freddie was pleased that at least someone in this place talked some sense and nodded his agreement. The interviews took a lengthy time as each employee was asked if they had seen anything or heard any gossip about the robbery. With every shake of the head they were led outside and the next was ushered into the office. By ten the next day the last person had been seen and they were still no further forward. Freddie was becoming irate and was about to vent his anger on Happy when the office door opened and Sheila Peterson stormed in.

"What the fucks going on here and where the hell is my husband?"

Turning towards Freddie she raised her head in a show of superiority.

"Who in god's name are you and what are you doing sitting in my husband's chair?"

Freddie rolled his eyes in Wally's direction.

"Fuck me if this ain't all I need. I've wasted almost two days with a bunch of fucking dribbly's and now I've got a fucking bloodsucking wife on my back."

Sheila was about to protest when Wally grabbed her roughly by the arm and shoved her out of the office and into the corridor.

"How dare you, take your hands off me! Who the hell do you think you are? You just wait until my husband hears about this I'll....."

Wally Evans didn't give the woman chance to finish her sentence. With one hand and as quick as a flash he held her up against the wall by her neck. Normally Wally wouldn't lay a hand on a woman, well not without extreme provocation but somehow this woman was different. This woman was the type to bleed a man dry and Wally could see the kind of life that poor old dear departed Roly must have had. The fear in Sheila Peterson's eyes gave him a buzz and although he knew he wouldn't really have hurt her, just sensing her fear was enough to tell him that he was getting the message across.

"Now you listen to me lady and listen good. Your husband ain't going to be around anymore and as far as this place is concerned, he sold out a long time ago. Now

139

go home and make the best of what you've got."
Sheila's lily white neck was becoming redder by the
second and Wally knew through experience that she
would probably be hoarse come tomorrow. Sheila was
about to stumble away when Wally once more grabbed
her arm.

"Don't have any daft fucking ideas about seeing the Old
Bill. You really don't want to mess with my Boss, he's
one nasty bastard. Understood?"

Sheila nodded and when Wally let go of her she bolted
towards the door. She wasn't stupid, in fact Sheila
Peterson (nee) White was more street wise than her
husband had ever given her credit for. Born on the
Primrose estate in Walthamstow, she had come across
these types of people her whole life and Sheila knew how
things worked. Hoping that there was still some cash in
their joint account Sheila made her way to the bank. If
she sold the house and down scaled they could still have
a reasonable standard of living. Tyron would have to
come out of his private school but when all was said and
done she still had far more now than when she had begun.
As for Roly, Sheila didn't care if she never set eyes on
him again and deep down she already knew that was
going to be the case. Wally Evans watched her walk
from the building and when he was convinced that she
wouldn't return, made his way back to the office. Inside
Freddie Gant just sat and stared at Happy and Fred. For
the first time in many years he didn't know how to
proceed. Boris wouldn't wait forever and as far as the
rest of the workforce were concerned, they had come up
with a big fat zero. Out of the blue Happy Bottle spoke
and Fred Blatch could have murdered him when he heard
what came out of his mouth.

"I told Mr Peterson it was that Vinny Frasier all along but

140

would he listen? All he kept saying was we couldn't be sure and....."
Freddie nodded towards the door and Fred Blatch felt relief at being allowed to leave. Taking on board all that he had heard, Fred hoped with all his heart that Jason really wasn't mixed up in any of this, that or he was as far away from the smoke as was humanly possible. When the door closed Wally Evans crossed the room in a flash and soon had the little man in the same kind of hold that had held Sheila Peterson only a few minutes earlier. This time as Wally pushed his hand upwards Happy's feet actually left the floor. Freddie stood up and walked around the desk until he was standing beside his man.
"Easy Wal, don't want to make another mistake now do we?"
Wally released his grip and Happy Bottle fell to the ground gasping for air. Freddie Gant bent low until his face was almost level with Happy's and with his index finger poked the man sharply in the temple.
"Now you'd better tell me everything and I fucking mean everything you little cunt. This time if I even think that you're skirting round the truth, then Wally here can do whatever he likes. I've just about had a fucking gutful of you; you've wasted my time and made me look a right cunt and no one makes me look a cunt, do they Wal?"
Wally Evans shook his head and grinned from ear to ear.
A second taste of blood in as many days, things were definitely looking up. Happy Bottle gulped in fear and without any further persuasion told all that he knew. He began from the very first day he set eyes on Jason and ended with seeing Vinny in the corridor just before the money had gone missing. When he'd at last told them everything he could, Happy was mentally exhausted and Freddie accepted that finally they had the truth. After
141

asking where these Frasier brothers could be found, Freddie turned to Wally and winked. It was the only signal to pass between the two men and the only one that was needed. Freddie left the room and heard Happy's first grunts of pain as he walked along the corridor. With another job well done Wally locked the office and joined his boss in the car.

"All sorted?"

"Sorted Boss. I'll come back tonight and get rid of the little cunt when the place is quiet, probably use the acid again I liked that. Now where to?"

"I think we'll take a drive over to Bethnal Green, Rickman Street to be more precise."

Wally Evans smiled as he started up the engine, things were beginning to happen and it was at times like these that he really came into his own.

CHAPTER FIFTEEN

After the prison ordeal Lisa Frasier had seemed to come to terms with things or at least for the time being and had even served drinks in the bar the previous night. It saddened Maude to see the girl desperately trying to act normal but she knew there were few words of comfort that she could offer. Now with another day dawning Maude Shelton realised that they had to get some kind of routine going, if not for the girl's sake then for her own sanity. It had been years since she had gone through anything as traumatic as this, many years in fact and then it had been to do with her own family. Maude shook the thoughts from her head, that was another story and one she didn't care to dwell on right now. Walking down the back hall she knocked gently on the door and entered when she heard Lisa's soft voice say, 'Come in'.

"Hello love, just wondered how you were feeling today?" Lisa rubbed the sleep from her eyes and Maude thought how vulnerable and childlike she looked.

"Not too bad but I didn't sleep very well last night. I think I'm going to call in sick and try to get a few more winks if that's alright with you?"

"Alright with me? Why ever shouldn't it be? Sometimes Lisa you do come out with the oddest of things."

"I'm sorry. It's just that I seem, or maybe we seem, to bring nothing but trouble to your door and you don't deserve it."

"And you do?"

"I suppose not but I really don't know what I would do without you Maude."

"Well the feelings mutual love. This little family set up we have ain't one sided you know? I need you two as

143

much as you need me."

"Thanks Duchess and I think I will call in sick."

"I don't blame you darling. Now I have to go down to the cash and carry but I should be back by opening time. If for some reason I ain't, then Sammy from the over sixties club said he'd open up so you're not to worry about anything all right?"

"Ok Maude and thanks."

"No thanks needed sweetheart now you just snuggle down and I'll pop in when I get back to see how you are." Before Maude Shelton had reached the end of the hallway Lisa's head had sunk back onto the pillow and she was snoring softly. The poor girl was absolutely exhausted but Maude couldn't work out why. True they'd both been through the mill and back again over the last few days but then surely it should have been Maude who was knackered, not some young slip of a girl. Honestly sometimes she didn't think the youth of today had any backbone.

Applying foundation thickly around her eyes, Maude tried to hide the dark circles that had appeared over the last couple of days. She hadn't been getting much sleep and was only too aware that at her age it could spell nothing but trouble. Pulling on her best cashmere coat she slipped quietly out of the Camels side door. As was her usual mode of transport Maude drove off to the cash and carry in the back of a pre booked black cab. Deep in thought and scrutinizing her list of crisps and nuts she didn't notice Vincent Frasier hiding around the corner. When he was confident that the coast was clear Vinny slipped into the back yard and after fumbling about in the outside shed, found the spare key. The information had been stored deep in his memory after he'd seen Jay retrieve it once and he gave himself a mental pat on

144

the back for being so clever. The Camel was graveyard
quiet as he walked along the hallway and stopping
outside his brother's room, Vinny put his ear to the door
listening for any sound of movement. Confident that he
hadn't been heard, he gently turned the brass door knob.
The smell of old beer and stale cigarettes hung in the air
but for some weird reason he found it sexual. The
thought that it was dirty and degrading just like the act he
was about to carry out spurred him on. For several
seconds he studied Lisa's face as she slumbered blissfully
unaware of what was to come. Vinny supposed she was
pretty in a plain sort of way but he still couldn't see what
his brother saw in her. On the odd occasion when he'd
paid Jason a visit Vinny could only ever remember her
whinging and whining. Quietly he began to undress and
when he was totally naked, pulled back the bedclothes
and climbed in. Instantly he could feel the warmth from
Lisa's body but his own coldness immediately woke his
sister in law. For a second what was happening didn't
register with Lisa and she just stared wide eyed. As soon
as she'd focused and worked out what was happening,
she opened her mouth as far as she could to scream. No
sound emerged and try as she might nothing came out,
she was paralysed with fear. Vinny realised his sister in
law had been struck mute and a leering smile crept over
his face which terrified her.
"About time we got to know each other a little better
Lisa! I've been thinking lately that Jay gets everything
he wants and as we are brothers and mum always taught
us to share, well you know what I mean. Now if you
struggle I'm going to hurt you and we don't want that
now do we?"
Lisa knew that her brother-in-law's interest in her was
nothing to do with lust or attraction. As with most rapists

and she had been exposed to this kind of abuse so many times in the past, Lisa could tell that Vinny wanted nothing more than to dominate and humiliate her. He hated her so much and his anger was such that just the sight of her could send him into a frenzy. For years he had held his feelings deep inside, telling himself that no matter how much she needed to be taught a lesson he wouldn't hurt his brother for the world. In reality Lisa knew that Vinny hadn't had the opportunity and that was the only reason she hadn't been subjected to this horrific act until now.

"Please Vinny don't do this, don't do it to me and don't do it to Jay."

"Jay! He couldn't care less about you. From day one you've tried to come between us and let me tell you, that ain't never going to fucking happen. You bewitched him you slut, well now I'm going to well and truly fucking break that spell"

Lisa continued to stare wide eyed at her attacker. She couldn't believe what she was hearing and what she knew was about to happen. Where was Jason when she needed him. After confronting her inner most demons and telling him every disgusting detail about her past how could he now let this happen? Suddenly and without warning a scream released itself from Lisa Frasier's mouth, a scream that was so piercing it made even Vinny jump. It stopped as soon as Vincent's fist hit her jaw and an agonising pain seared down the side of her face.

"I fucking told you I'd hurt you, now do as I say and we're going to get along just fine."

Lisa Frasier did as she was told and no further sounds emerged from her mouth but that didn't stop her resisting all the way. Holding her arms down Vinny used his knee to force Lisa's legs apart and his dirty nails scratched at

146

her wrists. Lisa fought with all her might and thrashed her legs around in all directions. This action managed to loosen the grip that his knee had on her but seconds later he had again pinned her down. This time his action trapped her skin and she winced in pain. Vincent was pleasantly surprised that he had risen for the occasion and put his excitement down to the fear that he was instilling. With one sharp movement he forced himself inside her but it was painful for them both. Lisa was dry and it felt like a hundred knives were being plunged deep within her. On the other hand pain was bringing Vincent Frasier to an early climax and he liked the feeling. As his body moved up and down he clasped a hand tightly over Lisa's mouth. Not to silence her but purely for the fact that he was mentally re-enacting a rape scene he had watched on a porn film a few days earlier. Even though Lisa's eyes were tightly closed it didn't stop the tears escaping and running down the sides of her cheeks. Just as she'd done all those years ago she tried her hardest to block out what was happening to her. This time no matter how much she willed it, the image of nice things just wouldn't appear. Desperately she prayed that Maude would forget something and come back early to rescue her but that wasn't about to happen either. After ejaculating once, Vinny still wasn't finished. He now roughly forced his fingers inside her, ramming as hard as he could as he desperately tried to get deeper and deeper. His weight was heavy and she knew that the tops of her legs would be bruised. Lisa's whole body ached with pain, this was nothing like the abuse of the past. Then she had been somewhat willing and had given herself up in the hope of pleasing her father. The bastard who now lay on top of her was helping himself to something that she had come to prize, something that she couldn't even give to her

147

own husband. Shame washed over her and she knew that Jason must never find out. It wasn't the fear of what he would do to his brother but the fact that he might never be able to forgive her even though she'd had no choice in the matter. Finally when Vinny released his hand and tried to kiss her she bit down hard on his lip. His face grimaced in pain and when she let go he could feel the blood begin to swirl in his mouth.

"You fucking bitch!"

Swiftly and before Lisa realised what was happening she felt the full force of his punch as it landed on her cheek for a second time. This was definitely going to bruise and Lisa knew that she would have to come up with a plausible excuse that Maude would believe. As his lip began to swell and bleed the pain only heightened his desire and Vincent Frasier was once more erect. Although he normally didn't have any desire for women, this rough sex was turning out to be pretty good and maybe it was something he could continue in Cambridge. After all he was sure there were plenty of old slappers out there who would be up for it even if it would mean having to dole out a few quid. Entering her again for the final time, Vincent Frasier raped her with such force that Lisa didn't think it would ever be over or that she would even survive. The pain was horrific and though she couldn't see it she knew that she was bleeding heavily. At long last and as if nothing had happened, Vinny calmly got off of his sister-in-law's bruised and battered body. Dressing in silence he didn't bother when he saw her pitiful tears. Vincent Frasier didn't bother about anything or anyone except himself.

"Don't start crying and pretending you didn't enjoy it because I know your fucking did. That's the trouble with fucking scrubbers like you, up for it one minute then

148

screaming assault the next. Well it won't fucking wash with old Vinny here, no way."

Lisa didn't offer any defence and just wanted her ordeal to be over as quickly as possible. Vinny had calculated that Lisa would keep her mouth shut for the fear of losing her husband if he found out. He was now positive that she wouldn't tell Jason and anyway after his brother was released from prison they probably wouldn't be coming back to the smoke again. Well not if he had his way and he had a knack of being able to twist Jason round his little finger. For some insane reason Vinny was confident that his brother would once more be by his side, that Lisa Murphy would be just a distant memory and that everything would turn out alright. As Lisa looked in her brother in laws direction she could see that he was staring back at her and she pulled the bedclothes up tightly around her neck.

"Don't fucking flatter yourself darling you weren't all that."

Closing her eyes Lisa hoped that he didn't want more and would leave her in peace, luckily her wish was granted. When she opened her eyes again Lisa felt instant relief when she saw that her attacker had gone. Struggling, she slowly lifted her tiny frame from the bed and made her way over to the mirror that hung on the back of the door. Tentatively she touched the side of her cheek and winced at the pain. It was clearly visible that the side of her face had already begun to swell and had a slight purple tinge. She decided to get dressed and when Maude got back she would make up an excuse of falling down the stairs after she'd had her morning bath. There was no reason for Maude Shelton not to believe the cock and bull story but as Lisa knew only too well, the woman was able to smell a rat at two hundred yards. Desperate to wash every last

149

bit of Vinny from her skin she ran a hot bath and scrubbed and soaked for over an hour. As she stepped out of the water she could see that it had turned red and she cautiously dabbed at herself with a towel. Her inner thighs were red raw and it hurt like hell to even walk. Convincing Maude was going to be a harder task than she'd first thought but then Lisa knew that she had little choice but to give it her best shot, that or blow her husband's family apart. As much as she hated Vinny and Vera, Lisa knew that deep down Jason loved them and breaking his heart was something she couldn't even contemplate doing.

As he quickly let himself out of the Camel, Vincent Frasier wore a wide grin. He was smug in the knowledge that he had once again got one over on someone. Passing the nearest bin he disposed of his mobile which would sever the only line of contact that anyone had with him. Strolling along in the warm sunshine he now felt calm and relaxed. In his mind at least, everything was now fine and back on track. Since talking to Jason he hadn't given Freddie Gant a second thought but suddenly the man now entered his head and he was scared. He hadn't got very much further when he realised that by throwing the phone away there was no way of speaking to his brother. He desperately wanted to hear from Jay but the dilemma was, that he also remembered during sex he had inadvertently let it slip about the dirty faggots he was staying with who owned a hotel in Cambridge. Now that Lisa knew where he was she could drop him right in it but deep down he was sure that she would keep her mouth shut, that or he would have to tell his brother all about their little tryst and she would avoid that from happening at any cost. Overly alert and on edge when anyone passed by, he cautiously walked back to the bin and retrieved the mobile. Glancing at his watch Vinny saw that he had plenty of time before his train left and for a minute toyed with the notion of paying his mother a visit. The idea only lasted a second before he hailed a cab and asked to be taken to Kings Cross station.

CHAPTER SIXTEEN

Vera Frasier was once more seated at the kitchen table and ready to tuck into her lunch. Although it had only been a few days since Vinny's disappearance the little money she had was fast running out and she was beginning to worry. She had her state pension but it would only just cover the basics. That said it didn't stop her indulging in good food whenever possible. When the boys were here cooking had been done on a strict budget but now, well now it was a bit more upmarket. Now was Vera Frasier's time and those two ungrateful bastards could just starve as far as she was concerned. Of course there was no way on earth that she would ever see that happen but for the time being these kind of thoughts were all that kept her going. The prime mackerel fillets had been grilled for three minutes on each side and being Vera's favourite she was salivating at the thought of them. Fresh hot bread and soft creamy butter sat touching the fish and the smell wafting up at her was delicious as she picked up her knife and fork to tuck in. The door bell ringing was instantly infuriating and Vera knew that if she put the mackerel in the oven to keep warm they would be ruined. For a second she considered ignoring the bell but the nosey part of her couldn't resist a peak through the window glass to catch a glimpse of whoever was calling. When she saw two well dressed men standing on her doorstep curiosity got the better of her. The notorious Freddie Gant was known to everyone in Bethnal Green but as Vera had never actually seen him she wasn't spooked. Positioning the safety chain as Vincent had shown her, she proceeded to open up the door just a few inches. Freddie Gant put on his best smile for the haggard looking old woman.

"Good morning Mrs Frasier. I wondered if I might take up a few minutes of your time."

"If you're selling I ain't buying and if you're from the council you can fuck off right now."

Freddie wanted to laugh, the woman reminded him so much of Pearl and he knew only too well that this type were a breed all to themselves and a force to be reckoned with.

"No no it's nothing like that I can assure you. I just need to have a quick chat with you about your boys."

His words were like music to Vera's ears and she couldn't release the door chain quick enough.

"Why the fuck didn't you say! Any friend of my lads is a friend of mine. Come on in and I'll put the kettle on Mr?"

Freddie Gant didn't respond to the question and stepped inside closely followed by Wally Evans. In the kitchen Vera proceeded to put the kettle on and turning to face her guests was shocked at the size of Wally. He hadn't seemed that big outside but now he almost filled the doorframe and she was starting to feel a little intimidated.

"Fuck me you're a big cunt!"

Wally Evans didn't bat an eyelid at her comment nor did he enter into any conversation. Instead he chose to remain in the doorway even after she had offered him a seat. Freddie on the other hand wanted to play safe, at least for the time being. Sitting down he politely accepted her offer of tea and once she had joined him began the conversation that would frighten his hostess almost to death.

"Now then Mrs Frasier do you know where your sons are?"

"Don't you?"

153

"I wouldn't be asking if I did, now would I?"

Vera placed her cup back on the table with such force that the china instantly cracked.

"Now look what you've made me fucking do! That was one of my best cups an all. If you're supposed to be their friend you should know where they are."

Freddie Gant was rapidly becoming irritated. The conversation was going nowhere and he really didn't want to resort to violence, not against an old woman but then again if needs must.

"Mrs Frasier I never said I was a friend of theirs. You see, how shall I put this? Your two boys have stolen something from me and I want it back. Now we can do this the hard way or the easy way, it's entirely up to them."

Vera stood up from the table and her face was scarlet with rage.

"You can just fuck off out of my house right now. Fucking coming in here and calling my boy's tea leafs! On your fucking bike Mr and take that gorilla with you."

Freddie was now standing and motioned with his eyes to Wally. Wally Evans stepped forward until he was level with the woman but towering over her. Placing both hands on her shoulders but using little force he pushed Vera back down into her seat and then stepped aside.

"Mrs Frasier I don't want to come across all heavy but believe me I will if I have to. Now Wally here could snap your scrawny little neck with one hand if I gave him the nod but we don't want to go down that road now do we?"

Vera could feel the onset of her angina and knew that if she didn't play ball, either the tosser behind would finish her off or her own heart would do the job for him.

"Look my boy went a couple of days or so ago and told

154

me nothing before he left. Maybe his brother's with him I don't know. I will tell you this for nothing though, those two bitches down at the Camel know more than they're letting on but I can't get nothing out of them. Maybe if you take the fucking hulk here along with you then you might get some answers. Now snap me neck if you want to but make up your bastard mind because me lunch is just about ruined because of you two."

Freddie Gant smiled, the old girl really had some balls and he liked that. The only problem this threw up was the fact that maybe her sons were as tough as her and the job in hand could turn out to be more difficult than he had at first thought. Motioning to Wally the two men left the flat and Vera once more sat down to her lunch without a second thought for anyone else. Vera Frasier was so much like her youngest son but it was something that she had never been able or wanted to see.

The Camel was quiet for a Tuesday and as yet no punters had walked through the door. Lisa was laid up in bed with a cold and Maude was manning the ship alone. She knew that by twelve thirty the place would be heaving as it was giro day for a lot of the regulars but for now she was enjoying the quiet. When the front door opened Maude didn't look up from her newspaper but spoke all the same.

"Morning what can I get you?"

When no reply came she removed her reading glasses and glanced up. The sight before her made Maude want to gasp but she kept her fear well hidden.

"Well well well, if it ain't little Freddie Gant and his playmate come to pay me a visit. I've been expecting you but I must say you took your fucking time. Old brain not as quick as it once was Fredrick?"

Freddie hated being called by his proper name and

155

Maude knew it would piss him off as soon as she said it.

"Hello Aunty Maude. Been keeping well I hope?"

"All the better for not seeing you now get out of me pub before I bleeding call the Old Bill."

"Now now Aunty, is that any way to welcome your long lost nephew?"

"Not lost for long enough as far as I'm concerned. Piss off Fredrick I ain't got anything to say to you."

Freddie walked over to the bar and took a seat on one of the stools. Wally followed but stood behind his boss, his eyes darting in all directions weighing up the place in case of trouble.

"I don't think that's true Aunty Maude. You see I've just paid a visit to Rickman Street and a certain old lady who lives there told me you know a lot more than you're letting on. We both know what I'm talking about so let's keep this short shall we?"

Maude tried to be as cool as she could and closing the paper poured two glasses of brandy and walked around to the other side of the bar. Taking a seat beside her nephew she offered him a glass, which out of politeness he accepted.

"How's your mum?"

"Wouldn't have a fucking clue, as you well know. I saw the old brass once a few years ago when she called round trying to squeeze a bit of cash out of me. I packed the old tart off with a flea in her ear and I ain't heard hide or hair from her since. With a bit of luck the bitch is dead in an alley somewhere."

Maude slowly shook her head from side to side.

"Don't look so fucking shocked Auntie Maude! Expected me to say I take her out to lunch every Sunday did you?"

"You're one nasty bastard Freddie Gant."

"So tell me something I don't already know."

"What on earth happened to you? You was a nice little chap as a kid now look at you, nothing but a bully backed up with ignorant twats like him standing behind you."

The words went straight over the top of Wally Evans's head, insults were like water off a ducks back to him.

"Fucking hell Maude, you know how I was dragged up and you ask me a daft question like that?"

"I agree Freddie you didn't have it easy but that should have made you go the other way not be like this."

"Should it now and where were you when I sat in a corner watching me own fucking mother turning a trick. Where were you when I had nothing to eat as the old bag had spent her last few quid on a bottle of gin? You sit here in your cosy fucking pub judging me, well where were you when I needed you?"

For a second and only a second Maude felt guilt begin to build up but was quickly brought back down to earth when she remembered why her long lost nephew was actually here.

"Look Freddie I wasn't responsible for you that was Pearls job. You know I cut all ties with your mother when she went on the game. By the time I had an inkling of what was happening to you it was too late."

Freddie didn't respond to her words and instead changed the subject altogether.

"Right, well now that we've got the obligatory family chat out of the way let's get down to business. You know why I'm here, so where are the thieving little slags?"

Maude Shelton walked around to the bar and poured two more brandies. She was aware of how formidable her nephew could be and knew she was going to have to tread very carefully if Jason was to stand a chance of survival.

157

"Look Freddie I know it's of no interest to you but all I ask is that you hear me out."

Freddie Gant shrugged his shoulders and glancing at his watch told Maude he wasn't a patient man and whatever she was about to say had better be good.

"I've known the boys for most of their lives and a more different pair you couldn't meet. Freddie you know I was never able to have kids of me own and well I suppose over the years Jason became like a surrogate son to me."

"Oh how my heart bleeds for you. Fucking funny that aunty when you had a nephew going through hell and you did nothing to help or stop it."

"Look Freddie that was a long time ago and we can spend the rest of the day raking over old coals but it won't change a thing. Now can I finish or what?"

His silence told her that she should continue.

"What I'm trying to tell you, is that Jason is a good man at heart. It's his brother Vinny that you really want."

"Maude it makes no fucking difference to me who I get, as long as my dosh is back where it belongs and someone is seen to be punished."

"Freddie, I know what they did was wrong and that Vincent Frasier is totally driven by greed but I will need time to sort this out. For the sake of family Freddie give us a bit of time will you?"

Freddie Gant stood up and after smoothing down the jacket of his suit, he handed her a card.

"One week Maude one fucking week! If I ain't got me money back by then, all hell is going to break loose family or no family. Call me when you have some news and it had better be fucking good!"

With that Wally Evans held open the door and Freddie Gant walked out of the Camel leaving Maude trembling, though her nephew would never have known. Seconds later Lisa walked into the room looking terrible.

"Who was that"?

"Oh no one you need to worry about. Now what are you doing out of bed love? You look absolutely terrible."

"Thanks."

"I didn't mean it like that and you know it but you are very pale love."

"I must admit Maude I have felt better. I think I'll go back and have another lay down, no matter what I do I can't seem to shake this cold off."

"You do that and if things haven't changed by tomorrow, me and you are going to talk about seeing a doctor young lady."

Lisa didn't argue, her head was splitting and all she wanted was peace and quiet and a warm bed. She hated lying to the older woman but the ruse of a cold was all she'd been able to think of and she wished deep down that it had been the real reason she was so down. Since Vinny's visit Lisa felt like she had a dark cloud hanging over her head and nothing she did was able to lift her mood. All she wanted was to be left alone, alone to sleep and she would have been happy to sleep for a hundred years if that's what it took. Maude on the other hand was desperate for Jason to get in touch and sleep was the last thing on her mind.

Back in the car Wally Evans turned to his boss and asked the question that he already knew the answer to.

"Where to next?"

"Somewhere I really don't want to go Wal, somewhere I really don't fucking want to go."

Without being told, Wally Evans knew where Freddie meant and starting the engine, pulled away into the traffic heading towards Whitechapel.

Boris Worzinze ran his corrupt business from the front

room of his council flat. The block had been purpose built by the local authority though many of the units had now passed over into the private sector. Nelson Street was a relatively quiet area and running vertical to Commercial Road was well situated for a swift getaway should the need arise. A detour of two roads, could in a few minutes see Boris crossing the Thames to Rotherhithe where he moored a small but exceptionally fast boat. Unlike Freddie Gant's place there was nothing cutting edge about the flat on Nelson Street. Only one room was furnished and contained a basic table, chairs, sofa and a computer. For all of his money the Russian still chose to live like a pauper and not draw attention to himself. There was always a man situated just inside the steel door though Boris insisted that they never did a stint longer than two hours on account of him wanting them to stay alert and not become complacent. After their allotted time they would be allowed to rest and another man would take over the shift. From the outside landing the flat resembled any other on the same floor but once a person was invited to step past the steel door it was a different story all together. As Wally and Freddie entered the stairwell and climbed the two flights of steps Boris's door came into sight. Wally knew that if need be he would protect his boss to the death but in reality was well aware that once inside he would be out numbered and wouldn't stand a cat in hells chance. Several minutes before, Boris had seen his guests arrive on the close circuit television that covered all the entrances, exits and car parks to the entire block of flats. Approaching the front door the visitors weren't kept waiting and were ushered inside immediately. Even though Freddie had been doing business with the Russian for a couple of years and it had been good business at that, he still hated

160

coming here. He hated feeling inferior to someone who wasn't even a native of his own country. In the narrow hallway the two men were scanned by one of the minders. A high-tech electric paddle, similar to the ones used at airports was effortlessly moved over Wally's body. When it came to Freddie, he opened out both sides of his jacket revealing the Berretta that he always carried in a shoulder sling. The minder stepped forward and removed the weapon leaving Freddie feeling vulnerable. Standing up, their host was over six and a half feet tall and almost as wide. Wally Evans was by no means small but compared to Boris he seemed only average. Freddie had to concentrate hard as Boris's accent was so strong that it was often difficult to understand what the man was saying. Today of all days it was paramount that he took in every word. Slowly Freddie revealed all that had happened regarding the money. He told of Roly and Happy's demise and the fact that he knew who had the money and it was just a case of retrieving it. The one thing he didn't report was going to see Maude. Call it family loyalty if you like but Freddie Gant didn't want the Russians paying his aunt a visit. For a few minutes Boris thought deeply and didn't comment on what he had just heard. That in its self made Freddie extremely nervous but finally when he did speak his words slightly shocked his guest.

"Sit with me Mr Gant and take drink of Vodka. Now we have done good business for long time and things have always gone smoothly, until this time no? If I go to my Bosses back in the homeland and tell them all that has happened they will not be pleased. We both know what would happen then! I do not see this as good business Freddie that is why I give you two weeks to sort mess out. I have no quarrel with these Frasier boys even

161

though they have my money. The responsibility of money, as I am sure you agree, lies with you. After two weeks if trouble not sorted, then the matter will be out of my hands. Now let us drink more Vodka and talk of friendship."

Wally, who had stood silently in the room for the entire meeting inwardly breathed a sigh of relief. Things weren't over, not by a long way but at least they had bought themselves some breathing space. An hour later and the two men were once again outside. Wally inhaled the smoggy air that was the life blood of good old London Town.

"That was a close shave Boss what are we going to do now?"

"A close shave! You daft cunt we ain't achieved nothing here today. Take me back to the office I need to think."

Wally did as he was told and decided that with the mood Freddie was in it was best to keep quiet. Back inside his Bridle street headquarters Freddie paced the floor and it wasn't a sight his minder liked seeing. Suddenly he stopped and slammed his fist into the highly polished desk, which over the last few days was becoming a regular occurrence.

"Fuck! fuck! fuck!!!!"

"What is it Boss, what's wrong?"

"Wally get a couple of bodies over here and then make me an appointment with Ritchie Foreman."

"Boss I really don't think we want to be getting fucking involved with the likes of the Foreman's."

Freddie Gant stared hard at his employee and Wally knew that he had overstepped the mark.

"I ain't got any fucking choice in the matter you twat! I need to raise some cash against one of the clubs to pay off Boris. At least with him off of our backs I can now

162

concentrate on the job in hand which is getting revenge and believe me Wal, this one I'm really going to take pleasure in."

CHAPTER SEVENTEEN

The meet with Ritchie Foreman had been arranged for three days time and Wally Evans had called in some hired help. The men were regulars at the local boxing club and without a shadow of a doubt could be trusted, an absolute must in their game. Normal business was managed and managed well by just Freddie and his sidekick. On the odd occasion that extra muscle was needed and this was definitely one of those times, then the heavies were asked along. The men who had been handpicked by Wally never asked any questions and after doing what was required of them, would each walk away a couple of hundred pounds better off. Freddie wasn't expecting any trouble with the Foreman's but as his old mum had taught him early on, being prepared is forewarned. Ritchie Foreman along with his two brothers Jed and Malc, ran the Foreman crew out of a small warehouse over in Charing Cross. Adams Street was perfectly located and backing directly onto the Thames, made the extra special deliveries that they sometimes received relatively easy. The warehouse had a large roller shutter at the front and a normal door to the side. Close circuit cameras were strategically placed so that any approach was monitored well in advance of arrival. Inside the building was just one large open space that housed an old settee and a couple of desks. A small kitchen area at one end supplied the endless brews of tea that were consumed throughout the day. Ritchie Foreman was teetotal and insisted on anyone working for him to be the same. Unbeknown to their brother, Jed and Malc often partook in a tipple but it was a fact never disclosed to Ritchie and it went without saying that it never occurred during working hours.

Tucked away in one corner and not visible to anyone who didn't know about it was a man hole. A continuous flow of water had been set up so that anything placed in the hole was instantly washed away into the Thames. The Foreman's weren't in the habit of disposing of their special deliveries but if it came to the crunch, then they at least had a way of appearing clean. As yet they had avoided any real interest from the Old Bill and that was how they wanted things to stay. When Ritchie Foreman had received the call from Wally he was more than a little intrigued. Aware of Freddie Gant but never actually having any dealings with him made Ritchie apprehensive. He couldn't see an attempted takeover on the cards as things had moved along smoothly between all the firms in the last few years and besides anyone who was anyone knew the Foreman's were more than a match for Gant. Every firm had their own manor and didn't intrude on another's patch. If on the odd occasion this taboo situation did arise through a payroll heist or a bank job, then the injured parties were entitled to a twenty percent cut of the takings. Ritchie Foreman was confident that this was nothing more than straightforward business and business was something he enjoyed. At exactly two pm on the day of the arranged meeting, Freddie's Jaguar followed by a blue Rover containing four menacing looking men pulled up outside the warehouse. Everyone got out of the cars but only Freddie and Wally approached the building. Aware that he was being watched Freddie Gant nodded his head in the direction of the nearest camera. Before he reached the side door it was already being held open for him. Freddie, followed by Wally, stepped inside and as was customary Wally glanced in all directions looking for anything suspect. Ritchie Foreman was seated on the old sofa and beckoned

165

for his guests to join him. Jed and Malc, who were Foreman's by blood but had none of their brother's brains or acumen, sat silently behind the desks. As Freddie approached Ritchie stood up and out of politeness offered his hand. When his guest readily accepted the offer things immediately became relaxed. Jed was instructed to make a brew and the two men sat down on the sofa and faced each other.

"So Freddie at last we get to meet!"

"And a pleasure it is Mr Foreman, although I wish it could have been under more social circumstances."

"Sometimes the best of friends meet through business and please Freddie call me Ritchie. We don't stand on ceremony round here, do we boys?"

Malc and the two minders now stood at the far end and were deep in hushed conversation but still turned and smiled. When Jed had delivered the refreshments and once more retreated to his desk, the conversation began in earnest.

"Now then Freddie what brings you to my neck of the woods?"

"Bit of a long story but I'll cut to the chase, I need to borrow some cash."

Ritchie Foreman didn't speak but nodded his head sagely.

"I have a good working relationship with the Russians but unfortunately I was recently fucking mugged off while holding some of my friend's wonga. Don't think I've gone soft Ritchie; nothing could be further from the truth. The cunt's are going to pay and pay dearly but as you know these things take time. Meanwhile if I could ease the pressure by paying off my friends, things would seem a whole lot better."

"Slippery cunts the Russians, personally I wouldn't entertain them but then that's your business not mine.

166

Now how much are we talking about here and over how long?"

"Five hundred K, over let's say six months."

"What interest are you looking to pay?"

Freddie smiled. He knew the score, new that the rate was already set and that the question was asked purely out of politeness.

"That Ritchie, as we both know has already been decided. Now I'm presuming your next question is what collateral am I offering? My clubs on Wardour Street and Macclesfield Street will more than cover it."

The Regal had been owned by Freddie for several years and was slightly more upmarket than the other. It catered mainly for tourists, offering meals and drinks and if you knew how to ask properly, ladies of the night. The Judges Den was at the other end of the spectrum and probably more what the general public imagined a Soho club to be. In this place everything appeared as it actually was. Watered down overpriced drinks and girls who had seen the best years of their lives sail by and who looked better in the clubs dim lights than they ever would in the cold light of day. As usual the clubs bouncers had been individually handpicked by Wally. They were all menacing to look at and whose size was so large, that no one dared to argue with them. Both places were run by managers but these had been selected by Freddie himself. He would not allow skimming of any kind and if he ever found out that a member of staff was trying to tuck him up, they were instantly removed and Wally would be allowed to flex his muscles when it came to dealing with them. Freddie Gant saw it as killing two birds with one stone as he liked to keep Wally fresh, a bit like letting a dog off its lead from time to time.

"All well and good Freddie but what if I don't want a

couple of clubs. Places in Soho are sometimes more trouble than they're worth. The girls are mostly dogs and there's always a punter ready to kick up a fucking stink. As far as Old Bill are concerned we have a good relationship, I grease a few palms and they leave me alone. Why would I want to go upsetting the proverbial apple cart for a poxy loan?"

"Then what can I offer you?"

Ritchie Foreman's next sentence took Freddie by surprise.

"Sam's."

"Sam's! Come on now Ritchie, I never even mentioned the place."

"I've done me fucking homework pal and the only way I'm prepared to bail you out of your little problem is if Sam's is on the table. Oh and by the way, I don't want it put up as collateral, I want the whole shooting bag lock stock and fucking barrel."

Sam's had been one of Freddie's first purchases in Soho and a place he held dear to his heart. Chapone Place was tucked away at the back of Dean Street and Sam's frontage was little more than twelve feet wide. It made no real income from sales but was a late night drinking den for most of London's underworld. The majority of robberies to hit the news headlines, including the Brinks Mat, had been planned from this very small place. To the men who frequented it Sam's was looked upon as a safe house. It was swept for bugs every few days so there was very little chance of any conversation being listened into. As the owner, Freddie was entitled to a cut from any blag that had been planned from inside his premises. Though not on paper, Sam's was extremely profitable and somewhere Freddie had sworn would always be his. As far as he was concerned to part with it could signal the end of his empire. Now he stood with back against the wall and no other option than to do the one thing he always said he wouldn't.

"Come on Ritchie, that place is worth far more than five hundred K."

"You're having a fucking laugh ain't you! I shouldn't think the takings cover your fucking overheads let alone make a profit."

"Ritchie we both know what I'm talking about here."

"Of course we do my friend but as we all know it's a buyer's market at the moment. These are the only terms I'm prepared to accept."

Freddie realised he had Hobson's choice in the matter and held out his hand to seal the deal. When Ritchie Foreman nodded in Jed's direction, a large holdall was brought up from under the desk. With the help of his brother Malc and the two minders, it was unzipped and five hundred thousand was meticulously counted out and placed into a second bag. Carrying a handle each they brought the bag over to Freddie. He declined the offer of a drink and motioned for Wally to pick up the cargo. Freddie Gant was aware that he had been well and truly shafted but as things stood could do nothing about it. He also knew that for all intent and purpose things could have been a lot lot worse. Even though the words stuck in his throat, he did what was expected of him and thanked his host for the deal before walking upright out of the building. Freddie may have been pissed off but there was no way anyone would have been able to tell that from his demeanour. Wally placed the bag in the boot of the Jag and walked over to the hired help to tell them that their work was over for the day. As if on auto pilot he didn't ask his boss where he wanted to go, instead he started the engine and headed in the direction

169

of Whitechapel. Once inside Boris's flat Wally stood the holdall at the man's feet and stepped backwards. Freddie sat when asked but didn't offer any conversation and Boris Worzinze could see that his guest was not a happy man.

"So my friend you have problem sorted?"

"Not quite but I will have soon. In the meantime I am returning what is rightfully yours and I hope this has not tarnished our business dealings for the future?"

Boris leaned forward and slapped Freddie hard on the back. Freddie Gant hated physical contact with anyone but knew better than to upset the Russian.

"Freddie you are my friend, now let us drink vodka and speak no more of this little problem."

As Boris poured the drinks, the smile that had been so welcoming only seconds earlier instantly disappeared and just when Freddie thought today couldn't get any worse it did.

"I have new shipment of workers next week, so it will be business like always."

"Bit of a problem there Boris I'm afraid."

"No no no Freddie there will be no problem. You drink vodka and we make plans."

Freddie Gant ran his fingers through his hair in frustration.

"Look mate, since we no longer have a manager at Kings there's no one to run the place. As you can imagine I have other things on my mind at the moment so if you could cut me a bit of slack it would be much appreciated."

Boris Worzinze face wore a hard calculating expression and Freddie Gant thinking back to what Ritchie had said, wished he'd never got mixed up with the foreigners in the first place.

"Freddie you are my friend no?"

Freddie Gant nodded in agreement.

"Good! Good! So here is what we do. My friends back home wish to buy factory from you and I sure you wish to keep my friends happy, no?"

Again Freddie nodded. In reality he couldn't care less about the place and would be more than happy to off load it, subject to an agreed price of course. In the beginning Kings had been very lucrative but as time moved on it was becoming a bit of a millstone around his neck. If the place got done over again and there was nothing to stop that happening, then he reasoned that he could end up with nothing. No, Freddie Gant would sell and just hoped that he wouldn't be too much out of pocket.

"My friends do not wish to, how is it you say in this country? ah yes shafting you. They happy to pay same as you Freddie. You accept offer my friend?"

Once Freddie Gant started to laugh he couldn't stop himself and all the time the Russian watched with a confused expression on his face.

"Oh Boris my old mukka. If only you knew the trouble I've been too today just to get your fucking cash. Now here I am and you're giving the whole fucking lot back to me. If it wasn't for the fact that I've had to let one of me clubs fucking go, then this would have turned out to be a blinder of a day."

Boris Worzinze didn't have the first clue what his guest was talking about but out of friendship and politeness he joined in with the laughter. At long last and after numerous amounts of alcohol had been consumed, Freddie Gant and Wally Evans were once more seated in the Jag.

"Back to the office Boss?"

"Yeah we had better get this little lot locked away then

171

you can take me to the Camel. I think another little family reunion is in order."

Maude had just cleared up the tea things and was then heading downstairs to prepare for opening when there was a loud banging on the pubs front doors. Taking the stairs two at a time, she was desperate to stop the noise for fear of waking Lisa. The poor girl had been through so much and all she wanted was to sleep. God only knew who was at the door but in the Smoke there was never much chance of any real peace and quiet. Maude reached the bar in record time, her breathing was laboured and she felt ready to keel over at any minute.

"Hold your bleeding horses whoever you are. Good god, anyone would think that it was a matter of life or..."

Opening the door and seeing her nephew stopped Maude dead in her tracks.

"Piss off Fredrick. You gave me a week. Now unless you're in a different bloody time zone I've still got a few days left."

Even addressing him with his real name couldn't upset Freddie today. Today he felt as though he'd been through the ringer and he was just happy to have come out unscathed and not too much out of pocket. Ignoring his Aunt and walking straight past her to the bar, he took a seat on one of the stools. Wally Evans followed his boss and as he passed Maude who was still holding open the door, winked at her. His small attempt at flirting didn't bother her; she had dealt with bigger, harder bastards than him on a regular basis and won. About to give him a mouthful, she thought again, maybe it wouldn't be such a bad idea to have a bit of an ally where her nephew was concerned. Instead of a sneer that would normally have been her response, Maude gave a thin smile. Closing the door she slid up the heavy bolts aware

170

that her regulars would start banging to be let in within a few minutes.

"Did you hear a word I just said or are you totally ignorant as well as being a bully?"

"Come on now Aunty I ain't here for a row. In fact I've come with some good news. I know I originally gave you a week but I'm not an unreasonable man and on reflection I think that you will need a lot longer."

Maude's eyes narrowed. She had always known Fredrick Gant was a slippery little bugger and all these years later he wasn't going to be any different.

"So?"

"I thought that within reason, you could take as long as you needed to bring the guilty culprits to me. Providing that is, you put this place up as let's say for arguments sake a sweetener."

"On your bike Fredrick, there ain't no way that I'm ever letting you get your grubby little hands on this place."

"How I see it Aunty Maude is that you ain't got much choice in the matter and if you want your precious Jason left out of this, then you will have to deliver his brother. Quite frankly I don't give a shit who pays as long as someone does. Now I ain't really interested in this shit hole you call a home Maude but if you have a little gentle pressure in place then you ain't going to give up so easily now are you?"

Freddie had worked out that the pub must be worth at least eight hundred grand and if things panned out he could stand to get a good earner out of it.

"The robbing little bastards owe me five hundred K! Now as you're so fucking close to one of them and you're prepared to try and take me on, here's the deal. Six months maximum and then if I ain't got me cash back I take this place. If on the other hand I do get back what's

173

mine, you will raise any shortfall that's missing plus interest."

Maude Shelton knew that she had no choice and in a strange way she could see that what he was offering her made sense. Even if everything was stacked up in Freddie's favour and there was nothing much in it for her, well the life of her boy, that's how she looked upon Jason, was all that mattered and she would have sold her soul for him if that's what it would take. As much as it riled her in the end she had to agree. Sharing a brandy to seal the agreement, Maude now felt a little better about the situation. She would do her utmost not to have to hand over the Camel but at least she now had time and with Jason away time was something she desperately needed. The idea of the Camel had come to Freddie like a bolt out of the blue. The place was popular and if he'd just lost Sam's, then maybe he could build up another place just as good. He didn't think for a minute that his aunt would ever be able to get back his cash or get one of the Frasier's to pay the price. As far as Freddie Gant was concerned the Camel was as good as his.

CHAPTER EIGHTEEN
Two months later

The Camel was heaving with punters and it took Maude all of her time to serve let alone fret about contact with Jason. He hadn't phoned for a couple of days and that concerned her. One less thing to worry about was that with Lisa being so sick the girl didn't keep whinging about when her husband would be home, which in the past few days had begun to wear Maude down. She had grown to love Lisa Frasier but the young woman could still be overly needy and grate on a person's nerves after a while. With all the will in the world Maude tried to be tolerant but it was becoming harder and harder as the days wore on. When the bar finally emptied at around 5pm, Maude wearily locked the front door and made her way up to the flat. After opening a can of chicken soup and placing it to simmer gently on the hob she took a seat at the table. Her hands were shaking as she glanced up at the clock. Every few seconds she willed with all her might for Jason to telephone. She had little more than two hours before reopening and that thought alone drained her. Maude was tired, more tired than she'd ever been in her life. When the soup was nicely warm she wearily headed back downstairs to the rear of the pub. Tapping gently on the door Maude didn't wait to be invited in. Lisa wasn't asleep and sat restlessly propped up in the bed. Beads of sweat stood out on her forehead and her hair was plastered to her skin. The room was hot but Lisa looked freezing cold.

"Here you are love, some nice chicken soup."

"Thanks Duchess but I don't think I could eat anything I....."

175

Maude Shelton didn't let her finish and placed the tray strategically across Lisa's lap.

"Nonsense! You must eat or you'll never get better. Now you try a few mouthfuls and we'll have a nice little chat."

With still no contact from Jay and call it a woman's intuition if you like but Maude had a bad gut feeling that things weren't right. She decided that the next step was to try again and pump Lisa for any information that she may have subconsciously forgotten.

"Now then love, when Jason last phoned you did he give anything away about where Vinny was staying?"

As Lisa cautiously sipped at the hot soup her doe eyes filled with tears. Maude didn't have time for this but knew that if she was to get anywhere, the girl had to be treated with kid gloves.

"Lisa don't cry we're only having a chat."

Placing the spoon down on the tray Lisa wiped her eyes with the back of her hands and sniffed loudly.

"I know but whenever I hear his name I can't help it, I hate him so much Maude. I'm sorry but I can't remember."

Maude Shelton was aware that Lisa had never got on with her brother in law but she couldn't for the life of her see where all this hatred had come from. Lately whenever Vinny's name was mentioned it was as if a red mist came over the girl.

"That's ok darling, now you get some rest and I'll call in again later before I open up."

Lisa Frasier just nodded before putting her head back on the pillow and closing her eyes. As Maude shut the door she gently shook her head from side to side. A few months ago and this pub was one of the happiest in the area. All the punters had commented on what a brilliant

176

atmosphere the place had. The married couple who lodged with her were so in love that your heart just wanted to melt at the sight of them and it was impossible for a little of their happiness not to rub off on a person. Now here they were just a short time later and everything was falling to pieces around them. For the first time in her Life Maude Shelton didn't know what to do about it, didn't know how to make things right and that fact alone made her angry. Maude was known for taking control of even the most difficult of situations but this time it was a different matter all together. Her nephew had given her a stay of execution as far as the boys were concerned but it still played heavily on her mind that he could pull the rug from under her at any time and take away the Camel. Time was quickly ticking by and she was still no further forward. At five to seven and just before opening up Maude Shelton popped her head around the bedroom door once more. Lisa was snoring softly which was a good sign but the soup had hardly been touched. Jason's wife was wasting away and nothing she had offered her could temp Lisa to eat. The girl was stubborn and Maude had repeatedly begged her to see a doctor but Lisa wouldn't hear of it. All she kept saying was 'it's just a cold' but her landlady was starting to think differently. The next morning, Maude was up bright and early and ready for the day. If she couldn't help Jason then the least she could do was take care of his wife. With two steaming hot mugs of tea she once more went down to the back room. As she opened the door the sight before her almost took her breath away. Lisa sat fully clothed on the edge of the bed. Dark circles encased her eyes and her beautiful hair was again plastered to her face with sweat. Looking up she managed a weak smile but it was barely visible.

177

"Right that does it young lady! We're off to the quacks and no more arguing."

Maude left the room but returned within a few minutes. "You're going to see Miles Crawford at 9.30 this morning. I'll come with you and we will get this sorted today. You can't go on like this Lisa; you look like the bleeding walking dead and no mistake!"

Lisa Frasier was petrified of the medical profession. She knew it was stupid and that it all stemmed from her childhood but all the same couldn't help feeling how she did. It would make things a bit easier to bear if Maude was with her but still the thought terrified her.

"Who is Miles Crawford?"

"Well sweetheart he's my own private doctor, has been for years and you'll get the best treatment possible. Now can you stand up or do you need me to hold you?"

Lisa slowly waved her hand, which silently told Maude she could manage. The black hackney was soon honking its horn and as the two women walked towards it Maude gave the driver a look of contempt. So fierce was the glare that the journey over to Harley Street was taken in silence. The huge imposing Georgian building resembled a house more than the surgery it had become in the last few years. As Maude took her arm Lisa could feel herself begin to tremble. On the wall and next to the shiny black door sat a large highly polished brass plate. Several different names were engraved onto it but it didn't make Lisa feel any better when she saw the name of Maude's personal doctor. Once inside they were shown to a luxurious waiting room and asked to take a seat. The soft classical background music that was playing seemed to relax Lisa a little and after a few seconds she turned to Maude and unexpectedly began to speak.

178

"You know when you asked me if I could remember anything about where Vinny was. Well when I couldn't sleep last night I began to go over in my mind all that's happened and I do remember a couple of things."
Suddenly Maude sat bolt upright in her chair and was all ears but Lisa wasn't immediately forthcoming which infuriated Maude.
"Well!"
Not able to say where the information had really come from, Lisa had to think quickly and the only idea she had was to say that Jason had told her.
"I think he said they were going to or Vinny was in a place called Cambridge and....."
The conversation was interrupted by a pretty young nurse.
"Excuse me Mrs Frasier but the doctor will see you now."
Maude Shelton naturally assumed that this snippet of information was from a plan the boys had decided on just before the robbery. Still totally oblivious to Vinny's recent visit she thought that Lisa had just plucked it from her memory. Both Lisa and Maude swung round in their seats. Lisa's turn was due to her fear but Maude's was out of sheer frustration. She knew they were only here for one reason but after the girl had begun to talk, Vinny's whereabouts was all that interested her.
Resigning herself to the fact that this conversation would have to wait she helped Lisa to her feet and led her through the double doors to where Miles Crawford sat behind a large oversized partner's desk. He immediately stood up but didn't walk around the table instead preferring to lean over and shake Lisa's hand.
"I'm Very pleased to meet you Mrs Frasier and Maude, a pleasure as always. Now how can I help you two

179

ladies?"

Maude waited for Lisa to speak and when no words were forthcoming she took over and told Dr Crawford how sick the girl had been and how she was getting worse not better. Miles Crawford just nodded and made notes as Maude talked. When she felt that she had covered everything and finally stopped talking, Dr Crawford asked to examine Lisa. He could sense that she was nervous and asked if she would prefer Maude to leave the room. Instantly she spoke but her words came out in almost a shout.

"No!!!"

Maude couldn't believe the girls response and her brow furrowed when she looked at Lisa.

"That's fine Mrs Frasier but I had to ask. Now if you would like to go behind that screen and undress you'll find a blanket on the bed to cover yourself."

"What take off everything?"

The alarm in her voice was noticed by all in the room.

"Good heavens no just down to your underwear."

As Lisa made her way behind the screen Maude gave an embarrassed smile and Miles a knowing nod. Ten minutes later and with Lisa now dressed and back in her seat Miles Crawford began to speak.

"Mrs Frasier I would like to do some further tests."

Maude instantly went into panic mode.

"Tests! What sort of tests?"

"Well Lisa's lymph nodes are swollen and I'd like to find out why. It could be something or nothing but its best to check it out. Now if you'd like to wait in reception I'll get the nurse to take a few blood samples. They will be back in a week or two and then you should at last have some answers."

"Now hold on there a minute sunshine. I ain't paying two

180

hundred quid a time to wait a week or two. If I was prepared to do that I would have gone to an NHS quack." Miles Crawford laughed out loud. Maude Shelton never ceased to shock and amaze him and her interpretation of the Queen's English was always a source of light relief from the upper class prat's who normally frequented his practise.

"As usual Maude, blunt and to the point. How about two days?"

"That's better, bugger me Miles you don't half take the piss sometimes. Don't know why I still use you after all these years but I suppose you're as good as any other quack."

After the bloods had been taken the two old friends shook hands and Dr Crawford said he would telephone with the results as soon as possible. The women left Harley Street and returned to the Camel, now both feeling slightly more relaxed about the situation. Lisa said she was feeling better already but Maude knew it was a lie. Maybe it was just wishful thinking on Lisa's part but right now Maude couldn't think about it, all she was interested in was finding out more information regarding where Vinny was.

"You get undressed and into bed and I'll make us a nice cup of rosie."

It was the fastest made brew in history and Maude was soon seated on the side of the bed next to Lisa.

"Right then love, we need to finish that conversation we was having at the surgery."

"Oh right but I'm really tired again now."

"I know you are and I wouldn't push you if it wasn't important."

Lisa smiled weakly.

"Well as I was saying, I think he's in Cambridge."

181

Maude rolled her eyes up towards the ceiling.

"I know you're trying love but bugger me Cambridge is a big place, where in Cambridge?"

Lisa tried desperately to think of something else but she felt so ill that all she really wanted was to go to sleep. None the less she could see that without more information Maude wasn't going anywhere.

"Well he did say that the place was run by two poof's, now what did he say their names were? I know one was called Trevor, that's it Trevor Hayes."

Maude gathered up the cups and walked towards the door.

"Well it's not much but I suppose it's something. Now you sleep while I get ready to open up."

The rest of the day passed in a whirl as Maude had one of her busiest Wednesdays on record. By 1pm she'd had to call on help in the form of her part time pot man Joey West. When the Camel at last closed for the afternoon it was 5pm and Maude Shelton was tired out. Since Jason's unexpected departure and Lisa's illness she was running the place almost single handed and didn't mind admitting it was wearing her out. She decided to take a lay down and it was the door being banged by a couple of regulars that woke her. Running down the stairs as fast as her legs would carry her, Maude was about to give out the biggest mouthful of abuse when she spied the large wall clock displaying 7.30pm. What should have been a quick cat nap had lasted two and a half hours. Letting in Don and Petey she proceeded to pour their preferred tipple without asking. When they were at last quiet and sitting at a booth, Maude took a second to take stock of what had happened today. She knew that finding out exactly where Vinny was staying was paramount but also finding the time to play detective was proving difficult. Maude then

182

toyed with the idea of getting the phone directories out in the bar and trying to do a bit of investigating while she served but then thought better of it. The reprieve she'd been given by Freddie was better than nothing but it still felt like a lead weight around her neck. However hard she willed it not too, time was passing fast and she knew he wouldn't wait forever. Every night just as she was beginning to fall asleep, visions of having to hand the keys to the Camel over to her nephew haunted her. The only trouble was these weren't just nightmares, Maude Shelton had to accept that it was turning into a real possibility. The possibility, that she was going to lose not only her business but her home. Another visit to Jason was on the horizon but Maude wanted to find out what was wrong with Lisa before she spoke to him again. After visiting Jason earlier and telling him about Freddie Gant she figured that finding out about his wife's deteriorating health may well be the one thing to tip him over the edge. Wisely she decided to wait at least for the time being. For a second she could picture herself throttling Vincent Frasier and that momentarily lifted her spirits. God he had a lot to answer for and she just hoped that he wasn't spending her nephew's money like it was going out of fashion.

At precisely 10.30am on Friday morning the telephone at the Camel burst into life. Maude had been bottling up but instantly stopped what she was doing and snatched up the receiver. For the first time ever she hoped that it wouldn't be Jason on the other end. For some reason and she didn't know why, Maude felt as though today she wouldn't be able to cope with it all.

"Hello."

"Hello Maude Miles Crawford here. I've received the test results back and I would like you and Mrs Frasier to

183

come in and see me as soon as possible."

"Can't you tell us over the phone?"

"No Maude I'm afraid I can't, now is 1.15 suitable?"

"Today?"

"Yes today."

Maude scratched at her chin, was she ever going to have any time to herself to locate Vinny.

"Well I suppose so but it's a bit short notice Miles."

Apart from saying he would see them both later, he didn't comment further. When Maude replaced the handset she suddenly realised that it must be something serious. Deciding to play it down at least as far as Lisa was concerned, she made some feeble excuse about Dr Crawford going away on holiday for a couple of months.

"So you see Lisa if we don't go today then we've got a long wait ahead of us. You do want to get better don't you?"

"Of course I do! What a stupid question to ask. When my Jay comes home I want to be in tip top condition."

"Glad to hear it. Now get yourself ready and I'll give Joey a call and see if he'll cover the lunchtime trade."

This time when the cab arrived it was Maude's turn to be nervous. Lisa on the other hand was pleased, at last she would find out what was wrong with her. Happy in the knowledge that after a few pills she would be back to her old self, made her light hearted on the drive through the city. On their arrival, unlike last time, they were not kept waiting. The receptionist showed the two women straight into Miles Crawford's office. Again he was seated at his desk but this time he got up and walked towards them. Maude could read the signs and knew they weren't good.

"Do take a seat ladies and I'll fetch my paperwork."

Crossing the room and opening up a highly polished filing cabinet Miles Crawford removed a magenta file

184

with the words 'Private & Confidential' printed boldly on the front. Maude could feel her palms becoming clammy and delved deep into her handbag for a tissue. When Dr Crawford at last began to speak nausea was beginning to pick up momentum in Maude's stomach.

"I'm afraid Mrs Frasier there's no easy way to say this so I won't beat about the bush. Your test results have come back showing that you have contracted a virus."

Maude let out a loud sigh.

"Bloody hell Miles talk about over icing the cake. A virus is that all? I thought you were going to tell the girl she was dying or something."

The expression on his face stopped Maude dead in her tracks and for a second the room was silent. Turning his attention to Lisa his face was grave.

"Mrs Frasier I am so very sorry but it's not good news I'm afraid. When you start to deteriorate we can try a cocktail of different drugs to help. Your life expectancy could be several years it just depends on how your body reacts and science is coming up with new and better treatments every year."

Maude had to swallow hard; she couldn't believe what she was hearing.

"Reacts! Whatever sort of virus is it Miles?"

Miles Crawford couldn't look either woman in the face and stared down at his file as he spoke.

"I asked for several sets of tests to be carried out. All except one came back negative. I'm afraid Mrs Frasier has contracted HIV."

"HIV! Whatever are you talking about you daft bugger. I think you need to take a bit more water with it mate. HIV! I've never heard anything so bleeding ridiculous in all my days."

"I can assure you Maude that I've gone over the results

185

and there is no doubt or possibility of a mistake."
Instantly Lisa started to cry, quietly at first and then deep heart wrenching sobs.

"I suggest you take her home Maude. It will take a while to sink and I know this must have come as a huge shock. I will contact you both in a few days and we will take things from there but at present there is very little we can do."

No other words were spoken, not in the surgery or on the journey back home. What was there to say, sorry seemed totally inadequate and Maude felt helpless. She would care for Lisa, there was no question about that but finding Vincent was now imperative. The girl would need nursing and the only person really capable of that was Jason. If his shit of a brother didn't bring back the loot, then it was a serious possibility that Maude would be planning a combined funeral for both Lisa and Jason. It broke hear heart to even think like this but it really could be on the cards if they didn't get Freddie Gant's money back.

CHAPTER NINETEEN

With the Camel now closed for the afternoon the place seemed eerily quiet. For Maude Shelton this was normally a time of day when she would relax and put her feet up but not today. In fact Maude silently wondered to herself if things would ever be relaxed again. She decided that for the time being it would be best to leave Lisa alone. She would call in later when the girl had been allowed some time to get her head round the devastating news. Now she was going to play her Miss Marple routine and find out what the hell was going on. Sitting at the kitchen table Maude had a pile of telephone directories laid out in front of her. For some reason British telecom always sent her four or five of London and the surrounding counties. Discarding a couple she soon placed her hand on the Cambridge edition. Maude knew that to look in the business section would be futile as she had no hotel name. Her only chance was in the residential and she just hoped that this Trevor Hayes bloke had been resident in that part of the world for a while at least. It did cross her mind that he may be ex-directory but she dismissed that idea instantly, a dead end was the last thing she needed. No, she had to stay positive, positive in the fact that come hell or high water she would succeed. There were several Hayes's listed but only one with the initial T. Nervously she dialled and when the phone at the other end was picked up she wanted to jump with joy at the words spoken to her.
"Cumberland Hotel how can I help you?"
Maude knew instantly that she had hit the jackpot on her first attempt. The man's voice was so camp that this had to be the place. Calming herself she laid her palms flat

on the table and took in a deep breath before she spoke.
"Oh yeah hello. I don't know if you can help me but I'm
trying to trace a guest of yours well at least I think he's a
guest. Vincent Frasier?"

"Vincent! Oh yes he's a guest here and what a lovely
man he is but I'm afraid he's out at work at the moment."
Trevor hated lying but as he always told Melvyn 'the
customers were the ones who provided their good
lifestyle'. If saying someone was nice when in reality
they were the pits was the price they had to pay, then in
his mind that was a small sacrifice. When Trevor had
done his best thespian rendition and said he liked Vinny
very much, he hadn't convinced the woman on the other
end of the line for a second. Luckily for him Maude
wasn't interested in what was thought of Vincent Frasier,
the only thing on her mind was tracking him down and
that she had succeeded at with relative ease.

"Can I ask him to call you?"

"That would be wonderful Mr Hayes. Could you tell him
it's Maude and that she needs to speak to him urgently?"
Ever the nosey one, Trevor couldn't help himself and
pushed the conversation further.

"Nothing to terrible I hope?"

Ever the wise old bird, Maude Shelton formed a mental
image of the man on the other end of the line and if she
had ever gotten the chance to meet him, would have
given herself a pat on the back for being spot on.

"No no definitely not but I really do need to speak to him
all the same. So if you would be so kind to ask him to
call me?"

"Certainly I will and can I just ask how you knew my
name?"

Maude had to think on her feet.

"Vincent speaks of you all the time when he calls home,

188

says what a lovely man you are."

If Maude could have seen the sight at the other end of the line she wouldn't have been able to stop laughing. Trevor Hayes was blushing and the woman's words had just made his day. It wasn't only the fact that he was attracted to his guest, at his age someone fancying him at all was a turn on. Many times over the years Melvyn had been heard to tell anyone who'd listen that his pet name for Trevor was Martini as he'd shag anyone, anyplace, any time. His extra marital sex was the one and only thing that he and Melvyn constantly bickered about.

"Now Mr Hayes it's imperative that Vincent gets the message today."

"Certainly, I'll deliver it personally as soon as he comes in."

"Thank you so much you've been really helpful."

"You don't have to thank me Maude, I can call you Maude? Rest assured this call will go directly from my lips to Vincent's. Listen to me, I mean Vincent's ears." Maude gathered that husband or not Trevor Hayes had a bit of a crush on anyone that showed an interest.

"Thanks and it's been nice having a chat with you."

"Likewise Maude. Bye for now."

As promised the message had been passed onto Vincent but Trevor hadn't received the response he'd anticipated. Vincent Frasier wore a look of horror when he realised that someone now knew where he was staying. He decided to think on the matter over night. Maude Shelton could give him up to Gant that was for sure but then Vinny couldn't really see why she'd do that. He would wait until the morning and then make a decision about what to do but one way or another he couldn't see himself staying in Cambridge much longer.

By 6pm and with still no word Maude was becoming

189

agitated. Although it went heavily against the grain she had placed a temporary closed sign on the door and decided to try and talk to Lisa. It would do little good but she at least had to try if only for her own peace of mind. The air in the room was thick with perspiration and the atmosphere was stifling. Drawing back the curtains Maude opened the small window to let in some fresh air.

"Hello sweetheart. How are you feeling?"

Lisa propped herself up in the bed and her reply shocked Maude.

"Oh just fucking hunky-dory. I mean I've just found out I'm at deaths door how, do you think I'm fucking feeling?"

"Lisa don't be like that with me, it's not my fault and I'm only trying to help. Now I've found out where Vinny is and I'm just waiting for him to call. Once he's back and sort's things out I'm sure it will ease your pain."

Lisa let out a cackle that made Maude spin round. The girl's next sentence came out in an almost hiss and fine droplets of spittle escaped from her mouth.

"Ease my pain? You don't think I'm going to tell him do you?"

"Why on earth not?"

"Why not!!!"

"Calm down darling. I know this is hard for you but you have to consider other people you know. The first person you need to tell is Jay."

"Tell Jay? No fucking way!"

"Don't be so silly of course you have to! Lisa you must tell him if only to protect him. I know how much you love Jason and you'd never risk infecting him."

Maude's last words didn't get the response she was expecting. Instead Lisa broke into a loud sarcastic laugh that culminated in near hysteria. The only thing Maude

190

Shelton could do was slap the girl hard on the cheek. Instantly there was silence as Lisa stared wide eyed into space.

"Now my girl, I think you and me need to have a little chat. I need you to tell me everything."

Lisa swallowed hard. It had been difficult telling Jason about her past but with Maude it was even harder. None the less she began and throughout the whole sorry tale of her childhood Maude remained expressionless. To have appeared judgmental in anyway would have made the girl clam up and that was one thing Maude couldn't afford to let happen.

"So you see there's no risk to Jay. We've never slept together and it definitely won't be on the cards now. The whole time we've been married I've longed to have the kind of closeness that only married couples share but no matter how hard I tried my body would just shut down. I was totally violated Maude and I can't bare anyone getting close to me not even my own husband. How sad is that?"

"It ain't sad darling."

"Ain't it? You must be the only person in the world that sees it like that."

"Do you think this virus was contracted when you was young then?"

"That's just it Maude it couldn't have been. A week or so after we got married and while I was still hopeful that one day I would be able to make love to my husband, I had some tests. I just wanted to make sure there was nothing from my past that could rear its ugly head and spoil things."

Maude placed her hand on Lisa's shoulder in a motherly way that made the girl begin to cry.

"But I don't understand? If you were clear and you

191

haven't slept with Jason then how could this possibly of happened? Oh Lisa please don't tell me that you've cheated on our boy?"

Immediately Lisa shrugged off Maude's hand and the look she gave the older woman was one of pure contempt.

"How can you even think that after everything I've just told you? I would die before I ever hurt Jay."

"Then how? I just don't understand."

"Vinny."

"Vinny?"

"Just after Jason got banged up he came back. You know the day you went to the cash and carry and I was still in bed with a cold."

"And you slept with him?"

Lisa recoiled in horror.

"Slept with him? There you go again. If having some bastard rape you is sleeping with them, then yeah I suppose I'm guilty."

"Oh Lisa!"

"Yeah that's right Maude he raped me, he fucking well raped me."

Maude Shelton wrapped her arms tightly around the tiny figure of a girl and she could see that pools of tears had begun to form in her beautiful doe like eyes.

"Oh Lisa! Oh dear God in heaven I'm so sorry!"

The two remained silent for a long time as Maude gently rocked Lisa back and forth in her arms. After a while Maude made Lisa take one of the sedatives that Miles Crawford had prescribed and when the girl was almost asleep she gently turned her round so that Lisa could lie down. After covering her tiny body with a soft blanket Maude quietly tiptoed from the room. Back in her flat she sat down at the table and placing her head in her

192

hands gently began to weep. No one had ever seen Maude Shelton cry and they weren't about to now but right at this moment she couldn't hold inside all the pain that she was feeling. The tears came thick and fast but after several minutes she wiped her eyes and sat up straight. This weak show of emotion wasn't helping anyone and suddenly Maude Shelton felt ashamed of herself. Things just seemed to be going from bad to worse and when the telephone suddenly burst into life she knew that her nerves wouldn't stand much more. Apprehensively she lifted up the receiver dreading who was on the other end. If at long last it was Vinny then she just didn't know what she would do.

"Hi Duchess it's Jay."

In the last week Jason had begun to telephone every couple of days from prison and whereas she normally couldn't wait to hear from him, today she just wished that BT could have cut her line off for some reason.

"How's my baby?"

Maude could feel her heart breaking and knew that to relay such horrendous news over the telephone would be nothing short of barbaric. Instead and although it really went against the grain she lied to her boy.

"She's fine love. Actually she's having a lay down as we've been really busy the last couple of days."

"Bless her heart don't wake her then. So how are things going with you Duchess?"

"Well Jay to tell the truth we've got a big problem. I haven't said anything before but I had a visit from Freddie Gant and his henchman. I didn't tell him where you were but initially he gave me just a week to get you and your brother back here. For some reason he's had a change of heart regarding the time limit but if I don't sort things out soon then there's going to be hell to pay. I

193

haven't heard from your brother and to be honest I'm at me wits end Jay."

The line was silent and Maude guessed that he was trying to think of what to do. Knowing that he needed a moment to gather his thoughts she didn't question his silence. After a short pause Jason responded.

"Well as far as I can see there's only one option. Tell Freddie Gant where I am and let me deal with it."

"Jason don't think because you're locked up in there that he can't get to you. If anything it will be far easier for him."

"Come on Duchess you don't think I'm that fucking naive do you? I'm planning that's exactly what he will do but remember one thing, he wants his money back so he ain't going to hurt anyone until he has it. At least in here I will be able to talk to him and possibly make a deal. If he has direct contact with me then he has no reason to see you or Lisa."

"But Jay you don't realise what he's capable of!"

"Listen Maude, none of us have a choice so please just call him and ask him to come and see me. Now I have to go darling there's a queue for the blower. Give Lisa a kiss and tell her I love her and will be in touch soon."

With that he was gone and as Maude replaced the handset she could feel the perspiration on her hands. Rummaging through her purse she pulled out the card that Freddie Gant had given her earlier. She could see by the Bridle Lane address that even though her nephew was successful he'd still never managed to break his ties with Soho. With slight hesitation she dialled the number. Maude Shelton was aware that if she'd hesitated much longer then this was one call that she wouldn't have made. As was common practice between the two, Wally Evans always answered the phone on his boss's behalf. He

194

normally repeated the caller's name out loud and looked towards Freddie to see if he would accept. This time he instinctively knew that it wouldn't be necessary and offering the phone to his boss he just said 'Maude Shelton'. Freddie Gant's face grimaced as things were now happening quicker than he would have liked and if his aunt did manage to locate the brothers too soon, then his plans could all go belly up. When Maude informed him as to Jason's whereabouts the smile dropped from his face.

"You're having a fucking laugh ain't you!"

"Fredrick I wouldn't laugh where my boy is concerned. Now I've told you what you wanted and I would thank you and your bleeding gorilla not to darken my door again."

"Wo hold on there a minute! You may have told me where he is but until I get my dosh back then our agreement still stands, do you hear?"

There was no reply to his statement as Maude had hung up. Crossing her arms and placing one fist under each armpit was the only way she could stop her hands from shaking. Opening up the Camel hadn't been on the list for tonight but suddenly she needed company, anything to take her mind off of the day's events and the image of what might be in the future. Unlike his aunt Freddie Gant wasn't frightened, he was totally furious.

"What's going on Boss?"

"What's going on? I'll fucking tell you what's going on Wal! That cunts only banged up in Belmarsh, how the fuck am I going to get at me money now!"

"But I thought that if she couldn't get your money and the scumbags who nicked it then you got the pub and that's what you wanted?"

"Of course I do you daft twat but I want me cash as well

195

or did you think I was just going to forget about it?"

"Well no but all the same I...."

"Wal don't try and be clever, just be here bright and early in the morning. I think a spot of prison visiting is called for and god help that littler bastard if he don't tell me what I need to hear."

"But we ain't got a visiting order"

"Don't need one, he's on remand. Now just make sure you're not late tomorrow."

With that Freddie Gant walked up to his flat without another word to his employee.

CHAPTER TWENTY

The black jaguar pulled into the large car park and after
Wally Evans had chosen an appropriate spot he got out
and opened the rear door for his boss. Freddie Gant
stepped from the car and smoothed down his Saville Row
suit. After placing his fine cashmere overcoat over his
shoulders he looked up at the imposing building that was
Belmarsh prison. Known to have the luck of the Irish or
that was what his adversary's had always said about him,
Freddie to date had never experienced a spell at her
majesties. He hoped this run of luck would continue for
many years to come but with how things had been going
in the last few months he wasn't sure if that would be the
case. The building resembled something from the eastern
block and appeared typically institutional. Silently he
wondered to himself how a person could ever adapt to
this hell hole once sentenced. It wasn't something that
he'd dwelled on that much in the past but now actually
standing outside, for the first time he thought about the
real possibility that one day he could actually be a
resident. He turned to face Wally as they walked along.
"Ever been here before Wal?"
"Yeah sure a lot of me old mukka's have done a stretch in
Belmarsh over the last few years."
"No I didn't mean that. Have you ever been banged up?"
"Not fucking likely Gov! If I had to do some bird then
I'd rather be sent to one of the old places like Pentonville
or the Scrubs."
Freddie Gant shook his head in amazement.
"Fuck you're a weird cunt Wal."
Wally Evans didn't reply and only gave his boss a
slightly vacant look that said 'I don't understand what you
197

mean'. Being his normal astute self Freddie had done
some investigating of his own regarding Jason Frasier's
charges. Only this morning and accompanied by Wally
he had paid Jason's solicitor Clive Heath a courtesy visit,
or that's what he preferred to call it. Wally had told the
secretary to be a good girl and pop out for coffee. When
she'd protested that she was busy and besides they had
drink facilities in the back room, Wally had given her one
of his menacing glares. It was enough to see the
secretary put her coat on and leave the office in record
time. Without knocking the two men had entered Clive
heaths office and crossing the room, stood directly in
front of the man's desk.

"Good morning Mr Heath. We're here regarding one of
your clients and I'd be grateful if you could provide us
with a bit of information."

To begin with Clive had come over arrogant and
dismissed any questions being asked regarding Jason.
"How the hell did you get in here? Miss Parsons should
have phoned before letting anyone through that door.
Now I'm sorry gentle men but it would be highly
unethical for me to discuss a client so if you don't mind I
have a lot to do today."

After nodding in the direction of his accomplice Freddie
Gant walked from the office and took a seat in the
waiting area. Thirty seconds alone in the room with
Wally Evans instantly changed Clive Heath's opinion
regarding ethics. He was soon giving Freddie every piece
of information he had on the case. Well aware that he
could have been disbarred for what he had just disclosed,
Clive also knew that he walked much better with two legs
and his knee caps intact. Given the choice as Wally had
put it, he decided that the disclosure option was for the
best, if not for Jason Frasier then at least for his own self

preservation. As Freddie Gant walked through the first set of steel gates at Belmarsh it felt as though someone had just walked over his grave and he gave a shiver. This outing didn't sit well with Wally Evans either and he quickened his pace so that he now walked level with his boss. In Soho Freddie demanded and received respect but not here, here he was just another mug on the visiting list. Having to sit alongside row after row of brasses, wives, mothers, snotty nosed kids and petty villains really went against the grain and he was relieved when his name was included in the first set of visitors to be called through. Closely followed by Wally he made his way along a narrow corridor and began the rigorous security checks that were now demanded but were in fact almost useless. About to continue into the open plan reception room that had been set aside for visitors he stopped dead in his tracks at the sound of Wally's voice.

"Get your fucking hands off me you ponce!"

One of the duty guards was in the process of patting this giant of a man down in search of any hidden weapons or drugs. When the guard had briefly touched Wally Evans inside leg he fiercely pushed the man away. Freddie rolled his eyes upwards, this was all he needed. Turning round he took in a deep breath and walked the few short steps back to where his employee stood. Three prison officers had now surrounded Wally and they were about to escort him out of the building when Freddie spoke up. "Wal just let the gentlemen get on with their jobs. I'm sorry about my friend but he had a bad experience some years ago and you can gauge by his reaction, that he's nervous if someone tries to get close to his balls!"

Freddie's words seemed to defuse the situation and the guards gave slight grins as they continued with their search. Wally grimaced at the touch but knew better than

199

to make another scene. Seconds later and the two men
entered the reception room and took seats on the same
side of a strategically placed table.

"What the fuck did you say that for Boss? They must
think I'm some kind of queer now."

"Look Wal, we're here for one reason only and you
starting world war fucking three aint it. I had to say
something or we would have both ended up back in the
car park. Now for fucks sake shut up about it and let's
get this over with. I don't want to spend a single minute
longer in this shit hole than I have to."

The opposite end of the room held an identical door
behind which sat Jason Frasier. He was aware who his
visitor was and to say he was apprehensive was an
understatement. After being led single file along with the
other prisoners, Jason was immediately able to pick out
from the room full of people exactly which one was
Freddie Gant. Having an oversized thug sitting next to
him had been a dead giveaway. Trying not to appear
nervous Jason made his way over to the table and took a
seat opposite Freddie and Wally. No words were spoken
for a few seconds as both men eyed each other up. Jason
noticed a few faces nod their heads in Freddie's direction
as they passed. Not being known by the guards was
certainly made up for by the inmates. Due to Jason being
on remand and as yet not guilty of a crime the
atmosphere in the room was slightly more relaxed than
on normal prison visits. Wally Evans was instructed to
go and purchase coffees for everyone and after giving
Jason a cold glare, did as he was told.

"So Mr Frasier you know why I'm here. I suppose my
aunt told you that I ain't a happy bunny at the moment?"

"Aunt?"

Freddie Gant smiled.

200

"You didn't know that even though we're estranged, dear old Maude was part of my clan? Well there's a first! Wonders will never fucking cease, the old bat has a bit of loyalty inside her after all. Now then to the point, ah cheers Wal!"

Jason accepted the steaming cup when it was pushed in his direction.

"As I was saying I ain't happy and you're the one who can put the smile back on my face."

"Am I supposed to feel threatened Mr Gant? You come in here with your animal on a lead and expect me to roll over in terror is that it?"

Freddie looked at Wally and smirked.

"This really ain't your day Wal is it?"

Not expecting an answer Freddie sharply turned to face Jason. The look on his face was now vicious and Jason understood how easily the man instilled fear.

"Let me ask you something Mr Frasier seeing as you've insulted my friend here in a not too flattering manner. Do you know what the difference is between an animal and a human being?"

Jason shrugged his shoulders.

"I'll tell you then, there's only one. Animals unlike human beings don't have the ability to lie. Now I'd say that puts them way above us wouldn't you? After all you're very good at fucking lying or so your wife and Aunty Maude must think. Now Wally here is as straight as a die, if he says he's going to break your fucking neck then he does just that. He don't lie or tell you something different. So when you call him an animal it's a backhanded kind of compliment wouldn't you say?"

Jason was about to speak but was silenced as Freddie Gant continued.

"You're probably wondering what you can do about any

201

of this mess while you're banged up in here and to tell the truth you're probably more than a little fucking relieved that you are here, am I right?"

Again Jason wasn't given chance to reply and all the time he was being spoken to he could feel Wally Evans's eyes boring into his skull.

"Well I have it on good information that you're about to be released. Your brief says the old girl you knocked down had dementia, so there's no way they can prove that she didn't just walk right out in front of you. Now how I see it is you have two choices when you get out of here. One is that you hand yourself over and Wally here will do his thing which I might add ain't very nice or you hand over that cunt of a brother of yours. Oh and before I forget, either scenario will be accompanied by my money. Think it over Mr Frasier but I will have been informed within a few hours of your release so don't even think about going on the fucking trot now will you?"

Freddie didn't wait for a reply and was up and heading towards the door before Jason or Wally even knew what was going on. Wally Evans stood up from the table but before he joined his boss leaned in forward so that his face was only millimetres away from Jason's. He didn't speak, he didn't need to. The action was enough and the smell of his breath from the strong coffee was rancid making Jason recoil in disgust. Finally reaching the outside and now able to inhale fresh air Freddie Gant once more felt human.

"Fetch the car Wal and get me away from this godforsaken fucking place as quick as you can."

Back in the relative safety of his cell Jason lay down on the bunk trying to take in what had just been said to him. Freddie Gant was a face and a well known one at that but he was insane if he thought that Jason could just hand over his brother. Another thing playing on his mind was the fact that Maude had decided to keep him in the dark about being related to a gangster. If as Freddie had said she was showing her family loyalty, then how safe was Lisa. Jason hated himself for even thinking such a thing. Maude had been so good to them but this news was like a bolt out of the blue and he felt as if he didn't really know the woman at all. He had no idea how he was going to sort things, he didn't have a clue but that night Jason prayed for his release like he'd never prayed for anything before.

By the first sound of cell doors banging open for breakfast Jason Frasier was already dressed and sitting on the side of his bed. The night had been long and restless and the only decision he'd reached was to try and see the governor about his release. Fortunately for him that wasn't necessary as a second later his own door was opened and one of the wing guards entered.

"Must be your lucky day Frasier. Get your things together you're out of here after breakfast."

Jason wanted to hug the man but thought better of it. In the dining hall breakfast was the last thing on his mind and he knew he wouldn't be able to manage much more than tea and toast. Word of his release had spread like wild fire on the wing and as he collected his food at the counter it seemed as if a thousand hands were patting him on the back. At just after nine thirty he was signed out and escorted towards the main gate. Men he had come to know in his short time of incarceration could be heard cheering from the barred windows. Some of the men Jason had liked and some he had come to loathe but one thing stood out above anything else, they all watched over each other. He could feel excitement beginning as butterflies did a crazy dance in the pit of his stomach.

203

The thought of seeing Lisa was a wonderful feeling but it was short lived and instantly replaced with feelings of anxiousness. Jason thought back to his visitors parting words 'I will have been informed within a few hours of your release, so don't even think about going on the trot' and a cold chill ran down his entire body. Standing on the side of the road with just a plastic bag holding his personal possessions Jason Frasier appeared a sad and lonely sight. His release was so swift that he hadn't had time to tell anyone or arrange to be picked up. Luckily he still had a twenty in his trouser pocket and that at least should be enough to get him a cab home. By the time he reached the Camel it was ten thirty. The draymen were pulling away after their weekly delivery and as he stepped into the yard Maude Shelton was just about to pick up a crate of mixers when for some reason she looked up.

"Oh Jason darling! Ain't you a sight for sore eyes."
After what he had learnt yesterday he assumed that she would be hostile. The one thing he wasn't expecting was for her to break down in floods of tears. This wasn't his Maude, the strong confident don't get in my way kind of Maude that he'd grown to love like a mother. Jason moved in closer and took the woman in his arms.

"Come on let's get you inside. I know I'm attractive to the opposite sex but don't you think this is a bit over the top?"
Maude couldn't help but give out a small giggle between sobs. She felt fear for the future but also pure relief that he was home where he belonged, at least for the moment. The two walked along the inner hall and up to her flat. Jason didn't even question Lisa's whereabouts as he naturally assumed that she was at work. Though in all honesty if he'd taken the time to think about it then he

would have realised that it would now be highly unlikely that she even had a job. Luckily for Maude all the commotion hadn't woken the girl and she would at least have some time to speak to her boy before he asked to see his wife.

"Eaten?"

"Only toast I couldn't fancy anything more. To tell the truth I'm fucking famished now."

"Bacon and egg do you?"

"Maude you're a queen and a fried slice wouldn't go a miss either."

"You could do with a wash love you have the smell of that place ingrained in your skin."

"Oh thanks a bunch."

"You know what I mean. To an East Ender that smell is more offensive than a sewer. The sooner we get you back smelling nice the better. Cuppa?"

"Mmmm lovely Duchess."

"So when did you find out you was getting released? If you'd have phoned I could have met you."

"Didn't know myself until breakfast time."

Jason was a little shocked that she didn't know he was being set free and wondered why her nephew hadn't warned her, still all that would be sorted out in a while. For now Jason Frasier was just happy to be home and eager to see his beautiful wife again. Placing the pan onto the stove Maude Shelton smiled to herself. It was a strange feeling because as she smiled a tear of sadness trickled down her cheek. She would feed her boy up as she'd dreamed of doing for the past few weeks. She'd run him a hot bath and make him comfortable as she always did, then she would have to do something she'd never done before. Maude Shelton would have to reveal the horrific truth of the last few days and break his heart.

205

If there was any other option, then she would have grasped it with both hands but there wasn't. Life at times can deal us all a bad hand and sometimes the blows are terrible but as she knew only too well, you just had to pick up the pieces and get on with living.

CHAPTER TWENTY ONE

Jason ate the hearty breakfast that Maude had prepared and enjoyed it like never before. Now laying back in the hot soapy bubbles of the bath he let his mind wander to thoughts of his wife. He couldn't wait to see her later that day and swore to himself that whatever happened, from now on he would always be there for her. He kept recalling all the events of the past few weeks and he felt ashamed of himself, ashamed that he'd not only abandoned Lisa but left Maude to sort out a mess that however much he might like to sugar coat it, was still a mess caused by him and Vinny. With her boy now happily soaking in his bath it gave Maude Shelton the time she needed to check on Lisa. Luckily she still had three of the sedatives left that Miles Crawford had provided. After thoroughly stirring one of them into the cup of hot chocolate she'd just made Maude went down to the backroom and tapped gently on the door. The voice that replied sounded so weak that Maude felt helpless.

"Come in."

Popping her head around the door Maude wrinkled her nose at the pungent smell that once more emerged from inside.

"Hi darling, how are you feeling?"

"A little better today thanks."

"Sure?"

"Yeah I really am."

Walking over to the bed Maude placed the cup on the side table and drew back the curtains. The bright sunlight made Lisa screw up her eyes. Turning back to look at the girl Maude could clearly see the beads of sweat that stood

out on her brow. This was a daily sight and one that
scared the woman far more than she would ever let on.
"Babe I just need to open the window up for a while. It's
really ripe in here and it can't be any good for you."
Lisa huddled down in the bed and pulled the covers up
tight around her neck.
"Sorry, it's just that I'm so cold all the time."
"I know darling that's why I've brought you some hot
coco. Get that down you and I'm sure it'll warm you
up."
Sitting on the side of the bed she didn't leave Lisa until
the cup was empty. Maude hated drugging the girl but
she had to be sure that she would have enough time to try
and explain things to Jason. Walking into the bar she
removed the temporary closed signs from the shelf and
placed one in each window by the doors. It was
something she didn't like doing and the customers were
going to kick up such a stink but right at this moment she
had no choice in the matter, no choice at all. When all
was said and done family came before anything and as far
as Maude Shelton was concerned Jason and Lisa Frasier
were the only family she had. Upstairs in the flat Jason
now felt refreshed and ready to take on the world no
matter what that entailed. As Maude entered the kitchen
he was adding two tots of brandy to the steaming hot tea
he'd just poured.
"Here we go Duchess! I think we need to talk and I
thought this would help us both to relax a little."
Maude sighed heavily which made Jason look up from
his cup but he didn't ask her what was wrong. Instead he
wanted an answer to the one thing that had been really
bugging him.
"Why didn't you tell me that you was related to Freddie
Gant?"

His question took Maude by surprise but then she figured if that little shit Fredrick had paid her boy a visit then it stood to reason he would stir things up as much as he could.

"I didn't tell you because he's not someone I consciously ever think about. As you know Freddie came here while you was banged up but before that I hadn't seen him in well over twenty years. You can pick your friends Jay but when it comes to family well that's a whole different ball game. I know it may sound harsh but Freddie Gant should have been drowned at birth. His mother would have done just as well to have held onto the afterbirth instead of keeping him. He's bad through and through and in all honesty it makes me ashamed to think that we are related. I can see by the look on your face that it's playing on your mind Jay but darling I really didn't think it mattered."

"Normally it wouldn't but now, well now I'm just wondering who your loyalties lie with. You see Duchess I need to know that Lisa's safe and always will be."

Instead of shock Maude's face portrayed nothing but hurt and he regretted the words as soon as they had left his mouth.

"Jay you don't even have to ask me that and it cuts me to the quick to think that you feel you need to."

"I'm sorry but when Gant came to Belmarsh he wasn't alone. I suppose by bringing his minder along he thought it would intimidate me"

"And did it?"

Jason smiled.

"Yeah a bit I suppose."

Maude placed her cup back onto the table and took both of Jason's hands in hers.

"Darling people like Freddie Gant are the scum of the

209

earth and you don't cross them, well not knowingly anyway. I've done all I can regarding my nephew and buying you some time but now it's out of my control. You know as well as I do that someone has to take a beating. The Freddie Gant's of this world can't be seen to let things go. I didn't step off the last banana boat Jay and I know Vinny got you both into this so why shouldn't he be the one to sort this out?"

"Under normal circumstances I might agree with that Duchess if it was only going to be a bit of a pasting but you know as well as I do that someone's not going to survive this. I realise I have a wife and responsibilities but all the same I don't think I can just hand over my brother like that."

Maude decided that to help him make up his mind and come to the only sensible conclusion he could, she must now tell him about Lisa. Still holding his hands they both looked down at the table when her palms became clammy and she began to shake.

"Duchess what is it?"

"Jason I want you to listen to me."

"I will but bleeding hell Maude, I ain't ever seen you like this before, whatever is it?"

"No Jason! I want you to really listen. I don't want you to speak or get up from this table. What I'm going to tell you will turn your world upside down and if there was any other way I...."

"Fuck me just tell me will you! For god's sake it can't be that bad, nobody's dead are they?"

"I can't Jay not until you promise to hear me out."

"Ok! Ok! I promise but you're starting to scare me now Duchess."

Maude Shelton stared long and hard into the eyes of the man that she had come to love as a son and began to tell him the story. It took some time to fully relay all that had happened. She had decided to play events down a bit and some details like the rape were kept to a minimum for the time being. To relay all the gory details wouldn't do anyone any good at this stage and although it was almost impossible, she was trying her hardest to limit the damage.

"Rape! What the hell are you talking about? Vinny would never do that to Lisa."

"I know it's hard to accept Jay and babe the last thing I want to do is hurt you but you have to let me finish, there's so much more you need to know and believe me it gets worse."

"Fucking worse!, Duchess how could it possibly get any worse?"

Maude gently leant over the table and placed her index finger onto his lips. Satisfied that she had silenced him she continued. Events like the visit to Miles Crawford's were explained in full detail and to begin with Jason's reaction wasn't readable. Maude put that down to shock and as much as she wanted to stop this sorry tale knew that she couldn't. The whole time her face never left his and eventually from those beautiful blue eyes she saw emerge so many different expressions of emotion. When she reached the end and her final words ended with H.I.V Jason Frasier at last broke down. His sobs were loud and heart wrenching and the one thing she was grateful for was the fact that at least Lisa wouldn't hear them. At the same time Maude realised that these feelings had to come out, that or her boy would go mad. She walked around the table and kneeling down took him in her arms. He clung to her and cried like a baby which made her feel totally and utterly useless. At that moment in time she pictured herself as the most evil woman in the world but

211

she also knew that this little lot wasn't over, not by a very
long way. Eventually his sobs subsided and as he looked
into Maude's face snot flooded from his nose. Like any
loving mother she pulled a tissue from her cuff and gently
wiped it away. Abruptly Jason stood up and taking in a
large lungful of air pushed back his shoulders. Maude
could see that now he had the truth he would be strong
just like she had known he would be, strong and able to
deal with things.

"Where is she?"

"Downstairs in your room love but she's asleep Jay and
very sick. Be careful what you say love the poor little
mare has really been through it lately."

He didn't reply but the look he gave, told her in no
uncertain terms that she shouldn't have even said that.
Maude stayed in the kitchen deciding that she wouldn't
go down until much later. They needed time alone and
that was exactly what she would give them. Gently he
tapped on the bedroom door. Fear began to rise inside
Jason as he thought of what was to come. He instantly
chastised himself for even thinking that way; Lisa was his
life and whatever happened he was going to look after
her. He had no experience of the disease and although he
knew she wouldn't have grown two heads, he really
didn't know what would greet him on the other side of
the door. Hesitantly he pushed hard on the wooden panel
and stepped inside. Lisa had been in a deep sleep but the
sound of the door opening woke her. Rubbing her eyes
she wearily tried to focus. It took a second or two for it
to sink in that Jay, her Jay was really here. Jason tried
desperately not to show how shocked he was but the look
on her face told him he wasn't doing a very good job.
Her eyes were dark and swollen from crying and her
normally beautiful bouncy hair was lank and greasy.

The room had a smell of perspiration and it was something under normal circumstances Lisa wouldn't have tolerated.

"Oh baby I'm so so sorry."

Lisa didn't speak, she didn't have anything to say and in any case she assumed that Maude had probably already said it all. Waiting for him to walk out and leave her, she sobbed out loud when he sat down beside her and took her in his arms.

"I'm here now and we're going to sort this out."

Lisa pulled away sharply.

"Sort this out? Jason I don't know what you've been told but I'm dying and there's nothing anyone can do about it."

He firmly grabbed hold of her elbows and stared deep into the beautiful eyes that had been the first thing he had fallen in love with.

"Lisa we're all dying it's just that some of us will go sooner than others. Now you can lie in that bed until the end or you can get up and try to enjoy life in whatever form it takes. I'm home now and once I've sorted that scumbag Vinny out, then we are going to make the most of what time we have left, however long that is."

Looking up into her husband's face Lisa Frasier smiled weakly.

"We could give it a try but Jay don't' do anything silly about Vinny will you. I couldn't bear to lose you again, not now."

Jason placed an arm around his wife's shoulder and propped himself up against the headboard.

"Don't you worry about that, I ain't got to do anything about him I promise. Someone else is more than willing to sort him out and maybe that's for the best. Now how about I go and run you a bath and fix you something to

213

eat?"

"Thanks Jay but I ain't got much of an appetite."

The look he gave her was all that she needed to see.

"Ok I'll give it a try."

Jason smiled then went up to the bathroom to prepare her bath. Five minutes later and he returned wearing the best smile he could muster.

"All done Babe! Now when you've had a soak me and Maude are going to fix you something nice to eat."

Lisa's eyes began to fill with tears and the only reply she could manage was a slow nod. Maude was startled when she saw the couple walk into the flat as she hadn't expected to set eyes on them for hours yet.

"I've just run Lisa a bath Duchess as she was getting a bit ripe."

Lisa playfully punched her husband and for a second the room was filled with laughter just as it had been a few months ago.

"Go have a soak babe and I'll see you in a minute, I've laid out a nice fresh dressing gown."

Maude and Jason didn't speak until they heard the bathroom door close and were sure Lisa couldn't hear them.

"How'd it go?"

Jason shrugged his shoulders and shook his head.

"I didn't think she'd be that bad Maude, fuck me it's only been a few weeks."

"I know it came as a shock to me as well but according to Miles Crawford the virus can take several different turns. Some people don't' show any signs for months, even years. While others like that unlucky little cow, show symptoms within weeks."

Sitting down at the table Jason put his head in his hands and Maude thought that he was about to cry again.

Seconds later, when he placed his hands in front of his face as though he was praying, she could see that he was actually deep in thought.

"Penny for them?"

Jason gave a weak smile.

"Duchess I know you've done a lot for me lately, more than anyone could ever ask in fact but there's one more thing I need you to do."

"Of course son, you only have to ask."

"I want you to contact Gant and arrange a meet."

"Jason that's not a good idea love. If he sees you alone there's no telling what he will do and I couldn't bare it if he hurt you. At least you had some kind of protection while you were banged up but outside, well that thug of his could wipe you out and no one would be any the wiser."

"Please Maude just trust me on this. I know he scares you, fuck me he'd scare the devil himself but we have to sort this out once and for all. God help me Maude, I have to sort this out if not for Lisa, then for me. Will you do it?"

"Pass me the phone."

Jason Frasier grinned as she did as he asked. It wasn't a grin of happiness but one of pure love for the woman who sat with him at the table in total unity. The call came through to Freddie Gant a few minutes later and as Wally had popped out on an errand it was answered by Freddie himself.

"Yeah?"

"Hi Fredrick it's your Aunt Maude."

"How nice to hear from you Aunty."

"Cut the sarcasm! Jason is home and against my better judgment I might add, he would like to come and see you."

215

"I knew he was out today but I didn't think he would be so punctual. Tell him to be at the Bridle Lane office at ten sharp tomorrow morning."

The line went dead before Maude had time to say anything else. Hanging up she was just about to try and talk Jason out of going when Lisa's footsteps could be heard on the landing. Jason put his index finger to his lips and as the door opened he gave Maude a knowing wink which went somewhere to reassuring her that he knew what he was doing.

"Hi babe, feel better?"

"Ummmm."

"Well at least you smell good now!"

"You really are a cheeky git Jason Frasier but I still can't stop loving you."

"Right, well you take a seat and I'll do us all some sandwiches. Hungry Maude?"

"Famished but now that I have my little family back again, food don't seem to matter that much. I've missed this."

"What?"

As she looked into Jason's face Maude grabbed Lisa's hand and squeezed it tightly.

"The three of us, being here like this."

"Well if I have anything to do with it Duchess, from now on that's just how it's going to stay."

Maude Shelton could see that he meant every word of what he was saying but whether he could make it happen was a different matter all together.

CHAPTER TWENTY TWO

The next morning when Jason woke the weather was dank and overcast. His whole body felt cold and clammy and he couldn't work out if it was just down to the weather or worse still the thought of what he was about to do. As he peered out of the window he knew that this could turn out to be one of the gloomiest days in his life. Jason had spent the night cramped up on the small sofa in the corner of the room and every muscle in his body ached. It wasn't that he didn't want to sleep with Lisa but her getting rest was the most important thing to him and as he'd been so fidgety of late he thought it was for the best. He had sat and watched her sleep until the early hours and alone in the dark he was finally able to release the tears that he'd struggled so hard to hold inside. His wife was so tired and worn out that she was oblivious to his pain and distress but that was fine with Jason. From this moment on he wanted nothing but smiles and happiness to surround her and he would go to any lengths to provide it. As the fresh morning light entered the room, he was once more overcome with grief and felt as though his heart would break. Hearing Maude approach the room, Jason Frasier quickly wiped away any tears that had won the battle to be released. Trying desperately not to spill the tray of teas, Maude was so deep in concentration that she didn't look into his eyes and see how red and puffy they were.

"Morning all sleep well?"

"Not too bad thanks. Lisa wake up babe Maude's here."

Had it not have been such a sad situation, the sight would have been comical as Lisa's tiny head popped up from underneath the covers. Her golden hair was a tangled mess and stuck out in all directions but at that moment in time Jason thought that he couldn't love her anymore than he did right now. Three of the world's most miss matched people sat together and drank tea, happy with just the fact that they had been reunited.

"So then Lisa what do you fancy doing today? I thought me and you could go up West and do a spot of shopping. Treat ourselves what do you say?"

Trying to smooth down her tussled hair and appear pretty to her husband, Lisa glanced in his direction as she spoke. "Thanks Maude that's very kind of you but I'd rather just stay here with Jay if you don't mind."

Jason Frasier and Maude Shelton looked at each other at exactly the same time and Lisa couldn't be off noticing the silent signals they were sending.

"What's going on you two?"

There was no answer to her question and she slammed her cup onto the bedside table.

"Jason I asked you a question, the least you could do is have the courtesy to answer. Well?"

"Look babe I have some business to sort out but after that I'm all yours. Now why don't you do as Maude suggests and do a bit of shopping."

"'Because I don't want to and don't think I don't know what you're up to Jason Frasier. You promised me you wouldn't do anything silly and less than twelve hours later you're doing just that. I know you think you have to take revenge for what was done to me but I'm the only one that really matters in all of this and if I can accept things, then so should you. Going after your brother won't accomplish anything."

"It'll make me feel better."

"Oh so once you've cleared your conscience everything's going to be fine is it?"

218

Jason stood up from the sofa and after stretching his aching back, walked over to the bed. He didn't sit beside his wife and she knew by the look on his face that this was one argument she wouldn't win.

"Lisa, no matter what you think I have to do this, that or I'll go fucking insane!"

"No you don't and don't you dare say it's for me because you know as well as I do that it would be a lie."

"I do have to do this and I'm not saying it's for you. Look why can't you just let me get on with it and then we can carry on as normal."

He regretted his choice of words the moment they came out of his mouth.

"I'm sorry I didn't mean that."

"Tough shit if you did Jay because nothings ever going to be normal around here again is it? I've been thinking and I want to offer you both a get out of jail card. If you choose to take it I really don't mind because if the shoe was on the other foot I don't know if I could cope with all of this."

Turning first to Maude, Lisa gave a loving smile that showed just how beautiful , sweet and caring she was.

"Maude you've been brilliant with me but you have a business to run and when we moved in here, looking after a dying bitch like me wasn't part of the deal."

"Lisa!"

"No Maude it's true. Now I've been happier here than anywhere else in my life but I've done a bit of research and there are several hospices that cater for AIDS patients. If it's alright with you I think I'll contact them later today."

It was now Maude Shelton's turn to walk over to the bed but unlike Jason she did sit down and taking Lisa's hand in hers gripped it tightly.

219

"Now you listen to me young lady and listen good. We are a family and families don't just take the good times, the bad are part of the package as well. As for you not knowing if you could deal with things had this of happened to Jay or me, well that's just rubbish. No one knows what they're capable of until the time comes and I think you of all people Lisa, would surprise us all."

"That's right Princess, Maude and me love you to bits and I thought you knew that by now. I don't want to hear any more talk of hospices and the likes. Later after I've sorted things we'll sit down and make plans for the future alright?"

Lisa reluctantly nodded her head but all this love still didn't stop her feeling a complete and utter burden.

Jason went out into the backyard in a desperate need for a smoke to calm his nerves but Maude remained seated on the bed.

"You have to let him do this love."

"Why Do I?"

"Lisa you still have a lot to learn. It's a man thing and if Jay doesn't do something he'll always regret it. Sweetheart you have to let him find his own way. As for you saying you're the only one that really matters in all of this, well that's just not true."

Lisa gave a sarcastic laugh as she spoke.

"I'm the one that's fucking dying here."

"Maybe you are darling but in reality we're all dying. Your life has been prematurely stolen from you and torn apart but don't you think ours hasn't been as well. It may be in a different way but we're suffering too you know."

Lisa Frasier didn't argue. For a start she was too tired and deep down she knew that as usual Maude was right.

The Hackney Maude had ordered the previous night was punctual and pulled up outside the pub at nine thirty

sharp. By the time Jason left Lisa was up and dressed
and both she and Maude hugged him tightly before he
walked out of the door. Turning towards the older
woman Lisa's eyes filled with tears.
"He is coming home Maude ain't he?"
"Of course he's coming home, what a daft thing to say.
Now come on let's get a move on those shops are
waiting."

As the cab drove along Shaftesbury Avenue Jason could
feel the tension and fear begin to build. He tried to make
idle chat with the driver but couldn't keep it up as he
entered the world of real criminals, a world that was
totally alien to him. Nothing was further from the truth.
Jason felt like a coward, a scab, the lowest of the low for
betraying his only brother to a face like Freddie Gant.
When the cab turned into Wardour Street Jason asked the
driver to pull over. He decided that walking the rest of
the way might give him time to compose himself. After
paying his fare Jason set off into a part of London that
he'd never stepped foot in before. Wardour Street was
filled with offices occupied by property developers,
interior designers and film and television companies.
When he passed a smart building with the name 'La
Plante Productions' emblazed above the doors Jason
smiled to himself. This was one name he did recognise
and for all intent and purpose what he was about to do
would have made a good story for this particular
company. Continuing along he passed the well know
nightclubs Trap, St Moritz and Camouflage. These
places seemed a world away from Camden Palace and the
others that he, Vinny, Mango, Pauly and Terry had been
so proud to frequent all those years ago. Turning left
onto Brewer Street, saw the scene change again with

Madam Jojo's club taking centre stage, flanked by restaurants and cafes, catering for all types and tastes. Weird names like Jumbo Eats, Kulu Kulu Sushi and Wok to Walk were mounted in bold letters above each of the premises and Jason thought to himself that whoever had come up with the names needed their heads testing. After continuing just a short distance further he glanced across the road and saw the sign for Bridle Lane. He could feel the bitter taste of bile begin to rise in his throat and would have given anything to have been able to turn around and walk away. Changing his mind wasn't an option and knowing it was something that definitely wasn't going to happen, he inwardly chastised himself for contemplating such a thought. Jason Frasier's legs felt like lead as he struggled to cross the road and a journey that should have taken seconds, seemed to last for minutes. The address he'd been given resembled a retail outlet more than an office. Its facade painted a shiny black gloss, looked menacing in the bright morning sunlight. Navy blinds over the window and door were pulled down tight to obscure anything that was happening on the other side. Trying the handle Jason wasn't surprised when he found the door locked. Nervously he rang the bell and waited to be let in. It was several seconds before he saw the door blind pulled back and a face peer out at him. Wally Evans looked just as frightening as he had on the prison visit and although Jason suspected that he could have a good row, he also guessed that Wally Evans had an IQ lower than the average goldfish. Holding open the door Wally didn't speak and Jason stepped inside without being asked. As the door closed behind him Jason heard the lock being engaged and turned back sharply. He knew that whatever happened from here on in, one way or another his fate was now sealed.

"Don't look so scared pal! Follow me the Guv'nor's waiting for you."

After passing the counter Jason was led into a back room where Freddie Gant sat behind a large highly polished desk.

"Well! Well! Well! Wally. Wonders will never fucking cease. He may be a robbing little bastard but at least he's a punctual one."

Freddie Gant laughed at his own joke but both Jason and Wally stayed silent. Jason's silence was out of pure contempt for the man sitting in front of him and Wally's was, well as usual Wally never really said much about anything. Freddie pointed to the chair that had been set out for him and Jason sat down.

"So then Mr Frasier what's it going to be?"

Jason stared blankly ahead. No matter how hard he tried he couldn't bring himself to say his brother's name, couldn't bear to just hand him over.

"Keep quiet for as long as you like mate but within the next few minutes, either I'll have your brother's whereabouts or your claret will be shed in this office. Now I don't really care which it is although I really would like me cash back and only one of those options will get it for me. If you choose to be a fucking hero and take the punishment then that's up to you because I can just go and see old aunty Maude and take her pub."

Jason's eyes opened wide in shock. He hadn't been told about the Camel and what Maude had agreed to do just in the hope of keeping him and Lisa safe.

"Don't tell me you weren't aware what the old gal has done for you? Stupid question really, I can see by the look on your face that you had no idea she'd put the pub up as collateral."

Jason just shook his head.

223

"Well there you fucking go mate! but that's life so what's it going to be you or him?"

"It's not as easy as that Mr Gant. Vinny's my flesh and blood and besides I have unfinished business with him. I need to see him and sort things out."

"What you really mean is buy more fucking time so the pair of you can do a runner with my money."

"No no! It's nothing like that."

Freddie's patience was fast running out and as he gave the usual nod in Wally Evan's direction Jason was alert enough to notice. Standing up he quickly backed himself into the corner of the room and put his hands up hoping to gain a few seconds of time.

"Please! Just hear me out. While I was banged up Vinny came back and raped my wife."

"Oh how my heart bleeds, she'll get over it."

"No she won't Mr Gant because the cunt infected her with H.I.V!"

Before Freddie could react and completely out of character Wally Evans voice could be heard.

"Fucking hell! Poor little cow!"

Freddie didn't chastise his employee for the interruption. As hard as he was Freddie Gant for the first time in his life felt real sympathy for another human being.

"If what you're saying is true and believe me I'll fucking check, then I can see your predicament. Wait in the front of the shop while I make a call."

Wally led Jay out and they both stood in silence waiting to be called back in. Freddie dialled the Camels number and luckily due to Lisa feeling unwell again the two women had cancelled their shopping trip.

"It's Freddie."

"I wondered when I'd hear from you, phoned to gloat have you? Well you listen to me Fredrick Ga...."

224

Freddie didn't give his aunt chance to complete her sentence.

"No I haven't and your precious boy is still intact, for the time being anyway. No the reason I phoned is to check out something he told me. Now I don't know if he's just concocted this little tale to get himself off the hook or whether it's the truth."

"Jason doesn't lie."

"Don't he now? Well we'll soon find out won't we. I want you to give me all the facts."

"What facts? I ain't got the foggiest idea what you're on about?"

"If he's telling the truth Aunty then you will be aware of everything."

Suddenly Maude realised that Jason had told her nephew about Lisa and the rape. She didn't exactly know why but accepted that her boy must have his reasons. Without further hesitation Maude Shelton relayed all the sorry details to her nephew. A few minutes later and Freddie Gants voice could be heard calling the two men back into his office. Once again he pointed to the chair and once again Jason silently took a seat.

"Seems your story is true Mr Frasier but as sad as it is, it don't give me back my money now does it?"

Jason swallowed hard.

"I can try and get it back for you or at least what's left of it."

As Freddie Gant's eyes narrowed Jason realised his last four words had been a mistake.

"I mean hopefully he won't have spent much but I need some time. I now know where he is but if you knew my brother you'd know that I have to get him on side, get him to trust me. I swear on my life that I won't try and shaft you, I have far too much at stake. As soon as I can

225

I'll call with a place you can find him but after that I want nothing more to do with it."

Freddie nodded his head.

"Ok you've brought yourself some breathing space but me and Wally will be keeping a watchful eye over your wife while you're away. Do you understand what I'm saying?"

"Yes I understand and thank you Mr Gant. I'm truly sorry for all the trouble my brother has caused you really I am."

Jason walked towards the door that Wally Evans now held open. About to step through and return to relative safety, he turned to face Freddie Gant one more time.

"I would ask one favour of you Mr Gant."

Freddie Gant grinned at the nerve of the man.

"You are one cheeky cunt Frasier but fire away."

"When it's all over will you let me know?"

Freddie didn't speak but he did nod his head in a way that told Jason his request would be granted. Out on the street Jason felt nothing but pure relief as if a weight had been lifted. He was well aware that the worst was yet to come and he had no idea how he was going to react when he saw his brother again. For the moment he would savour the calm and decided to take a walk before returning to the Camel and his dying wife. As Wally Evans relocked the door and made his way back to the office he was smiling. For once the good guy was getting a result and it was something he was happy to see, that and the fact that when he got hold of Vincent Frasier he would take revenge like never before.

"Well done boss that was a fucking lovely gesture, you're a real diamond geezer for doing that."

"I don't know about that Wal, I think I need me fucking head examining. Maybe I'm getting soft in my old age."

"Never but a bit of compassion goes a long way and if this ever gets out it won't do your street cred any harm. People love a story that pulls at the heart strings and that fucker certainly pulled at mine."

Freddie Gant stood up and walking around the desk, proceeded to pat Wally on the back.

"Street cred? That remains to be seen old pal that remains to be seen."

CHAPTER TWENTY THREE

Lisa stood in the back hall nervously biting her finger nails. When Jason's key could be heard turning in the lock she ran towards the door and hardly gave him time to step inside before she flung her arms around his neck.

"Thank god, oh baby thank god you're home."

Jason laughed and playfully pulled her arms from his neck.

"Of course I am, where else did you think I'd go. Mind you I did toy with the idea of going off with that little blonde heiress that keeps stalking me but then I thought against it besides no one makes a cuppa like you."

Lisa punched him in the shoulder and he reeled back in mock pain.

"Just you remember Jason Frasier that as sick as I am I can punch as good as any woman."

As soon as the words were out of her mouth the relaxed moment was spoiled. They looked at each other and knew that from now on this was how things were going to be. From now on, they would both be treading on egg shells every single day. He hugged her close and she nestled into his chest never wanting him to let him go. This was a new feeling to Jason Frasier but sadly it was a feeling that wouldn't last very long. He'd hoped for years that one day he would be able to hold his wife and that she would be willing for him to do so but he would never have wished for it under these circumstances.

"Where's the Duchess?"

"Up in the flat, she'll be so pleased to see you. We didn't get any shopping done so we can go and cheer her up if you like."

"Lisa I need to have a quiet word with Maude alone."

Lisa pulled away sharply.

"You're shutting me out again Jay, what's going on?"

"Nothing babe but I just have a few loose ends to tie up and then I'll be all yours."

Lisa Frasier smiled up at him. She was imagining that in a few minutes everything would be sorted out and she would at last have her husband to herself. It had seemed like forever since they had spent any quality time together and her excitement was such that she didn't feel she could wait much longer, little did she know that Jason's tying up a few loose ends would mean several days away from her.

"Ok babe but don't be too long will you?"

He didn't answer but gave her a wink that sent shivers down her spine. Her feelings weren't of a sexual nature, that part of life had long since been shut down by her own body. No Lisa's feelings were ones of pure love, safe in the knowledge that for as long as she lived she would never be alone again, for however long that was.

Maude Shelton was lying on the settee when Jason entered the flat. Sitting up she was about to stand when he stopped her.

"Don't get up Duchess you look really comfy."

Maude couldn't enter into idle chit chat she was too desperate to know what had occurred with her wayward nephew.

"So?"

"Well for once I think things are going my way."

"For god's sake, why ever did you tell that ponce about Lisa?"

"I didn't have any choice if I wanted to walk out of there alive, anyway I think Gant has a heart in there after all."

Maude Shelton rubbed at her brow.

"I doubt that very much. In all the years I've known him

229

I ain't never seen an ounce of humanity in the little wanker."

Jason laughed. With all that was going on Maude was still able to raise a smile from him.

"So what happens now?"

"Now I have to go and see my brother and hand him over to Gant on a plate. Believe me Duchess if there had been any other way I would have taken it. Right up until I walked in the fucking place I didn't know if I could go through with it but then I thought of Lisa and what he had done to her. Then it somehow didn't seem so wrong but I don't know how I'm going to feel when it actually comes down to it."

"You could always change your mind son."

"That ain't an option. He more or less told me that while I'm away he's going to make sure Lisa don't go anywhere and besides there's this place to think about."

Maude couldn't hide the surprise and her face showed it.

"Yeah, I know that you put this place up as collateral and for that alone I will be eternally grateful."

"I don't want gratitude Jay this place is nothing without you and Lisa. After Geoff died I thought I was happy, thought I could build a new life for myself but I wasn't kidding anyone. I was lonely Jay, lonelier than you could ever imagine and when you came back into me life everything seemed brighter. Maybe deep down what I did was for selfish reasons but I'd do it again without batting an eyelid. This could still all go tits up and I could lose this place but you know what Jay? I don't give a toss as long as I've got you two."

Jason hugged the older woman as if she was his mother. For an instant he thought of his real mum and was filled with guilt that he hadn't given Vera a second thought in all of this. Fleetingly she had entered his head but as

230

quick as she'd appeared he made the image disappear. "Duchess you've been there for me more than my own mother and as far as I'm concerned that's exactly what you are."

Maude Shelton's eyes brimmed with tears; she'd waited years hoping that one day he'd look upon her in that way. "Have you told Lisa you're going away?"

"Not yet. I'll do it in a minute but I ain't looking forward to it I can tell you."

When Jason entered their room Lisa lay on the bed in her pyjamas and fluffy dressing gown which made her look so snugly and inviting. Lying down beside her he felt so close to her, so in tune with her suffering and knew that if he didn't pull himself together, then any second his own heart would break. This nightmare wasn't real, it couldn't be happening. Long ago Jason had realised that life was a bitch but to do this to Lisa after all that she'd been through in her short time on earth was more than cruel, it was downright sadistic.

"Did you sort everything out with Maude?"

"Yeah, now shush and go to sleep."

"I don't care if I never sleep again as long as you're beside me."

Jason held onto his wife as tightly as was comfortable. Tomorrow would be time enough to break her heart; now was for closeness and cuddles. If things didn't go to plan then tonight could end up being their last together and Jason wanted to make the most of it. For the first time in days they both slept soundly and when Jason woke he was still holding his wife in his arms. Lisa stirred and he kissed her tenderly on the lips.

"Morning babe."

"Morning! I had a wonderful dream last night Jay."

"Did you sweetheart?"

231

"Yeah, we were at the beach and the sun was shining and it was just perfect. We walked along the sand and the wind was in our hair and we were so free Jay. I wish we could be in that dream for real."

"Maybe we will one day honey. Now how about you put some clothes on and we have some breakfast?"

"Ok."

When Lisa reappeared she was washed dressed and ready for the day but Jason's next sentence knocked her for six.

"I have to go away for a few days love."

"Away! But you said that once you'd tied up a few loose ends then that was it."

"And it will be but those ends are going to take a couple of days to sort out. Oh Lisa don't look at me like that."

"How do you expect me to look? Jay my life is running out and you just seem to be avoiding the inevitable. Don't you want to spend some time with me?"

"It's not that babe but it's just something I have to do. Trust me on this please!"

"I ain't got much choice in the matter have I?"

Lisa wasn't convinced; she loved and trusted her husband but a sixth sense told her things weren't right. Brushing those feelings to the back of her mind she smiled at him. Since the day they had married Lisa Frasier had known that Jason, her beautiful loving Jay would never knowingly hurt her for the world.

"Do whatever you have to babe as long as you swear you'll come back to me?"

"I swear! Nothing could stop me being with you but I have to sort this out."

Within half an hour they'd eaten and Jason had packed a small overnight bag. Walking him to the door Lisa suddenly stopped and turned towards her husband.

"I know to try and stop you would just tear us apart but

232

promise me one thing."

"What?"

"Don't take any chances Jay."

"I promise."

With those last words he was gone and she wondered if this was the end.

As Lisa broke her heart to Maude and relayed all that had happened, Jason was boarding a train to Cambridge. A train, that would seal his brother's fate and begin a nightmare for him. The journey was non descript and as the carriage chugged along all that Jason could think of was betrayal. He was aware that he had to have retribution for Lisa but at the same time he had known Vinny all of his life and in a way it was ironic. Jason Frasier had spent his whole life protecting his brother, would have died for him in fact, now here he was having a hand in Vinny's death. He'd never been a religious sort but as the train moved forwards Jason stared out of the window at the sky above and silently asked God why. Ok he'd been a jack the lad and at times, brought trouble home to his mothers door, albeit small misdemeanours. Now in the cold light of day, after everything was put into perspective, he hadn't been too bad, just gone off the rails a bit that was all. For some reason he felt as though God was punishing him but for the life of him Jason couldn't think why.

When the train pulled into the station there was a lot less movement on the platform than back home in the Smoke. Asking directions from a friendly looking porter he was told that his destination was only a few roads away. Everywhere was relatively quiet and hassle free and as the weather was fine he decided against a taxi and opted to walk instead. Carrying just his small overnight bag he made his journey to The Cumberland Hotel. On arrival

Jason was warmly greeted by Trevor Hayes whose eyes lit up when the handsome stranger walked in.

"Good day Sir and how can I be of help?"

"I'm here on a short visit and I thought I'd surprise my brother. I believe he's a guest of yours?"

"And who might that be Sir?"

"Vincent Frasier."

Just as he had in the telephone conversation with Maude, Trevor Hayes plastered on a smile and proceeded to go on about what a nice man Vincent was and how it had been a pleasure having him as a guest. For a moment Jason thought there must be another Vincent Frasier staying here, that or his brother had gone through a personality transplant. He stood patiently and listened as the man continued to babble on but was finally rescued when Melvyn Hayes appeared from the back room.

"Trevor! For goodness sake you've been going on and on for the last five minutes! Give your mouth a rest for a moment. I'm sorry about my husband but he does tend to get a little over excited when we have a new guest."

Jason couldn't believe his ears, did this man just say 'my husband'. He wanted to laugh but knew that would be an insult to the people and after all he did need a favour and they were being very welcoming.

"Vincent's out at work at the moment but if you'd like to wait in his room, I'm sure that would be fine. It's a double so there's plenty of room."

"Melvyn and I have even slept in there and it's very spacious and......"

Melvyn Hayes slammed his hand down onto the counter. "There you go again! Trevor do stop running on and please don't interrupt when I'm speaking to a guest. Now then Mr Frasier as I was saying before I was so rudely interrupted."

Jason's ears had taken quite a bashing and by now he wasn't listening to a word being said. He desperately struggled to hold the laughter inside and wondered how Vinny had coped staying here, what with him always having been so homophobic or at least that was what Jason had been led to believe. After being shown to room ten and told that Vincent didn't usually return from work for another couple of hours, Jason lay on the bed and decided to take a nap. He slept for the whole two hours and was only woken by the sound of the door being opened. Sitting up he wiped the sleep from his eyes and was in time to see his brother enter with a look of sheer horror on his face. Vincent Frasier didn't say a word he just stared as if he was seeing a ghost sitting on his bed. As Jason looked deep into his brother's eyes, all the hatred of the last few days started to build up. Just the image of his brother raping his wife was enough to make him feel physically sick and there and then he was quite capable of committing murder. Instead of allowing those feelings to surface he held back his repulsion and instead smiled.

"Nice to see you as well mate!"

Vinny took a few steps further into the room but still kept enough distance for an easy escape. He eyed up his brother wearily but was unable to tell if he knew what had occurred. At the same time Jason could feel the tension and for a second feared that Vinny may turn and run.

"Vin whatever's the matter? Cat got your fucking tongue or what?"

"No it's just a bit of a shock that's all, you know you turning up here out of the blue."

"Yeah I know sorry about that mate. When I got released from clink Maude and Lisa started giving me a load of

235

fucking ear ache. So I thought to myself that a few days away wouldn't go amiss and who better to go and see than me baby brother. If it's going to cause you a problem I can always go?"

"Nah mate of course not."

"Well come here then and give us a hug. It's good to see you bro."

As Jason wrapped his arms around Vincent his brother immediately reciprocated the show of emotion but if Vinny could have seen the sneer on Jason's face it would have been a different story.

"It's great to see you too Jay but you're not going to ask me to take the fucking loot back are you?"

"What to Gant? No, he can go fuck himself but I must admit things did get a little hairy back in the Smoke for a while. When he realised that I didn't know where you were he kind of left things alone but I don't think he's going to give up looking for you."

Vinny nodded in the direction of the wardrobe.

"I've hardly touched the money so he's going to have a hard job. What say we get out of this shithole of a country and start fresh somewhere new?"

"Let's just see how things go Vin, I ain't made any firm plans yet."

Hearing that the cash was almost intact and now knowing where it was kept was like music to Jason's ears. For the time being all he had to do was play his part of the doting brother just a bit longer.

"I was thinking, until we sort things out how about having a bit of fun? I almost went fucking stir crazy in Belmarsh, so I could do with spreading me wings a bit. While I was waiting for you to get back I looked at some of the tourist leaflets. Did you know that Newmarket race course is only fifteen miles away, fancy a little flutter tomorrow?"

Vincent Frasier smiled from ear to ear.

"Now you're talking bro! I knew you'd come back to me Jay, I knew that little whore wouldn't keep you happy forever."

It took every ounce of strength Jason had to hold his rage inside but he was sure Vinny hadn't noticed any change in his expression.

"What say I have a shower and then we go grab a bite to eat? It's the weekend tomorrow and the world is our oyster."

"Sounds good to me."

While Vincent Frasier cleaned himself up Jason stepped out into the hall and dialled Freddie Gants number. It only rang once before the receiver was snatched up by Wally Evans.

"Yeah?"

On hearing Jason's voice Wally was taken aback that the man had done the business so soon. He listened to everything that was said and when Jason told him that they would be at the Rowley Mile course at Newmarket the following day he grinned. It was arranged that Jason would stand somewhere around the parade ring ten minutes before the first race, so that Wally could get a good look at Vinny. Replacing the receiver, Wally turned towards his boss.

"Fancy a little day trip to the races tomorrow Gov?"

CHAPTER TWENTY FOUR

The mini cab that had been booked for ten that morning was punctual and the brothers chatted away on the drive over to Newmarket. Jason did his best to act normal as he didn't want anyone to think things were strained. If people were interviewed at a later date, and that included their driver, he wanted everything to look as it should be. He was well aware that questions would probably be asked and that the Old Bill might even get involved, so he knew he had to cover his tracks and try to act like the perfect brother.

Approaching the course and leaning forward in his seat Jason inquired as to any good hotels the driver might be able to recommend.

"Bit pricey in these parts mate but the Rutland Arms isn't too bad. Out on your jollies are you?"

"That's right and if we have a few jars too many then we might just crash here tonight."

"Might we?"

This revelation was news to Vinny and for a second he became a bit suspicious and eyed Jason with caution.

"Well I don't know about you Vin but being as I've only got a few days of freedom planned I'm going to make the most of it."

The driver laughed out loud. They were all mug punters and all the same no matter where they came from.

"Got a reprieve from the old woman have you mate?"

"Yeah something like that."

"Well then I don't blame you, in fact I might even park the cab up and have a bit of a flutter with you two boys. I'm lucky in that respect; I'm single see and only have myself to please."

238

Inwardly Jason groaned, this was all he needed but to try and put the bloke off might seem a little odd so instead of protesting he just smiled. As luck would have it things panned out exactly as Jason had hoped. The long driveway on the approach to the Rowley Mile course was jam packed with traffic. Rooting about in the glove compartment for his fake disabled parking badge the driver took his eyes off the road for a second and crunch; he went straight into the back of the car in front. The car behind immediately slammed on its brakes but it was too late and it rear ended the taxi. All three drivers instantly got out of their vehicles and were arguing fiercely as to whose fault it was. Vinny stared at Jason and started to laugh.

"Fucking twats! Fancy walking the rest of the way? I can see buildings at the end so it can't be that far. It's certainly going to be quicker than waiting for these Muppets to sort themselves out."

Strolling over to the driver, whose face was growing redder with every second, the brothers settled their fare and made a hasty retreat.

"Bit of fucking luck that Jay. I thought were going to get saddled with that tosser for the rest of the day."

Jason breathed a sigh of relief but for totally different reasons to that of his brother.

"Me too. Mind you I wouldn't have minded staying around for a few more minutes , there's going to be a right row. Our driver looked fit to burst and I thought the guy from the car in front was going to crack him one any second."

"Bit like your normal Saturday night down the Camel then."

Jason laughed. His brother always seemed to be able to bring a smile to his face and instantly his guts felt as

239

though they were being ripped out at the thought of what he was about to do. They continued to stroll along but now they were silent as both took in the beautiful open view of the countryside. When they finally arrived at their destination Jason was spitting feathers and in dire need of a drink. The pedestrian entrance stretched out before them like some Victorian avenue from an old movie. Red tarmac covered the ground and a sea of green ornate street lamps were evenly distributed along both sides.

"Fuck me Vin, this is a bit posh ain't it?"

Vinny grinned.

"We're in a different league now bro, we have money and plenty of it! No more slumming it for us. From now on we're going to live like fucking millionaires."

"Don't get carried away mate we ain't won the lottery."

"Maybe not but for however long Gants money lasts us it's going to fucking seem like we have."

Vincent Frasier slapped his brother on the back as he pulled a large wad of twenty pound notes from his jacket pocket.

"Here you are! Just a little taster of what's to come."

Apart from saying thanks, Jason couldn't bring himself to enter into more conversation. It was getting harder by the minute and took all of his steel just to appear normal. Passing the old grandstand and the new Millennium one, they proceeded towards the member's enclosure.

"Vinny what are you doing? We can't get in there."

"Watch and learn Jay, watch and learn."

Soon they were approached by a steward who asked for their members badges. Vincent Frasier casually removed a crisp twenty pound note from the roll he was holding and pressed it into the man's palm. As if by magic the gate was held open for them and as they passed through.

240

Jason could only shake his head, he knew that Vinny could have paid for an upgrade and that he was just being flash but then that was Vinny all over. It had always been the same, whatever his brother wanted he always got well not this time he would make sure of that. Several buildings encircled the parade ring and were built in red brick with a fusion of Georgian and deco architecture. Jason Frasier's scanned each one and his eyes darted in all directions looking for Wally Evans. For a second he thought he could make out the man's figure but it turned out to be just another race goer. The weather wasn't exceptionally warm but even so he could feel himself begin to perspire and hoped that his brother wouldn't notice. A life size bronze of some famous horse or another stood on a granite plinth for all to see and Vinny walked over to it. Stretching out his hand he gave the statue a rub for luck before heading back to where Jason stood.

"Fancy a flutter on the first race bro?"

"Nah I think I'll just stand here and get a feel for things. Maybe on the next one but you go ahead mate. Feeling lucky?"

"When you're by my side I'm always lucky Jay and besides there's a bloke on the building site who's in a syndicate."

"So?"

"Well as it happens they've been waiting for a particular horse to run. Lightning Strike's it's called and apparently its running times have been bleeding phenomenal, can't lose."

"Fuck me Vin, if I had a tenner for every time I've heard that one I'd be a millionaire!"

"Honest Jay it's a dead cert, no ways it going to lose. I need to keep an eye out because they said there's going to

241

be a big bet laid on it so we need to get the early price. I'm just going to take a gander at the set up, back in a minute."

Jason watched as his brother walked towards the rows of on course bookies and again a massive feeling of guilt began to well up inside him. It would be strange to most but as much as Jason Frasier hated his brother for all that he'd done he also loved him dearly. Suddenly realisation hit him that this would probably be the last day they would ever spend together, in this life anyway. Turning back to the ring he once more began to scan the crowd and instantly spotted Freddie Gant standing at the rails opposite. Smartly dressed in a three piece suit, his outfit was topped off by a trilby style hat and camel coat. Jason thought he looked more like a horse owner or trainer than the gambler he was trying to portray. As the two men's eyes met Freddie gently gave a nod of his head in recognition, a nod that to most would have gone unnoticed. Wally Evans as always stood close behind his boss and he too had seen Jason.

"There we go all done! Now we've just got to wait for the fucking cash to come rolling in."

Jason had been concentrating so hard that his brother's words made him jump.

"Fuck me you're a bit twitchy ain't you?"

Jason had to think fast.

"No not at all Vin. I was deep in thought about Lisa and got a bit carried away."

"Not that little bitch again, I don't know why you fucking bother just forget about her."

Jason stared across the ring, desperate to see if the two men had clocked his bother.

"I'm trying mate, really trying."

Wally Evans nodded his head and Jason knew that he had

completed his part of the task and that the plan was now in motion and totally out of his hands. He felt helpless and even though he knew that nothing could stop things deep down he so desperately wanted to try. The only way he was able to deal with his demons was to dismiss the thought of him and Vinny running every time the idea came into his head. Nudging it aside he replaced the thought with visions of Lisa and what she had been through and would continue to go through for the rest of her life. The next hour seemed to be the longest in history for Jason Frasier. He placed a bet but his heart wasn't in it, luckily Vinny's was and he almost screamed with enthusiasm when his horse came in. Standing close to the finish line, the roar from the crowds as the winning horse approached was amazing and each time Vincent Frasier acted like a small child. His excitement would normally have been infectious but nothing he did could get his brother to join in.

"Fuck me Jay you're about as much fun as a wet weekend in Clacton. I'm starting to wonder why you even fucking suggested a day out in the first place. Come on, have another flutter, maybe your luck might be on the turn. Enjoy yourself for once!"

Jason knew that if he didn't buck his ideas up Vinny would start to suspect something, so reluctantly he smiled and placed an arm around his brother's shoulder.

"That's better! Now you just follow old Vinny and you won't go wrong."

As Vincent pushed another large bundle of notes in his brother's direction Jason prayed that Freddie Gant had taken a break from watching them. If the man thought they were throwing his cash away then there was no telling what he might do right here in front of everyone.

"What's this?"

"Five grand."

"Fucking five grand!, are you barmy or what?"

"Look Jay, just trust me on this. Go over there to the bookie and place it all on 'Lightning Strike's at six to one."

"All of it?"

"Yes all of it. Bet you've never put that much on a nag before have you? Go on mate go see what it feels like you'll enjoy it."

Jason slowly walked to where the bookies had all set up their pitches. Every few seconds he would glance back over his shoulders to look at his brother and see Vinny nodding his head and flicking his hands as if to say 'Go on'. Vincent Frasier thought the scene was hilarious and continued laughing about it for several minutes. Standing in front of the small pitch that brightly displayed in bold letters 'The Punters Choice', Jason stared up at the long list of horse's names. His mind was blank and he couldn't for the life of him remember what the nag was called.

"What's it to be guv'nor?"

"I can't remember mate. Me brothers given me this but I've forgot which horse. I know he said something about a six but that's about it."

When the bookie spotted the bundle of cash his eyes saw nothing but pound signs and he was desperate not to lose the punt.

"Well there's 'Strike A Lite' at twelve to one, its number six on the list so it could be that I suppose?"

Jason really wasn't sure but if he went back without placing the bet then Vinny would be really pissed off. Today was bad enough, without having to continue with his brother in a foul mood.

"Yeah Ok mate. I think that one rings a bell."

244

Jason reluctantly handed over the money and after getting his ticket pushed it into his pocket and walked back to where Vincent stood.

"There you go mate, weren't that hard now was it?"

Just before the off Vinny suggested that they move down to the front for a better view. The horses were led towards the stalls but for some reason Lightning Strike's started to play up and no matter how hard the handler leading him tried, the horse just wouldn't go into the stalls. After the third attempt Lightning Strike's was withdrawn and the race started without him. Vincent Frasier cursed and stamped his feet to such a degree that people started to look at him. It wasn't the fact that he'd lost the money but purely that he couldn't bear to lose at anything he did.

"Calm down Vin!"

"Fucking calm down?"

As the race reached the final furlong the crowd went into overdrive and the sound was deafening. The tannoy announced that the winner was number six Strike A Lite.

"We've won Vin! We've only gone and bleeding won!"

"What you talking about that was Strike A Lite. Our horse was fucking Lightning Strike's."

"Bit of a confession there I'm afraid. See when I went to put the bet on I was in two minds about the amount and forgot what the horse was called. Seems I placed it on the wrong nag, here have a butchers."

Jason removed the betting slip from his pocket and the brothers both inspected it before screaming with joy which forced everyone to turn and look at them.

"That's sixty five grand! I could kiss you Jay. You know bro you always seem to do right by me no matter what."

Jason Frasier didn't have to have a sixth sense to know

245

that they were being continually watched. As Freddie
Gant monitored the two through his binoculars he could
see that by their behaviour they must have had a nice
little touch. Jason scanned the course but could no longer
see Gant or his side kick. It made him feel uneasy as he
had no idea how things were supposed to pan out.
Naively he had imagined that it would be at the race
course but thinking about it now that would have been
impossible. As the day drew to a close and the brothers
once more made their way along the red tarmac walkway
Jason's eyes darted in all directions.
"You're a bit fucking jumpy Jay! What's the matter?"
Jason could have kicked himself. He had fought tooth
and nail all day to keep his composure and now when
things were possibly coming to a close he was letting his
guard down.
"Nah I'm alright mate. I was just looking for a taxi that's
all."
Vincent Frasier watched his brother out of the corner of
his eye. He knew Jason too well and things weren't right
but here they were surrounded by thousands of people so
he couldn't see how it was anything to be suspicious
about. Within a few minutes they struck gold and had
jumped into the first available minicab. Jason seemed to
relax a bit and Vinny noticed this which made him realise
that he had probably read his brother all wrong.
"Right Jay, lets enjoy ourselves!"
"How about a club, there's a couple of good ones in
Cambridge."
"Nah, I quite fancied staying round here tonight and
having a few jars. I'm probably going to head back to the
smoke tomorrow so let's make a night of it here, what do
you think?"
"Yeah, why not. Can you remember the name of the

hotel that prat from this morning recommended?"

"Yeah. Driver, can you take us to the Rutland Arms please."

The Frasier brothers along with their driver, were totally unaware of the black Jaguar that had been discreetly following them since they had left the course. Freddie Gant sat solemnly in the front passenger seat and Wally Evans was in the back. The car was being driven by one of the bodies that Freddie hired from time to time. Tony Dwyer had a wife, three kids and one on the way, so any extra work was always welcome. He was well aware what Freddie Gant and his henchman were capable of and sometimes it didn't sit well with Tony. The only way he could be a party to any of their kind of skulduggery, was by reminding himself that putting food on the table for the kids was more important than some little ponce getting a slap. Besides he'd always had a saying and it was one he strongly believed in, 'Live by the sword, die by the sword' and anyone mixed up with and prepared to cross the likes of Freddie Gant probably deserved all that was coming to them. Less than ten minutes later the cab pulled up outside a rather posh Georgian building in the heart of Newmarket. It had once been a coaching inn but over recent years had promoted itself to a more up market establishment.

"This looks a bit of alright Jay! Right tasty."

Entering the elaborate foyer Jason headed in the direction of the reception. Vinny followed close behind but couldn't resist poking his head into the grand panelled dining room.

"This'll do for me Jay. A full English served up in there tomorrow will go down a real treat."

Jason didn't reply, he couldn't. He felt a lump form in his throat at the thought of this being Vinny's last day on

247

earth.

"Can I help you Sir?"

The young girl seated behind the desk had a pleasant homely face and she smiled genuinely as she spoke.

"I was wondering if you had a room for the night for me and my brother. We don't mind sharing so a double will do."

"Let's have a look. Yes we can accommodate you tonight Sir are there any special requests?"

Vinny moved in beside his brother and the sound of his smarmy voice suddenly irritated Jason like never before.

"Can we have a safety deposit box?"

"No problem Sir. Now is there anything else I can help you with?

"Nah we're pretty easy going sweetheart."

Jason remembered the instructions he'd received from Wally Evans and smiling at the receptionist inquired if there were any good clubs nearby?

"There's De Nero's and club M, I can personally recommend either. When you leave the Hotel, turn right and they're about half a mile down the road. If you'd like I could order you a taxi?"

Jason jumped in before Vinny had chance to open his mouth again.

"No that's fine darling the walk will do us good."

"Then here is your key and I just have to remind you that this is a totally non smoking establishment but there is a designated smoking area at the side of the building should you wish to use it. I hope you both enjoy your stay at the Rutland Arms."

Vinny snatched the key from the young woman's hand and his manner wasn't friendly.

"Fuck me! We're paying a king's ransom for a poxy room and we can't even have a smoke in it. Come on Jay

248

let's put the cash away and then get out of here."
Vincent Frasier was in desperate need of a cigarette and
as they turned the corner of the building and headed
towards the smoking area Jason saw the black Jag and
knew that things were about to kick off. Leaning up
against the wall, Vinny had just lit up a Marlboro and was
inhaling deeply as the car pulled up in front of them.
While the brothers had been booking in Wally Evans had
thoroughly cased the outside of the hotel. Satisfied that
there was no close circuit television, at least not on this
side of the building, he was happy to proceed. Vinny had
no reason to be alarmed as he'd never seen Freddie Gant
or Wally before. Wally got out of the back door and
Freddie tipped his hat in recognition of Jason. At that
moment the cigarette fell from Vinny's mouth.
"Fucking hell!"
Those were the only words to escape Vinny's mouth
before he was bundled into the back of the car. When
Freddie beckoned for Jason to get in as well his heart
skipped a beat. This wasn't supposed to happen but there
was little he could do now. If Freddie Gant was going to
renege on the deal they had made and Jason's life was
about to end as well then so be it because right at this
moment Jason Frasier felt so bad that he didn't really care
if he lived or died. The only thing he would really regret
and regret deeply, was not being able to say goodbye to
Lisa and Maude. The Jag pulled away at a slow pace so
as not to draw attention to the occupants and driving
along the main road there was nothing but silence inside
the car. Jason was just waiting to see what would happen
and Vinny was so paralyzed with fear that he wouldn't of
been able to speak even if he'd wanted to. He had
already worked out who the men were but hadn't or
couldn't accept that his own brother had set him up.

249

Finally he managed one word to his brother.
"Why?"
Wally instantly elbowed Vinny hard in the ribs; he
wouldn't allow any conversation to take place and one
look in Jason's direction told the man not to bother
answering. Just as the receptionist had said, the clubs
were less than half a mile away from the hotel. Freddie
had connections in Newmarket going way back and
happened to be on friendly terms with the owners of club
M. Pulling round the back and into the car park Tony
Dwyer stopped the car and switched the headlights off.
Due to the earliness of the evening the car park was
deserted and Freddie had it on good authority that they
wouldn't be disturbed. Freddie Gant now turned around
in his seat to face the men. He wore a thin hard smile but
his manner was gentle as he spoke.
"Well! Well! Well! We meet at last Vincent."
Vinny was again about to open his mouth when Wally
grabbed a handful of his hair and yanked his head
backwards.
"Don't speak cunt, not until Mr Gant tells you that you
fucking can."
Vinny swallowed hard but it was difficult and he tried
desperately to turn his head sideways to look at his
brother. Wally's grip was vice like and it was
impossible.
"Secure his hands Wal, then me you and Jason here are
going to take a little walk."
Wally Evans felt in his pocket and pulled out a long
plastic cable tie. Swiftly he tied Vinny's wrists together,
so tightly in fact that there was little chance of blood
being able to circulate let alone allow him to escape.
Leaning forward he handed Tony a handgun.
"If this slimy cunt moves an inch, shoot him!"

As he looked down at the Beretta 8mm automatic Tony saw his hand begin to shake. He hadn't signed up for this, a good kicking was one thing but murder? Still he knew better than to protest or he could easily end up in the same boat as the man sitting in the back seat. Freddie Gant wasn't known for his compassion and Tony wanted to live long enough to see his baby born. Freddie got out and held open the door for Jason. Stepping out of the car he took one last look at his brother whose eyes were now pleading for help.

"Please Jay why?"

Jason Frasier's brow furrowed and his face became hard. With or without Freddie Gant's permission he had no intention of entering into a conversation with Vinny and as he closed the door he had only two parting words.

"For Lisa!"

Jason slammed the door so hard that Tony Dwyer thought it was about to come off its hinges. Tony turned to face his prisoner and could see that the man was now crying. For a second his heart went out to Vincent Frasier, for all the good it would do him. Freddie and Jason made their way over to the clubs rear exit and all the while Jason could feel Wally Evans close behind.

"Worried Jason?"

"Do you know something Mr Gant, for some reason I ain't. If you're going to wipe me out then there ain't much I can do about it. The one consolation I'll have, if only for a short time, is knowing that I got retribution for my Lisa."

Freddie Gant grinned.

"Well it must be your lucky day because I have no intention of going back on me word. Now sooner or later there may be some heat come down and I want you to have a plausible story to tell the Old Bill if necessary.

You and your brother were on a night out and you got hit from behind, when you came round Vinny was nowhere to be seen."

"Ok Mr Gant and thanks."

"Don't fucking thank me you cheeky cunt and your lot ain't over with yet. Remember I want my money back and you'd better make it soon."

Jason didn't hear anymore. As Wally brought his fist complete with brass knuckle duster down hard on the back of Jason's skull he passed out. It would be a further two hours before he was found by a pair of the clubs waitresses who'd popped outside for a crafty cigarette before their shift began. Coming round Jason looked up at the girls but everything seemed to be swirling and he couldn't hear what they were saying to him.

"Come on mate you've had a bit of a shock. We've phoned the police and an ambulance, they'll be here in a minute. Get mugged did you?"

Looking at her friend the woman shook her head.

"I tell you something for nothing Alice, it's fucking coming to something when a person can't be out alone at night."

"I wasn't on my......."

"What are you saying love I can't understand you?"

Jason Frasier passed out again. Blood had run down his neck and was now congealed and dried. The girls didn't like the look of the injury and prayed that either of the emergency services would get here soon. Waking up in Newmarket general hospital, Jason put his hand up and felt the bandage that was wrapped tightly around his skull. He had the mother of all headaches but in the grand scale of things considered himself lucky. Jason wasn't on a ward but still in accident and emergency department so he wasn't surprised when two policemen looked round from the other side of the curtain.

"Hello Mr Frasier how are you feeling?"

"A bit sore, how's my brother?"

"Brother?"

Jason realised that Freddie's little plan had turned out well and he proceeded to explain that after a day at the races they had been on a night out and got mugged or at least he thought that's what had happened. Stan Harding, the senior of the two policemen instantly put out an APB of Vinny's description but told Jason there was little more they could do at this stage. Jason provided his home address and told them that all being well once he'd had an x-ray and was released he would head back to the Camel. Stan Harding reassured Jason that when and if they had any news it would be passed onto his local station at Bethnal Green and Jason would be informed immediately.

At just after one am Jason Frasier discharged himself from hospital. He did as he'd said and went home to London but not before a detour to the hotel to empty the safety deposit box. He then went on to Cambridge to collect the holdall that Vinny had hidden in the wardrobe. The holdall that Freddie Gant was so desperate to have returned and the one that Jason's life depended on.

CHAPTER TWENTY FIVE

The journey back to London would take less than an hour and a half. Freddie Gant was relaxing in the front seat and pulled his hat down over his face. Vinny thought he was sleeping but as usual he was wide awake and alert to every word that was being said. Tony Dwyer didn't utter a word, preferring to keep his nose out of business that didn't concern him and just concentrate on his driving. It was raining quite heavily and the last thing they needed was to be involved in an accident. Vincent Frasier was still seated in the back with Wally Evans. The cable ties were starting to cut deep into his wrists and a slight numbness had begun to set in. Vinny was desperate for a pee but his captures had no intention of stopping for a toilet break. He held on for as long as he could but finally the need to relieve himself was overwhelming. The interior of the car was chilly and when the hot urine was released a fine steam rose in the air. Freddie Gant removed his hat and sniffed.

"Fucking hell whatever's that smell?"

"Sorry Boss seems our little friend here has pissed himself."

"Oh that's just fucking brilliant that is. I've got the finest calf leather upholstery and it's now impregnated with that twats piss!"

Vinny could see his knees visibly begin to shake and he wondered just how long he could hold onto his other bodily fluids. He'd always been so good at dishing out pain but when it came down to himself it was a totally different story. He thought back to when he was a boy, when going to the dentist had been or at least as far as he was concerned, a life or death experience. Poor Vera had literally had to drag him there by the scruff of his neck. How he wished his dear old mum was here now. Up until this moment he hadn't missed her at all but right now he would have sold his soul to the devil to be tucked up in their little flat with Vera waiting on him hand and foot. The thought brought a smile to his face which really annoyed Wally Evans.

"Something funny cunt? Smile while you can sunshine because once we get back to the smoke you won't be so fucking smug."

Vinny didn't reply and instead stared straight ahead trying to focus and stay calm as he watched the wipers glide back and forth. As the first lights of the city started to appear it was just past nine thirty. The rain had at long last subsided and Tony Dwyer had begun to relax, so much so that he spoke for the first time in the entire journey.

"Brilliant! We're nearly home."

Freddie Gant laughed out loud.

"Fuck me Tone you sound as if you've been to outer Mongolia instead of eighty miles down the fucking road. I tell you what Wal, you can't half pick them."

Wally Evans also laughed which made Tony feel slightly embarrassed.

"Nah it ain't that Mr Gant but there's no place like home and if homes the Smoke then that's even better. I know we weren't far away but it still felt like the fucking sticks to me. I can't abide fucking carrot crunchers and all that boooootiful crap."

Wally couldn't resist a joke at the driver's expense.

"Tone you watch too much telly me old mukka. What'd you think fucking Bernard Matthews was going to pop up with a turkey under his fucking arm or what?"

Freddie Gant shook his head in amazement.

255

"You twat Wal, that's fucking Norfolk not Suffolk!"
"Norfolk, Suffolk. It's all the same to me Gov. They're all bleeding inbreeds as far as I'm concerned."
Everyone in the car except Vinny burst into fits of giggles. For Vinny time was running out and he was more than aware of that fact.
"Where are we heading Mr Gant?"
"You can take me back to Soho then it's wherever Wally wants to go. To be honest I ain't really interested as long as he gets rid of that piece of shit sitting in the back fucking soiling me seats."
"Soho it is then."
"Oh and Tone? Once you've dropped Wally off try and clean the motor will you. It fucking stinks in here."
Fifteen minutes later and the Jag arrived outside the Bridle Lane office. Getting out of the car Freddie Gant just closed the door and walked inside the building. He didn't give Vinny Frasier a second glance or even a second thought. As far as he was concerned it was just another little problem that would soon be sorted out.
Tony Dwyer drew away from the kerb and waited for directions from Wally. He wasn't the least bit surprised when he was told to go over to Hackney. Over the years Tony had gotten used to driving to all manner of places and this one wasn't out of the ordinary. A couple of times he'd been asked to take Wally and some other faces to farms in various parts of the country. Now that had been scary and he'd always stayed in the motor but the sound coming out of the barns was horrendous and at times he didn't think they were even human. Whatever happened inside these buildings never got talked about and as far as Tony was concerned he was happy for it to stay that way. The traffic was relatively light for the time of night and when they reached Cambridge Heath Wally

gave Tony Dwyer directions to Cassland Road and the Kings factory. Long before that Vinny had realised where they were going. It felt strange to know he was so close to his mother and that this was probably the last sight he would ever have of his home turf. Pulling up outside the factory Wally roughly dragged Vinny from the car and snatched up a Sports bag that had been stored under the front seat. After slamming the door he tapped on the cars roof, a signal to the driver that he could now leave and Tony Dwyer didn't need to be told twice. He hadn't had any conversation with the rear seat passenger and he was now sure that he never would. Pure relief washed over him as he pulled away into the night. Freddie Gant had sold Kings Lock stock and barrel to the Russians but unbeknown to them Wally Evans had kept hold of a spare key. Boris Worzine didn't mess around and had the place up and running again immediately after the sale but as yet hadn't reinstalled a twilight shift. Unlike Freddie, the Russians didn't keep so much as spare change on the property so that even after the robbery there was no need for added security. As far as Boris Worzine was concerned, the fewer people sniffing about the place the better. Wally removed a pair of thin surgical gloves from his pocket and placed them on his hands. He was always so careful regarding any evidence he might accidently leave for the Old Bill. With Tony now safely out of sight Wally cut Vinny's ties. Instantly adrenalin rushed through Vinny's veins and he knew that it was now or never if he wanted to make a run for it. He didn't get more than one foot in front of the other before Wally kicked at the back of his knees and brought him crashing to the ground.

"Try that again cunt and I'm going to make you suffer like you couldn't even imagine."

257

Removing another cable tie from his pocket Wally proceeded to re secure Vinny's hands again. This time he did it so that they were now behind his back. Wally frogmarched Vinny across the concrete yard but instead of going into the office he led his prisoner round the back to the old store shed. Vinny was now in so much pain as his arms had somehow twisted into an unnatural position behind his back. Almost at breaking point and in a strained voice he cried out.

"If you're going to stick the fucking boot in just get on with it will you."

"Now don't be impatient Vincent everything comes to those who wait."

Producing a key from his pocket, Wally grinned but the illumination from the bulkhead light on the wall made him look nothing but menacing. Even though he had the key the door wouldn't budge an inch. Grabbing hold of a handful of Vinny's hair he pushed upwards which made Vinny go onto the tip of his toes in pain but gave Wally more control. The place hadn't been used much over the years and everything had swelled or seized with age. Even his visit earlier in the week to check things out hadn't made much difference and Wally Evans found himself having to push hard on the door several more times. Finally he gave one last shove and the door creaked and gave up trying to compete with his heavy frame. While fighting to gain entry he never once eased his grip on Vinny's hair and several times as he banged against the door he pulled Vinny up with even more force. It was cold and dank and a musty smell hit Vincent Frasier's nostrils as soon as the night air seeped inside. Wally switched the light on and Vinny could see a solitary bulb hanging bleakly from the ceiling. A stainless steel table, similar to those used in the catering or hospital trade, had been placed in the middle of the room and directly beneath the light. Suddenly Vincent Frasier felt his bowls release and the overpowering stench filled the room. He wasn't ashamed or humiliated, in fact the only emotion he now felt was sheer and utter panic. Wally Evans began to cackle in an almost inhuman way.

"You dirty cunt, that fucking stinks."

Originally and before taking his final orders from Freddie, Wally had planned on some sick ritual incorporating Vinny's private parts. His boss had reminded him that no matter how disgusted they both felt regarding the things Vincent had done, that really wasn't any of their business. At first Wally had been more than a little disappointed but had cheered up when Freddie had given him precise instructions as to what he wanted done to Vincent Frasier. Wally placed his bag on the steel table and removed a pair of overalls, the type that painter s and workmen use. The material was light weight but durable and stepping inside them Wally pulled up the zip completely covering his clothes.

"Do they suit me?"

Again Wally cackled out loud.

"This ain't just to keep my suit clean you know. When I start releasing your claret I don't fancy catching a dose of that HIV you've been spreading about."

Vinny's eyes opened wide but strangely not at the mention of being harmed. He didn't for the life of him know what Wally Evans was talking about and it showed on his face.

"Don't tell me you didn't fucking know? Ha ha well that's fucking blinding that is, the fucking icing on the cake so to speak."

Wally pulled up an old bentwood chair that had been resting against the wall. After testing it for strength he

259

roughly forced Vincent down onto it. Wally placed a large piece of duct tape across Vinny's mouth, now he wouldn't even be able to plead for his life. Suddenly he straddled his victim and sat on his legs, the two men's faces were only centimetres away from each other. Vinny tried to turn his head away but was stopped when Wally again grabbed a large handful of his hair. Vinny could smell and feel the man's breath on his face. He was desperate for space as he fought the beast sitting on top of him with as much force as he could muster. For a second but only that, Vincent believed he was gaining ground as Wally Evans seemed to tire. Maybe it was all his years of violence starting to catch up with him but magically from out of nowhere his captor produced a syringe.

"Now then sonny, I think you're getting a little uptight don't you. A mild sedative is all you need."

Without any hesitation Wally Evans smoothly pushed the hypodermic straight into Vincent Frasier's neck.

"Now that's better, don't you agree?"

In seconds Vincent Frasier was calm beyond belief, his body seemed weightless and he knew he wouldn't be able to walk a single step without help. As every ounce of his mobility drained away Vincent stared straight ahead and the only thing he could manage was a single tear.

"Let me tell you a little story young Vincent, then probably you'll realise why your punishment is so severe and why I'm going to enjoy every minute of inflicting it."

Wally waited for some kind of response, some recognition of fear but there was none.

"Are you sitting comfortable cunt? Right then I'll begin. There was once a right tosser of a bloke, a real nasty bastard who had a diamond geezer of a brother. Now this nasty bastard wanted everything that the older brother had, including a taste of his Mrs. One day this nasty bastard just walked in and raped the woman, as cool as a cucumber he was and he didn't have any regard for her suffering or feelings. Anyway to cut a long story short as I'm sure you'd rather I got on with the matter in hand, he left her not only feeling ashamed and degraded but also with HIV. Now the poor cow ain't got long to live and her husband's heartbroken. Got anything to say in your defence?"

There was a moment's silence.

"Didn't think so. Now then let's get down to business." Even if he hadn't been drugged or silenced by the tape, Wally Evans had no intention of letting Vincent speak. There was absolutely nothing he could say that would have been able to justify what he'd done to the girl let alone stealing his boss's money. Several years earlier Freddie had carried out some business with a Manchester firm and Wally had been loaned out as a heavy. Unusually for him he had struck up a friendship with one of the other guys who was a martial arts fanatic. Seth Mumby had trained in several of the arts but his favourite was Ninjutsu. The speciality of this Japanese art was to embrace bushido, espionage and commando warfare. A ninja concealed his name, objectives and techniques, even to the point of death but for some reason Seth had allowed Wally into his inner sanctum. The lessons Wally learned had stood him in good stead over the years but none more so than now.

"Right, now let's begin. I'm going to wipe your eyes out young Vincent and there ain't a fucking thing you can do about it."

Wally placed his hands onto Vinny's cheeks and positioned a thumb in the corner of each eye. Pressing firmly in an almost hooking motion he didn't stop until they had both popped out and lay dangling down each cheek. Even through the duct tape Vinny began to emit a low muffled kind of scream and it was a sound Wally took pleasure in hearing. Unzipping the overalls just enough to reach inside his jacket pocket, Wally removed a stiletto switch blade knife and proceeded to cut off one eyeball and place it in the palm of his hand. With the remaining eye hanging by a thin thread of tissue Vinny was still able to see. Looking down he saw his severed eyeball sitting on his torturers hand and Vinny passed out. Wally didn't like to work alone and always preferred his victims to watch him carry out his work, almost to the end at least. Reluctantly, he gave Vinny a few moments before throwing water in his face to revive him. As Vincent Frasier came round Wally severed the other eye.

"Well you won't be fucking infecting anyone else now, not unless you can do rape by brail you cunt!"

Swiftly Wally pulled his victims head forward and placing the knife at the base of Vinny's neck, slowly but firmly pushed it in an upward movement into his brain. Blood seepage was minimal and death instantaneous. Standing up from the chair Wally took a moment to admire his work. He'd done a good neat job and a feeling of pride overcame him. Remembering his directive, he cut Vincent's cable tie and the body fell forward. Removing a large razor sharp meat cleaver from his bag he cut off the hands with a single blow to each. It would have been easy to dispose of the evidence by throwing everything in the acid tank just as he'd done with Roly Peterson but he'd had strict instructions from the boss that he must clean up and place the body in the stairwell of the Rickman Street flats. Freddie Gant wanted everyone to know that he had taken his revenge, credibility was everything in this game and Wally's actions would secure it in bucket loads. It would be the talk of the manor for years to come and everyone would know that if you coveted any of Freddie Gants possessions you would lose your eyes, steal from him and it would be your hands along with your life. Wally Evans placed Vinny's body in a large black plastic bag. Glancing down at the eyeballs and hands, he decided that there was no need to hold onto them. Spying a supermarket carrier that had been left on one of the shelves he placed the body parts inside and walking over to the tank, threw them in. He watched for a few seconds as the bag and contents began to bubble then slowly sink. An old Vauxhall Nova purchased from Jake the scrap man earlier in the week was already parked at the side of the factory. Picking up the body Wally left through the side gate and when he reached the car struggled with the dead weight as he placed it into the boot. With just a small amount of blood to wash away the job was nearly complete. The place had been well thought out and a high pressure hose connected to a tap on the outside wall did the job perfectly. Removing his overalls, Wally placed the tools of his trade back into the sports bag and after renewing his medical gloves with fresh, locked the door and climbed into the car. He was careful to remember the lights as the last thing he needed was a pull from the Old Bill, now that would really have upset the apple cart. It was just past midnight and the residents of Rickman Street were well and truly in a deep slumber. Switching off the lights and engine, Wally glided the car towards the pavement. He wasn't unduly worried about being seen by Joe public as everyone on this manor knew only too well what would happen to them if they even thought of speaking to the law let alone actually doing it.

263

It was also a fact that fighting and burning out cars was somewhat of a past time for the local youths, so whatever was happening outside was nothing out of the ordinary. The day had taken its toll on Wally Evans and he was now more than a little tired. Removing the carcass from the boot, he threw the body onto the floor and gave it a kick for good measure as he left. Retrieving the holdall he pulled out a small can of petrol and liberally doused the inside of the Vauxhall. Using the remaining petrol he led a trail down the street and after lighting a match and throwing it down, swiftly strolled away. Wally Evans didn't need to look back to make sure that the car burned, he heard the explosion as he turned the corner and made his way home.

CHAPTER TWENTY SIX

Betty Dale along with her husband Rodney, had been residents of the Rickman Street flats for nearly as many years as the Frasier family. She'd seen the boys grow into men and had encountered many a run in with their mother Vera. The two women had never been what anyone would deem friends but as the years passed they had agreed to a kind of tolerance that saw them nod to each other if their paths ever crossed on the stairs. Betty's job, cleaning at one of the offices on the Mile End Road over in Stepney Green, called for her to start each morning at six thirty sharp. She didn't mind getting up early as it meant she was home by nine and had enough time to prepare breakfast before her Rodney got up. Rodney Dale hadn't worked in years and his proclamation regarding his injured back to anyone who'd listen, was never taken seriously except by his devoted wife. A bit of buying and selling of illegal contraband, along with Betty's wage just about kept them afloat. Rodney slept on and off for most of the day preferring to sit up late into the night watching movies or doing deals for tobacco and cartons of cigarettes over the telephone. Every penny that he brought into the home no matter how small, always had Betty fussing and cooing over him. She was totally oblivious to the fact that he used her and was nothing but a lazy slob. Somehow the weird set up seemed to work and they both muddled along with few words of complaint.

At precisely six am on the morning after Wally Evans had left his calling card on Rickman Street, all hell broke loose. Betty Dale as usual was one of the first residents in the block to be up and about. As she left the flat she called out to Rodney who was tucked up under the duvet and informed him that she would see him later but there was no reply. She descended the concrete steps but didn't get more than a few yards when she spied the black plastic bag and glancing at her watch, knew that she had enough time for a closer look. Ever the nosey one and always open to a freebie Betty bent down and tore an inspection hole in the plastic. Her screams seemed to echo so loud around the stairwell, that much to Rodney's annoyance woke even him. Doors began banging and people shouted for the silly bat to shut up as they were trying to get some kip. When the neighbours chastising failed to silence her, Rodney finally hauled his backside out of bed and pulling on his towelling robe went to see what all the fuss was about. He was met with the sight of Betty huddled on the floor sobbing her heart out. Rodney bent down and placed his hand on her shoulder.

"Whatever's the matter you silly mare?"

Betty Dale was in too much shock to speak and could only manage to point in the direction of the bag. Ever the hero, to his wife at least, Rodney poked at the black plastic with his foot until it fell over onto one side. Instantly Vincent Frasier's face could clearly be seen through the hole that had been made a few minutes earlier. The blood stained empty sockets stared back up at Rodney and he almost tripped over.

"Holy shit!"

His words once more set Betty off and she again became hysterical. Rodney's face was as white as a ghost and shakily he took hold of his wife's arm and helped Betty to her feet.

"Come on let's get you inside love, you're in shock. I'll phone the Old Bill and then make you a hot drink."

Back in the warmth and safety of her own home Betty
Dale started to recover from her ordeal. The more she
thought about it, the more she realised just who the likely
culprit might be and that idea scared her more than the
sight of Vincent's Frasier's tortured body. Rodney
appeared with two steaming mugs and his wife looked at
him wide eyed.
"There's no way we can phone the Old Bill Rod. You do
know who's at the heart of all this don't you?"
Rodney Dale shook his head in bewilderment.
"Of course you do, you daft twat. Whose name kept
getting mentioned in the Kings robbery?"
Suddenly the penny dropped and Rodney was on the
same wave length as his wife.
"Fucking Nora B, we don't want to be getting involved
with the likes of Freddie Gant now do we but then again
we can't leave that poor fucker down there like that.
What if his old mum finds him? I mean I know you two
ain't ever been bosom buddies but if she's the one to find
him it could give the old girl a heart attack!"
"I don't give a shit about her Rod. This is all about self
preservation and if we don't look out for ourselves, no
one else will. I never did like them Frasier's and if
they're mixed up with Freddie Gant then we're staying
well clear. Did you hear what I said Rod?"
Rodney Dale began to pace the floor. He may have been
a layabout but he still knew right from wrong and this
was so very wrong.
"Will you stop fucking walking up and down or we'll end
up having to buy a new carpet."
Turning to face his wife Rodney looked directly into her
eyes and his face was grave.
"Betty no matter what you say I can't leave that poor sod
laying out there. Now I'm going to call the Old Bill,
267

withhold our number and just tell them there's a stiff on the landing. No one will ever know we saw anything alright?"

Betty Dale thought for a second before nodding her agreement to her husband. It took the local force less than ten minutes to attend. By London standards this was a record but in all honesty was probably just due to the early hour. After fully opening the bag and realising what its contents were, the stairwell was instantly cordoned off. The two young constables, who had been the first to arrive at the flats, instantly vomited up their breakfast. They were only there to direct residents, as even though it was a crime scene people still had to be given access in and out of their homes. PC Gary Clarke was as white as a sheet and as he stood guard, had to face away from the corpse as he dry heaved every time he looked at it. Mohamed Adhere was newer to the force than his colleague but seemed to handle murder scenes much easier. After his initial shock and sickness he had pulled himself together and taken charge of things.

"Hold on in there Gary, you'll get through this. Scene of crimes are on the way and then we'll get relieved."

PC Clarke was now panting rapidly, this seemed to be the only action that stopped him continually retching.

"I know mate but did you see the poor sod! Someone had taken his eyes out."

"Look just don't think about it, concentrate on something else."

"Like what?"

"Oh fuck me I don't know, anything mate so long as you stop throwing up."

It was only a few minutes later that DI's Nick Graves and Peter Wilson arrived. The two original constables where replaced with fresh men and Gary and Mohamed were

268

told to return to the station and begin writing their reports. Nick Graves had been on the force for over thirty years and at least twenty of those had been spent in homicide. Pete Wilson was relatively new to the division and eager to learn, hung onto his colleagues every word. Bending down Nick inspected the gruesome find without batting an eyelid. On a scale of one to ten this probably rated a six but he'd seen far worse over the years.

"Looks like the act of a weirdo to me. When I first got the call I thought it was going to be a gang land killing but I don't think so, not now anyway."

"How so Nick?"

"Well someone's taken their time over this one."

"But I thought a lot of them did, I mean they ain't against castration or pulling the odd tooth now are they?"

"Have a look at this though, its choice. I mean someone's really taken their time, really enjoyed it and by the looks of things, are skilled in the art of torture. No this is a psycho if you ask me and maybe there's more to come."

"Well that's my fucking leave out the window! Sandra's going to do her nut."

Nick Graves laughed. He'd been single for the last ten years and intended to stay that way.

"Pete you really are under the thumb mate, I don't know how you stick it."

Peter Wilson was about to argue the point further when two white vans pulled up.

"S.O.C.O are here Nick so I guess we can get back to the station now. Pardon the pun but I could murder a cuppa."

Since the arrival of the police Rodney Dale had been leaning over the stair rails, desperate to have a nose in what was going on. As Nick Graves glanced upwards Rodney darted back and hoped that he hadn't been seen.

269

It wasn't his lucky day and D.I Graves had clocked him at least two seconds earlier. Racing up the stairs in record time he was able to put his hand out and stop Rodney Dale from closing his front door.

"Hold on a minute Mr?"

"Here, what the fuck are you doing Copper?"

"I saw you looking over the rails and wondered if you could help with our inquiries Sir?"

"It wasn't me pal, you've got the wrong fella. I only just opened the door to pick me milk up."

Nick Graves started to lose his patience. Time was precious in a murder case and he could do without timewasters like this. He forcibly pushed Rodney up against the wall and with his forearm pressed against the man's chest.

"Don't take me for a mug mate, I saw you. Now you can help me out here or back at the station, the choice is yours?"

Suddenly Betty's voice could be heard calling from the living room.

"Rod what's going on?"

Rodney Dale began to panic and knew he was getting in much deeper than he wanted.

"It's alright love just going to get some milk, old Percy ain't delivered again. Won't be long."

Lowering his voice to almost a whisper he spoke in the direction of Nick's ear.

"Alright but let's go outside. If me old woman hears us there'll be hell to pay and you really don't want to be messing with the likes of my Betty I can tell you!"

Back outside on the landing D.I Graves asked whether Rodney knew the victim.

"How should I know I ain't seen him have I?"

Nick Graves looked the man up and down, all the time

trying to work out if he was lying. Confident that he was he asked Rodney Dale to see if he could identify the body.

"Oh fuck me mate I don't know about that. Do you know what it's like to live round these parts? You don't get involved in anyone else's business, not if you know what's good for you."

"I'm not asking you to. All I want is for you to take a quick look and see if you know him. Scouts honour that's all I want and I won't press you for any more information. If you do what I ask you can go back home and forget we ever spoke."

Rodney Dale thought for a moment and realised that if he didn't comply things could get a whole lot messier and if he was seen being carted off in a police car, well it didn't bare thinking about.

"Ok."

As he made his way down the stairs Rodney Dale tried to psych himself up into showing a face that was shocked and horrified at what he was seeing but his attempt at amateur dramatics wasn't needed. Behind the plastic sheeting that had been erected to keep prying eyes at bay, Vincent Frasier's body was now openly exposed.

"Oh my god!"

"I know it's not a pretty sight Sir, but if you could just focus on the face and try and not to think about anything else."

Rodney Dale closed his eyes and after taking a few seconds to compose himself, walked from the tent and headed back up to the flat. Nick Graves followed in hot pursuit and once again managed to catch the man as he entered the flat.

"What the fucks going on? Do you know him or not?"
Rodney Dale anxiously rubbed his palm backwards and

forwards across his mouth as he spoke.
"Yeh I do, his names Vinny Frasier and his old mum lives upstairs. This lot is going to kill the poor cow."
"What number?"
"Oh fuck me I can't remember but it's a red door. Now I did what you asked and I'd be grateful if you'd leave me in peace. I don't want any of this coming back on me or mine."
"Any of what?"
Rodney glared at the policeman and the look was enough to tell D.I. Graves that come hell or high water he wouldn't get anything else out of the man. Nick Graves reasoned that the question had at least been worth a try.
"Ok mate you go back inside and thanks for your help."
Returning to his colleague his face resembled that of a cat that had got the cream.
"Come on Pete we need to get to the station like yesterday! I've found out who he is and the real work starts here."
Their office in Bethnal Green police station which was situated just off Roman Road, took less than five minutes to get to. Once there it didn't take long for Vincent Frasier's name to be bandied about. When the information was entered into the system a warning flag appeared. Nick Graves saw that the victim had been listed as a missing person and knew that there was going to be a lot more to this story than meets the eye.
Telephoning Suffolk police he was soon transferred to Stan Harding. The man relayed all that had occurred the previous evening regarding the mugging and gave any other information that he felt relevant to the case. When Jason's name and address came up Nick Graves realised that he might be onto something. Over at the Camel Maude had been up and about with the larks.

She had heard Jason come home at around five am that morning and her mind was filled with all kinds of scenarios of what had happened. Unable to get anymore sleep she'd decided to clean behind the bar and was deep in thought when a loud knock on the front doors brought her crashing back to reality. The noise had been so loud and unexpected that it had made her knock a bottle of stout clean off the shelf. The glass shattering was a nuisance but the brown liquid now dripping off her best skirt was even worse. Grabbing the nearest bar towel she dabbed at the stain as she made her way over to the door.

"Who's there at this time of the morning?"

"Police Mrs Shelton, we'd like to have a word."

This was all she needed and Maude couldn't believe that more trouble was coming to her door. If Jason had got involved in something else then she wasn't aware of it and being ill prepared made her nervous. After opening the door just wide enough to check their identities, she let the men in when Nick Graves showed his warrant card.

"Take a seat lads! Can I get you a drink?"

Pete Wilson smiled and was about to accept when his partner spoke up.

"Thanks but no. It's too early and besides we're on duty."

Sitting herself down beside the younger of the officers, Maude eyed them both up suspiciously.

"Fair enough. So what can I do for you?"

"Do you have a Jason Frasier staying on the premises?"

"Come on now boys, what's all this about? I ain't going to commit myself to saying anything until you tell me."

"All in good time Mrs Shelton. Now do you or do you not have a Jason Frasier staying here?"

"I do indeed officer. Him and his wife live in my back room, though I doubt very much if they're awake yet.

Would you like me to go and see?"

"In a minute Mrs Shelton but I'd like to ask you a few questions first."

"What about?"

"Do you know a Vincent Frasier?"

Maude now had an inkling of where this was going but not to what depth.

"Of course I know Vinny. Why?"

"What sort of a person was he?"

"Was he? You're talking in the past tense! What's happened?"

"I can't really discuss that with you Mrs Shelton, at least not until I've spoken to Jason. I just wanted to get a feel for what sort of person he was."

"There you bloody go again but I suppose you ain't going to tell me anything are you?"

D.I Graves gently shook his head.

"Alright then, I get the message loud and clear. Well you want to know about Vinny Frasier, he is an evil piece of work! Pardon my French but he was a complete and utter wanker."

Maude Shelton's words took both officers by surprise, so much so that it brought a smile to Pete Wilson's face.

"If you can find anyone on the manor who'll talk to you then they would all say the same. Vincent's a nasty bloke who's just horrible in every sense of the word, just like his mother as you'll find out soon enough. Now do you want me to wake Jason?"

"Not yet Mrs Shelton. Tell me about Jason, what sort of person is he?"

Maude smiled for the first time since the policemen's arrival.

"Jay! He's the salt of the earth, do anything for anyone would Jason. Got himself a lovely little wife and as far

274

as I know don't have much to do with that brother of his."

Maude had been careful not to mention Lisa's illness. If Jay wanted them to know then it was up to him to say. "Well thank you very much Mrs Shelton. If you could fetch Jason now that would be really helpful."

Doing as she was asked Maude made her way out to the back and along the hall. Gently tapping on the door she took a second to gather herself before she spoke in a hushed tone.

"Jay! Jay are you up?"

After last night's escapade Jason Frasier had fallen into a deep sleep but the sound of her voice jolted him awake and he rubbed at his eyes with the backs of his hands. By the time he'd retrieved the cash and got back to London it had been the early hours of the morning and getting off to sleep had at first been difficult. Thoughts of Vinny and what may be happening to him whirled around in Jason's head. Lisa had gotten out of bed when he came in and even though he protested, she insisted on making tea and having a chat. By the time they finally got into bed it was really late and she was exhausted, so much so that she was still in a deep sleep now. Getting out of bed he pulled on a pair of boxers and opened the door. Jason didn't speak and holding a finger up to his lips, told Maude not to say anything until the door was closed and they were standing in the hall.

"What's up?"

"The Old Bill are here and they want to speak to you. They keep asking questions about Vinny as if he's dead." Maude waited for a response but apart from a shrug of the shoulders, Jason Frasier said nothing as he walked into the bar. Nick Graves stood up as a sparsely dressed Jason entered the room.

275

"Have you found anything out about the mugging yesterday?"

"I'm afraid that's not why we're here Sir."

"Then what's all this about guv'nor, because you've dragged me out of bed and to tell the truth I'm knackered."

"Not been home long Sir?"

Jason smiled.

"Well by the time I got released from the hospital and got back here it was pretty late. My wife is sick at the moment so we were up a lot of the night."

"Hospital! What hospital?"

"It's Ok Duchess, just a spot of bother I got into last night. I'll explain it all later."

Hearing his words Maude instantly knew that something bad had occurred and that Jason was mixed up in it somewhere along the line. D.I Graves on the other hand thought the complete opposite. If the man had the alibi of being admitted to hospital, then he very much doubted that he'd seen his brother after.

"I'm sorry to hear that Sir and even sorrier that I have to bring you bad news."

Jason knew what was coming, was even prepared for it but to anyone else's eyes it would appear a complete shock.

"A body has been discovered this morning and we believe it to be that of your brother Vincent."

"Oh my god! Then it is to do with the mugging?"

Jason feigned shock and almost fainted as he fell down onto a seat in one of the booths.

"How? What happened?"

"That's what we're trying to find out Mr Frasier."

"Fucking hell! I mean we hadn't been that close of late but I didn't think the last time I'd see him was after a day at the races. What about mum, has anyone spoken to mum?"

"Calm down Mr Frasier. Everything will be taken care of but for now what we really need is for you to come to the morgue and formally identify your brother."

The policeman's words frightened Jason. He didn't know what Freddie had done to Vinny or what state he would be in and the thought terrified him.

"I don't know if I can do that, no I'm sure I can't."

"Well if you don't Mr Frasier, it will have to be your mother. Do you think she would be up to it?"

Jason thought for a second. As despicable as Vera had been to him and Lisa he couldn't let the poor old girl go through that.

"No! Definitely not. Can you give me a while to get showered and dressed?"

Nick Graves handed Jason a card.

"We need to do this soon, so my direct number is on there and if you call before you leave I can make sure I meet you at St Thomas's hospital."

"St Thomas's, but that's over Lambeth way."

"I know Sir and I am sorry but it's the only morgue with any space at the moment."

Both officers shook Maude and Jason's hands before leaving and once outside Pete Wilson turned to Nick.

"So do you think he's involved?"

"No I don't think so, you saw how shocked he was. I'm pretty good at reading people and I think he was genuine enough. That said, I do think we should talk to him some more about what happened in Newmarket but for now we'll leave him to come to terms with his loss."

Back inside the Camel Maude wanted to make sure that the men were truly on their way and waited a few seconds before she spoke.

277

"Are you involved in this?"

Jason's eyes narrowed and became hard.

"Best you don't ask Duchess, best you don't ask."

"Well I am fucking asking Jay and while you are living under my roof, the least you can do is keep me up to date regarding what's going on."

"I know and I'm sorry but really you don't want to know about this one, trust me."

"Well are you going to the morgue then?"

"Of course I am but I have something important to do first."

"What could be more important than identifying your own brother?"

Jason Frasier turned sharply to face her and Maude could see that he was angry.

"Returning Freddie Gants cash, after all Vinny ain't going anywhere now is he?"

As Jason walked away, Maude Shelton could see that something had changed in her boy. Something she didn't like and hoped with all her heart that it would quickly disappear.

CHAPTER TWENTY SEVEN

Jason crept back into the bedroom and dressed as quietly as he could. Lisa was sleeping and her angelic face made him smile. Even though her illness was taking its toll, to him she looked exactly as she had the first day he saw her at Kings. God that seemed like so long ago now and for a minute he struggled with the realisation of just where they had ended up and what was to come in the future. Opening the wardrobe he surveyed the holdall that he'd placed there only a few hours earlier. Up until now he hadn't bothered to look inside but knowing this was his last chance he slowly unzipped it and parted the sides. Just as Vinny had said the money had hardly been touched. A few of the bound piles had been lifted from the top but that was about all. Jason quickly sifted through the cash and reckoned, give or take a few hundred, it was roughly ten thousand short. Jason knew that Freddie would be pleased the money had been returned and hopefully he wouldn't count it out straight away. For a second there was a tempting thought to remove a few bundles but something deep within wouldn't allow him to, it would feel as though somehow he was responsible for Lisa's illness. Jason knew the idea was ridiculous but he couldn't help how he felt, after all, if he'd been stronger willed and denied Vinny's request, then the robbery wouldn't have occurred and none of this sorry mess would ever have happened. Leaning over, he reached inside his jacket pocket and pulled out their winnings from the races. Counting out exactly ten thousand he placed the money inside the holdall and zipped it up. He could just about force himself to accept the rest of the cash, not for himself, this was for Lisa and her alone. It would enable him to take her anywhere she wanted to go and to be happy, if only for a while. Jason took down a shoe box from the top of the wardrobe and emptying out the contents he put the remaining cash inside. The few old photographs that Lisa had kept in the box were placed neatly back on top and on inspection no one would guess what the dilapidated box contained. Lifting up the bag, Jason turned when he heard her stir.

"Jay is that you?"

"No it's your secret lover come to whisk you away from all this, now go back to sleep."

Lisa gave a quiet giggle but turned over and within a few seconds she had drifted back into a deep sleep. After pulling on his coat Jason Frasier hoisted the bag up and placed the strap over his shoulder. Thinking that he could slip out and be back before anyone noticed, he was surprised to see Maude waiting for him in the hallway.

"All set?"

"If that's what you want to call it."

He walked towards the door but stopped as she spoke.

"Jay, don't tell me you're going to walk about with that lot in broad daylight. God above, can you imagine what would happen if you really did get mugged? I think that's one tale Freddie Gant wouldn't have any sympathy for. Now go and wait in the bar and I'll call a cab."

Jason did as he was told and ten minutes later he sat back for what he hoped would be his last journey into this part of London. When the driver attempted to engage in conversation Jason's only replies were either yes or no. After several minutes of trying, the driver at last gave up and much to Jason's relief he was now left in peace. It was just before ten and Soho wasn't yet busy. The few people who were milling around were only interested in their own daily business and totally ignorant of what was going on right under their noses. As was the norm, Freddie Gant had walked out and bought his daily paper and then stopped off at a small cafe for coffee and croissants. He was known for not taking chances but as mean as the streets of Soho could be, he felt far safer travelling the few hundred yards on his own manor than anywhere else in London. It was usual for Wally to accompany him but today Freddie felt like a little piece and quiet. As much as he valued his number one, Wally Evans could talk a load of twaddle sometimes. Freddie was about to open the office front door when the black hackney pulled up. Ever vigilant regarding his own self preservation his hand quickly went inside his jacket breast and rested on his handgun. The relative safety he felt in the area was continually overshadowed by the chance of a slip up by some young punk wanting to make a name for himself. When he spied Jason Frasier struggling out of the cab with the holdall, he relaxed his grip. Freddie didn't speak to his visitor or offer to help with his cargo. The only act of kindness he showed was to hold the door open for his guest to walk inside. Seeing that the person entering wasn't his boss, Wally Evans was up like a shot and only backed off when he heard Freddie's voice.

"Calm down Wal! It's only our little friend come to pay me what he owes."

Instantly Jason felt a rage of pure hatred begin to build up inside him. Here stood the two men who had murdered his brother and they were being sarcastic and calling him their friend. Walking through to his office Freddie Gant took a seat behind his desk and Jason struggled in behind him with the bag.

"Wal make a cuppa will you, he looks parched."

Placing the bag on the floor, Jason sat in the chair that was offered and stared coldly into Freddie Gants eyes. The look didn't faze Freddie in the least, he'd seen it too many times over the years and by some of the hardest villains. Leaning forward he placed his hands flat onto the leather surface of the desk.

"There ain't no point you having a fucking attitude with me pal. I can see that you'd like to slit our throats if you had half a fucking chance but just remember one thing Jason, if you and that scumbag of a brother hadn't robbed me in the first place then we wouldn't be sitting here now. Lose the high and fucking mighty act because as far as your brothers' demise is concerned, you had just as much a hand in it as Wally or me."

Jason could feel the first tears begin to sting his eyes and he tried desperately to hold them back.

"Do you have a brother Mr Gant?"

"Nah and can't say I ever fucking wanted one, especially if they'd been anything like yours."

Wally emerged from the front with three mugs of the finest china blend and placed them onto the desk. It was as if he was now a different person from the man who had carried out such torture on another human being just a few hours earlier. As Jason turned to face him Wally Evans now felt sympathy for the man's loss.

"Did he suffer?"

"You don't want to know son and I ain't going to fucking tell you any porky's. I suppose you'll hear the truth soon enough anyway."

Jason inhaled deeply. He'd hoped that they would at least lie to him. Freddie Gant again leaned forward.

"Have you heard from the Old Bill?"

"They came to the pub earlier, want me to go and identify Vinny today."

282

"But nothing else? No clues as to who they think it might be?"

"Not as far as I know. Maybe they think it's got something to do with the mugging but I ain't sure. I expect they'll want to have another chat before too long though."

Jason suddenly looked in Wally's direction.

"I think they're under the impression it was some kind of psychopath."

Instead of feeling insulted Wally Evans felt his heart swell. That kind of street cred didn't come easily and it was even more valuable if it came from the Old Bill. Still he could see that the man was hurting and he didn't want to poor salt on his wounds.

"Well Mr Gant if that's all, I would like to get back to my wife."

"Hold on there a minute my old sunshine we ain't discussed my cash yet. How much is in there?"

"I haven't got a clue Mr Gant. To be honest with you I ain't been that interested not with all that's been going on. Now I hope you've got back what my brother took but if it's short then there's nothing I can do about it. If you want to make me pay, then I'd be grateful if you'd just get on with it because I need to get back."

Wally Evans had never heard anyone speak to his boss like that before and deep down he admired Jason for his bravery. How Freddie would handle it was another matter and Wally waited with baited breath.

"You really are one cheeky cunt Frasier but I hear what you're saying. I suppose in the long run you did do me a favour bringing me back anything at all. That brother of yours has already settled the debt so as far as I'm concerned we're even."

Jason stood up and was about to leave when Freddie Gant

283

spoke again.

"Jason just a word of advice son. Don't ever fucking cross me again, because next time I won't be so fucking soft."

Jason didn't reply but the look he gave said he understood only too well. With the door insight he kept walking and didn't look back. When Wally Evans was sure that the man had left he turned to his boss.

"Do you think he had a dip in the bag, helped himself to a few quid like?"

"Quite possibly Wal but that's something we'll never know."

"I could find out for you Boss if you like."

"Sometimes Wally you just have to know when to quit and looking on the bright side, at least we've got a lot of it back. After all's said and done the little bastard could have done a runner if he'd wanted to."

Outside as he inhaled the fresh morning air Jason suddenly felt as though he was going to pass out. Staggering along the pavement he stopped at the first cafe he came to, the one that Freddie Gant had sat in just a half hour earlier. As he almost fell into the chair the owner eyed him suspiciously. Jack Greeves had run his small establishment for over thirty years and the likes of Gant and Evans were always welcome visitors. Jack wouldn't have dared say anything derogatory about his two most regular customers but this bloke looked weird and could be on drugs for all Jack knew. Jason was perspiring heavily, he hadn't told Maude his fears but in all reality he didn't think he would get out of Freddie Gants place alive. Now the relief was finally hitting home and the sensation made him feel light headed.

"Just a coffee please and could you make it extra strong."

Jack Greeves took the order himself and all the time he

kept a close eye on his customer. The young waitress
made the drink but it was delivered by the owner himself.
Jack placed the cup down onto the table but offered no
words of welcome to Jason. The lack of a smile or kind
word went unnoticed as Jason was too deep in thought.
After taking several sips to calm his nerves he then pulled
Nick Graves card along with a mobile phone from his
pocket. After studying it for several seconds Jason
finally dialled the number.
"Detective Graves speaking."
"Hello its Jason Frasier here. I'd like to come and see my
brother now if that's ok."
"Sure, how long will you be."
"Well I'm in Soho at the moment so I expect I could be
there about eleven thirty if that's any good."
As soon as the words were out of his mouth Jason
instantly regretted them. He couldn't for the life of him
think what had possessed him to tell the policeman where
he was but now that the damage had been done, well he
would just have to try and cover his tracks if he was ever
questioned about it. Nick Graves agreed to meet Jason at
St Thomas's main entrance forty five minutes later.
Replacing the phone Nick couldn't help but wonder what
the man was doing that could possibly be more important
than identifying his brother. Come to that he couldn't
think why Jason Frasier would want or need to be in
Soho that early in the morning. He decided to file this in
his memory bank for a later date but something about this
case was beginning to stink. He couldn't put his finger
on anything and no new information had come to light
but he'd always had a sixth sense about most of his cases
and there was definitely something wrong here.
By the time Jason had finished his drink he was starting
to feel his old self again and after paying for his coffee he

hailed a taxi, and headed to the hospital. As it pulled up outside the main entrance Jason looked out of the window and could see Nick Graves leaning up against the wall smoking a cigarette. St Thomas's was a huge cube shaped building and Jason strained his neck upwards to see the top. Scanning the horizon the London eye could easily be seen and he thought that if you had to be in hospital then this would be as good as any, unless you were in his brother's situation. The two men shook hands and entered the building with Nick Graves taking the lead. He'd visited this place many times over the years and it never seemed to change. Suddenly a hoard of student doctors came rushing down the corridor, all white coats flapping and with their heads in the clouds. To avoid a collision Jason and Nick had to step to the side. "Fucking tosser's."

Nick Graves's words shocked Jason for a second but he didn't make any comment. The men continued along until they reached an area that seemed so much quieter than the rest of the hospital. Jason realised that this was the place and he could feel himself begin to shake.

"Just take a seat over there Mr Frasier and I'll go check if they're ready for us."

Jason without question did as he was asked and in all honesty was grateful for the seat. Several minutes later and when he had just about decided to give up and go home as his nerves couldn't stand much more, Nick Graves reappeared.

"Mr Frasier, if you would like to follow me."

Standing up Jason breathed in deeply as he tried to steady himself. Walking towards the swing doors an image of Vinny's face unrecognisable from a horrendous beating began to invade his mind. Nick Graves instantly realised what was happening and he grabbed hold of Jason's

286

elbow as they entered the viewing room. Looking through the glass panel Jason could see the outline of his brother's body which was still covered from head to toe in a white sheet.

"You all right?"

"I will be when we get this over with but thanks for asking."

D.I Graves gave a wave in the direction of the mortuary assistant who then proceeded to pull back the sheet and reveal Vincent Frasier's face. Immediately Jason gasped but not out of horror. His shock was purely from the fact that his brother appeared so peaceful. Apart from his ashen colour there were no marks on Vinny's face and that alone gave Jason a sense of relief. The morticians had cleaned up his brother's face, inserted two glass marbles and closed his eyelids so for all intent and purpose Jason wouldn't have known that his brother's eyes had long since been removed.

"I know what you were expecting Mr Frasier all relatives have the same thought, well those that have to do this anyway."

A lone tear dropped onto Jason's cheek but he quickly wiped it away.

"For some reason I expected him to be all battered and bruised, not look like he was asleep. How did he die?"

"Jason are you sure you're ready to hear all the gory details, because I can't paint a pretty picture about it."

Jason Frasier glared at the detective and for a split second Nick Graves saw something that made him wonder if this man was as blameless as he was making out.

"Look the injuries were, let's just say gruesome to say the least. Now I know it's ridiculous but I have to ask this question all the same. Is this the remains of your brother, Vincent Frasier?"

Jason nodded then swiftly left the room. He couldn't bear to stay in there a moment longer and was in desperate need of fresh air. Nick Graves gave the all clear to the assistant before leaving to search for Jason. Finally he located the man leaning up against the wall outside the hospital's main doors.

"Do you want a lift home Mr Frasier?"

"If you don't mind."

The two men got into Nick Graves car and began the journey back to Bethnal Green. Jason was the first to try and make conversation but it was strained to say the least.

"I need to go and check on my wife before I go and see my mother, unless your lot have told her already?"

"No, as far as I'm aware she doesn't know yet. We weren't in a position to tell her until you'd identified the body."

Jason shot the man a hurt look which Detective Graves immediately picked up on.

"I'm sorry, I mean your brother."

When the car had pulled up outside the Camel and as Jason was about to get out he once again felt the man's hand on his arm.

"We really will need to take a statement from you at some time and I would prefer if it was sooner rather than later. You've got my card, call me as soon as you can."

Jason didn't reply and after closing the car door, wearily entered the back yard of the pub.

CHAPTER TWENTY EIGHT

Entering through the back of the Camel, Jason poked his head round the bedroom door and was surprised to find the bed neatly made and no sign of his wife. The bar should have been full of regulars by now but as he walked in it was deserted. Reaching for a glass, he offered it up to one of the optics and drew down two shots of whisky. The golden liquid instantly burnt his throat as he swallowed and Jason took a moment to savour the warmth. Suddenly tears started to fall and they came so thick and fast that Jason Frasier didn't think they would ever stop. He could taste the saltiness mixed with the watery snot that now flowed freely from his nose. Jason made no attempt to wipe the mess away until he heard Maude Shelton's voice call out from the flat above. Looking around for a tissue, the only thing to hand was an old bar towel but he didn't care. After wiping his face to remove any trace of tears, he threw the now offending item into the wash basket that Maude kept tucked away in the corner.

"Did you hear me, I said Jason is that you?"

"Yeah it's me Duchess, now coming."

Making his way up the stairs Jason was dreading seeing Lisa and Maude. He was physically and emotionally drained and all he wanted was to fall into bed and sleep. That wasn't going to happen and he knew that after going through everything with the two women upstairs, he would then have to go over it all again with his own mother.

"There you are! We were starting to get a bit worried. How did it all go?"

"Terrible Maude, just terrible."

"Sit down son and I'll make you a nice cup of tea."
Lisa gently took hold of her husband hands and stared
deeply into his eyes.
"Maude's told me about the police Jay, was it him?"
Jason's voice was almost a whisper and the only word he
spoke was 'Yeah'.
"I'm so sorry Jay; I know how much you loved him."
Just as in the bar, he could again feel the tears begin to
build up but this time he did everything he could to hold
them at bay. Yes her words were true but how could she
say them so calmly about a man who had robbed her of
any future. She really was an angel and looking into her
beautiful eyes, Jason's finally couldn't stop the tears from
falling. These tears weren't for Vinny or for any feelings
of guilt, no these were tears of pure love for the woman
that he was so proud to call his wife.
"Oh don't babe or you'll start me off."
Maude placed the three mugs of tea on the table and took
a seat opposite Jason. When things had gotten too
emotional in the past, Maude's way of handling the
situation was to get back to business. Now more than
ever she realised that she had to put this into practice and
calmly she spoke.
"So what now?"
Jason Frasier puffed out his cheeks in a gesture that said
'where do we start'.
"I suppose the first thing is a visit to my mum."
"Can't it wait until the morning love, you look done in?"
"I am Maude but as much as I hate her sometimes, my
mum has a right to know about Vinny. It's not fair to
keep it from her and if she heard the news from anyone
else, well I wouldn't be able to forgive myself."
The idea of seeing her mother-in-law filled Lisa with
nothing but dread but she also knew that if her husband

needed her, then come hell or high water she would be there for him.

"Do you want me to come with you?"

Jason clasped her hand tightly and smiled.

"No love you're alright. The Duchess will come with me, if that's alright with you Maude?"

"Of course it is, you don't even have to ask."

"Lisa you have a lay down and get some rest. The last thing you need is for Vera to throw one of her fits on you and I ain't in any doubt that's exactly what she'd do."

At precisely four that afternoon, Jason Frasier and Maude Shelton set off for the Rickman Street flats and as it wasn't too far from the Camel they had decided to walk. Reaching the building Jason gasped out loud when he saw the area was still partially cordoned off with tape.

"This is where they found him Duchess. They left the poor bastard on his own manor for the world and his wife to see."

"What did you expect from the likes of Gant?"

"What? What are you talking about?"

Maude didn't reply. Now well aware that her boy was heavily involved in whatever had happened to Vinny, she knew that when he was ready he would tell her everything. Climbing the stairwell they reached the walkway that led to Jason's former home. Six flats were housed in the section and four of them were now occupied by either brasses or dealers. It was all so different from when the boys had been growing up, then it had been a nice place to live. A couple of the flats had reinforced steel doors, so it was easy to tell where the dealers lived and the brasses didn't bother much with homemaking so their places just looked unkempt but not Vera Frasier's flat. Her front door gleamed in the late afternoon sunshine and the high gloss red step that she

291

prided herself on had been newly painted. Knocking on the door, Jason gave Maude a sideways glance as he waited for a reply. Vera had been in the middle of watching countdown and even though she wasn't really bright enough to solve any of the conundrums, she fancied the presenter like mad. Des Lynam was everything Vera desired in a man but had never found. When she heard someone at the door she immediately became angry. What with kids burning out cars and the amount of police sirens she'd heard today, now there was some stranger at her door, was she ever going to get any peace.

"Hang on, hang on I'm coming."

Opening the door, Vera was momentarily speechless at the sight of her son but true to form it didn't take her long before she was back to her old vindictive self.

"Well well well. Look what the fucking cats dragged in."

"Afternoon to you as well Mum!"

Jason didn't wait to be invited in and walked straight past his mother into the kitchen. Vera was immediately behind him and it was Maude who closed the front door and followed them both inside. Jason placed the kettle on the stove and turned to face his mother.

"Well make yourself at fucking home why don't you!"

"Sit down mum we need to talk."

"What's the little whore finally left you? I must admit she hung in there a lot longer than I would have given her credit for."

Jason didn't respond as he knew his mother was only trying to bait him; instead he gently shook his head and sat down. Vera studied the face of her eldest son and could see that he was troubled in a way that she'd never seen before. Taking a seat, her tone became soft and a small part of the caring mother that she once was started to emerge.

"Come on son, whatever's the matter? You look done in."

"Oh mum I don't know where to start."

Maude Shelton had remained in the doorway and was leaning up against the frame. She had stayed silent for the last few minutes but now decided that it was time to give Jason some support.

"Jason, start at the beginning love."

Maude wasn't sure exactly how much Jason wanted his mother to know but reasoned that it wouldn't be that much. Her words were like a red rag to a bull as far as Vera Frasier was concerned.

"Oh I wondered when you'd fucking pipe up! Never have been able to keep your nose out of my business have you. Anyway Jason what the hell is she doing here?"

"Moral support Vera, something you've never given your son."

"Get out of my place you old tart and don't....."

Jason slammed his fist down onto the table.

"Enough Mum! Maude is here for me not you and she'll go when I do. If you'll just shut up for a minute I've got some bad news to tell you and it's going to break your heart."

For the first time ever Vera did as she was asked and remained silent.

"Mum, Vinny's dead."

Vera Frasier snorted in a comical sort of way that dismissed his sentence out of hand.

"Don't be so fucking daft. Why would you say such a thing to your own mother? It's nothing short of bleeding cruel!"

"Mum believe me I ain't trying to be cruel, it's the truth I'm telling you."

293

Vera shook her head from side to side in a defiant manner that told the other two people in the room that she wouldn't accept what she was being told, couldn't accept it.

"Please mum don't do this."

"No no it's not true. No! No! Noooooooooo you've got it wrong, not my Vincent!"

Jason could see that he wasn't getting anywhere but he had to make her take on board what he was saying, had to make his mother understand that her youngest son was never coming home again. As it had been for the whole of his life, Jason would need to take a firm hand that or his mother would walk all over him while continuing to dismiss anything he said.

"Well deny it for as long as you like mother but I was the one who had to identify him earlier today and whether you believe it or not, it was my brother lying on that slab."

Without any further argument Vera Frasier began to sob. The sound was so heart wrenching that even Maude took pity on the woman. Kneeling down she took Vera in her arms and held her close. The sight of his mother's grief hurt Jason more than he could ever have imagined possible. Deep down he knew that however nasty Vera could be and there was no denying that fact, she truly loved her sons and none more so than Vinny. The woman who had brought Jason into the world and taught him many valuable lessons, seemed to shrink and age before his eyes. She wasn't strong like she used to be, couldn't take on the world anymore and if need be fight it. Standing in the kitchen of the Rickman Street flat, all Jason Frasier saw was an old woman whose heart had just been ripped out and there was nothing he could do to make things better. It seemed like forever before Vera's

294

tears at last began to subside. Her face was so pale that Maude considered calling a doctor but the other woman wouldn't hear of it.

"Thank you for your kindness Maude Shelton but me and my boy will be just fine, now if you don't mind, I think we need to be on our own for a while."

Maude looked at Jason who just gave a single nod of his head.

"Well I'll be off then, let me know if you need anything."

"I'll walk you to the door Duchess."

Outside on the landing Jason pulled the door until it was almost closed.

"Maude I need to stay with her, just for tonight."

"Of course you do son, I wouldn't have expected anything less. Don't you worry about a thing, I'll go home and explain to Lisa and we'll see you soon, Ok?"

Leaning forward she placed a kiss tenderly on his cheek before turning and disappearing down the stairwell.

"Jason! Jason where are you?"

"Right here mum, I'm now coming."

Closing the front door behind him, Jason Frasier leant heavily onto the woodwork. This was his duty and he had to be here but unlike a lot of sons, in reality he wanted to be as far away from his mother as possible.

Entering the kitchen Jason could see that Vera had regained her composure and was now almost back to her old self.

"Sit down son; we've got a lot of talking to do."

Without argument Jason Frasier did as his mother asked.

"Tell me all you know."

"That ain't much mum. I had a visit from the Old Bill this morning telling me they'd found a body that they believed was Vinny."

"Has this little lot got anything to do with what went on

at Kings?"

To say Jason was shocked was an understatement.

"What do you know about Kings?"

"Give me some fucking credit boy, I may be old but I ain't fucking senile. Everyone knows what went on and who was behind it. Where did they find my Vinny?"

"At the bottom of the stairs ."

"Downstairs! You mean to tell me, that the rotten fuckers left my boy in a dirty stairwell?"

Jason didn't answer and just lowered his head.

"That Freddie Gant is going to pay for this."

Alarm bells began to ring in Jason's head, they were so loud that he thought he'd be deafened.

"Freddie Gant! How do you know about him mum?"

"It's common knowledge that he was the face behind the company. People do talk you know."

"Well I think it'd be best for all concerned if you didn't bandy that name about."

Vera stood up, her face red and contorted with rage.

"Don't you dare fucking come in here telling me what to do. That cunt has taken my baby away and he's going to pay. Now either you do something about it or I will."

"Do something about it! Do you know who you're talking about here? Fucking hell mum, men like Gant eat people like us for breakfast and think nothing of it."

"So he just gets away with it, I don't think so. I'm fucking telling you now Jay, something's got to be done."

"You can do what you like mother but I have Lisa to think about."

"You're putting that fucking little whore before your own flesh and blood?"

Jason walked towards the door, this conversation was draining him and he didn't know how much more he could take.

296

"Look mum there's a lot you don't know."

"Well then tell me!"

"I can't and believe you me it's for your own good. I hope you can accept this Mum and that you will be alright but now I need to get back to my wife. Regarding Vinny, well you can do what you like but I'm staying well out of it. We both know it don't bode well for anyone who takes the name of Freddie Gant in vain. Think long and hard mum, after all nothing you do or say will bring Vinny back."

"Make me feel a whole fucking lot better though."

"Will it mum, will it really?"

Vera didn't answer and Jason knew that this was something they would never see eye to cye on. He could see that his mother had some of her old self back again and her anger and not her hurt would enable her to cope with the next few days. Not waiting for the argument to continue, Jason Frasier decided that even though he'd told Maude he wouldn't be home until the morning it would be best for all concerned if he didn't stay the night after all. Walking out of his mothers flat he headed into the cold evening air and began the journey back to the Camel. He hoped with all his heart that Vera would have second thoughts and decide to let the matter drop but deep down Jason knew his mother to well and like a dog with a bone she would never let it drop.

297

CHAPTER TWENTY NINE

It had been a long night and Detective Inspector Nick Graves was slumped over his desk when his partner arrived for work.

"Don't tell me you spent the night here?"

Nick sat up in his chair and arching his back raised his arms in a lengthy stretch.

"I called in a favour and Gerry Tollit over at St Thomas's did a night autopsy for me. I'm waiting on the results."

"What autopsy?"

"Vincent Frasier's."

"Whatever's the matter with you Nick, the body was only found yesterday so why the hurry?"

"I know it was Pete but there's just something about this one and I don't mean what state the corpse was in. After the identification yesterday I came to the conclusion that the brother is involved somewhere along the line and it's really bugging me."

"What do you mean?"

"That I don't know yet but I'm looking forward to unravelling the mystery."

After a knock at the door and as PC Clarke who had been one of the first officers at the scene walked in, the conversation was momentarily halted.

"Autopsy report Sir."

"Thanks Clarke just put it down on the desk."

To Gary Clarke the Detectives attitude seemed like he really couldn't care less about the results and the young constable wondered why he'd bothered racing up two flights of stairs. As soon as Nick Graves and Pete Wilson were once again alone the papers were snatched up.

"Fuck me! Calm down mate you'll give yourself a heart

attack."

"I want to play this one close to my chest Pete. This station always seems to leak anything of interest and I might add, sometimes not to the right type of people."

"Here you go again, there's always some kind of underworld conspiracy with you."

Nick Graves ignored the comment and standing up headed towards the door.

"Get your coat."

"For fucks sake Nick, I ain't even had a coffee yet. Sandra forgot to do the weekly shop again, lazy cow!"

"D I Wilson I ain't the least bit interested in your domestic set up, now are you coming or not?"

Not waiting for a reply Nick headed out of the office, fully aware that his partner would be right behind him. In the car park he threw his colleague the keys.

"You drive it will give me time to glance over the report."

"Where to?"

"I think it's about time we paid a visit, see how the old girl's holding up."

The journey was taken in silence, except for the three occasions when DI Graves was heard to say 'Fuckin hell!' or 'Oh my god!' After his statement of exclamation had been made for a third time Pete Wilson couldn't stand the suspense any longer.

"Are you going to share it with me or just keep on teasing me?"

Nick Graves didn't look up from the papers on his lap. "Share what?"

"Come on Nick don't be a prat what's it say?"

"Well Gerry Tollit has put the cause of death down to the brain injury which was caused by a sharp blade being inserted into the base of the skull, real professional like

299

so no surprises there but Vincent Frasier was also HIV positive."

"Gay attack?"

"I don't think so but there is something else he's added."

"What?"

"The poor cunt was alive when his eyes were removed. The hands were post-mortem though so I suppose that's one blessing if you can call it that."

"God in heaven help us! What a way to go."

"I can think of better ways to leave this earth I can tell you. We're here now and not a word to the old girl about any of this."

"Fucking Nora Nick, whatever do you take me for?"

Just as Jason and Maude had found earlier, the stairwell was still cordoned off but there was no police attachment. S.O.C.O had done all that they could but thanks to Wally's astuteness and planning there was very little evidence to be found at the scene.

Vera Frasier had just settled down with a fresh cup of tea in readiness for the Jeremy Kyle show when the knock came at her door. True since she'd received the news about her Vinny not much could hold her interest, except for the odd TV programme that was and this happened to be one of them. She loved the way that the host got everyone arguing and if you were really lucky they even threw a few punches.

"Here we go again. Oh bollocks, fuck off I aint answering."

Nick Graves pressed his ear to the door and on hearing the television knocked again but this time even harder.

"Alright, alright I'm coming."

Looking through the side glass she immediately recognised the two men as plod. It seemed to be something inbuilt where an East Ender could pick out

Old Bill from the largest of crowds. After cursing under her breath Vera opened up but was none to friendly.

"You took your bleeding time getting here but then why should I have expected anything else. As far as you lot are concerned my boy was just another low life wasn't he?"

"Mrs Frasier I wondered if we might have a few words?" Nothing more was said and the three people just stood staring at each other in awkward silence.

"Well?"

"I meant inside Mrs Frasier."

Vera didn't invite them in, instead she just turned round and made her way back to the living room. Nick Graves and Pete Wilson both shrugged their shoulders at the same time and followed the woman through. Vera had sat back down in her chair and was staring deeply at the television screen.

"Would you mind if I turned that off, only we need to speak to you about your son."

"Can't imagine what you'd have to say that ain't been bleeding said already. Someone killed my baby and they're going to pay. If my eldest don't sort it then I will, even if it takes the last fucking breath in me body I swear I'll have revenge for my boy!"

Nick Graves sat down on a small pouffe directly facing Vera.

"Do you mean to tell me that you know who did this terrible thing Mrs Frasier?"

"Of course I fucking do, the whole of the East End knows."

"Then why don't you tell us and let us deal with it."

"Because we sort things out for ourselves round these parts. We don't need the Old Bill poking their sodding noses in and pouring salt on peoples wounds."

301

While he took a moment to think about where to go from here, Nick Graves glanced up at his partner and saw Pete standing open mouthed in surprise. Nick decided to change tactics and in a sympathetic manner knelt down beside the woman.

"Believe it or not Mrs Frasier I'm East End as well and I'm only too aware of how you do things. Putting that aside let me just ask you one question. You've just lost one son, do you really want to see the other one banged up for the rest of his natural?"

Vera Frasier turned from the screen to face the man before her. The idea of Jason going to prison hadn't even occurred to her and now brought to her attention, was something she would have avoided at all costs.

"Jason wouldn't have anything to do with it!"

"Then all you have to do is give me a name and we will do the rest."

"Yeah! Like sit on your fucking arses and do nothing as usual."

"That would not happen Mrs Frasier. I can assure you we will do our utmost to bring to justice whoever's responsible for your son's death."

"Don't make me laugh!"

Vera didn't want to continue talking to the men and standing up motioned for the two policemen to go. Nick Graves could see that he was wasting his time and that this line of questioning wasn't getting him anywhere so it took him by surprise when at the front door and just as they were about to leave, the woman said a name 'Freddie Gant'. Back in the car Nick Graves turned to his partner.

"Well that was a fucking turn up for the books."

"What now?"

"Back to base I think. We need to do a bit of digging

302

regarding Gant. I'm aware that he's a well known face but what we need to find out is how he's involved in this little lot."

The station was its usual buzzing self. Rumours of who was to blame for the Frasier murder were circulating the place at ten to the dozen. The two detectives didn't participate in conversation with the other officers except for the obligatory nod of hello. Once back in the relative privacy of the investigation room Nick Graves switched on his computer and typed in the name of Freddie Gant. "Well well well!"

Pete Wilson, who'd been collecting coffee from the vending machine was intrigued.

"Is he on the system?"

"On the system? Of course he's on the system you daft sod. As I said before he's a known face but for some reason he ain't ever been pulled in. Apparently the Flying Squad have had the Foreman gang under surveillance for the past six months and this Gant and a few heavies were seen coming out of Foreman's place not too long ago."

"Fucking hell Nick the Foreman's aren't to be messed with. Right nasty bastards they are."

Nick Graves couldn't believe what he was hearing.

"Fuck me Pete you're a copper, not some newspaper hack who can be frightened off. What are you telling me you're too fucking scared to look into this?"

"I didn't say that."

"Then get your coat because we're going to pay our Mr Gant a little visit."

Freddie was seated behind his desk reading one of the daily's when a knock at the door made him look up. Wally Evans had been dozing on a sofa out in the front but was out of his seat in a second. Pulling the door blind

303

to one side he instantly recognised the Old Bill and unlocked the door.

"Yeah?"

"D.I Graves Mr?"

Wally didn't offer his name and stared coldly at the two men.

"This is my colleague Detective Wilson and we're here to have a word with a Mr Gant if he's available."

"Wait here."

Wally walked to the inner office but Freddie had already heard the conversation.

"For fucks sake Wal let them in. We don't want to antagonise our boy's in blue, now do we?"

Doing as he was asked Wally led the men through to where his boss sat with a welcoming smile on his face.

"Gentlemen I've been told you would like a word, please take a seat. Wally fetch us some teas would you."

Nick graves held up his hand.

"Thank you but no, we haven't got a lot of time so if we could just get down to the matter in hand."

"And what matter might that be Detective?"

Nick Graves tried to weigh the man up but was coming up with a big fat zero. Freddie Gant was a player and knew the Old Bill's tactics only too well. As hard as the man in front of him tried to read him, Freddie wasn't giving anything away. Pete Wilson on the other hand stood silently behind his partner and Nick knew that it was through fear that he didn't utter a single word. That said, it still annoyed him somewhat but then Pete had a young wife and the promise of a family so Nick could see why he didn't want to take any unnecessary risks.

"We are currently investigating a murder and have been told that you have had dealings with the victim."

Freddie Gant raised his eyebrows in a show of

bewilderment.

"And who are you talking about or do you want me to start play guessing games?"

"Vincent Frasier."

"Name don't ring a bell."

"Well we have it on good authority that....."

Freddie Gant sat back in his leather chair in a relaxed manner.

"Hang on a minute, I do know who you're talking about but I don't know him personally. I am however familiar with Jason Frasier and I know he has a brother called Vinny if that's any help to you."

"And just how do you know Jason Mr Gant?"

Freddie smiled and Nick could sense that although the show of recognition was supposed to come across as genuine he was in fact being mocked.

"He lives at the back of my aunt's pub over in Bethnal green officer! Now I ain't got a clue who's been telling you a load of crap about me knowing this Vincent character but I can assure you there ain't an ounce of truth in it. I'm from the East End officer and not wanting to blow my own fucking trumpet, have done quite well for myself. That said there's always someone ready to do you down. Jealousy's a terrible thing don't you think? Now if there ain't anything else I really do have a busy day. Wally, would you show the gentlemen out."

Freddie once more started to read his paper and as Wally held open the office door, Freddie made no further acknowledgment of the two policemen. After seeing the men out and making sure that the front door was securely locked Wally Evans returned to the back office.

"What do you think Boss?"

"I think Wally my old pal, that someone's been shouting their fucking mouth off and I intend to find out who it is."

305

"Jason?"

"Nah he's got too much to lose. Makes no odds anyway, they ain't got nothing on us but it still pisses me off big-time to think that anyone's got the nerve to talk about me behind me back. We need to nip this in the bud and as quickly as possible! Hand me the phone."

His conversation with Freddie Gant had infuriated Nick Graves but he was also aware that unless he got anymore information from the Camel, then he was flogging a dead horse.

"Where to now Nick?"

"Let's see, it's nearly lunchtime. I think we deserve to take our break at a certain pub over in Bethnal Green don't you?"

The Camel was unusually quiet but not through a lack of punters. There were as many regulars as normal but as they had all heard of Jason's loss, were out of respect being extra quiet. Jason and Lisa were in the back watching television and Maude Shelton had just rung up a sale on the till when Nick Graves and Pete Wilson walked in.

"Hello gents didn't expect to see you two so soon."

"Mrs Shelton is Jason about?"

"He was a while ago; I'll just pop and see where he is. Take a seat! I won't be long."

Hurriedly she made her way to the back room and called out to Jason. Maude didn't want to go in as she would have had to explain to Lisa that the police were here again and the girl really didn't need any more stress. Jason popped his head round the door and saw his landlady silently beckon for him to join her. Closing the door he could see that Maude wore a look of concern.

"What's up Duchess you look like you've seen a ghost?"

"Jay the coppers are here again."

306

"Now what?"

Maude pointed towards the closed bedroom door with her index finger and then placed it to her lips which silently told Jason to keep his voice down so that Lisa wouldn't hear.

"I don't know but I think it'll be best if you take them up to the flat."

Five minutes later and Jason Frasier along with the two policemen were seated at Maude Shelton's kitchen table.

"Mr Frasier I ain't going to beat around the bush, we paid Freddie Gant a visit this morning."

Jason couldn't hide the look of surprise on his face but surprise was the only thing that the two men would get out of him. Inwardly he wondered how they had made the link, he knew only too well that Freddie wouldn't have said a word and would have denied all knowledge of having any association with Vinny.

"So?"

"You're not denying that you know him then?"

"I don't think there's anyone in the East End, come to that the whole of the Smoke who's not heard of Freddie Gant and besides he's my landlady's nephew."

"I wasn't aware of that fact Jason, not until Mr Gant informed us of it but you had an expression of fear on your face when his name was mentioned."

"I take it you don't know that much about Freddie Gant, because if you did you would know full well why people fear him."

Before Nick Graves had a chance to ask any further questions Maude Shelton entered the kitchen.

"Gentlemen I think that's quite enough for today if you don't mind. Jason's had a great loss and is having difficulty coming to terms with things. Now if this could wait until after the funeral we would be grateful."

"Mrs Shelton, why didn't you mention that Freddie Gant was your nephew?"

"'Because it had no relevance or are you trying to tell me that he's involved in all of this?"

"I didn't say that."

"Well sonny it wouldn't surprise me to find out he was but no one's going to talk to you, at least not anyone who's got any real information. I would have thought that someone in your position would have known about Freddie and his firm years ago."

Nick Graves appeared almost embarrassed by her comment.

"I can assure you Mrs Shelton we know all about your nephew."

"Obviously not enough though! I suggest you go back to your station, do a little digging and then put this to bed once and for all."

"But I have to ask if......"

"I don't care what you have or haven't got to ask. You leave my boy alone. Now out with the pair of you before I really lose me rag and put in a complaint of harassment."

Nick Graves knew he couldn't push the matter as he really didn't have anything to go on but he was determined not to let the matter drop. Returning to the station the two officers were met with an almost eerie silence as they walked inside. About to ascend the stairs they were stopped by W.P.C Farren who'd been on desk duty and had hardly been able to contain herself when she'd seen the men arrive back.

"Sir! Sir! Hang on a minute."

"What is it Julie only we have a lot of work on."

"You've got to go see the guv'nor straight away. Seems he's had a visitor today and your name got mentioned

308

several times."

"Who was the visitor?"

Julie Farren's chest swelled with pride as she spoke the man's name.

"None other than Commander Bowers from the Yard."

Nick Graves frowned in bewilderment. Climbing the stairs as quickly as he could and at the same time frantically pulling at his tie trying to straighten it, showed just how worried he was. Pete Wilson didn't make a single comment and followed closely behind his colleague as they made their way to the Chief's office in silence. Passing the incident room, the two men walked along a corridor that was flanked on either side by smaller rooms set aside for the higher ranks. The chief's office was situated right at the bottom of the corridor and was not much more than a four sided glass box with blinds. As Nick and Pete got closer they could see him sitting behind his desk.

"Fuck me Pete whatever's going on?"

"Ain't got a clue mate but I know he don't look in a mood to be messed with."

"Yeah and I've seen that look before. Take my word for it there's going to be trouble!"

Nick tapped lightly on the door and waited to be called in.

"Ah! D.I Graves glad you could make it. D.I. Wilson you won't be needed."

Pete remained in the doorway for a second until a sideways glance from his colleague told him to get the hell out.

"Please take a seat Nick. While I've been waiting I took the opportunity to read up on your file and I see you're about due for a promotion."

"Well that's nice to hear Sir but why has it come about

now?"

"Nick there are many things that go on in the Met that are hard to understand and often it's for the best if you don't even try. Now I'm aware of your investigation into the Frasier case and that you paid a certain Freddie Gant a visit."

Nick Graves sighed as he realised what was coming next.

"I want you to leave Mr Gant alone. Completely forget about him as far as this investigation is concerned."

"But Sir he could be the main suspect in all of this."

"I don't think you heard me clearly enough Detective Graves, leave the man alone! Now I don't wish to come across all heavy handed but if you persist in this matter your career will suffer. I'm sure you're aware by now that today I received a visit from the Commander."

"Pardon me Sir but I can't see what that has to do with one of our murder cases."

For a second the room was silent and Nick could feel the tension that was building up.

"It is not for a DI to question his superiors but I will make an exception just this once and explain a few key points. I could allow you to continue with the case but I can guarantee that months of hard work would be wasted as a criminal conviction would never happen. It's obviously gang related and spending thousands of pounds of public money on wasted man hours wouldn't go down well with the Commissioner. Now I assume you are astute enough to realise that the Commander can fuck up a man's career with just a phone call."

Nick wasn't given a chance to respond to the last statement.

"Good! Obviously you will need to go through the motions of investigating this case as we don't need the family complaining that we haven't done our best but

310

anything you may or may not uncover must be brought directly to me. I will then take a look at things and decide what action to take if any. Now are we in agreement that I will not have to speak to you a second time regarding this matter?"

Accepting defeat didn't sit well with Nick Graves but he knew that when the men at the top closed ranks, there was little anyone could do to change things. Without another word but with a wave of his hand the Chief motioned for Nick to leave the office. A few seconds later and when he was back behind his own desk, Nick was in the middle of mulling over all that had been said when Pete entered the room.

"What did he say?"

Nick repeated word for word everything that had been said by the Chief and Pete Wilson just shook his head in amazement.

"So Gant gets off scot free?"

"There ain't much I can do about it Pete. I mean I could try and push things but we'd both just end up back on the beat."

"Fuck me! Sandra would skin me alive if that happened."

As hard as he tried Nick couldn't help but laugh and slapped his friend on the back.

"Come on mate I'll buy you a pint. I suppose sometimes you just have to let sleeping dogs lie and this is one of them times."

"He's still an evil bastard though Nick!"

"Indeed he is Pete and Mr Freddie Gant may have gotten away with this one but favours run out sooner or later and I'm going to be right there when they do."

Within an hour of Nick being given his orders the telephone in Freddie Gants office began to ring. Lifting

311

the receiver he heard only two words 'all sorted'.
Freddie leaned back in his chair and smiled to himself.
The damning photographs of Bowers that had sat tucked
away in his safe for so many years had at last come in
useful. As instructed Nick Graves had carried out his
investigations to the letter. Starting at the beginning he
had travelled to Newmarket but after a meeting with Stan
Harding, he'd learned that there was no evidence
regarding the mugging. Returning to London Nick
instructed four beat policemen to carry out a door to door
inquiry in the hope that someone would have seen
something. In true East End fashion, this drew a blank
just as he knew it would. Studying the forensic report
didn't get him anywhere either. Oh there was quite a bit
of detail regarding the knife's probable length and width
and Gerry Tollit had even hazarded a guess as to the
make but with no actual weapon it was another dead end.
Finally after two weeks of getting nowhere and Vera
Frasier constantly on the telephone regarding her sons
remains Nick Graves gave permission for the body to be
released and began to scale down the investigation. It
really went against the grain to know that he'd been
outsmarted by a villain but Nick Graves continued to
remind himself that every dog has its day and sooner or
later that day would come for him, at least as far as
Freddie Gant was concerned.

CHAPTER THIRTY

Still seated in his mothers flat, the cigarette that Jason
had lit on returning from the funeral was now totally
burned down and only the filter and a long line of ash
remained. Glancing up to the kitchen window he could
see that the skyline now had a warm orange glow and
when he noticed the wall clock displaying seven pm,
wondered where the day had gone. After settling Lisa
down he'd only meant to stay for a short while but
without realising it most of the day from the funeral
onwards had somehow passed him by. He had sat as still
as a statue and relived his whole life in a matter of hours
and now all he felt was a total emptiness at how things
had turned out. In the early years Jason Frasier had never
been one to make plans and was always happy to go with
the flow wherever life took him. Not once could he ever
have imagined the horrendous trail of events that would
see him back at his mother's Rickman Street flat where it
had all began. Those happy carefree days Jason had
spent with Mango and the others now seemed like a
million years ago and he felt old, far far older than his
years. Jason was suddenly brought back to the present by
the sound of the flat door slamming shut and hearing his
mother's footsteps thunder down the hall. Years of
experience had taught him how to read her every move
and just by her walk he could tell that Vera Frasier's
mood was black. As the kitchen door swung open with
so much force that it slammed against the adjoining work
surface, Jason rolled his eyes in anticipation at what was
to come.

"And where the fuck have you been?"

"Don't start mum. I needed to bring Lisa back to

313

somewhere quiet and after I got a drink and sat down, well the time just seemed to fly by. I was thinking back to when me and Vin was kids and....."

"Don't give me any of that sentimental old fucking clap trap. It was only your brother's funeral today in case you'd forgotten! You couldn't even be bleeding bothered to go to his wake."

"Mum it wasn't like that. Vinny's gone now but we're all still here and if you hadn't noticed, Lisa ain't too well at the moment."

"Lisa Lisa Lisa! I'm sick to my back teeth hearing that little bitches name and don't think I don't know that she had something to do with it all. I ain't fucking daft Jay and you're all keeping something from me but I'll get to the bottom of it."

Jason stood up and pushed the chair away with such force it fell over.

"Will you just leave it alone mother, it's like you're constantly picking at a fucking sore."

"Don't you dare speak to me like that."

"Well someone's got to. You go on and on about what a good boy your Vinny was and all the time people are taking the piss out of you. Vinny was a bastard Mum and if you knew half of what he'd got up to you'd be ashamed of him."

"Never! My boy was a perfect son in every way."

"Perfect! Don't make me laugh. Your precious Vinny was so perfect that he almost got me killed as well. So fucking perfect that he raped my wife and left her with a terrible disease."

"How could you Jason! Your brother was a wonderful person and he didn't have no fucking disease. If he had then it was probably that little whore in the next room who gave it to him. Raped indeed! I did my homework

314

when you first married her and I know all about them Murphy's. That disgusting tart was a Tom before she was fifteen, bet you didn't know that fucking little gem now did you?"

"Mum I know everything there is to know about my wife and there ain't nothing about her that I'm ashamed of. If you had of done your homework properly then you would have known that it was her own father who put her on the game?"

"A likely story and I bet that little snippet came from her didn't it?"

Jason stood up and walking into the hall, turned to his mother one last time.

"I'm to knackered to argue with you mum, so I'm going to turn in but I have to say that you really are the most evil old bitch I've ever come across. Goodnight!"

It was a first for Vera Frasier and she remained totally silent, stunned by her sons last words. After laying Vinny to rest she had hoped that her eldest would come back to take care of her but somehow that didn't seem likely now and the idea of being alone scared the hell out of her. Still Vera reasoned she had always been able to twist her boys around her little finger and this time would be no exception. No, she would turn in and have an early night, tomorrow was a whole new day and it would be better to start working on her son fresh from a good night's sleep.

Even before the dawn chorus had got into full swing Vera Frasier was up and about. She was washed and dressed by six am which was almost unheard of for her and by eight she had prepared a full English breakfast. Even though it seriously went against the grain she had also included food for her daughter in law. Although she was

315

desperate for her son to get up, Vera knew better than to wake him and when Jason finally made an appearance a half hour later she was seething but did her best not to show it.

"Morning son. Is her ladyship getting up or shall I throw hers in the bin?"

"Don't be like that mum, Lisa's just having a wash then she'll be through."

Jason and his mother sat down at the table and had just begun to eat when Lisa entered the kitchen. Vera stayed seated, adamant that she wasn't about to wait on her whore of a daughter-in-law and it was Jason who immediately stood up to retrieve his wife's breakfast from the oven. Vera offered no words of welcome or friendship to the girl and things were strained from the off.

"So what time are you moving your stuff in son?"

"Sorry?"

Lisa didn't say a word but the alarm on her face spoke volumes.

"When are you going to get all your things from the Camel?"

"We ain't."

"Don't be so fucking daft, of course you are."

"No mum we're not. I thought you understood that me and Lisa only came back here to be with you for the funeral. Our home is with Maude at the Camel."

"Fucking Maude! What's she ever done for you?"

"Well to start with she's been more of a mother than you ever have."

Lisa couldn't stand how things were going and immediately left the table in a desperate attempt to seek solace in the bedroom.

"Now look what you've done."

316

"For god's sake Jason when are you going to wake up and smell the coffee. That little bitch is twisting you round her little finger and you're too fucking daft to see it."

Jason pushed his plate in his mothers direction and the contents spilled over onto the table top.

"That's it! I've tried, lord knows I've tried but there's just no pleasing you mother. Well as far as I'm concerned you can sit here and wallow in self pity for your precious lost boy. Come to that, as far as I'm concerned you can fucking rot because you won't be seeing me or my wife again."

"Please yourself. You always was a selfish little bastard and don't think I'll miss that little slut in the next room either!"

Vera Frasier regretted the words as soon as they'd left her mouth but she was far too stubborn to apologise.

Entering the bedroom Jason wasn't surprised to find Lisa packed, dressed and sitting on the end of the bed.

"Ready babe?"

His wife only smiled but was on her feet in seconds. Leading her by one hand and carrying their bag with the other the couple exited the flat without a word of goodbye to Vera Frasier. There was no chance of her running after them and she remained sitting at the kitchen table with a face full of rage. As they hurried along the landing Jason looked at his wife and smiled.

"Come on, I'm going to treat you to a slap up breakfast."

"That's alright Jay I ain't that hungry anyway."

"Well I am and after having to put up with that old cow, I think we both deserve it. Let's get a cab and go somewhere real posh."

"Can we afford it Jay?"

Not wanting to let on about the money he had recently

acquired Jason played things down.

"I don't care if we can't sweetheart. Today is for us and what we want and to hell with the cost or my bitch of a mother!"

Three hours later and after filling their stomach's to bursting point and then taking a long walk to work the food off the couple made their way home. The Camel was its usual bustling self and as they walked in through the front door Maude Shelton's face was a picture.

"Come on in you two, I'll get you both a drink. To be honest I didn't think you'd last this long with that crazy old bag."

Jason laughed and Lisa slightly dropped her head as she puffed out her cheeks and exhaled deeply.

"I'm going for a lay down if that's alright darling, only I'm feeling a bit tired."

Jason kissed his wife tenderly on the forehead and then watched her frail frame as she slowly walked in the direction of their room.

"How's she been Jay?"

"Not good Duchess and having to stop with mum didn't help. I suppose in hindsight it was a bad idea but I just thought that with all that had happened, the old girl might have been a bit different with her, a bit friendlier you know?"

"And I take it she wasn't?"

"Nah, if anything she was more vicious than ever. We had an almighty bust up just before we left and I told the old bitch she wouldn't ever see me or Lisa again."

Maude topped up Jason's Guinness and poured herself a brandy.

"And did you mean it or was it just in the heat of the moment?"

"I meant it alright! She's my own mother Maude but

318

right at this minute, going to the moon wouldn't be far enough away from her."

Maude Shelton sipped at her brandy but didn't speak as she was deep in thought about how to put her plan into action. It was a plan Maude had dreamed of for a long time now and a few months ago, before all this upset had happened, one she'd been in the process of making happen. Maude now realised that there would never be a better time to push ahead with things.

"Jason could you mind the place for a while only I need to pop out for a couple of hours."

"Yeah no problem, let me just check on Lisa and then I'm all yours."

Thirty minutes later, Maude Shelton's taxi pulled up in Bridle Lane. She had toyed with the idea of phoning ahead and then thought better of it. Maude realised that her nephew might not be there but if he was and she'd telephoned in advance he may have made up some excuse not to see her. Knocking on the door she waited patiently for Wally Evans to go through the routine of slightly pulling back the blind to see who was there. When he finally opened up she didn't wait to be invited inside.

"Is he in?"

"If you'd like to take a seat Mrs Shelton I'll just go and see."

"Oh don't give me any of that old twaddle, get out of my way."

Maude marched straight through to the rear and into Freddie Gants office.

"Well fuck me if it ain't Auntie Maude."

"Fredrick."

"This family stuffs starting to wear a bit thin if you don't mind me saying. I don't mind a visit every decade but

I've seen you more times in the last few months than I have all my life and it's getting a bit too much to take."

"Cut the crap Fredrick I've got a proposition for you."

"Fire away Auntie I'm all ears."

"I want you to buy the Camel."

Freddie Gant pushed back in his leather chair and laughed.

"And why on earth would I want to do that?"

"Because it's a good deal. Now I had the place valued early in the year and they told me I could get at least seven hundred and fifty grand for it."

"So why don't you just put it on the market?"

"Because I want a quick sale. Now apart from it being in a prime location that's about to go under extensive regeneration, it's a good little earner. You can have it for seven hundred."

Freddie lifted his arms above his head and stretched as he spoke.

"Six fifty and I might think about it."

Maude was more than happy with the amount. She'd known that she'd be screwed down before she even suggested a figure and six fifty was exactly what she was hoping for. Not wanting to seem to keen she thought for a moment.

"Six fifty but no thinking about it. Deal or no deal?"

Freddie leant across the table and shook his aunt's hand. Since losing Sam's to Ritchie Foreman he'd been looking for somewhere else and the Camel would do just fine. Originally he'd thought the place would be his soon anyway but when he'd got back his cash that idea had diminished fast. True it wasn't Soho but the East End was in a different way as good as the West End. The locals knew how to keep their mouths shut while at the same time watching out for anything suspicious. His

320

reputation was already strong in Bethnal Green so it wasn't as if he was starting from scratch. All in all things couldn't have turned out better.

"So what's on the horizon for you now then Auntie?"

"I'm getting out of London. I'm too long in the tooth for this game and I think the quieter life will be much more to my liking. Now even though I'd love to stay and chat Fredrick, I'm sure you have better things to do. I'll wait to hear from your solicitor but don't take too long about it or I might just change my mind."

"Aunty Maude we've shaken on it and as anyone will tell you, my word is my bond."

With that Maude walked out of the office and once outside a wide grin spread across her entire face. From behind Wally Evans had eyed the woman up and down and she really was in good shape for her years.

Relocking the door he sighed at what might have been before joining his boss in the back.

"What's happening Guv'nor?"

"We're back in business Wal my old mate that's what's happening. The old girl has just sold me her pub and we're going to open up another Sam's."

"Do you think the other firms will want to use the East End instead of Soho?"

"Once they realise that the old Sam's is being run by the Foreman's there won't even be standing room at the Camel. I think this calls for a celebration Wal, go put the kettle on."

After a quick visit to her solicitor's Maude returned home to find Jason putting the final bolt across for afternoon closing. She banged loudly on the door and he was about to shout out 'We're closed' when he recognised Maude's silhouette through the glass. Swiftly he opened up, glad that she was back.

"Alright Duchess?"

"More than alright son! Come on upstairs I need a word and bring that bottle of brandy with you."

Jason's brow furrowed, to say he was curious was an understatement. Grabbing the bottle as he'd been asked he made his way upstairs to find out what all the cloak and dagger stuff was about and what his landlady had been up to.

"So what's with all the secrecy and where have you been?"

"I paid a visit to Freddie Gant."

"What!"

"Now don't start worrying everything's going to be fine. I think you and that little wife had better start packing in the next few days."

"Packing?"

"Yes my darling packing, we're moving out!"

"Duchess do you think that's such a good idea? I mean shouldn't we let the dust settle first, let things get back to normal, whatever normal's going to be from now on."

"What about that poor little mare downstairs? Do you really want to see her end her days in some grubby little back street pub?"

"No but....."

"Then it's settled, we're moving and as far as I'm concerned it can't come soon enough."

CHAPTER THIRTY ONE

One week later

Jason and Maude were up with the larks. They had both been too excited to sleep properly the previous night. 'Closed until further notice' signs had been placed in the Camels windows and Maude was busy cleaning down the shelves and polishing the bottles. Jason had just finished washing and stacking the ashtrays when he turned to face his landlady with a quizzical look on his face which didn't go unnoticed.

"What?"

"Duchess why are we doing all this? I mean it ain't as if Freddie Gants going to care if the place is spick and span."

"Probably not Jason but I do. I've always run a tight tidy ship and that's the way I intend to leave things. The Camels been good to me over the years not only as a business but as my home and I guess I'd feel like I betrayed it if I walked out leaving it dirty"

Tenderly hugging the woman that he had come to love Jason Frasier smiled.

"You're one of a kind Duchess, one of a kind."

"Oh get away with you, you daft sod! Now I take it that you still ain't told Lisa that today's the day we move?"

"Not yet. I was going to do it first thing but she was still sleeping when I got up so I suppose I'd better go do it now."

Jason wiped his hands on a bar towel and handing it to Maude stopped for a second.

"What's wrong Son?"

"Now that it's come to the crunch and we're actually

323

going, well what if she don't want to go Maude?"

"Don't give in before you've even tried son."

A hard knock on the front door brought the conversation to a temporary halt as Maude Shelton bellowed out in her loudest voice 'We're shut can't you bleeding read?'.

"Mrs Shelton it's the police open up."

Maude and Jason looked at each other in unison and rolled their eyes upwards.

"Now what?"

"Only one way to find out Son, let's open up and see what they've got to say."

Holding open the door, Jason waited for the officer to be followed in by his partner but Nick Graves was alone. The man walked over to the bar and by the look on his face Maude could tell that he wasn't here on official business.

"Morning Detective. Drink?"

Normally it would have been a definite no but this time Nick Graves nodded and accepted the double brandy that was passed over the bar.

"Fancy one Jay?"

Jason grinned; he wasn't usually a daytime drinker but when all was said and done, today was special.

"Why not, as long as you join us."

After pouring two more drinks Maude at last turned her attention to the policeman.

"Now what can I do for you Detective?"

Jason locked the front door and joined the only other two people in the bar. Slowly sipping his drink he didn't enter into conversation after deciding it was best for Maude to handle things, for the time being at least. Nick Graves savoured his brandy for several seconds before he replied and Maude could tell that whatever was on his mind didn't sit well with the man.

324

"I just thought you both might like to know that for all intent and purpose, the case has been closed."

He waited to see if any shouting would begin, in fact he hoped that they would call for the case to be kept open until the killer had been caught. When there was no response of any kind he finally continued.

"I'm really not sure what involvement the two of you had in Vincent Frasier's murder but...."

His words automatically hit a nerve with Jason and he didn't allow the man to finish.

"Now you look here copper I ain't got a fucking clue what you're on about but just because you ain't getting anywhere with my brother's murder, don't give you the right to come in here and start laying down aspersions."

Maude sensed that things could easily get out of hand and the last thing she wanted was for Jason to start running off at the mouth in the heat of the moment.

"Calm down Jay and listen to what the man has to say."

"I'm sorry Mr Frasier, perhaps I phrased that wrongly but I know you two are in a lot deeper than you're letting on. Don't get me wrong, I'm not accusing you of being directly involved with what happened to your brother. I'm already convinced that a certain Freddie Gant played a big hand in that matter. Besides, in all honesty and between you me and the gatepost I can't take this any further. The men at the top have told me that I have to put this to bed and leave Gant alone."

"Then best you do as you've been asked detective."

Maude's face was expressionless as she spoke and Nick Graves could see that she was a wise old bird.

"Officer of the law or not my nephew is not the kind of man you want to mess with. Freddie is far from the proverbial driven as far as all this is concerned but don't think that Vinny was an angel because he wasn't.

Vincent Frasier wasn't happy to be a spectator in life, he craved to be a player and we all know that when you play with fire Mr Graves you get burnt. Now if that's all we have a lot of work to do!"

"Going somewhere, a holiday perhaps?"

Even as Maude continued to speak Jason guided Nick Graves in the direction of the door.

"You could say that but I think this will be rather more permanent. Now you take care Detective and for your own sake stay away from the likes of Freddie Gant. Men like him are the scum of the earth but for every one you put away there's three ready to take their place. Life's too short and too ungrateful for getting into all that Mr Graves and believe you me, if you try and go after my nephew your life will be just that."

Nick Graves nodded his understanding and he even appreciated the woman's words of concern but as for Freddie Gant, he was high on Nick's list of villains to put away. Justice ran through his veins and as much as he wanted to heed her advice he knew that deep down he wouldn't be able to take it. One way or another he would have Freddie Gant if it was the last thing he did. When Jason had closed the door and pulled the bolt across he leaned against the glass and breathed out a sigh of relief.

"What do you think he really wanted Duchess?"

"I don't know what you mean?"

"Well he didn't come here for the good of his health now did he?"

Maude couldn't help but smile.

"He wanted nothing more than what he said love and that was basically to tell us that you're off the hook. Now just thank your lucky stars and go and tell that wife of yours that we'll be out of here by the end of the day."

Euston station was abuzz with people as all colour and

creeds jostled for trains to all corners of the country. The thick smell of diesel hung in the air and every few seconds a mystery voice burst into life from the tannoy system announcing delays or warnings about abandoned luggage. Lisa Frasier gripped her husband's hand tightly as they walked along the platform in search of a vacant carriage. Jason was having difficulty keeping hold of his wife and steering the trolley that was steeped high with suitcases.

"Here you two! This one will do."

Maude Shelton had already climbed the step and taken a seat as Jason struggled to unload all of their worldly possessions but deep down he didn't mind. Seeming to just accept his lot and muddle through for the best part of forty years, the thought suddenly hit home that this little adventure was one he'd desperately needed and wanted all his life but had never realised.

"I can manage Lisa you go and sit with the Duchess." Since he'd told her a few hours earlier that they were moving she hadn't once questioned him and that in its self worried Jason. Maybe she didn't care or perhaps she wasn't feeling well again and he wondered if taking her away from all that she knew was a fair thing to force her into. Over the last few weeks whenever he'd had a moment of doubt regarding anything he was about to do, he'd thought of Vinny and everything seemed to fall into place, today would be no exception. When Jason had finally loaded all of the luggage he took the seat next to his wife and opposite Maude.

"Well babe it looks like we're really going!"

"I'm scared Jay."

"Whatever of?"

"The future, leaving London, just about everything really."

327

Maude leant forward and clasped both of Lisa's hands in hers.

"My darling, you ain't got nothing to be scared about. Regardless of all that's happened we would probably have ended up doing this anyway. You're here with the two people who care most about you in the whole world so there's nothing to be frightened of. Now let's enjoy ourselves, we've got a long journey ahead of us."

"Where are we going to Maude?"

"That's for me to know and you to find out. Ain't that exciting!"

All three people in the carriage laughed and Maude hoped with all her heart that this was how things would be from now on. The trio changed trains twice before they reached their destination and by the time they pulled into Falmouth town they were all exhausted. The welcome sign made no difference either way to Lisa Frasier. Having never been out of London before and loosing most of her education due to her father, she might as well have come to Timbuktu for all it meant to her. The day was drawing to a close and in the dim lights the busy seaside town didn't look that appealing to Jason. Still he reasoned that Maude knew best and he would wait until tomorrow before passing judgement. Even though it was overly expensive, Maude Shelton had pre booked two rooms at the Castle hotel. The grand foyer was warm and welcoming and Jason gazed round in amazement.

"Don't get to fond of it love its only for a couple of nights."

"Then where?"

"Like I told Lisa, you'll just have to wait and find out. Now I'm going to turn in as I'm knackered and by the looks of her you two should do the same."

Lisa was standing up but Maude could see that the girl was almost asleep on her feet. The journey must have really taken it out of her but Lisa hadn't complained once. Inwardly Maude was worried but she didn't relay her fears to Jason. His wife seemed to be getting sicker by the day and Maude feared time was running out fast. All three slept soundly that night and in the morning, Jason thinking he was the first up was surprised to see a note from Maude pushed under his bedroom door.

'Jay I've got a few things to do today so you and Lisa amuse
yourselves and I'll see you both tonight.
Love Maude'

Waiting for Lisa to wake was frustrating but there was no way Jason would hurry her. From now on whatever Lisa Frasier wanted, Lisa Frasier would get. At just before ten am she at last lifted her head from the pillow and after a quick shower the couple dressed and went down to breakfast.

"So babe! What would you like to do today?"

"Just have a look about and see what our new homes like I suppose."

They spent the next couple of hours walking the streets of Falmouth and even though it wasn't said; neither found the area that nice. In reality apart from being near to the sea, the place wasn't that different from London. True the traffic and noise was less than in the Smoke and the place was a typical holiday resort but deep down after all they'd been through Jason wanted his wife to have peace and she certainly wouldn't get it here. He decided that as soon as Maude returned he would pull her to one side and explain that even though he was grateful for all she'd done for them, there was no way they could stay here. The hours seemed to drag by and Maude Shelton finally returned at nine o'clock that night. After seeing Lisa off to bed an hour earlier Jason had decided to wait for Maude in the bar area and that's exactly where she found him. Sitting all alone he looked a sorry sight and she could instantly tell by the look in his eyes that he wasn't happy.

"What's up Son?"

"Sit down Duchess I need to talk to you."

"And I know exactly what you are going to say but before you start let me explain a couple of things." Jason nodded for her to continue.

"This ain't where we'll be living you know. I can tell by the look on your face that you hate it already and I would too but we had to have a place to stay while I crossed the t's and dotted the i's. Now that's all done we can at last go to our new home. Go get Lisa."

"What now?"

"No time like the present and besides, the owners are waiting for us so they can hand the keys over."

"But Lisa's turned in for the night Maude."

Standing up Maude Shelton was already walking away from her seat as she spoke.

"Don't worry about that. It's not far and if you get a move on Lisa can be tucked up in her new bed by ten." Jason stood up wearily and sighed, this trip was turning out to be anything but peaceful. Just as Maude had said the place wasn't far and even though it was almost dark when the taxi entered the village of Maenporth, Jason could see that it was really rural. Through the diming light they passed fields of laying cows and narrow roads flanked on either side by high hedging, Jason could sense that this place was instantly more attractive than Falmouth. The Smugglers Cove public house sat nestled on a small hill just above the beach. Getting out of the

car Lisa jumped when she heard the waves crashing onto
the sand and Jason pulled her close to him. The pub was
small but friendly and filled to the rafters with regulars
who were all eager to welcome the new landlady. It was
all too much for Lisa Frasier and she began to cry.
"Come on babe let's get you upstairs. Maude I'll be back
in a minute, I really need to get her to bed."
Maude Shelton had already taken her rightful place
behind the bar and when she shouted 'Drinks on the
house everyone' an almighty cheer erupted. Shouting
above the noise she told Jason that his room was directly
at the top of the stairs. The large oak bed almost filled
the room and it appeared extra high due to the three
mattresses that were perched on top of it. The place was
oldie worldly and beautiful but Lisa took no notice, all
she wanted was to fall into bed and after being helped to
undress, that's exactly what she did. When he was sure
that his wife was sleeping, Jason Frasier went down stairs
and joined in the merriment. He liked the place straight
away, though he didn't say too much preferring to wait
until the cold light of day before voicing his opinion.
Jason slept like a log and only woke when he heard
Maude knocking at the door. Reaching over he was
alarmed to find that his wife was missing.
"Maude! Maude!"
Instantly Maude entered and rushed over to the bedside.
"Where is she Maude, has something happened?"
"Follow me son, I think you need to see this."
Drawing back the curtains revealed a small balcony that
looked directly onto the cove and the sandy beach below.
Stepping out onto the wooden deck Jason could hardly
believe his eyes. In the distance he could see Lisa
running along the sand. Her arms were outstretched and
the wind blew her long hair in all directions.

331

"But how?"

"I don't know love, maybe it's the sea air but she looked radiant this morning."

"She had a dream once you know, she dreamed of exactly this."

Suddenly Jason stopped talking and Maude could see the onset of tears in his eyes.

"What's wrong?"

"This is fantastic Duchess but things can't stay this way can they. When I think of what's to come, well it breaks my heart in two."

Maude Shelton grabbed Jason firmly by the arms and pulled him to face her.

"Now you listen to me and listen good, for however long she has left her life will be perfect."

"And then what Maude, what do I do then?"

"Then we run this place together, just the two of us. We will never forget her Jason, neither of us will ever let that happen but life is for living. You only have to look down there on that beach to see that and if Lisa can do it then so can you."

Jason Frasier hugged the woman tightly and whispered the words that Maude Shelton had always longed to hear.

"I love you mum, I can call you that can't I?"

"Oh Son of course you can, I've waited years to hear it."

THE END

EPILOGUE

2008 THREE YEARS LATER

On a sunny day two years after moving to Cornwall, Lisa
Frasier passed away. With her last breath she told Jason
that they had been the best two years of her life. The
funeral was a sad affair and it took him a long while to
accept that she had finally gone. Without Maude there
was no doubting that Jason would have crumbled. Now
they ran the Smugglers Cove together and made an
excellent team. They were loved by all the regulars and
never gave a second thought to London and all the pain
that had been caused there. They were often mistaken for
mother and son by the numerous holiday makers who
would call in for a cold beer on a warm afternoon.
Neither Jason or Maude ever bothered to correct the
mistake, in fact it was something they welcomed. Jason
knew he would never marry again, after Lisa there was
no one who could come up to scratch but in the ensuing
years it wouldn't stop Maude Shelton from trying to pair
him off at any opportunity. When she'd worked her way
through the barmaids she had moved onto the cleaner and
was at present trying to set him up with the local librarian
Miss Francesca Bootle, now that Jason couldn't wait to
see. If the truth was told he didn't really mind Maude's
interfering and on some of the long winter nights even
enjoyed female company but that was as far as it would
ever go. Often, especially on hot sunny afternoons when
he strolled along the sand his thoughts would turn to
Vinny. Sometimes the guilt still cut deeply but it was
also at those times he remembered all that his beautiful
girl had gone through. Thinking of the suffering she had
endured in the last few months of her life always made

him realise that the choice he had made regarding his brother had definitely been the right one.

After his Aunt left London, Freddie Gant had lasted precisely three years in business. The Camel had been refurbished and was doing equally as well as his original club on Chapone Place. True it had gutted him to lose Sam's but sometimes it was good to have a change and all in all Freddie was forced to accept that the turn of events had probably worked out for the best in the long run. Things had been running smoothly and Freddie had more money than he could poke a stick at, so when out of the blue he started to do deals with the Foreman's it caused his sidekick Wally Evans to have a lot of sleepless nights. It was through one of those so called deals that a misunderstanding had occurred and ultimately led to a full scale turf war. True Freddie Gant was a well known face but when it came to the Foreman's he was a small fish in a big pond. The body of Wally Evans along with that of his boss had been found in Epping Forest. Sitting upright in the front of Freddie's brand new range rover, they both had a single gunshot to the forehead. Maude was the first person to be told of his demise. For reasons known only to him Freddie had left instructions with his solicitor that should anything ever happen to him she was to be informed before anyone else. Maude Shelton didn't return to London for the funeral. For some strange reason and Maude didn't know if it was an oversight on her nephews part or just the fact that he was arrogant enough to think he was invincible but Freddie had never had a Will drawn up. Now to add insult to injury Fredrick Gant would be turning in his grave to hear that on his death his mother Pearl had inherited all of his shops and clubs. Good clothes and money would never change the woman and many nights while well inebriated she could be heard raising a glass to her son and thanking god that he was dead.

Vera Frasier would remain in her Rickman street flat for the rest of her days. Even when she became totally housebound and her only visitors, apart from her carer's, were the postman and milkman, she would always seize the opportunity to talk about her precious Vinny and how he was murdered. Chinese whispers had begun to circulate in the East End of how Freddie Gant was planning to take over the Foreman Empire. It was never discovered if these whispers had filtered their way back to Ritchie Foreman but on hearing of Freddie's demise, Vera Frasier had worn a smile for weeks. From the day he walked out of her home Jason's name never again left her lips and as far as Vera Frasier was concerned both her sons were now dead. She never got to visit The Smugglers Cove or learn of her daughter in laws death but to her that was a small price to pay. Keeping her boy Vinny's name pure and not tainting it with the likes of Lisa Frasier and Freddie Gant was all that she cared about.

Detective Chief Inspector Nick Graves received his promotion on the recommendations of Commander Bowers. Arresting Freddie Gant had still been on his 'To do list' and he was in no doubt that one day he would succeed. When he received news of the double gangland murders a part of him felt cheated but at the same time her remembered Maude Shelton's final words 'Life's too short and to ungrateful for getting into all that'. Nick decided that perhaps he'd had a lucky escape and maybe it was time to move on to pastures green.

As for Maude Shelton, she was now more content than she'd ever been. True she missed Lisa terribly but having Jason by her side softened the loss and running the pub together was her dream come true. Occasionally when The Smugglers Cove was quiet and she had time to herself, Maude would recall all that had happened. Her mind sometimes wondered if Lisa had been totally truthful regarding the tests she was supposed to have taken shortly after her marriage. Smiling to herself Maude would instantly dismiss those thoughts. In the grand scale of things did it really matter who gave who the disease. After all Maude reasoned, Vincent Frasier had finally gotten what he deserved!

Printed in Poland
by Amazon Fulfillment
Poland Sp. z o.o., Wrocław